PENGUIN CLASSICS

SERIES ADVISOR: PAUL POPLAWSKI

THE FOX
THE CAPTAIN'S DOLL
THE LADYBIRD

DAVID HERBERT LAWRENCE was born into a miner's family in Eastwood, Nottinghamshire, in 1885, the fourth of five children. His first novel, *The White Peacock*, was published in 1911. In 1912 Lawrence went to Germany and Italy with Frieda Weekley, the German wife of a professor at Nottingham University College, where Lawrence had studied; she divorced, and they were married on their return to England in 1914. Lawrence had published *Sons and Lovers* in 1913; but *The Rainbow*, completed in 1915, was suppressed, and for three years he could not find a publisher for *Women in Love*, which he first completed in 1917. After the First World War he travelled extensively in Europe, Australia, America and Mexico. He returned to Europe from America in 1925, and lived mainly in Italy and France. His last novel, *Lady Chatterley's Lover*, was published in 1928 but was banned in England and America. In 1930 he died in Vence, in the south of France, at the age of forty-four.

HELEN DUNMORE is a novelist, poet, short story and children's writer. Her published work includes eight collections of poetry, the most recent being *Out of the Blue, New and Selected Poems*, nine novels and three collections of short stories. In her first novel, *Zennor in Darkness*, she wrote about D. H. Lawrence's stay in Zennor during the First World War. The book won the McKitterick Prize, and her third novel, *A Spell of Winter*, won the inaugural Orange Prize for Fiction. *The Siege* was shortlisted for the Whitbread Prize for Fiction and the Orange Prize for Fiction. Helen Dunmore is a Fellow of the Royal Society of Literature.

PAUL POPLAWSKI is a Senior Lecturer at the University of Leicester. He is a member of the editorial board of the Cambridge Edition of Lawrence's Works and his recent publications include the revised third edition of *A Bibliography of D. H. Lawrence* (Cambridge, 2001), and *Encyclopedia of Literary Modernism* (Greenwood, 2003).

D. H. LAWRENCE

The Fox
The Captain's Doll
The Ladybird

Edited by DIETER MEHL
With Notes by DAVID ELLIS
With an Introduction by HELEN DUNMORE

PENGUIN BOOKS

PENGUIN CLASSICS

Published by the Penguin Group
Penguin Books Ltd, 80 Strand, London WC2R ORL, England
Penguin Group (USA) Inc., 375 Hudson Street, New York, New York 10014, USA
Penguin Group (Canada), 90 Eglinton Avenue East, Suite 700, Toronto, Ontario, Canada M4P 2Y3
(a division of Pearson Penguin Canada Inc.)
Penguin Ireland, 25 St Stephen's Green, Dublin 2, Ireland (a division of Penguin Books Ltd)
Penguin Group (Australia), 250 Camberwell Road, Camberwell,
Victoria 3124, Australia (a division of Pearson Australia Group Pty Ltd)
Penguin Books India Pvt Ltd, 11 Community Centre,
Panchsheel Park, New Delhi – 110 017, India
Penguin Group (NZ), cnr Airborne and Rosedale Roads, Albany,
Auckland 1310, New Zealand (a division of Pearson New Zealand Ltd)
Penguin Books (South Africa) (Pty) Ltd, 24 Sturdee Avenue,
Rosebank, Johannesburg 2196, South Africa

Penguin Books Ltd, Registered Offices: 80 Strand, London WC2R ORL, England

www.penguin.com

First published 1923
Cambridge University Press edition published 1992
Published with new editorial material in Penguin Books 1994
This edition published with new Chronology, Introduction, Further Reading,
A Note on the Texts in Penguin Classics 2006

015

Copyright © the Estate of Frieda Lawrence Ravagli, 1992
Explanatory Notes copyright © David Ellis, 1994
Introduction copyright © Helen Dunmore, 2006
Chronology and A Note on the Texts copyright © Paul Poplawski, 2006
All rights reserved

The moral right of the introducer and the editor has been asserted

Printed in England by Clays Ltd, St Ives plc

ISBN-13: 978-0-141-44183-2

www.greenpenguin.co.uk

MIX
Paper from
responsible sources
FSC® C018179

Penguin Books is committed to a sustainable
future for our business, our readers and our planet.
This book is made from Forest Stewardship
Council™ certified paper.

Contents

Chronology

1885 11 September: David Herbert Lawrence born in Eastwood, Nottinghamshire, third son of Arthur John (coalminer) and Lydia Lawrence.

1898–1901 Attends Nottingham High School.

1901 October–December: Clerk at Nottingham factory of J. H. Haywood; falls ill.

1902–5 Pupil-teacher in Eastwood and Ilkeston; meets Chambers family, including Jessie, in 1902.

1905–6 Uncertificated teacher in Eastwood; starts to write poetry, shows it to Jessie.

1906–8 Studies for teaching certificate at University College, Nottingham; begins first novel *The White Peacock* in 1906.

1907 Writes first short stories; first published story, 'A Prelude', appears in the *Nottinghamshire Guardian* (under Jessie's name).

1908–11 Elementary teacher at Davidson Road School, Croydon.

1909 Jessie sends selection of Lawrence's poems to the *English Review*; Ford Madox Hueffer (editor) accepts five and recommends *The White Peacock* to a publisher. Writes 'Odour of Chrysanthemums' (–1911) and first play, *A Collier's Friday Night*.

1910 Engaged to Louie Burrows; death of his mother. First drafts of *The Trespasser* and 'Paul Morel' (later *Sons and Lovers*).

1911 *The White Peacock* published. Second draft of 'Paul Morel'; writes and revises short stories. 'Odour of Chrysanthemums' published. Third draft of 'Paul Morel' (–1912). Falls seriously ill with pneumonia (November–December).

1912 Recuperates in Bournemouth; in February, breaks off engagement, returns to Eastwood and resigns teaching post. Meets Frieda Weekley (née von Richthofen), the wife of a professor at Nottingham University, and in May goes with her to Germany and then to Italy for the winter. *The Trespasser* published. Revises 'Paul Morel' into *Sons and Lovers*.

1913 Drafts Italian essays and starts to write 'The Sisters' (which will become *The Rainbow* and *Women in Love*). *Love Poems* published.

April–June in Germany; writes 'The Prussian Officer' and other stories. *Sons and Lovers* published (May). Spends the summer in England with Frieda, then they return to Italy. Works on 'The Sisters'.

1914 *The Widowing of Mrs Holroyd* (play) published (USA). Finishes 'The Wedding Ring' (latest version of 'The Sisters') and returns to England with Frieda; her divorce finalized, they marry on 13 July. At the outbreak of war (August), Methuen & Co. withdraw from their agreement to publish 'The Wedding Ring'. War prevents return to Italy; lives in Buckinghamshire and Sussex. Rewrites 'The Wedding Ring' as *The Rainbow* (–1915).

1915 Writes 'England, My England'; works on essays for *Twilight in Italy*. Moves to London in August. *The Rainbow* is published in September but withdrawn in October, and prosecuted as obscene and banned a month later. Hopes to travel to USA with Frieda but at the end of December they settle in Cornwall (–October 1917).

1916 Rewrites the other half of 'The Sisters' material as *Women in Love*; it is finished by November but refused by several publishers (–1917). Reading American literature. *Twilight in Italy* and *Amores* (poems) published.

1917 Begins work on *Studies in Classic American Literature* (hereafter *Studies*). Revises *Women in Love*. Expelled from Cornwall with Frieda in October under Defence of the Realm Act; they return to London. Begins the novel *Aaron's Rod*. *Look! We Have Come Through!* (poems) published.

1918 Lives mostly in Berkshire and Derbyshire (–mid 1919). *New Poems* published; first versions of eight *Studies* essays published in periodical form (–1919). War ends (November). Writes *The Fox*.

1919 Revises *Studies* essays in intermediate versions. Revises *Women in Love* for Thomas Seltzer (USA). In November leaves for Italy.

1920 Moves to Sicily (February) and settles at Taormina. Publication of *Women in Love* in USA, *Touch and Go* (play), *Bay* (poems) and *The Lost Girl* in England.

1921 Visits Sardinia with Frieda and writes *Sea and Sardinia*. *Movements in European History* (textbook) and *Women in Love* published in England; *Psychoanalysis and the Unconscious* and *Sea and Sardinia* published in USA. Travels to Italy, Germany and Austria (April–September) and then returns to Taormina. Finishes *Aaron's Rod*, writes *The Captain's Doll* and *The Ladybird*, revises *The Fox*.

Chronology

1922 February–September: Travels with Frieda to Ceylon, Australia and USA. *Aaron's Rod* published; writes *Kangaroo* in Australia. Arrives in Taos, New Mexico, in September; rewrites *Studies* (final version). *Fantasia of the Unconscious* and *England, My England and Other Stories* published. Moves to Del Monte Ranch, near Taos, in December.

1923 *The Ladybird* (with *The Fox* and *The Captain's Doll*) published. Travels to Mexico with Frieda. *Studies* published in August (USA). Writes 'Quetzalcoatl' (early version of *The Plumed Serpent*). *Kangaroo* and *Birds, Beasts and Flowers* (poems) published. Rewrites *The Boy in the Bush* from Mollie Skinner's manuscript. Frieda returns to England in August; Lawrence follows in December.

1924 In France and Germany, then to Kiowa Ranch, near Taos. *The Boy in the Bush* published; writes 'The Woman Who Rode Away', *St. Mawr* and 'The Princess'. Death of his father. Goes to Mexico with Frieda.

1925 Finishes *The Plumed Serpent* in Oaxaca; falls ill, nearly dies and is diagnosed with tuberculosis. Returns to Mexico City and then to Kiowa Ranch. *St. Mawr Together with The Princess* published. Travels via London to Italy. *Reflections on the Death of a Porcupine* (essays) published; writes *The Virgin and the Gipsy* (–January 1926).

1926 *The Plumed Serpent* and *David* (play) published. Visits England for the last time; returns to Italy and writes first version of *Lady Chatterley's Lover*, then second version (–1927).

1927 Tours Etruscan sites with Earl Brewster; writes *Sketches of Etruscan Places*; writes first part of *The Escaped Cock* (second part in 1928). Suffers series of bronchial haemorrhages. *Mornings in Mexico* (essays) published. Starts third version of *Lady Chatterley's Lover*.

1928 *The Woman Who Rode Away and Other Stories* published. Finishes, revises and privately publishes third version of *Lady Chatterley's Lover* in limited edition (late June); distributes it through network of friends but many copies confiscated by authorities in USA and England. Travels to Switzerland for health, and then to Bandol in the south of France. *The Collected Poems of D. H. Lawrence* published; writes many of the poems for *Pansies*.

1929 Organizes cheap Paris edition of *Lady Chatterley's Lover* to counter piracies. Typescript of *Pansies* seized by police in London. Travels to Spain, Italy and Germany; increasingly ill. Police raid exhibition of his paintings in London (July). Expurgated (July) and unexpurgated (August) editions of *Pansies* published; *The Escaped Cock* published. Returns to Bandol.

1930 2 March: Dies of tuberculosis at Vence, Alpes Maritimes, France, and is buried there. *Nettles* (poems), *Assorted Articles*, *The Virgin and the Gipsy* and *Love Among the Haystacks & Other Pieces* published.

1932 *Sketches of Etruscan Places* published (as *Etruscan Places*). *Last Poems* published.

1933–4 Story collections *The Lovely Lady* (1933) and *A Modern Lover* (1934) published.

1935 Frieda has Lawrence exhumed and cremated, and his ashes taken to Kiowa Ranch.

1936 *Phoenix* (compilation) published.

1956 Death of Frieda.

1960 Penguin Books publish the first unexpurgated English edition of *Lady Chatterley's Lover*, following the famous obscenity trial.

Introduction

In his Preface to his poems, Wilfred Owen wrote 'My subject is War, and the pity of War.'[1] Few readers would do anything but agree. Owen's subject, manifestly and palpably, is War, and succeeding generations have assented to Owen's own understanding of himself as a writer.

D. H. Lawrence is not often considered as a writer whose subject is war, nor is he much compared to poets and memoirists such as Wilfred Owen, Siegfried Sassoon, Robert Graves or Isaac Rosenberg. Born in 1885, Lawrence was twenty-eight when the First World War broke out. Unlike younger writers such as Graves, who went from school to the trenches, notebook in pack, Lawrence had already established himself as a writer. By 1914 *The White Peacock*, *The Trespasser* and *Sons and Lovers* had been published, and Lawrence was at work on the novel which became *The Rainbow*. He had published one play (and written five more), fifteen short stories and his first poetry collection, *Love Poems and Others*. His expressive, fluid and voluminous correspondence made a more private, but equally significant impact on his contemporaries.

In both style and subject matter, Lawrence had already broken much new ground. Readers and critics recognized in *Sons and Lovers* or in a story such as 'Odour of Chrysanthemums' a voice which took them into unknown territory with assurance, and in language which glowed with life. The originality of Lawrence's prose is breathtaking, even now in the twenty-first century. His style is so direct that a reader is immediately captivated and drawn into the narrative, while at the same time a sustained, richly developed imagery allows his prose to take root in the imagination and bear fruit there. The cadences of his speaking voice, so quick, vital and rhythmic, are unmistakable even in this small fragment from a letter to Lady Cynthia Asquith in 1913, about scrubbing a floor:

> Lord what a time we've had, scrubbing it. It was no use calling on Ellide, the girl. She had never seen a scrubbing brush used. So I tied my braces round my waist and went for it. Lord, to see the dark floor flushing

crimson, the dawn of deep red bricks arise from out this night of filth, was enough to make one burst forth into hymns and psalms. 'Ah', cries Ellide, 'l'aria e la pulizia' – 'air and cleanliness are the two most important things in this life'. She might as well have said nectar and ambrosia, for all she knew of 'em.[2]

This young writer who knew all about scrubbing floors was a thrill and a challenge, but he was not yet a threat. Very probably his early readers enjoyed the sense of adventure and privileged insight that Lawrence gave them. The life of mining families in Nottinghamshire and Derbyshire was as remote as that of Trobriand Islanders from most literate middle- and upper-class readers. Lawrence's writing offered authentic, first-hand experience of the working lives that fed the great engine of pre-war British prosperity. While he was a newcomer who needed welcome and nurture from such critical insiders as Edward Garnett, he was no naive 'discovery'. From the outset of his writing career, Lawrence possessed an authoritative experience, viewpoint and language.

A sign of Lawrence's early self-confidence and inner strength was that he gave up the teaching career he had been working towards for years, to live frugally but independently by his writing. Although there were health reasons too, this was an enormous step for a young man of Lawrence's background. It is easy to forget how many writers of that time were sustained by private incomes. Lawrence's self-confidence and social mobility, together with a complex, ironic or sometimes sparklingly humorous awareness of social class, are evident in the three novellas collected here.

The outbreak of war ruptured Lawrence's life and work, as it ruptured those of almost all his contemporaries. Not only would the First World War transform Lawrence's personal life and affect his entire future, leading him eventually into exile from England, but it would also transform his writing and the way it was regarded by the reading public. Lawrence almost immediately understood the connection between the way working men were treated as part of the machinery of production and the way that they would be treated in wartime as part of the machinery of destruction. As John Worthen notes in his biography of D. H. Lawrence, *The Life of an Outsider*, Lawrence wrote a prescient article about how this modern war would be fought, and that in it the fighting man would be 'attached to the machines as the subordinate part thereof, as the butt is the part of a rifle.'[3]

This denatured, dehumanized vision of man at war is central to Lawrence's writing from 1914 onwards, and critical to an understanding of these three novellas. They deal with death, wounding, destruction of the mind and spirit by the experience of war, and the struggle to reshape life in the aftermath of slaughter. They also focus subtly but insistently on the social and political changes brought about by the war, such as the growth of the power of the state, and the diminution of the individual.

In *The Ladybird*, the three main characters have between them suffered imprisonment, serious wounds, loss of home and country, and repeated bereavements. Lady Daphne's two beloved brothers have been killed in the war, as were the brothers of Lawrence's friend Lady Cynthia Asquith, who was a model for this character. Lady Daphne's mother is a mater dolorosa, struggling to uphold her moral and spiritual standards in an atmosphere of belligerent demonization of the enemy. Count Dionys, a German officer who has barely survived his wounds, wishes only for death. Lady Daphne's husband Basil has been scarred by his experiences to such an extent that on his return he fills his wife with fear. The story is saturated with the atmosphere of this war which has swallowed so many lives, and is now drawing to its close. It is relevant that just before the Armistice, and before suffering a breakdown, Cynthia Asquith wrote in her diary: 'One will have to look at long vistas again . . . and one will at last fully recognise that the dead are not only dead for the duration of the war.'[4]

In *The Captain's Doll*, Lawrence examines the defeated nations after the First World War. He knew Germany well, and through his wife Frieda, a von Richthofen by birth, he became acquainted with the pre-war German officer class. The story is set chiefly among aristocratic German women of this class, now dispossessed by defeat, forced to scrabble for a living in an occupied land. Lawrence drew on his wife Frieda and her sisters Johanna and Else as models for Hannele and Mitchka, and the description of their lives is intimate, domestic and understanding, down to the details of gestures, jokes, contrivances, love affairs, the cut of a swimsuit or the way a woman wears a hat.

Again, the war is everywhere. The power of the occupying British army is absolute, despite surface courtesies between former enemies of a similar social class. Later, when the story moves to the idyllic landscape of the Austrian Alps, it remains clear that beneath the Gemütlichkeit there lie poverty, despair, politicking and corruption. Peasants weigh out their paper money, which inflation has rendered almost worthless. A new generation strides the mountains, bare-kneed and booted, anaesthetizing itself with hectic exertion and the cult of nature:

> And the young Tannhäuser, the young Siegfried, this young Balder beautiful strode climbing down the rocks, marching and swinging with his alpenstock. And immediately after the youth came a maiden, with hair on the wind and her shirt-breast open, striding in corduroy breeches, rumpled worsted stockings, thick boots, a knapsack and an alpenstock. (p. 131)

As they tramp, the ramblers greet one other with the *Bergheil!* that will all too soon change to the *Heil Hitler!* Lawrence makes no bones about the social and political chaos of these ruined lands, and the likely consequences; his foresight is almost uncanny, given that the story was written as early as 1921.

But while Lawrence could be caustic about nature worship, one of the great strengths of these stories is their superb and original description of the landscapes, birds, beasts and flowers among which his people live and through which, if they are fortunate, they come to understand themselves. Captain Hepburn's outing with Hannele to see the glacier begins as a commonplace tourist trip, but both the journey and the language make a leap into pulsating, vivid reality as the glacier comes into sight.

> On the left rose the grey rock, but the glacier was there too, sending down great paws of ice. It was like some great, deep-furred ice-bear lying spread upon the top heights, and reaching down terrible paws of ice into the valley; like some immense sky-bear fishing in the earth's solid hollows, from above. (p. 140)

The fearsomeness of the glacier is beautifully contrasted with the dogged, self-willed struggle of the tourists to get a foothold on it. Even dignified Captain Hepburn is prepared to scramble up the ice, throwing down his coat ahead of him to get a grip, and 'going ridiculously as on four legs'. But when he reaches the brim of the glacier, he finds a place of death.

> It would seem as if the ice breathed through these great ridged gills. One could look down into the series of gulfs, fearful depths, and the colour

burning that acid, intense blue, intenser as the crack went deeper. And the crests of the open gills ridged and grouped pale blue above the crevices. It seemed as if the ice breathed there.

The wonder, the terror, and the bitterness of it. Never a warm leaf to unfold, never a gesture of life to give off. A world sufficient unto itself in lifelessness, all this ice. (p. 143)

This is a key moment in the story, where the real glacier is implicitly allied to the glacial movement of death over a living society. The 'warm leaf' of existence has been crushed.

Lawrence writes brilliantly in all three novellas about the way in which war has altered his characters' perception of death. Far from being remote and to be avoided at all costs, death has become an automatic recourse, the first solution reached for in an impasse. Just as Count Dionys in *The Ladybird* longs for his own death, characters in both *The Captain's Doll* and *The Fox* long for the deaths of others. In each story, a violent and perhaps accidental death removes a character who is an obstacle to other characters having what they desire. Lawrence very subtly shows how sudden, violent death has become a routine part of domestic life.

Captain Hepburn's wife reaches too far from a window to bring in 'a certain little camisole' which is drying there ... or perhaps that is not quite the whole story. Young Henry Grenfel, in *The Fox*, offers to fell a tree on the smallholding of two women, Nellie March and Jill Banford, one of whom he loves and one of whom he loathes. He realizes there is a risk that a heavy branch will fall on Jill Banford, whom he hates and wishes to remove. In his own mind he is able to pass off the risk as fate, to be decided by a power which acts through him. When the tree falls, the scene is written as if a force beyond Henry really is behind the axe:

There was a moment of pure, motionless suspense, when the world seemed to stand still. Then suddenly his form seemed to flash up enormously tall and fearful, he gave two swift, flashing blows, in immediate succession, the tree was absolutely severed, turning slowly, spinning strangely in the air and coming down like a sudden darkness on the earth. (p. 65)

The final simile strongly echoes the first Book of Genesis. 'The earth was waste and void; and darkness was upon the face of the deep: and the Spirit of God moved upon the face of the waters. And God said, Let there be light, and there was light.' Lawrence knew the Authorized Version of the Bible well, and his reference to one of its most famous passages is surely deliberate. But in *The Fox*, the power that seems superhuman creates darkness and death, not light and life.

In both *The Captain's Doll* and *The Ladybird*, these 'accidental' deaths fail to achieve quite the effect desired by those who have perhaps connived at them. Captain Hepburn's way to Hannele is now clear, but instead of taking it he first returns to England to fulfil his duties with half-hearted conventionality:

> So he went to England, to settle his own affairs, and out of duty to see his children. He wished his children all the well in the world—everything except any emotional connection with himself. (p. 114)

After the death of Banford, March and Henry Grenfel have each other, but remain at a loss and consumed with a sense of failure.

Interestingly, violent deaths which fail to produce the right result, and to which other characters cannot respond with adequate emotion, are also a striking feature of the detective novels which were hugely popular in the 1920s and 1930s. Agatha Christie, for example, published *The Mysterious Affair at Styles* in 1920. Possibly a reading public which was all too familiar with the chaos of violent death found comfort in the highly structured, indeed formalized version created by the detective novel.

In these three novellas, Lawrence certainly shows a detective novelist's insouciance about the eruption of death in the midst of everyday life. When Captain Hepburn eventually returns to Munich from England in search of Hannele, he finds that she has disappeared, and Mitchka is dead, 'shot in a riot in Salzburg' (p. 117). There is no apparent mourning for Mitchka, even from her close friend Hannele. Perhaps Lawrence is suggesting that these sudden deaths do not need to be distinguished, because death has become the norm during four years of mass slaughter. To stay alive and to live fruitfully or with any optimism is so difficult, however, that it requires total concentration. But Lawrence also seems to suggests that this lack of response to violent death implies a tragic atrophy in the power of human beings to feel for one another. If Mitchka and Mrs Hepburn are memorialized at all, it is in Captain Hepburn's climb to the glacier's kingdom of lifelessness.

War, death, mechanization and the atrophy of human existence are so closely connected in these novellas that they cannot be separated. Certain passages are overt condemnations of industrialized death-dealing, and make the connection between this and the more general mechanization and industrialization of life in the early twentieth century. In *The Ladybird*, Lady Daphne questions Count Dionys:

> 'You want more war?' she said to him bitterly.
>
> 'More trenches? More Big Berthas, more shells and poison-gas, more machine-drilled science-manœuvred so-called armies? Never. Never. I would rather work in a factory that makes boots and shoes. And I would rather deliberately starve to death than work in a factory that makes boots and shoes.' (p. 177)

But Lawrence also develops his argument about the impact of a mechanized society on the individual in lighter and more humorous ways. When Captain Hepburn in *The Captain's Doll* finally expounds his view of love to Hannele, the couple must shout, scream and bawl their dialogue above the noise of the car in which they are riding. Finally, Hannele is hurled forward on top of the driver by a sudden swerve of the car. This is a comic passage, but it is also full of pain. The driver of the car smiles at his own children with 'warm, manly blue eyes' but looks on the tourists 'with his sharp, metallic eye of a mechanic' (pp. 128, 148).

Relationships are not only weakened, but they are very often not entered on at all. Daily life is gnawed down to the point that it is a cause of surprise when excellent bread is produced from this shattered land. Similarly, in *The Ladybird*, the collapse of the ample, confident pre-war aristocratic life into which Lady Daphne was born is symbolized by her present home, a 'rather ugly flat' with a 'narrow doorway'. Instead of a live fire there is only an electric fire, by which Lady Daphne sits, always ill and 'far too thin' (p. 160). This 'thinness' is also a dominant characteristic of Banford, in *The Fox*. Her lack of full-bodied existence extends to the loss of her first name, and she is described as 'a small, thin, delicate thing with spectacles' (p. 7).

Banford and her friend March have set up house together, like thousands of their contemporaries in an era when the men these women might have married were already dead. Their decision to run a smallholding does not suit their natures or talents, but again they are like thousands of their contemporaries in making it. An unspoken need to make things grow and thrive is hampered by their ineffectuality.

Heifers run away, the fox eats the poultry. All the characters in *The Fox* seem to have forgotten how to live, down to the smallest everyday detail. Their actions, like their emotions, appear random and spasmodic. They are like survivors of some immense wreck, clinging to one another, but the embrace is far from warm.

Even the young soldier, Henry Grenfel, who derides the two women's ineptitude, has no solution. He longs only to escape to Canada. Equally, after Banford is killed, March envies her dead friend, and realizes that she herself will never be able to pluck the 'blue' flower of happiness without falling into a 'bottomless gulf' (p. 69). She, too, yearns for sleep and death.

Henry Grenfel's desire to move westward echoes the longing that Lawrence himself expresses repeatedly in his wartime letters. He wanted a double emigration. He longed to leave England physically, and go overseas, but also to escape the social organization which he believed was breaking down around him, and build another. Lawrence may never have achieved his ideal community, the 'Rananim'[5] centred on a band of like-minded friends, but he did carry out his resolve to leave England. His belief that the England he loved had in some fundamental sense ceased to exist was formed early in the war. He wrote to Cynthia Asquith on 28 November 1915:

> I am struggling like a fly on a treacle paper, to leave this country. I am hoping to be able to scrape together a little money, so that we can go to Florida straight . . . I would like to go to a land where there are only birds and beasts and no humanity, nor inhumanity-masks.[6]

After 1919, Lawrence never lived permanently in England again, but neither did he settle within any other society. He became the outsider, the observer, the infinitely receptive vagabond of his later fiction, poetry and travel writing.

For many years Lawrence returned to the task of understanding himself and his native land in relation to the war that he believed had driven him abroad. These three novellas were completed towards the end of 1921. Lawrence had had six years to reflect on the material which he had first used in a story called *The Thimble*, written in 1915, and eventually refined, expanded and transformed into *The Ladybird*. *The Captain's Doll* also draws on and relates to an earlier story called 'The Mortal Coil', published in 1917, and *The Fox* is an amplified final version of a much shorter story.

Introduction

All three novellas are concerned not only with what war does to individuals who fight in it, but with the corruption of entire societies. They draw on a particular historical moment, when to be male and under middle age was to be taken from home, work, friends and family, and immersed in a world of mud, cold, death and mutilation. Lawrence did not share that front-line experience. The closest he got to military life was at Bodmin barracks in 1916, where he was finally given a complete exemption from all military service, on health grounds. He wrote to Catherine Carswell on 9 July 1916:

> I had to join the Colours in Penzance, be conveyed to Bodmin (60 miles), spend a night in barracks with all the other men, and then be examined. It was experience enough for me, of soldiering. I am sure I should die in a week, if they kept me. It is the annulling of all one stands for, this militarism, the nipping of the very germ of one's being . . . The sense of spiritual disaster everywhere was quite terrifying . . . Yet I liked the men. They all seemed so *decent*.[7]

Lawrence recoiled from his experience within the machinery of mass conscription, not because he felt that he should be immune, but because he believed that the entire process of waging war in this way was a violation of human dignity, sense and feeling, and a fatal undermining of the 'England' he recognized and trusted. He observed from a civilian's viewpoint, while the boundaries between civilian and military life were deliberately dissolved throughout the years of 1914–18. Britain entered the war years with a relatively small professional army, augmented it with mass volunteering at the outbreak of war, and finally introduced conscription in 1916, against considerable opposition. By the end of the war 662,000 British soldiers had died, 1,600,000 were wounded, and 140,000 were missing, believed killed.

Lawrence's letters from the period refer with outrage and pity to friends joining up, and to the deaths of brothers, husbands and sons. Meanwhile military and state control over civilian life grew immeasurably. The Defence of the Realm Act (DORA) was passed without debate in August 1914. It gave extensive powers to the government, among which were the power to control reporting of events, censor printed material, imprison without trial, to take control of economic resources, restrict civilian residence, regulate the food supply and curtail licensing hours.

It is this climate of suspicion and demonization of the enemy that

Lawrence explores so effectively in *The Ladybird*. Lady Daphne's mother, old Lady Beveridge, has lost two sons in battle, but still strives to forgive. She has resolved that 'She would be swept into no general hate' (p. 157), although her behaviour and values are already meeting with ridicule rather than respect. It is while visiting wounded, imprisoned German officers that she meets Count Dionys once again, whom she has known well before the war. Through this meeting, Lady Daphne and Count Dionys become friends. An individual act, which goes against the social current, bears fruit.

A year later in 1922, Lawrence would confront his horror of wartime England head-on in the chapter of his novel *Kangaroo* (1923) entitled 'The Nightmare'. The obliteration of sensitive, mutually respectful behaviour between individuals by a system which encourages mass war hysteria is described through tiny, often absurd incidents.

> He and Harriet did all their own work, their own shopping. One wintry afternoon they were coming home with a knapsack, along the field path above the sea, when two khaki individuals, officers of some sort, strode after them. 'Excuse me,' said one, in a damnatory officious voice. 'What have you got in that sack?'
>
> 'A few groceries,' said Lovat.
>
> 'I would like to look.'
>
> Somers put the sack down on the path. The tall and lofty officer stooped and groped nobly among a pound of rice and a piece of soap and a dozen candles.
>
> 'Ha!' he cried, exultant. 'What's this? A camera!'
>
> Richard peeped in the bag at the groping red military hands. For a moment he almost believed that a camera had spirited itself in among his few goods, the implication of his guilt was so powerful. He saw a block in brown paper.
>
> 'A penn'orth of salt,' he said quietly, though pale to the lips with anger and insult.[8]

This passage reveals a very interesting piece of self-knowledge. Somers, a character strongly based on Lawrence himself, almost believes that he is actually a spy without knowing it, because 'the implication of his guilt was so powerful'.

This sense of unreality and inability to trust one's own perceptions and experience is something that pervades the consciousness of almost all the characters in *The Fox*, *The Ladybird* and *The Captain's Doll*.

Lady Daphne clings to her own beauty, because this at least is something she can measure in the mirror, but she does not trust her own marriage, her feelings or her future. Even her relationship with her mother is cold and mechanical. Nellie March sleepwalks through her life, stirring a little at the death of her closest friend, but then relapsing into passivity. Even at the most basic level, characters must battle to assert that they possess reality. Captain Hepburn fears Hannele's desire to make a doll of him, without realizing that the army has already done so. The doll is not like him, he is like the doll: 'She heard his step, and looked again. He was like the doll, a tall, slender, well-bred man in uniform' (p. 78).

The Fox, The Ladybird and *The Captain's Doll* are as wonderful to read as they are disturbing in their violence, their ruthlessness and bitter humour. These novellas are kin to the poetry of Wilfred Owen: their subject is War, and the pity of War.

Helen Dunmore

NOTES

1. *The Collected Poems of Wilfred Owen*, ed. C. Day Lewis (London: Chatto & Windus, 1972).

2. D. H. Lawrence, *The Letters of D. H. Lawrence*, Vol. II, *June 1913–October 1916*, ed. George J. Zytaruk and James T. Boulton (Cambridge University Press, 1981), p. 88.

3. John Worthen, *D. H. Lawrence, The Life of an Outsider* (London: Allen Lane, 2005), p. 149. 'With the Guns' was published in the *Manchester Guardian* of 18 August 1914.

4. Lady Cynthia Asquith, *Diaries 1915–1918* (London: Hutchinson & Co., 1968), p. 480.

5. Rananim was the name Lawrence gave to his proposed community of like-minded individuals. Rananim was a sustaining vision, but never a reality.

6. Lawrence, *Letters*, Vol. II, p. 454.

7. Ibid., p. 625.

8. D. H. Lawrence, *Kangaroo*, ed. Bruce Steele (Cambridge: Cambridge University Press, 1994), p. 223.

Further Reading

CRITICAL STUDIES OF LAWRENCE'S WORK

The following is a selection of some of the best Lawrence criticism published since 1985.

Michael Bell, *D. H. Lawrence: Language and Being* (Cambridge University Press, 1992). Philosophically-based analysis of Lawrence's work.

Michael Black, *D. H. Lawrence: The Early Fiction* (Macmillan, 1986). Very close analytical approach to Lawrence's fiction up to and including *Sons and Lovers*.

James C. Cowan, *D. H. Lawrence: Self and Sexuality* (Ohio State University Press, 2002). Sensitive and intelligent psychoanalytical study.

Keith Cushman and Earl G. Ingersoll, eds., *D. H. Lawrence: New Worlds* (Fairleigh Dickinson, 2003). Gathers essays about Lawrence and America.

Paul Eggert and John Worthen, eds., *Lawrence and Comedy* (Cambridge University Press, 1996). Collects essays concerning Lawrence's uses of satire and comedy.

David Ellis, ed., *Casebook on 'Women in Love'* (Oxford University Press, 2006). Essays of modern criticism.

David Ellis and Howard Mills, *D. H. Lawrence's Non-Fiction: Art, Thought and Genre* (Cambridge University Press, 1988). Collection which examines in particular Lawrence's writing of the 1920s.

Anne Fernihough, *D. H. Lawrence: Aesthetics and Ideology* (Oxford University Press, 1993). Wide-ranging enquiry into the intellectual context of Lawrence's writing.

Anne Fernihough, ed., *The Cambridge Companion to D. H. Lawrence* (Cambridge University Press, 2001). Usefully wide-ranging collection.

Louis K. Greiff, *D. H. Lawrence: Fifty Years on Film* (Southern Illinois University Press, 2001). Detailed account and analysis of screen adaptations.

Further Reading

G. M. Hyde, *D. H. Lawrence* (Palgrave Macmillan, 1990). Brief but provocative account of all Lawrence's writing.

Earl G. Ingersoll, *D. H. Lawrence, Desire and Narrative* (University Press of Florida, 2001). Postmodern approach to the major fiction.

Paul Poplawski, ed., *Writing the Body in D. H. Lawrence: Essays on Language, Representation, and Sexuality* (Greenwood Press, 2001). Gathers modern essays.

N. H. Reeve, *Reading Late Lawrence* (Palgrave Macmillan, 2004). Especially finely written account of Lawrence's late fiction.

Neil Roberts, *D. H. Lawrence, Travel and Cultural Difference* (Palgrave Macmillan, 2004). Valuable post-colonial study of Lawrence's travel-related writings 1921–5.

Carol Siegel, *Lawrence Among the Women: Wavering Boundaries in Women's Literary Traditions* (University Press of Virginia, 1991). Important and wide-ranging feminist reassessment of Lawrence.

Jack Stewart, *The Vital Art of D. H. Lawrence* (Southern Illinois University Press, 1999). Insightful study of Lawrence and the visual arts.

Linda Ruth Williams, *Sex in the Head: Visions of Femininity and Film in D. H. Lawrence* (Harvester Wheatsheaf, 1993). Feminist approach to selected works of Lawrence.

John Worthen and Andrew Harrison, eds., *Casebook on 'Sons and Lovers'* (Oxford University Press, 2005). Essays of modern criticism.

Peter Widdowson, ed., *D. H. Lawrence* (London and New York: Longman, 1992). Useful collection surveying contemporary theoretical approaches to Lawrence.

REFERENCE, EDITIONS, LETTERS AND BIOGRAPHY

The standard bibliography of Lawrence's work is *A Bibliography of D. H. Lawrence*, 3rd edn., ed. Warren Roberts and Paul Poplawski (Cambridge University Press, 2001). A useful reference work is Paul Poplawski's *D. H. Lawrence: A Reference Companion* (Greenwood Press, 1996) which gathers material up to 1994 and includes comprehensive bibliographies for most of Lawrence's works; Poplawski's 'Guide to further reading' in the *Cambridge Companion to D. H. Lawrence* goes up to 2000.

Further Reading

Lawrence's letters – arguably including some of his very best writing – have been published in an eight-volume complete edition, edited by James T. Boulton and published by Cambridge University Press.

Lawrence's work has now been almost completely published in the Cambridge Edition; thirty-three volumes have appeared and are variously available in paperback and hardback. The edited texts from a number of the volumes have also been published by Penguin.

A biographical work on Lawrence still worth consulting is the magnificent three-volume *D. H. Lawrence: A Composite Biography*, ed. Edward Nehls (University of Wisconsin Press, 1957–9). Between 1991 and 1998, Cambridge University Press published a three-volume biography which remains the standard work: John Worthen, *D. H. Lawrence: The Early Years 1885–1912* (1991), Mark Kinkead-Weekes, *D. H. Lawrence: Triumph to Exile 1912–1922* (1996) and David Ellis, *D. H. Lawrence: Dying Game 1922–1930* (1998). The most recent single-volume modern biography is that by John Worthen, *D. H. Lawrence: The Life of an Outsider* (Penguin Books, 2005).

A Note on the Texts

The texts in this edition are those established for *The Fox / The Captain's Doll / The Ladybird*, ed. Dieter Mehl (Cambridge University Press, 1992). This contains an apparatus of all the changes made to the base-texts, a full discussion of the editorial decisions taken, and a detailed account of the complex history of textual transmission, including locations for all surviving manuscript and typescript sources.

The Fox

Lawrence wrote the manuscript of the first version (located at University of Nottingham) in Derbyshire during November–December 1918. He revised the typescript and this was published in *Hutchinson's Story Magazine* (8 October 1920).

In November 1921, Lawrence heavily revised the other copy of the typescript (University of Texas at Austin), completely replacing and substantially extending the original ending. When this was retyped, Lawrence revised each of the two new typescripts slightly differently in the winter of 1921; one was used for the text published in the volume *The Ladybird / The Fox / The Captain's Doll* by Martin Secker in England (March 1923) and the other was used for the text published by the *Dial* in four numbers (May–August 1922) and by Thomas Seltzer (USA) in his volume *The Captain's Doll / Three Novelettes* (April 1923), for which Lawrence slightly revised the proofs.

The original manuscript of the first version has been adopted as the base-text for the first part of the story, and the combined heavily revised typescript and manuscript for the ending. Both have been emended from later states where revisions by Lawrence can with reasonable confidence be distinguished from typing and printing errors and house-styling. The ending of the first version is included in an Appendix.

The Captain's Doll

The manuscript (University of Tulsa) was written in Sicily during

A Note on the Texts

October–November 1921. Lawrence revised the typescripts (both unlocated), and one was used to produce a clean typescript (Bucknell University); the other was probably used for Secker's edition (see above).

The base-text is the manuscript, very slightly emended to incorporate corrections made by Lawrence in the first typescripts and revisions which can with reasonable confidence be attributed to him in proof.

The Ladybird

The manuscript (New York Public Library) was written in Sicily during November–December 1921 and revised heavily. Lawrence corrected both typescripts (neither survives) before sending them on 9 January 1922 to his English and American agents, who supplied them to Secker and Seltzer respectively.

The base-text is the manuscript, emended to incorporate the corrections which can with reasonable confidence be attributed to Lawrence either in the typescripts or in proof.

Paul Poplawski

THE FOX

THE CAPTAIN'S DOLL

THE LADYBIRD

The Fox

The two girls were usually known by their sur-names, Banford and March. They had taken the farm together, intending to work it all by themselves: that is, they were going to rear chickens, make a living by poultry, and add to this by keeping a cow, and raising one or two young beast. [Unfortunately things did not turn out well.]

Banford was a small, thin, delicate thing with spectacles. She, however, was the principal investor, for March had little or no money. Banford's father, who was a tradesman in Islington, gave his daughter the start, for her health's sake, and because he loved her, and because it did not look as if she would marry. March was more robust. She had learned carpentry and joinering at the evening classes in Islington. She would be the man about the place. They had, moreover, Banford's old grandfather living with them at the start. He had been a farmer. But unfortunately the old man died after he had been at Bailey Farm for a year. Then the two girls were left alone.

They were neither of them young: that is, they were near thirty. But they certainly were not old. They set out quite gallantly with their enterprise. They had numbers of chickens, black Leghorns and white Leghorns, Plymouths and Wyandots: also some ducks: also two heifers in the fields. One heifer, unfortunately, refused absolutely to stay in the Bailey Farm closes. No matter how March made up the fences, the heifer was out, wild in the woods, or trespassing on the neighbouring pasture, and March and Banford were away, flying after her, with more haste than success. So this heifer they sold in despair. Then, just before the other young beast was expecting her first calf, the old man died, and the girls, afraid of the coming event, sold her in a panic, and limited their attentions to fowls and ducks.

In spite of a little chagrin, it was a relief to have no more cattle on hand. Life was not made merely to be slaved away. Both girls agreed in this. The fowls were quite enough trouble. March had set up her carpenter's bench at the end of the open shed. Here she worked, making coops and doors and other appurtenances. The fowls were

7

housed in the bigger building, which had served as barn and cowshed in old days. They had a beautiful home, and should have been perfectly content. Indeed, they looked well enough. But the girls were disgusted at their tendency to strange illnesses, at their exacting way of life, and at their refusal, obstinate refusal, to lay eggs.

March did most of the out door work. When she was out and about, in her puttees and breeches, her belted coat and her loose cap, she looked almost like some graceful, loose-balanced young man, for her shoulders were straight, and her movements easy and confident, even tinged with a little indifference, or irony. But her face was not a man's face, ever. The wisps of her crisp dark hair blew about her as she stooped, her eyes were big and wide and dark, when she looked up again, strange, startled, shy and sardonic at once. Her mouth, too, was almost pinched as if in pain and irony. There was something odd and unexplained about her. She would stand balanced on one hip, looking at the fowls pattering about in the obnoxious fine mud of the sloping yard, and calling to her favourite white hen, which came in answer to her name. But there was an almost satirical flicker in March's big, dark eyes as she looked at her three-toed flock pottering about under her gaze, and the same slight dangerous satire in her voice as she spoke to the favoured Patty, who pecked at March's boot by way of friendly demonstration.

Fowls did not flourish at Bailey Farm, in spite of all that March did for them. When she provided hot food for them, in the morning, according to rule, she noticed that it made them heavy and dozy for hours. She expected to see them lean against the pillars of the shed, in their languid processes of digestion. And she knew quite well that they ought to be busily scratching and foraging about, if they were to come to any good. So she decided to give them their hot food at night, and let them sleep on it. Which she did. But it made no difference.

War conditions, again, were very unfavourable to poultry keeping. Food was scarce and bad. And when the Daylight Saving Bill was passed, the fowls obstinately refused to go to bed as usual, about nine o'clock in the summer time. That was late enough, indeed, for there was no peace till they were shut up and asleep. Now they cheerfully walked around, without so much as glancing at the barn, until ten o'clock or later. Both Banford and March disbelieved in living for work alone. They wanted to read or take a cycle-ride in the evening: or perhaps March wished to paint curvilinear swans on porcelain,

8

with green background, or else make a marvellous fire-screen by processes of elaborate cabinet-work. For she was a creature of odd whims and unsatisfied tendencies. But from all these things she was prevented by the stupid fowls.

One evil there was greater than any other. Bailey Farm was a little homestead, with ancient wooden barn and two-gabled farm-house, lying just one field removed from the edge of the wood. Since the war the fox was a demon. He carried off the hens under the very noses of March and Banford. Banford would start and stare through her big spectacles with all her eyes, as another squawk and flutter took place at her heels. Too late! Another white leghorn gone. It was disheartening.

They did what they could to remedy it. When it became permitted to shoot foxes, they stood sentinel with their guns, the two of them, at the favoured hours. But it was no good. The fox was too quick for them. So another year passed, and another, and they were living on their losses, as Banford said. They let their farm-house one summer, and retired to live in a railway-carriage that was deposited as a sort of out-house in a corner of the field. This amused them, and helped their finances. None the less, things looked dark.

Although they were usually the best of friends, because Banford, though nervous and delicate, was a warm, generous soul, and March, though so odd and absent in herself, had a strange magnanimity, yet, in the long solitude, they were apt to become a little irritable with one another, tired of one another. March had four-fifths of the work to do, and though she did not mind, there seemed no relief, and it made her eyes flash curiously sometimes. Then Banford, feeling more nerve-worn than ever, would become despondent, and March would speak sharply to her. They seemed to be losing ground, somehow, losing hope as the months went by. There alone in the fields by the wood, with the wide country stretching hollow and dim to the round hills of the White Horse, in the far distance, they seemed to have to live too much off themselves. There was nothing to keep them up—and no hope.

The fox really exasperated them both. As soon as they had let the fowls out, in the early summer mornings, they had to take their guns and keep guard: and then again, as soon as evening began to mellow, they must go once more. And he was so sly. He slid along in the deep grass, he was difficult as a serpent to see. And he seemed to circumvent the girls deliberately. Once or twice March had caught sight of the white tip of his brush, or the ruddy shadow of him in the deep grass, and she had let fire at him. But he made no account of this.

One evening March was standing with her back to the sunset, her gun under her arm, her hair pushed under her cap. She was half watching, half musing. It was her constant state. Her eyes were keen and observant, but her inner mind took no notice of what she saw. She was always lapsing into this odd, rapt state, her mouth rather screwed up. It was a question, whether she was there, actually consciously present, or not.

The trees on the wood-edge were a darkish, brownish green in the full light—for it was the end of August. Beyond, the naked, copper-like shafts and limbs of the pine-trees shone in the air. Nearer, the rough grass, with its long brownish stalks all agleam, was full of light. The fowls were round about—the ducks were still swimming on the pond under the pine trees. March looked at it all, saw it all, and did not see it. She heard Banford speaking to the fowls, in the distance—and she did not hear. What was she thinking about? Heaven knows. Her consciousness was, as it were, held back.

She lowered her eyes, and suddenly saw the fox. He was looking up at her. His chin was pressed down, and his eyes were looking up. They met her eyes. And he knew her. She was spell-bound. She knew he knew her. So he looked into her eyes, and her soul failed her. He knew her, he was not daunted.

She struggled, confusedly she came to herself, and saw him making off, with slow leaps leaping over some fallen boughs, slow, impudent jumps. Then he glanced over his shoulder, and ran smoothly away. She saw his brush held smooth like a feather, she saw his white buttocks twinkle. And he was gone, softly, soft as the wind.

She put her gun to her shoulder, but even then pursed her mouth, knowing it was nonsense to pretend to fire. So she began to walk slowly after him, in the direction he had gone, slowly, pertinaciously. She expected to find him. In her heart she was determined to find him. What she would do when she saw him again she did not consider. But she was determined to find him. So she walked abstractedly about on the edge of the wood, with wide, vivid dark eyes, and a faint flush in her cheeks. She did not think. In strange mindlessness she walked hither and thither.

At last she became aware that Banford was calling her. She made an effort of attention, turned, and gave some sort of screaming call in answer. Then again she was striding off towards the homestead. The red sun was setting, the fowls were retiring towards their roost. She watched them, white creatures, black creatures, gathering to the barn. She watched them spell-bound, without seeing them. But her automatic intelligence told her when it was time to shut the door.

She went indoors to supper, which Banford had set on the table. Banford chatted easily. March seemed to listen, in her distant, manly way. She answered a brief word now and then. But all the time she was as if spell-bound. And as soon as supper was over, she rose again to go out, without saying why.

She took her gun again and went to look for the fox. For he had lifted his eyes upon her, and his knowing look seemed to have entered her brain. She did not so much think of him: she was possessed by him. She saw his dark, shrewd, unabashed eye looking into her, knowing her. She felt him invisibly master her spirit. She knew the way he lowered his chin as he looked up, she knew his muzzle, the golden brown, and the greyish white. And again, she saw him glance over his shoulder at her, half inviting, half contemptuous and cunning. So she went, with her great startled eyes glowing, her gun under her arm, along the wood edge. Meanwhile the night fell, and a great moon rose above the pine trees. And again Banford was calling.

So she went indoors. She was silent and busy. She examined her gun, and cleaned it, musing abstractedly by the lamp-light. Then she went out again, under the great moon, to see if everything was right. When she saw the dark crests of the pine-trees against the blond sky, again her heart beat to the fox, the fox. She wanted to follow him, with her gun.

It was some days before she mentioned the affair to Banford. Then suddenly, one evening, she said:

"The fox was right at my feet on Saturday night."

"Where?" said Banford, her eyes opening behind her spectacles.

"When I stood just above the pond."

"Did you fire?" cried Banford.

"No, I didn't."

"Why not?"

"Why, I was too much surprised, I suppose."

It was the same old, slow, laconic way of speech March always had. Banford stared at her friend for a few moments.

"You saw him?" she cried.

"Oh yes! He was looking up at me, cool as anything."

"I tell you," cried Banford—"the cheek!—They're not afraid of us, Nellie."

"Oh no," said March.

"Pity you didn't get a shot at him," said Banford.

"Isn't it a pity! I've been looking for him ever since. But I don't suppose he'll come so near again."

"I don't suppose he will," said Banford.

And she proceeded to forget about it: except that she was more indignant than ever at the impudence of the beggars. March also was not conscious that she thought of the fox. But whenever she fell into her odd half-muses, when she was half rapt, and half intelligently aware of what passed under her vision, then it was the fox which somehow dominated her unconsciousness, possessed the blank half of her musing. And so it was for weeks, and months. No matter whether she had been climbing the trees for the apples, or beating down the last of the damsons, or whether she had been digging out the ditch from the duck-pond, or clearing out the barn, when she had finished, or when she straightened herself, and pushed the wisps of hair away again from her forehead, and pursed up her mouth again in an odd, screwed fashion, much too old for her years, then was sure to come over her mind the old spell of the fox, as it came when he was looking at her. It was as if she could smell him, at these times. And it always recurred, at unexpected moments, just as she was going to sleep at night, or just as she was pouring the water into the teapot, to make tea—there it was, the fox, it came over her like a spell.

So the months passed. She still looked for him unconsciously, whenever she went towards the wood. He had become a settled effect in her spirit, a state permanently established, not continuous, but always recurring. She did not know what she felt or thought: only the state came over her, as when he looked at her.

The months passed, the dark evenings came, heavy, dark November, when March went about in high boots, ankle deep in mud, when the night began to fall at four o'clock, and the day never properly dawned. Both girls dreaded these times. They dreaded the almost continuous darkness that enveloped them on their desolate little farm near the wood. Banford was physically afraid. She was afraid of tramps, afraid lest someone should come prowling round. March was not so much afraid, as uncomfortable and disturbed. She felt discomfort and gloom in all her physique.

Usually, the two girls had tea in the sitting room. March lighted a fire at dusk, and put on the wood she had chopped and sawed during the day. Then the long evening was in front, dark, sodden, black outside, lonely and rather oppressive inside, a little dismal. March was content not to talk, but Banford could not keep still. Merely listening to the wind in the pines outside, or the drip of water, was too much for her.

One evening the girls had washed up the tea-things in the kitchen, and March had put on her house-shoes, and taken up a roll of crochet-work, which she worked at slowly from time to time. So she lapsed into silence. Banford stared at the red fire, which, being of wood, needed constant attention. She was afraid to begin to read too early, because her eyes would not bear any strain. So she sat staring at the fire, listening to the distant sounds, sound of cattle lowing, of a dull, heavy, moist wind, of the rattle of the evening train on the little railway not far off. She was almost fascinated by the red glow of the fire.

Suddenly both girls started, and lifted their heads. They heard a footstep—distinctly a footstep. Banford recoiled in fear. March stood listening. Then rapidly she approached the door that led into the kitchen. At the same time they heard the footsteps approach the back door. They waited a second. The back door opened softly. Banford gave a loud cry. A man's voice said softly:

"Hello!"

March recoiled, and took a gun from a corner.

"What do you want?" she cried, in a sharp voice.

Again the soft, softly-vibrating man's voice said:

"Hello! What's wrong?"

"I shall shoot!" cried March. "What do you want?"

"Why, what's wrong? What's wrong?" came the soft, wondering, rather scared voice: and a young soldier, with his heavy kit on his back, advanced into the dim light. "Why," he said, "who lives here then?"

"We live here," said March. "What do you want?"

"Oh!" came the long, melodious wonder-note from the young soldier. "Doesn't William Grenfel live here then?"

"No—you know he doesn't."

"Do I?—Do I?—I don't, you see.—He *did* live here, because he

13

was my grandfather, and I lived here myself five years ago.—What's become of him then?"

The young man—or youth, for he would not be more than twenty, now advanced and stood in the inner doorway. March, already under the influence of his strange, soft, modulated voice, stared at him spell-bound. He had a ruddy, roundish face, with fairish hair, rather long, flattened to his forehead with sweat. His eyes were blue, and very bright and sharp. On his cheeks, on the fresh ruddy skin were fine, fair hairs, like a down, but sharper. It gave him a slightly glistening look. Having his heavy sack on his shoulders, he stooped, thrusting his head forward. His hat was loose in one hand. He stared brightly, very keenly from girl to girl, particularly at March, who stood pale, with great dilated eyes, in her belted coat and puttees, her hair knotted in a big crisp knot behind. She still had the gun in her hand. Behind her, Banford, clinging to the sofa-arm, was shrinking away, with half-averted head.

"I thought my grandfather still lived here?—I wonder if he's dead."

"We've been here for three years," said Banford, who was beginning to recover her wits, seeing something boyish in the round head with its rather long, sweaty hair.

"Three years! You don't say so!—And you don't know who was here before you?"

"I know it was an old man, who lived by himself."

"Ay!—Yes, that's him!—And what became of him then?"

"He died.—I know he died—"

"Ay! He's dead then!"

The youth stared at them without changing colour or expression. If he had any expression, besides a slight baffled look of wonder, it was one of sharp curiosity concerning the two girls, sharp, impersonal curiosity, the curiosity of that round young head.

But to March he was the fox. Whether it was the thrusting forward of the head, or the glisten of fine whitish hairs on the ruddy cheek-bones, or the bright, keen eyes, that can never be said: but the boy was to her the fox, and she could not see him otherwise.

"How is it you didn't know if your grandfather was alive or dead?" asked Banford, recovering her natural sharpness.

"Ay, that's it," replied the softly-breathing youth. "You see I joined up in Canada, and I hadn't heard for three or four years.—I ran away to Canada."

"And now have you just come from France?"

"Well—from Salonika really."

There was a pause, nobody knowing quite what to say.

"So you've nowhere to go now?" said Banford rather lamely.

"Oh, I know some people in the village. Anyhow, I can go to the Swan."

"You came on the train, I suppose.—Would you like to sit down a bit?"

"Well—I don't mind."

He gave an odd little groan as he swung off his kit. Banford looked at March.

"Put the gun down," she said. "We'll make a cup of tea."

"Ay," said the youth. "We've seen enough of rifles."

He sat down rather tired on the sofa, leaning forward.

March recovered her presence of mind, and went into the kitchen. There she heard the soft young voice musing:

"Well, to think I should come back and find it like this!"

He did not seem sad, not at all—only rather interestedly surprised.

"And what a difference in the place, eh?" he continued, looking round the room.

"You see a difference, do you?" said Banford.

"Yes—don't I!"

His eyes were almost unnaturally clear and bright, though it was the brightness of abundant health.

March was busy in the kitchen preparing another meal. It was about seven o'clock. All the time, while she was active, she was attending to the youth in the sitting-room, not so much listening to what he said, as feeling the soft run of his voice. She primmed up her mouth tighter and tighter, puckering it as if it was sewed, in her effort to keep her will uppermost. Yet her large eyes dilated and glowed in spite of her, she lost herself. Rapidly and carelessly she prepared the meal, cutting large chunks of bread and margarine—for there was no butter. She racked her brain to think of something else to put on the tray—she had only bread, margarine, and jam, and the larder was bare. Unable to conjure anything up, she went into the sitting room with her tray.

She did not want to be noticed. Above all, she did not want him to look at her. But when she came in, and was busy setting the table just behind him, he pulled himself up from his sprawling, and turned to look over his shoulder. She became pale and wan.

The youth watched her as she bent over the table, looked at her slim, well-shapen legs, at the belted coat dropping around her thighs, at the knot of dark hair, and his curiosity, vivid and widely alert, was again arrested by her.

The lamp was shaded with a dark-green shade, so that the light was thrown downwards, the upper half of the room was dim. His face moved bright under the light, but March loomed shadowy in the distance.

She turned round, but kept her eyes sideways, dropping and lifting her dark lashes. Her mouth unpuckered, as she said to Banford:

"Will you pour out?"

Then she went into the kitchen again.

"Have your tea where you are, will you?" said Banford to the youth—"unless you'd rather come to the table."

"Well," said he, "I'm nice and comfortable here, aren't I? I will have it here, if you don't mind."

"There's nothing but bread and jam," she said. And she put his plate on a stool by him. She was very happy now, waiting on him. For she loved company. And now she was no more afraid of him than if he were her own younger brother. He was such a boy.

"Nellie," she called. "I've poured you a cup out."

March appeared in the doorway, took her cup, and sat down in a corner, as far from the light as possible. She was very sensitive in her knees. Having no skirts to cover them, and being forced to sit with them boldly exposed, she suffered. She shrank and shrank, trying not to be seen. And the youth, sprawling low on the couch, glanced up at her, with long, steady, penetrating looks, till she was almost ready to disappear. Yet she held her cup balanced, she drank her tea, screwed up her mouth and held her head averted. Her desire to be invisible was so strong that it quite baffled the youth. He felt he could not see her distinctly. She seemed like a shadow within the shadow. And ever his eyes came back to her, searching, unremitting, with unconscious fixed attention.

Meanwhile he was talking softly and smoothly to Banford, who loved nothing so much as gossip, and who was full of perky interest, like a bird. Also he ate largely and quickly and voraciously, so that March had to cut more hunks of bread and margarine, for the roughness of which Banford apologised.

"Oh well," said March, suddenly speaking, "if there's no butter to put on it, it's no good trying to make dainty pieces."

Again the youth watched her, and he laughed, with a sudden, quick laugh, showing his teeth and wrinkling his nose.

"It isn't, is it," he answered, in his soft, near voice.

It appeared he was Cornish by birth and upbringing. When he was twelve years old he had come to Bailey Farm with his grandfather, with whom he had never agreed very well. So he had run away to Canada, and worked far away in the West. Now he was here—and that was the end of it.

He was very curious about the girls, to find out exactly what they were doing. His questions were those of a farm youth: acute, practical, a little mocking. He was very much amused by their attitude to their losses: for they were amusing on the score of heifers and fowls.

"Oh well," broke in March, "we don't believe in living for nothing but work."

"Don't you?" he answered. And again the quick young laugh came over his face. He kept his eyes steadily on the obscure woman in the corner.

"But what will you do when you've used up all your capital?" he said.

"Oh, I don't know," answered March laconically. "Hire ourselves out for landworkers, I supppose."

"Yes, but there won't be any demand for women land-workers, now the war's over," said the youth.

"Oh, we'll see. We shall hold on a bit longer yet," said March, with a plangent, half sad, half ironical indifference.

"There wants a man about the place," said the youth softly.

Banford burst out laughing.

"Take care what you say," she interrupted. "We consider ourselves quite efficient."

"Oh," came March's slow, plangent voice, "it isn't a case of efficiency, I'm afraid. If you're going to do farming you must be at it from morning till night, and you might as well be a beast yourself."

"Yes, that's it," said the youth. "You aren't willing to put yourselves into it."

"We aren't," said March, "and we know it."

"We want some of our time for ourselves," said Banford.

The youth threw himself back on the sofa, his face tight with laughter, and laughed silently but thoroughly. The calm scorn of the girls tickled him tremendously.

"Yes," he said, "but why did you begin then?"

"Oh," said March, "we had a better opinion of the nature of fowls then, than we have now."

"Of Nature altogether, I'm afraid," said Banford. "Don't talk to me about Nature."

Again the face of the youth tightened with delighted laughter.

"You haven't a very high opinion of fowls and cattle, have you?" he said.

"Oh no—quite a low one," said March.

He laughed out.

"Neither fowls nor heifers," said Banford, "nor goats nor the weather."

The youth broke into a sharp yap of laughter, delighted. The girls began to laugh too, March turning aside her face and wrinkling her mouth in amusement.

"Oh well," said Banford, "we don't mind, do we Nellie?"

"No," said March, "we don't mind."

The youth was very pleased. He had eaten and drunk his fill. Banford began to question him. His name was Henry Grenfel—no, he was not called Harry, always Henry. He continued to answer with courteous simplicity, grave and charming. March, who was now not included, cast long, slow glances at him from her recess, as he sat there on the sofa, his hands clasping his knees, his face under the lamp bright and alert, turned to Banford. She became almost peaceful, at last. He was identified with the fox—and he was here in full presence. She need not go after him any more. There in the shadow of her corner she gave herself up to a warm, relaxed peace, almost like sleep, accepting the spell that was on her. But she wished to remain hidden. She was only fully at peace whilst he forgot her, talking with Banford. Hidden in the shadow of her corner, she need not any more be divided in herself, trying to keep up two planes of consciousness. She could at last lapse into the odour of the fox.

For the youth, sitting before the fire in his uniform, sent a faint but distinct odour into the room, indefinable, but something like a wild creature. March no longer tried to reserve herself from it. She was still and soft in her corner like a passive creature in its cave.

At last the talk dwindled. The youth relaxed his clasp of his knees, pulled himself together a little, and looked round. Again he became aware of the silent, half-invisible woman in the corner.

"Well," he said, unwillingly, "I suppose I'd better be going, or they'll be in bed at the Swan."

"I'm afraid they're in bed anyhow," said Banford. "They've all got this influenza."

"Have they!" he exclaimed. And he pondered. "Well," he continued, "I shall find a place somewhere."

"I'd say you could stay here, only—" Banford began.

He turned and watched her, holding his head forward.

"What—?" he asked.

"Oh well," she said, "propriety, I suppose—". She was rather confused.

"It wouldn't be improper, would it?" he said, gently surprised.

"Not as far as we're concerned," said Banford.

"And not as far as *I'm* concerned," he said, with grave naïveté. "After all, it's my own home, in a way."

Banford smiled at this.

"It's what the village will have to say," she said.

"I see," he answered. And he looked from one to another.

"What do you say, Nellie?" asked Banford.

"I don't mind," said March, in her distinct tone. "The village doesn't matter to me, anyhow."

"No," said the youth, quick and soft. "Why should it?—I mean, what should they say?"

"Oh well," came March's plangent, laconic voice, "they'll easily find something to say. But it makes no difference, what they say. We can look after ourselves."

"Of course you can," said the youth.

"Well then, stop if you like," said Banford. "The spare room is quite ready."

His face shone with pleasure.

"If you're quite sure it isn't troubling you too much," he said, with that soft courtesy which distinguished him.

"Oh, it's no trouble," they both said.

He looked, smiling with delight, from one to another.

"It's awfully nice not to have to turn out again, isn't it?" he said gratefully.

"I suppose it is," said Banford.

March disappeared to attend to the room. Banford was as pleased and thoughtful as if she had her own young brother home from France. It gave her just the same kind of gratification to attend on him, to get out the bath for him, and everything. Her natural warmth and kindliness had now an outlet. And the youth luxuriated in her sisterly attention. But it puzzled him slightly to know that March was silently working for him too. She was so curiously silent and obliterated. It seemed to him he had not really seen her. He felt he should not know her if he met her in the road.

That night March dreamed vividly. She dreamed she heard a singing outside, which she could not understand, a singing that roamed round the house, in the fields and in the darkness. It moved her so, that she felt she must weep. She went out, and suddenly she knew it was the fox singing. He was very yellow and bright, like corn. She went nearer to him, but he ran away, and ceased singing. He seemed near, and she wanted to touch him. She stretched out her hand, but suddenly he bit her wrist, and at the same instant, as she drew back, the fox, turning round to bound away, whisked his brush across her face, and it seemed his brush was on fire, for it seared and burned her mouth with a great pain. She awoke with the pain of it, and lay trembling as if she were really seared.

In the morning, however, she only remembered it as a distant memory. She arose and was busy preparing the house and attending to the fowls. Banford flew into the village on her bicycle, to try and buy food. She was a hospitable soul. But alas, in the year 1918 there was not much food to buy. The youth came downstairs in his shirt-sleeves. He was young and fresh, but he walked with his head thrust forward, so that his shoulders seemed raised and rounded, as if he had a slight curvature of the spine. It must have been only a manner of bearing himself, for he was young and vigorous. He washed himself and went outside, whilst the women were preparing breakfast.

He saw everything, and examined everything. His curiosity was quick and insatiable. He compared the state of things with that which he remembered before, and cast over in his mind the effect of the changes. He watched the fowls and the ducks, to see their condition, he noticed the flight of wood-pigeons overhead: they were very numerous; he saw the few apples high up, which March had not been able to reach; he remarked that they had borrowed a draw-pump, presumably to empty the big soft-water cistern which was on the north side of the house.

"It's a funny, dilapidated old place," he said to the girls, as he sat at breakfast.

His eyes were wide and childish, with thinking about things. He did not say much, but ate largely. March kept her face averted. She, too, in the early morning, could not be aware of him, though something about the glint of his khaki reminded her of the brilliance of her dream-fox.

During the day the girls went about their business. In the morning, he attended to the guns, shot a rabbit and a wild duck that was flying high, towards the woods. That was a great addition to the empty larder. The girls felt that already he had earned his keep. He said nothing about leaving, however. In the afternoon, he went to the village. He came back at tea-time. He had the same alert, forward-reaching look on his roundish face. He hung his hat on a peg with a little swinging gesture. He was thinking about something.

"Well," he said to the girls, as he sat at table. "What am I going to do?"

"How do you mean,—what are you going to do?" said Banford.

"Where am I going to find a place in the village, to stay?" he said.

"I don't know," said Banford. "Where do you think of staying?"

"Well—" he hesitated—"At the Swan they've got this Flu, and at the Plough and Harrow they've got the soldiers who are collecting the hay for the army: besides in the private houses. There's ten men and a corporal altogether billeted in the village, they tell me. I'm not sure where I could get a bed."

He left the matter to them. He was rather calm about it. March sat with her elbows on the table, her two hands supporting her chin, looking at him unconsciously. Suddenly he lifted his clouded blue eyes, and unthinking looked straight into March's eyes. He was startled as well as she. He too recoiled a little. March felt the same sly, taunting, knowing spark leap out of his eyes as he turned his head aside, and fall into her soul, as it had fallen from the dark eyes of the fox. She pursed her mouth as if in pain, as if asleep too.

"Well, I don't know—" Banford was saying. She seemed reluctant, as if she were afraid of being imposed upon. She looked at March. But, with her weak, troubled sight, she only saw the usual semi-abstraction on her friend's face. "Why don't you speak, Nellie?" she said.

But March was wide-eyed and silent, and the youth, as if fascinated, was watching her without moving his eyes.

"Go on—answer something," said Banford. And March turned her head slightly aside, as if coming to consciousness, or trying to come to consciousness.

"What do you expect me to say?" she asked automatically.

"Say what you think," said Banford.

"It's all the same to me," said March.

And again there was silence. A pointed light seemed to be on the boy's eyes, penetrating like a needle.

"So it is to me," said Banford. "You can stop on here if you like."

A smile like a cunning little flame came over his face, suddenly and involuntarily. He dropped his head quickly to hide it, and remained with his head dropped, his face hidden.

"You can stop on here if you like. You can please yourself, Henry," Banford concluded.

Still he did not reply, but remained with his head dropped. Then he lifted his face. It was bright with a curious light, as if exultant, and his eyes were strangely clear as he watched March. She turned her face aside, her mouth suffering as if wounded, and her consciousness dim. Banford became a little puzzled. She watched the steady, pellucid gaze of the youth's eyes, as he looked at March, with the invisible smile gleaming on his face. She did not know how he was smiling, for no feature moved. It seemed only in the gleam, almost the glitter of the fine hairs on his cheeks.

Then he looked with quite a changed look, at Banford.

"I'm sure," he said in his soft, courteous voice, "you're awfully good. You're too good. You don't want to be bothered with me, I'm sure."

"Cut a bit more bread, Nellie," said Banford uneasily; adding: "It's no bother, if you like to stay. It's like having my own brother here for a few days. He's a boy like you are."

"That's awfully kind of you," the lad repeated. "I should like to stay, ever so much, if you're sure I'm not a trouble to you."

"No, of course you're no trouble. I tell you, it's a pleasure to have somebody in the house besides ourselves," said warm-hearted Banford.

"But Miss March?" he said in his soft voice, looking at her.

"Oh, it's quite all right as far as I'm concerned," said March vaguely.

His face beamed, and he almost rubbed his hands with pleasure.

"Well then," he said. "I should love it. I should love it, if you'd let me pay my board, and help with the work."

"You've no need to talk about board," said Banford.

One or two days went by, and the youth stayed on at the farm. Banford was quite charmed by him. He was so soft and courteous in

22

speech, not wanting to say much himself, preferring to hear what she had to say, and to laugh in his quick, half mocking way. He helped readily with the work—but not too much. He loved to be out alone with the gun in his hands, to watch, to see. For his sharp-eyed, impersonal curiosity was insatiable, and he was most free when he was quite alone, half-hidden, watching.

Particularly he watched March. She was a strange character to him. Her figure, like a graceful young man's, piqued him. Her dark eyes made something rise in his soul, with a curious elate excitement, when he looked into them, an excitement he was afraid to let be seen, it was so keen and secret. And then her odd, shrewd speech made him laugh outright. He felt he must go further, he was inevitably impelled.—But he put away the thought of her, and went off towards the wood's edge with the gun.

The dusk was falling as he came home, and with the dusk, a fine, late-November rain. He saw the fire-light leaping in the window of the sitting-room, a leaping light in the little cluster of dark buildings. And he thought to himself, it would be a good thing to have this place for his own. And then the thought entered him shrewdly: why not marry March? He stood still in the middle of the field for some moments, the dead rabbit hanging still in his hand, arrested by this thought. His mind waited in amazement—it seemed to calculate—and then he smiled curiously to himself in acquiescence. Why not? Why not indeed? It was a good idea. What if it was rather ridiculous? What did it matter? What if she was older than he? It didn't matter. When he thought of her dark, startled, vulnerable eyes he smiled subtly to himself. He was older than she, really. He was master of her.

He scarcely admitted his intention even to himself. He kept it as a secret even from himself. It was all too uncertain as yet. He would have to see how things went.

Yes, he would have to see how things went. If he wasn't careful, she would just simply mock at the idea. He knew, sly and subtle as he was, that if he went to her plainly and said: "Miss March, I love you and want you to marry me," her inevitable answer would be: "Get out. I don't want any of that tomfoolery." This was her attitude to men and their "tomfoolery." If he was not careful, she would turn round on him with her savage, sardonic ridicule, and dismiss him from the farm and from her own mind, for ever. He would have to go gently. He would have to catch her as you catch a deer or a woodcock when you go out shooting. It's no good walking out into the forest and saying to the deer: "Please fall to my gun." No, it is a slow, subtle battle. When you really go out to get a deer, you gather yourself together, you coil yourself inside yourself, and you advance secretly, before dawn, into the mountains. It is not so much what you do, when you go out hunting, as how you feel. You have to be subtle and cunning and absolutely fatally ready. It becomes like a fate. Your own fate overtakes and determines the fate of the deer you are hunting. First of all, even before you come in sight of your quarry, there is a strange battle, like mesmerism. Your own soul, as a hunter, has gone out to fasten on the soul of the deer, even before you see any deer. And the soul of the deer fights to escape. Even before the deer has any wind of you, it is so. It is a subtle, profound battle of wills, which takes place in the invisible. And it is a battle never finished till your bullet goes home. When you are *really* worked up to the true pitch, and you come at last into range, you don't then aim as you do when you are firing at a bottle. It is your own *will* which carries the bullet into the heart of your quarry. The bullet's flight home is a sheer projection of your own fate into the fate of the deer. It happens like a supreme wish, a supreme act of volition, not as a dodge of cleverness.

He was a huntsman in spirit, not a farmer, and not a soldier stuck in a regiment. And it was as a young hunter, that he wanted to bring down March as his quarry, to make her his wife. So he gathered himself subtly together, seemed to withdraw into a kind of invisibility. He was not quite sure how he would go on. And March was suspicious as a hare. So he remained in appearance just the nice, odd stranger-youth staying for a fortnight on the place.

He had been sawing logs for the fire, in the afternoon. Darkness came very early: it was still a cold, raw mist. It was getting almost too dark to see. A pile of short sawed logs lay beside the trestle. March came to carry them indoors, or into the shed, as he was busy sawing the last log. He was working in his shirt sleeves, and did not notice her approach, she came unwilling, as if shy. He saw her stooping to the bright-ended logs, and he stopped sawing. A fire like lightning flew down his legs, in the nerves.

"March?" he said, in his quiet young voice.

She looked up from the logs she was piling.

"Yes?" she said.

He looked down on her in the dusk. He could see her not too distinctly.

"I wanted to ask you something," he said.

"Did you? What was it?" she said. Already the fright was in her voice. But she was too much mistress of herself.

"Why—" his voice seemed to draw out soft and subtle, it penetrated her nerves—"why, what do you think it is?"

She stood up, placed her hands on her hips, and stood looking at him transfixed, without answering. Again he burned with a sudden power.

"Well," he said and his voice was so soft it seemed rather like a subtle touch, like the merest touch of a cat's paw, a feeling rather than a sound. "Well—I wanted to ask you to marry me."

March felt him rather than heard him. She was trying in vain to turn aside her face. A great relaxation seemed to have come over her. She stood silent, her head slightly on one side. He seemed to be bending towards her, invisibly smiling. It seemed to her fine sparks came out of him.

Then very suddenly, she said:

"Don't you try any of your tomfoolery on me."

A quiver went over his nerves. He had missed. He waited a moment to collect himself again. Then he said, putting all the strange softness into his voice, as if he were imperceptibly stroking her:

"Why, it's not tomfoolery. It's not tomfoolery. I mean it. I mean it. What makes you disbelieve me?"

He sounded hurt. And his voice had such a curious power over her; making her feel loose and relaxed. She struggled somewhere for her own power. She felt for a minute that she was lost—lost—lost. The word seemed to rock in her as if she were dying. Suddenly again she spoke.

"You don't know what you're talking about," she said, in a brief and transient stroke of scorn. "What nonsense! I'm old enough to be your mother."

"Yes I do know what I'm talking about. Yes I do," he persisted softly, as if he were producing his voice in her blood. "I know quite well what I'm talking about. You're not old enough to be my mother. That isn't true. And what does it matter even if it was. You can marry me whatever age we are. What is age? What is age to me? And what is age to you! Age is nothing."

A swoon went over her as he concluded. He spoke rapidly—in the rapid Cornish fashion—and his voice seemed to sound in her somewhere where she was helpless against it. "Age is nothing!" The soft, heavy insistence of it made her sway dimly out there in the darkness. She could not answer.

A great exultance leaped like fire over his limbs. He felt he had won.

"I want to marry you, you see. Why shouldn't I?" he proceeded, soft and rapid. He waited for her to answer. In the dusk he saw her almost phosphorescent. Her eyelids were dropped, her face half-averted and unconscious. She seemed to be in his power. But he waited, watchful. He dared not yet touch her.

"Say then," he said. "Say then you'll marry me. Say—say?" He was softly insistent.

"What?" she asked, faint, from a distance, like one in pain. His voice was now unthinkably near and soft. He drew very near to her.

"Say yes."

"Oh I can't," she wailed helplessly, half articulate, as if semi-conscious, and as if in pain, like one who dies. "How can I?"

"You can," he said softly, laying his hand gently on her shoulder as she stood with her head averted and dropped, dazed. "You can. Yes, you can. What makes you say you can't? You can. You can." And with awful softness he bent forward and just touched her neck with his mouth and his chin.

"Don't!" she cried, with a faint mad cry like hysteria, starting away and facing round on him. "What do you mean?" But she had no breath to speak with. It was as if she was killed.

"I mean what I say," he persisted softly and cruelly. "I want you to marry me. I want you to marry me. You know that, now, don't you? You know that, now? Don't you? Don't you?"

"What?" she said.

"Know," he replied.

"Yes," she said. "I know you say so."

"And you know I mean it, don't you?"

"I know you say so."

"You believe me?" he said.

She was silent for some time. Then she pursed her lips.

"I don't know what I believe," she said.

"Are you out there?" came Banford's voice, calling from the house.

"Yes, we're bringing in the logs," he answered.

"I thought you'd gone lost," said Banford disconsolately. "Hurry up, do, and come and let's have tea. The kettle's boiling."

He stooped at once, to take an armful of little logs and carry them into the kitchen, where they were piled in a corner. March also helped, filling her arms and carrying the logs on her breast as if they were some heavy child. The night had fallen cold.

When the logs were all in, the two cleaned their boots noisily on the scraper outside, then rubbed them on the mat. March shut the door and took off her old felt hat—her farm-girl hat. Her thick, crisp black hair was loose, her face was pale and strained. She pushed back her hair vaguely, and washed her hands. Banford came hurrying into the dimly-lighted kitchen, to take from the oven the scones she was keeping hot.

"Whatever have you been doing all this time?" she asked fretfully. "I thought you were never coming in. And it's ages since you stopped sawing. What were you doing out there?"

"Well," said Henry, "we had to stop up that hole in the barn, to keep the rats out."

"Why I could see you standing there in the shed. I could see your shirt sleeves," challenged Banford.

"Yes, I was just putting the saw away."

They went in to tea. March was quite mute. Her face was pale and strained and vague. The youth, who always had the same ruddy, self-contained look on his face, as though he were keeping himself to himself, had come to tea in his shirtsleeves as if he were at home. He bent over his plate as he ate his food.

"Aren't you cold?" said Banford spitefully. "In your shirtsleeves."

He looked up at her, with his chin near his plate, and his eyes very clear, pellucid, and unwavering as he watched her.

"No, I'm not cold," he said with his usual soft courtesy. "It's much warmer in here than it is outside, you see."

"I hope it is," said Banford, feeling nettled by him. He had a strange, suave assurance, and a wide-eyed bright look that got on her nerves this evening. He watched her.

"But perhaps," he said softly and courteously, "you don't like me coming to tea without my coat. I forgot that."

"Oh, I don't mind," said Banford: although she *did*.

"I'll go and get it, shall I?" he said.

March's dark eyes turned slowly down to him.

"No, don't you bother," she said in her queer, twanging tone. "If you feel all right as you are, stop as you are." She spoke with a crude authority.

"Yes," said he, "I *feel* all right, if I'm not rude."

"It's usually considered rude," said Banford. "But we don't mind."

"Go along, 'considered rude'," ejaculated March. "Who considers it rude?"

"Why you do, Nellie, in anybody else," said Banford, bridling a little behind her spectacles, and feeling her food stick in her throat.

But March had again gone vague and unheeding, chewing her food as if she did not know she was eating at all. And the youth looked from one to another with bright, watchful eyes.

Banford was offended. For all his suave courtesy and soft voice, the youth seemed to her impudent. She did not like to look at him. She did not like to meet his clear, watchful eyes, she did not like to see the strange glow in his face, his cheeks with their delicate fine hair, and his ruddy skin that was quite dull and yet which seemed to burn with a curious heat of life. It made her feel a little ill to look at him: the quality of his physical presence was too penetrating, too hot.

After tea the evening was very quiet. The youth rarely went into the village. As a rule he read: he was a great reader, in his own hours. That is, when he did begin, he read absorbedly. But he was not very eager to begin. Often he walked about the fields and along the hedges alone in the dark at night, prowling with a queer instinct for the night, and listening to the wild sounds.

Tonight however he took a Captain Mayne Reid book from Banford's shelf and sat down with knees wide apart and immersed himself in his story. His brownish fair hair was long, and lay on his head like a thick cap, combed sideways. He was still in his shirt-sleeves, and bending forward under the lamplight, with his knees stuck wide apart and the book in his hand and his whole figure absorbed in the rather strenuous business of reading, he gave Banford's sitting-room the look of a lumber-camp. She resented this. For on her sitting-room floor she had a red Turkey rug and dark stain round, the fire-place had fashionable green tiles, the piano stood open with the latest dance-music: she played quite well: and on the walls were March's handpainted swans and water-lilies. Moreover, with the logs nicely, tremulously burning in the grate, the thick curtains drawn, the doors all shut, and the pine-trees hissing and shuddering in the wind outside, it was cosy, it was refined and nice. She resented the big, raw, long-legged youth sticking his khaki knees out and sitting there with his soldier's shirt-cuffs buttoned on his thick red wrists. From time to time he turned a page, and from time to time he gave a sharp look at the fire, settling the logs. Then he immersed himself again in the intense and isolated business of reading.

March, on the far side of the table, was spasmodically crochetting. Her mouth was pursed in an odd way, as when she had dreamed the fox's brush burned it, her beautiful, crisp black hair strayed in wisps. But her whole figure was absent in its bearing, as if she herself was miles away. In a sort of semi-dream she seemed to be hearing the fox singing round the house in the wind, singing wildly and sweetly and like a madness. With red but well-shapen hands she slowly crochetted the white cotton, very slowly, awkwardly.

Banford was also trying to read, sitting in her low chair. But between those two she felt fidgetty. She kept moving and looking round and listening to the wind and glancing secretly from one to the other of her companions. March, seated on a straight chair, with her knees in their close breeches crossed, and slowly, laboriously crochetting, was also a trial.

"Oh dear!" said Banford. "My eyes are bad tonight." And she pressed her fingers on her eyes.

The youth looked up at her with his clear bright look, but did not speak.

"Are they, Jill?" said March absently.

Then the youth began to read again, and Banford perforce returned to her book. But she could not keep still. After a while she looked up at March, and a queer, almost malignant little smile was on her thin face.

"A penny for them, Nell," she said suddenly.

March looked round with big, startled black eyes, and went pale as if with terror. She had been listening to the fox singing so tenderly, so tenderly, as he wandered round the house.

"What?" she said vaguely.

"A penny for them," said Banford sarcastically. "Or twopence, if they're as deep as all that."

The youth was watching with bright clear eyes from beneath the lamp.

"Why," came March's vague voice, "what do you want to waste your money for?"

"I thought it would be well spent," said Banford.

"I wasn't thinking of anything except the way the wind was blowing," said March.

"Oh dear," replied Banford. "I could have had as original thoughts as that myself. I'm afraid I *have* wasted my money this time."

"Well, you needn't pay," said March.

The youth suddenly laughed. Both women looked at him: March rather surprised-looking, as if she had hardly known he was there.

"Why, do you ever pay up on those occasions?" he asked.

"Oh yes," said Banford. "We always do. I've sometimes had to pay a shilling a week to Nellie, in the winter time. It costs much less in summer."

"What, paying for each other's thoughts?" he laughed.

"Yes, when we've absolutely come to the end of everything else."

He laughed quickly, wrinkling his nose sharply like a puppy and laughing with quick pleasure, his eyes shining.

"It's the first time I ever heard of that," he said.

"I guess you'd hear of it often enough if you stayed a winter on Bailey Farm," said Banford lamentably.

"Do you get so tired, then?" he asked.

"So bored," said Banford.

"Oh!" he said gravely. "But why should you be bored?"

"Who wouldn't be bored?" said Banford.

"I'm sorry to hear that," he said gravely.

"You must be, if you were hoping to have a lively time here," said Banford.

He looked at her long and gravely.

"Well," he said, with his odd young seriousness, "it's quite lively enough for me."

"I'm glad to hear it," said Banford.

And she returned to her book. In her thin, frail hair were already many threads of grey, though she was not yet thirty. The boy did not look down, but turned his eyes to March, who was sitting with pursed mouth laboriously crochetting, her eyes wide and absent. She had a warm, pale, fine skin, and a delicate nose. Her pursed mouth looked shrewish. But the shrewish look was contradicted by the curious lifted arch of her dark brows, and the wideness of her eyes; a look of startled wonder and vagueness. She was listening again for the fox, who seemed to have wandered farther off into the night.

From under the edge of the lamplight the boy sat with his face looking up, watching her silently, his eyes round and very clear and intent. Banford, biting her fingers irritably, was glancing at him under her hair. He sat there perfectly still, his ruddy face tilted up from the low level under the light, on the edge of the dimness, and watching with perfect abstract intentness. March suddenly lifted her great dark eyes from her crochetting, and saw him. She started, giving a little exclamation.

"There he *is*!" she cried involuntarily, as if terribly startled.

Banford looked round in amazement, sitting up straight.

"Whatever has got you, Nellie?" she cried.

But March, her face flushed a delicate rose colour, was looking away to the door.

"Nothing! Nothing!" she said crossly. "Can't one speak?"

"Yes, if you speak sensibly," said Banford. "Whatever did you mean?"

"I don't know what I meant," cried March testily.

"Oh Nellie, I hope you aren't going jumpy and nervy. I feel I can't stand another *thing*!—Whoever did you mean? Did you mean Henry?" cried poor frightened Banford.

"Yes, I suppose so," said March laconically. She would never confess to the fox.

"Oh dear, my nerves are all gone for tonight," wailed Banford.

At nine o'clock March brought in a tray with bread and cheese and tea—Henry had confessed that he liked a cup of tea. Banford drank a glass of milk, and ate a little bread. And soon she said:

"I'm going to bed, Nellie. I'm all nerves tonight. Are you coming?"

"Yes, I'm coming the minute I've taken the tray away," said March.

"Don't be long then," said Banford fretfully. "Goodnight Henry. You'll see the fire is safe, if you come up last, won't you?"

"Yes Miss Banford, I'll see it's safe," he replied in his reassuring way.

March was lighting the candle to go to the kitchen. Banford took her candle and went upstairs. When March came back to the fire she said to him:

"I suppose we can trust you to put out the fire and everything?"—She stood there with her hand on her hip, and one knee loose, her head averted shyly, as if she could not look at him. He had his face lifted, watching her.

"Come and sit down a minute," he said softly.

"No, I'll be going. Jill will be waiting, and she'll get upset if I don't come."

"What made you jump like that this evening?" he asked.

"When did I jump?" she retorted, looking at him.

"Why just now you did," he said. "When you cried out."

"Oh!" she said. "Then!—Why, I thought you were the fox!" And her face screwed into a queer smile, half ironic.

"The fox! Why the fox?" he asked softly.

"Why one evening last summer when I was out with the gun I saw the fox in the grass nearly at my feet, looking straight up at me. I don't know—I suppose he made an impression on me." She turned aside her head again, and let one foot stray loose, self-consciously.

"And did you shoot him?" asked the boy.

"No, he gave me such a start, staring straight at me as he did, and then stopping to look back at me over his shoulder with a laugh on his face."

"A laugh on his face!" repeated Henry, also laughing. "He frightened you, did he?"

"No, he didn't frighten me. He made an impression on me, that's all."

"And you thought I was the fox, did you?" he laughed, with the same queer, quick little laugh, like a puppy wrinkling its nose.

"Yes I did, for the moment," she said. "Perhaps he'd been in my mind without my knowing."

"Perhaps you think I've come to steal your chickens or something," he said, with the same young laugh.

But she only looked at him with a wide, dark, vacant eye.

"It's the first time," he said, "that I've ever been taken for a fox. Won't you sit down for a minute?" His voice was very soft and cajoling.

"No," she said. "Jill will be waiting." But still she did not go, but stood with one foot loose and her face turned aside, just outside the circle of light.

"But won't you answer my question?" he said, lowering his voice still more.

"I don't know what question you mean."

"Yes, you do. Of course you do. I mean the question of you marrying me."

"No, I shan't answer that question," she said flatly.

"Won't you?" The queer young laugh came on his nose again. "Is it because I'm like the fox? Is that why?" And still he laughed.

She turned and looked at him with a long, slow look.

"I wouldn't let that put you against me," he said. "Let me turn the lamp low, and come and sit down a minute."

He put his red hand under the glow of the lamp, and suddenly made the light very dim. March stood there in the dimness quite shadowy, but unmoving. He rose silently to his feet, on his long legs. And now his voice was extraordinarily soft and suggestive, hardly audible.

"You'll stay a moment," he said. "Just a moment." And he put his hand on her shoulder.—She turned her face from him. "I'm sure you don't really think I'm like the fox," he said, with the same softness and with a suggestion of laughter in his tone, a subtle mockery. "Do you now?"—And he drew her gently towards him and kissed her neck, softly. She winced and trembled and hung away. But his strong young arm held her, and he kissed her softly again, still on the neck, for her face was averted.

"Won't you answer my question? Won't you now?" came his soft, lingering voice. He was trying to draw her near to kiss her face. And he kissed her cheek softly, near the ear.

At that moment Banford's voice was heard calling fretfully, crossly from upstairs.

"There's Jill!" cried March, starting and drawing erect.

And as she did so, quick as lightning he kissed her on the mouth, with a quick brushing kiss. It seemed to burn through her every fibre. She gave a queer little cry.

"You will, won't you? You will?" he insisted softly.

"Nellie! *Nellie!* Whatever are you so long for?" came Banford's faint cry from the outer darkness.

But he held her fast, and was murmuring with that intolerable softness and insistency:

"You will, won't you? Say yes! Say yes!"

March, who felt as if the fire had gone through her and scathed her, and as if she could do no more, murmured:

"Yes! Yes! Anything! Anything you like! Anything you like! Only let me go! Only let me go! Jill's calling."

"You know you've promised," he said insidiously.

"Yes! Yes! I do!—" Her voice suddenly rose into a shrill cry. "All right, Jill, I'm coming."

Startled, he let her go, and she went straight upstairs.

In the morning at breakfast, after he had looked round the place and attended to the stock and thought to himself that one could live easily enough here, he said to Banford:

"Do you know what, Miss Banford?"

"Well what?" said the goodnatured, nervy Banford.

He looked at March, who was spreading jam on her bread.

"Shall I tell?" he said to her.

She looked up at him, and a deep pink colour flushed over her face.

"Yes, if you mean Jill," she said. "I hope you won't go talking all over the village, that's all." And she swallowed her dry bread with difficulty.

"Whatever's coming?" said Banford, looking up with wide, tired, slightly reddened eyes. She was a thin, frail little thing, and her hair, which was delicate and thin, was bobbed, so it hung softly by her worn face in its faded brown and grey.

"Why what do you think?" he said, smiling like one who has a secret.

"How do I know!" said Banford.

"Can't you guess?" he said, making bright eyes, and smiling, pleased with himself.

"I'm sure I can't. What's more I'm not going to try."

"Nellie and I are going to be married."

Banford put down her knife, out of her thin, delicate fingers, as if she would never take it up to eat any more. She stared with blank, reddened eyes.

"You what?" she exclaimed.

"We're going to get married. Aren't we Nellie?" and he turned to March.

"You say so, anyway," said March laconically. But again she flushed with an agonised flush. She too could swallow no more.

Banford looked at her like a bird that has been shot: a poor little sick bird. She gazed at her with all her wounded soul in her face, at the deep-flushed March.

"Never!" she exclaimed, helpless.

"It's quite right," said the bright and gloating youth.

Banford turned aside her face, as if the sight of the food on the table made her sick. She sat like this for some moments, as if she were sick. Then, with one hand on the edge of the table, she rose to her feet.

"I'll *never* believe it, Nellie," she cried. "It's absolutely impossible!"

Her plaintive, fretful voice had a thread of hot anger and despair.

"Why? Why shouldn't you believe it?" asked the youth, with all his soft, velvety impertinence in his voice.

Banford looked at him from her wide vague eyes, as if he were some creature in a museum.

"Oh," she said languidly, "because she can never be such a fool. She can't lose her self-respect to such an extent." Her voice was cold and plaintive, drifting.

"In what way will she lose her self-respect?" asked the boy.

Banford looked at him with vague fixity from behind her spectacles.

"If she hasn't lost it already," she said.

He became very red, vermilion, under the slow vague stare from behind the spectacles.

"I don't see it at all," he said.

"Probably you don't. I shouldn't expect you would," said Banford, with that straying mild tone of remoteness which made her words even more insulting.

He sat stiff in his chair, staring with hot blue eyes from his scarlet face. An ugly look had come on his brow.

"My word, she doesn't know what she's letting herself in for," said Banford, in her plaintive, drifting, insulting voice.

"But what has it to do with you, anyway?" said the youth in a temper.

"More than it has to do with you, probably," she replied, plaintive and venomous.

"Oh has it! I don't see that at all," he jerked out.

"No, you wouldn't," she answered, drifting.

"Anyhow," said March, pushing back her chair and rising uncouthly. "It's no good arguing about it." And she seized the bread and the teapot, and strode away to the kitchen.

Banford let her fingers stray across her brow and along her hair, like one bemused. Then she turned and went away upstairs.

Henry sat stiff and sulky in his chair, with his face and his eyes on fire. March came and went, clearing the table. But Henry sat on, stiff with temper. He took no notice of her. She had regained her composure and her soft, even, creamy complexion. But her mouth was pursed up. She glanced at him each time as she came to take things from the table, glanced from her large, curious eyes, more in curiosity than anything. Such a long, red-faced sulky boy! That was all he was. He seemed as remote from her as if his red face were a red chimney-pot on a cottage across the fields, and she looked at him just as objectively, as remotely.

At length he got up and stalked out into the fields with the gun. He came in only at dinner-time, with the devil still in his face, but his manners quite polite. Nobody said anything particular: they sat each one at the sharp corner of a triangle, in obstinate remoteness. In the afternoon he went out again at once with the gun. He came in at nightfall with a rabbit and a pigeon. He stayed in all evening, but hardly opened his mouth. He was in the devil of a temper, feeling he had been insulted.

Banford's eyes were red, she had evidently been crying. But her manner was more remote and supercilious than ever, the way she turned her head if he spoke at all, as if he were some tramp or inferior intruder of that sort, made his blue eyes go almost black with rage. His face looked sulkier. But he never forgot his polite intonation, if he opened his mouth to speak.

March seemed to flourish in this atmosphere. She seemed to sit between the two antagonists with a little wicked smile on her face, enjoying herself. There was even a sort of complacency in the way she laboriously crochetted, this evening.

When he was in bed, the youth could hear the two women talking and arguing in their room. He sat up in bed and strained his ears to hear what they said. But he could hear nothing, it was too far off. Yet he could hear the soft, plaintive drip of Banford's voice, and March's deeper note.

The night was quiet, frosty. Big stars were snapping outside, beyond the ridge-tops of the pine-trees. He listened and listened. In the distance he heard a fox yelping: and the dogs from the farms barking in answer. But it was not that he wanted to hear. It was what the two women were saying.

He got stealthily out of bed, and stood by his door. He could hear no more than before. Very, very carefully he began to lift the doorlatch. After quite a time he had his door open. Then he stepped stealthily out into the passage. The old oak planks were cold under his feet, and they creaked preposterously. He crept very very gently up the one step, and along by the wall, till he stood outside their door. And there he held his breath and listened. Banford's voice:

"No, I simply couldn't stand it. I should be dead in a month.

36

Which is just what he would be aiming at, of course. That would just be his game, to see me in the churchyard. No Nellie, if you were to do such a thing as to marry him, you could never stop here. I couldn't, I couldn't live in the same house with him. Oh-h! I feel quite sick with the smell of his clothes. And his red face simply turns me over. I can't eat my food when he's at the table. What a fool I was ever to let him stop. One ought *never* to try to do a kind action. It always flies back in your face like a boomerang."

"Well he's only got two more days," said March.

"Yes, thank heaven. And when he's gone he'll never come in this house again. I feel so bad while he's here. And I know, I know he's only counting what he can get out of you. I *know* that's all it is. He's just a good-for-nothing, who doesn't want to work, and who thinks he'll live on us. But he won't live on me. If you're such a fool, then it's your own lookout. Mrs Burgess knew him all the time he was here. And the old man could never get him to do any steady work. He was off with the gun on every occasion, just as he is now. Nothing but the gun! Oh I do hate it. You don't know what you're doing, Nellie, you don't. If you marry him he'll just make a fool of you. He'll go off and leave you stranded. I know he will. If he can't get Bailey Farm out of us—and he's not going to, while I live. While I live he's never going to set foot here. I know what it would be. He'd soon think he was master of both of us, as he thinks he's master of you already."

"But he isn't," said Nellie.

"He thinks he is, anyway. And that's what he wants: to come and be master here. Yes, imagine it! That's what we've got the place together for, is it, to be bossed and bullied by a hateful red-faced boy, a beastly laborer. Oh we *did* make a mistake when we let him stop. We ought never to have lowered ourselves. And I've had such a fight with all the people here, not to be pulled down to their level. No, he's not coming here.—And then you see. If he can't have the place, he'll run off to Canada or somewhere again, as if he'd never known you. And here you'll be, absolutely ruined and made a fool of. I know I shall never have any peace of mind again."

"We'll tell him he can't come here. We'll tell him that," said March.

"Oh, don't you bother, I'm going to tell him that, and other things as well, before he goes. He's not going to have all his own way, while I've got the strength left to speak. Oh Nellie, he'll despise you, he'll despise you like the awful little beast he is, if you give way to him. I'd

37

no more trust him than I'd trust a cat not to steal. He's deep, he's deep, and he's bossy, and he's selfish through and through, as cold as ice. All he wants is to make use of you. And when you're no more use to him, then I pity you."

"I don't think he's as bad as all that," said March.

"No, because he's been playing up to you. But you'll find out, if you see much more of him. Oh Nellie, I can't bear to think of it."

"Well it won't hurt you, Jill darling."

"Won't it! Won't it! I shall never know a moment's peace again while I live, nor a moment's happiness. No, Nellie—" and Banford began to weep bitterly.

The boy outside could hear the stifled sound of the woman's sobbing, and could hear March's soft, deep, tender voice comforting, with wonderful gentleness and tenderness, the weeping woman.

His eyes were so round and wide that he seemed to see the whole night, and his ears were almost jumping off his head. He was frozen stiff. He crept back to bed, but felt as if the top of his head were coming off. He could not sleep. He could not keep still. He rose, quietly dressed himself, and crept out on to the landing once more. The women were silent. He went softly downstairs and out to the kitchen.

There he put on his boots and his overcoat, and took the gun. He did not think to go away from the farm. No, he only took the gun. As softly as possible he unfastened the door and went out into the frosty December night. The air was still, the stars bright, the pine-trees seemed to bristle audibly in the sky. He went stealthily away down a fence-side, looking for something to shoot. At the same time he remembered that he ought not to shoot and frighten the women.

So he prowled round the edge of the gorse cover, and through the grove of tall old hollies, to the woodside. There he skirted the fence, peering through the darkness with dilated eyes that seemed to be able to grow black and full of sight in the dark, like a cat's. An owl was slowly and mournfully whooing round a great oak-tree. He stepped stealthily with his gun, listening, listening, watching.

As he stood under the oaks of the wood-edge he heard the dogs from the neighbouring cottage, up the hill, yelling suddenly and startlingly, and the wakened dogs from the farms around barking answer. And suddenly, it seemed to him England was little and tight, he felt the landscape was constricted even in the dark, and that there were too many dogs in the night, making a noise like a fence of sound, like the network of English hedges netting in the view. He felt the fox didn't have a chance. For it must be the fox that had started all this hullabaloo.

Why not watch for him, anyhow! He would no doubt be coming sniffing round. The lad walked downhill to where the farmstead with its few pine-trees crouched blackly. In the angle of the long shed, in the black dark, he crouched down. He knew the fox would be coming. It seemed to him it would be the last of the foxes in this loudly-barking, thick-voiced England, tight with innumerable little houses.

He sat a long time with his eyes fixed unchanging upon the open gateway, where a little light seemed to fall from the stars or from the horizon, who knows. He was sitting on a log in a dark corner with the gun across his knees. The pine-trees snapped. Once a chicken fell off its perch in the barn, with a loud crawk and cackle and commotion. That startled him, and he stood up, watching with all his eyes, thinking it might be a rat. But he *felt* it was nothing. So he sat down again with the gun on his knees and his hands tucked in to keep them warm, and his eyes fixed unblinking on the pale reach of the open gateway. He felt he could smell the hot, sickly, rich smell of live chickens on the cold air.

And then—a shadow. A sliding shadow in the gateway. He gathered all his vision into a concentrated spark, and saw the shadow of the fox, the fox creeping on his belly through the gate. There he went, on his belly like a snake. The boy smiled to himself and brought the gun to his shoulder. He knew quite well what would happen. He knew the fox would go to where the fowl-door was boarded up, and sniff there. He knew he would lie there for a minute, sniffing the fowls within. And then he would start again prowling under the edge of the old barn, waiting to get in.

The fowl-door was at the top of a slight incline. Soft, soft as a shadow the fox slid up this incline, and crouched with his nose to the boards. And at the same moment there was the awful crash of a gun reverberating between the old buildings, as if all the night had gone smash. But the boy watched keenly. He saw even the white belly of the fox as the beast beat his paws in death. So he went forward.

There was a commotion everywhere. The fowls were scuffling and crawking, the ducks were quark-quarking, the pony had stamped wildly to his feet. But the fox was on his side, struggling in his last tremors. The boy bent over him and smelt his foxy smell.

There was a sound of a window opening upstairs, then March's voice calling:

"Who is it?"

"It's me," said Henry; "I've shot the fox."

"Oh goodness! You nearly frightened us to death."

"Did I? I'm awfully sorry."

"What ever made you get up?"

"I heard him about."

"And have you shot him?"

"Yes, he's here," and the boy stood in the yard holding up the warm, dead brute. "You can't see, can you? Wait a minute." And he took his flash-light from his pocket, and flashed it on to the dead animal. He was holding it by the brush. March saw, in the middle of the darkness, just the reddish fleece and the white belly and the white underneath of the pointed chin, and the queer, dangling paws. She did not know what to say.

"He's a beauty," he said. "He will make you a lovely fur."

"You don't catch me wearing a fox fur," she replied.

"Oh!" he said. And he switched off the light.

"Well I should think you'll come in and go to bed again now," she said.

"Probably I shall. What time is it?"

"What time is it, Jill?" called March's voice. It was a quarter to one.

That night March had another dream. She dreamed that Banford was dead, and that she, March, was sobbing her heart out. Then she had to put Banford into her coffin. And the coffin was the rough wood-box in which the bits of chopped wood were kept in the kitchen, by the fire. This was the coffin, and there was no other, and March was in agony and dazed bewilderment, looking for something to line the box with, something to make it soft with, something to cover up her poor dead darling. Because she couldn't lay her in there just in her white thin nightdress, in the horrible wood box. So she hunted and hunted, and picked up thing after thing, and threw it aside in the agony of dream-frustration. And in her dream-despair all she could find that would do was a fox skin. She knew that it wasn't right, that this was not what she could have. But it was all she could find. And so she folded the brush of the fox, and laid her darling Jill's head on this, and she brought round the skin of the fox

40

and laid it on the top of the body, so that it seemed to make a whole ruddy, fiery coverlet, and she cried and cried and woke to find the tears streaming down her face.

The first thing that both she and Banford did in the morning was to go out to see the fox. He had hung it up by the heels in the shed, with its poor brush falling backwards. It was a lovely dog-fox in its prime, with a handsome thick winter coat: a lovely golden-red colour, with grey as it passed to the belly, and belly all white, and a great full brush with a delicate black and grey and pure white tip.

"Poor brute!" said Banford. "If it wasn't such a thieving wretch, you'd feel sorry for it."

March said nothing, but stood with her foot trailing aside, one hip out, her face wax pale and her eyes big and black, watching the dead animal that was suspended upside down. White and soft as snow his belly: white and soft as snow. She passed her hand softly down it. And his wonderful black-glinted brush was full and frictional, wonderful. She passed her hand down this also, and quivered. Time after time she took the full fur of that thick tail between her hand, and passed her hand slowly downwards. Wonderful sharp thick splendour of a tail! Wonderful! And he was dead! She pursed her lips, and her eyes went black and vacant. Then she took the head in her hand.

Henry was sauntering up, so Banford walked rather pointedly away. March stood there bemused, with the head of the fox in her hand. She was wondering, wondering, wondering over his long fine muzzle. For some reason it reminded her of a spoon or a spatula. She felt she could not understand it. The beast was a strange beast to her, incomprehensible, out of her range. Wonderful silver whiskers he had, like ice-threads. And pricked ears with hair inside.—But that long, long slender spoon of a nose!—and the marvellous white teeth beneath! It was to thrust forward and bite with, deep, deep into the living prey, to bite and bite the blood.

"He's a beauty, isn't he?" said Henry, standing by.

"Oh yes, he's a fine big fox. I wonder how many chickens he's responsible for," she replied.

"A good many. Do you think he's the same one you saw in the summer?"

"I should think very likely he is," she replied.

He watched her, but he could make nothing of her. Partly she was so shy and virgin, and partly she was so grim, matter-of-fact, shrewish. What she said seemed to him so different from the look of her big, queer dark eyes.

"Are you going to skin him?" she asked.

"Yes, when I've had breakfast, and got a board to peg him on."

"My word what a strong smell he's got! Pooo!—It'll take some washing off one's hands. I don't know why I was so silly as to handle him."—And she looked at her right hand, that had passed down his belly and along his tail, and had even got a tiny streak of blood from one dark place in his fur.

"Have you seen the chickens when they smell him, how frightened they are?" he said.

"Yes, aren't they!"

"You must mind you don't get some of his fleas."

"Oh fleas!" she replied, nonchalant.

Later in the day she saw the fox's skin nailed flat on a board, as if crucified. It gave her an uneasy feeling.

The boy was angry. He went about with his mouth shut, as if he had swallowed part of his chin. But in behaviour he was polite and affable. He did not say anything about his intentions. And he left March alone.

That evening they sat in the dining-room. Banford wouldn't have him in her sitting-room any more. There was a very big log on the fire. And everybody was busy. Banford had letters to write, March was sewing a dress, and he was mending some little contrivance.

Banford stopped her letter-writing from time to time to look round and rest her eyes. The boy had his head down, his face hidden over his job.

"Let's see," said Banford. "What train do you go by, Henry?"

He looked up straight at her.

"The morning train. In the morning," he said.

"What, the eight-ten or the eleven-twenty?"

"The eleven-twenty, I suppose," he said.

"That is the day after tomorrow?" said Banford.

"Yes, the day after tomorrow."

"Mmm!" murmured Banford, and she returned to her writing. But as she was licking her envelope, she asked:

"And what plans have you made for the future, if I may ask?"

"Plans?" he said, his face very bright and angry.

"I mean about you and Nellie, if you are going on with this

business. When do you expect the wedding to come off?" She spoke in a jeering tone.

"Oh, the wedding!" he replied. "I don't know."

"Don't you know anything?" said Banford. "Are you going to clear out on Friday and leave things no more settled than they are?"

"Well, why shouldn't I? We can always write letters."

"Yes of course you can. But I wanted to know because of this place. If Nellie is going to get married all of a sudden, I shall have to be looking round for a new partner."

"Couldn't she stay on here if she was married?" he said. He knew quite well what was coming.

"Oh," said Banford, "this is no place for a married couple. There's not enough work to keep a man going, for one thing. And there's no money to be made. It's quite useless your thinking of staying on here if you marry. Absolutely!"

"Yes, but I wasn't thinking of staying on here," he said.

"Well that's what I want to know. And what about Nellie, then? How long is *she* going to be here with me, in that case."

The two antagonists looked at one another.

"That I can't say," he answered.

"Oh go along," she cried petulantly. "You must have some idea what you are going to do, if you ask a woman to marry you. Unless it's all a hoax."

"Why should it be a hoax?—I am going back to Canada."

"And taking her with you?"

"Yes, certainly."

"You hear that, Nellie?" said Banford.

March, who had had her head bent over her sewing, now looked up with a sharp pink blush on her face and a queer, sardonic laugh in her eyes and on her twisted mouth.

"That's the first time I've heard that I was going to Canada," she said.

"Well, you have to hear it for the first time, haven't you?" said the boy.

"Yes, I suppose I have," she said nonchalant. And she went back to her sewing.

"You're quite ready, are you, to go to Canada? Are you, Nellie?" asked Banford.

March looked up again. She let her shoulders go slack, and let her hand that held the needle lie loose in her lap.

"It depends entirely on *how* I'm going," she said. "I don't think I want to go jammed up in the steerage, as a soldier's wife. I'm afraid I'm not used to that way."

The boy watched her with bright eyes.

"Would you rather stay over here while I go first?" he asked.

"I would, if that's the only alternative," she replied.

"That's much the wisest. Don't make it any fixed engagement," said Banford. "Leave yourself free to go or not after he's got back and found you a place, Nellie. Anything else is madness, madness."

"Don't you think," said the youth, "we ought to get married before I go—and then go together, or separate, according to how it happens?"

"I think it's a *terrible* idea," cried Banford.

But the boy was watching March.

"What do you think?" he asked her.

She let her eyes stray vaguely into space.

"Well I don't know," she said. "I shall have to think about it."

"Why?" he asked, pertinently.

"Why?"—She repeated his question in a mocking way, and looked at him laughing, though her face was pink again. "I should think there's plenty of reasons why."

He watched her in silence. She seemed to have escaped him. She had got into league with Banford against him. There was again the queer sardonic look about her, she would mock stoically at everything he said or which life offered.

"Of course," he said, "I don't want to press you to do anything you don't wish to do."

"I should think not, indeed," cried Banford indignantly.

At bedtime Banford said plaintively to March:

"You take my hot bottle up for me, Nellie, will you."

"Yes, I'll do it," said March, with the kind of willing unwillingness she so often showed towards her beloved but uncertain Jill.

The two women went upstairs. After a time March called from the top of the stairs: "Goodnight Henry. I shan't be coming down. You'll see to the lamp and the fire, won't you!"

The next day Henry went about with the cloud on his brow and his young cub's face shut up tight. He was cogitating all the time. He had wanted March to marry him and go back to Canada with him. And he had been sure she would do it. Why he wanted her he didn't know. But he did want her. He had set his mind on her. And he was convulsed with a youth's fury at being thwarted. To be thwarted, to be thwarted! It made him so furious inside, that he did not know what to do with himself. But he kept himself in hand. Because even now things might turn out differently. She might come over to him. Of course she might. It was her business to do so.

Things drew to a tension again towards evening. He and Banford had avoided each other all day. In fact Banford went in to the little town by the 11.20 train. It was market day. She arrived back on the 4.25. Just as the night was falling Henry saw her little figure in a dark-blue coat and a dark-blue tam-o'-shanter hat crossing the first meadow from the station. He stood under one of the wild pear trees, with the old dead leaves round his feet. And he watched the little blue figure advancing persistently over the rough, winter-ragged meadow. She had her arms full of parcels, and advanced slowly, frail thing she was, but with that devilish little certainty which he so detested in her. He stood invisible under the pear-tree, watching her every step. And if looks could have affected her, then she would have felt a log of iron on each of her ankles as she made her way forward. "You're a nasty little thing, you are," he was saying softly, across the distance. "You're a nasty little thing. I hope you'll be paid back for all the harm you've done me for nothing. I hope you will—you nasty little thing. I hope you'll have to pay for it. You will, if wishes are anything. You nasty little creature that you are."

She was toiling slowly up the slope. But if she had been slipping back at every step towards the Bottomless Pit, he would not have gone to help her with her parcels. Aha, there went March, striding with her long land stride in her breeches and her short tunic! Striding down hill at a great pace, and even running a few steps now and then, in her great solicitude and desire to come to the rescue of the little Banford. The boy watched her with rage in his heart. See her leap a ditch, and run, run as if a house was on fire, just to get to that creeping dark little object down there! So, the Banford just stood still and waited. And March strode up and took *all* the parcels except a bunch of yellow chrysanthemums. These the Banford still carried. Yellow chrysanthemums!

"Yes, you look well, don't you," he said softly into the dusk air. "You look well, pottering up there with a bunch of flowers, you do. I'd make you eat them for your tea, if you hug them so tight. And I'd give them you for breakfast again, I would. I'd give you flowers. Nothing but flowers."

He watched the progress of the two women. He could hear their voices: March always outspoken and rather scolding in her tenderness, Banford murmuring rather vaguely. They were evidently good friends. He could not hear what they said till they came to the fence of the home meadow, which they must climb. Then he saw March manfully climbing over the bars with all her packages in her arms, and on the still air he heard Banford's fretful:

"Why don't you let me help you with the parcels?" She had a queer plaintive hitch in her voice.—Then came March's robust and reckless:

"Oh I can manage. Don't you bother about me. You've all you can do to get yourself over."

"Yes that's all very well," said Banford fretfully. "You say *Don't you bother about me* and then all the while you feel injured because nobody thinks of you."

"When do I feel injured?" said March.

"Always. You always feel injured. Now you're feeling injured because I won't have that boy to come and live on the farm."

"I'm not feeling injured at all," said March.

"I know you are. When he's gone you'll sulk over it. I know you will."

"Shall I?" said March. "We'll see."

"Yes, we *shall* see, unfortunately.—I can't think how you can make yourself so cheap. I can't *imagine* how you can lower yourself like it."

"I haven't lowered myself," said March.

"I don't know what you call it, then. Letting a boy like that come so cheeky and impudent and make a mug of you. I don't know what you think of yourself. How much respect do you think he's going to have for you afterwards?—My word, I wouldn't be in your shoes, if you married him."

"Of course you wouldn't. My boots are a good bit too big for you, and not half dainty enough," said March, with rather a miss-fire sarcasm.

"I thought you had too much pride, really I did. A woman's got to hold herself high, especially with a youth like that. Why he's impudent. He's impudent. Even the way he forced himself on us at the start."

"We asked him to stay," said March.

"Not till he'd almost forced us to.—And then he's so cocky and self-assured. My word, he puts my back up. I simply can't imagine how you can let him treat you so cheaply."

"I don't let him treat me cheaply," said March. "Don't you worry yourself, nobody's going to treat me cheaply. And even you aren't, either." She had a tender defiance, and a certain fire in her voice.

"Yes, it's sure to come back to me," said Banford bitterly. "That's always the end of it. I believe you only do it to spite me."

They went now in silence up the steep grassy slope and over the brow through the gorse-bushes. On the other side the hedge the boy followed in the dusk, at some little distance. Now and then, through the huge ancient hedge of hawthorn, risen into trees, he saw the two dark figures creeping up the hill. As he came to the top of the slope he saw the homestead dark in the twilight, with a huge old pear-tree leaning from the near gable, and a little yellow light twinkling in the small side window of the kitchen. He heard the clink of the latch and saw the kitchen door open into light as the two women went indoors. So, they were at home.

And so!—this was what they thought of him. It was rather in his nature to be a listener, so he was not at all surprised whatever he heard. The things people said about him always missed him personally. He was only rather surprised at the women's way with one another. And he disliked the Banford with an acid dislike. And he felt drawn to the March again. He felt again irresistibly drawn to her. He felt there was a secret bond, a secret thread between him and her, something very exclusive, which shut out everybody else and made him and her possess each other in secret.

He hoped again that she would have him. He hoped with his blood suddenly firing up that she would agree to marry him quite quickly: at Christmas, very likely. Christmas was not far off. He wanted, whatever else happened, to snatch her into a hasty marriage and a consummation with him. Then for the future, they could arrange later.—But he hoped it would happen as he wanted it. He hoped that tonight she would stay a little while with him, after Banford had gone upstairs. He hoped he could touch her soft, creamy cheek, her strange, frightened face. He hoped he could look into her dilated, frightened dark eyes, quite near. He hoped he might even put his hand on her bosom and feel her soft breasts under her tunic. His heart beat deep and powerful as he thought of that. He wanted very much to do so. He wanted to make sure of her soft woman's breasts under her tunic. She always kept the brown linen coat buttoned so close up to her throat. It seemed to him like some perilous secret, that her soft woman's breasts must be buttoned up in that uniform. It seemed to him moreover that they were so much softer, tenderer, more lovely and lovable, shut up in that tunic, than were the Banford's breasts, under her soft blouses and chiffon dresses. The Banford would have little iron breasts, he said to himself. For all her frailty and fretfulness and delicacy, she would have tiny iron breasts. But March, under her crude, fast, workman's tunic, would have soft white breasts, white and unseen. So he told himself, and his blood burned.

When he went in to tea, he had a surprise. He appeared at the inner door, his face very ruddy and vivid and his blue eyes shining, dropping his head forward as he came in, in his usual way, and hesitating in the doorway to watch the inside of the room, keenly and cautiously, before he entered. He was wearing a long-sleeved waistcoat. His face seemed extraordinarily a piece of the out-of-doors come indoors: as holly-berries do. In his second of pause in the doorway he took in the two women sitting at table, at opposite ends, saw them sharply. And to his amazement March was dressed in a dress of dull, green silk crape. His mouth came open in surprise. If she had suddenly grown a moustache he could not have been more surprised.

"Why," he said, "do you wear a dress, then?"

She looked up, flushing a deep rose colour, and twisting her mouth with a smile, said:

"Of course I do. What else do you expect me to wear, but a dress?"

"A land-girl's uniform, of course," said he.

"Oh," she cried nonchalant, "that's only for this dirty mucky work about here."

"Isn't it your proper dress, then?" he said.

"No, not indoors it isn't," she said. But she was blushing all the time as she poured out his tea. He sat down in his chair at table, unable to take his eyes off her. Her dress was a perfectly simple slip of bluey-green crape, with a line of gold stitching round the top and round the sleeves, which came to the elbow. It was cut just plain, and round at the top, and showed her white soft throat. Her arms he knew, strong and firm-muscled, for he had often seen her with her sleeves rolled up. But he looked her up and down, up and down.

Banford, at the other end of the table, said not a word, but piggled with the sardine on her plate. He had forgotten her existence. He just simply stared at March, while he ate his bread and margarine in huge mouthfuls, forgetting even his tea.

"Well I never knew anything make such a difference!" he murmured, across his mouthful.

"Oh goodness!" cried March, blushing still more. "I might be a pink monkey!"

And she rose quickly to her feet and took the teapot to the fire, to the kettle. And as she crouched on the hearth with her green slip about her, the boy stared more wide-eyed than ever. Through the crape her woman's form seemed soft and womanly. And when she stood up and walked he saw her legs move soft within her moderately short skirt. She had on black silk stockings and small, patent shoes with little gold buckles.

No, she was another being. She was something quite different. Seeing her always in the hard-cloth breeches, wide on the hips, buttoned on the knee, strong as armour, and in the brown puttees and thick boots, it had never occurred to him that she had a woman's legs and feet. Now it came upon him. She had a woman's soft, skirted legs, and she was accessible. He blushed to the roots of his hair, shoved his nose in his teacup and drank his tea with a little noise that made Banford simply squirm: and strangely, suddenly he felt a man, no longer a youth. He felt a man, with all a man's grave weight of responsibility. A curious quietness and gravity came over his soul. He felt a man, quiet, with a little of the heaviness of male destiny upon him.

She was soft and accessible in her dress. The thought went home in him like an everlasting responsibility.

"Oh for Goodness' sake say something somebody," cried Banford fretfully. "It might be a funeral."—The boy looked at her, and she could not bear his face.

"A funeral!" said March, with a twisted smile. "Why, that breaks my dream."

Suddenly she had thought of Banford in the wood-box for a coffin.

"What, have you been dreaming of a wedding?" said Banford sarcastically.

"Must have been," said March.

"Whose wedding?" asked the boy.

"I can't remember," said March.

She was shy and rather awkward that evening, in spite of the fact

49

that, wearing a dress her bearing was much more subdued than in her uniform. She felt unpeeled and rather exposed. She felt almost improper.

They talked desultorily about Henry's departure next morning, and made the trivial arrangement. But of the matter on their minds none of them spoke. They were rather quiet and friendly this evening. Banford had practically nothing to say. But inside herself she seemed still, perhaps kindly.

At nine o'clock March brought in the tray with the everlasting tea and a little cold meat which Banford had managed to procure. It was the last supper, so Banford did not want to be disagreeable. She felt a bit sorry for the boy, and felt she must be as nice as she could.

He wanted her to go to bed. She was usually the first. But she sat on in her chair under the lamp, glancing at her book now and then, and staring into the fire. A deep silence had come into the room. It was broken by March asking, in a rather small tone:

"What time is it, Jill?"

"Five past ten," said Banford, looking at her wrist.

And then not a sound. The boy had looked up from the book he was holding between his knees. His rather wide, cat-shaped face had its obstinate look, his eyes were watchful.

"What about bed?" said March at last.

"I'm ready when you are," said Banford.

"Oh very well," said March. "I'll fill your bottle."

She was as good as her word. When the hot-water bottle was ready, she lit a candle and went upstairs with it. Banford remained in her chair, listening acutely. March came downstairs again.

"There you are then," she said. "Are you going up?"

"Yes, in a minute," said Banford. But the minute passed, and she sat on in her chair under the lamp.

Henry, whose eyes were shining like a cat's as he watched from under his brows, and whose face seemed wider, more chubbed and cat-like with unalterable obstinacy, now rose to his feet to try his throw.

"I think I'll go and look if I can see the she fox," he said. "She may be creeping round. Won't you come as well for a minute, Nellie, and see if we see anything?"

"Me!" cried March, looking up with her startled, wondering face.

"Yes. Come on," he said. It was wonderful how soft and warm

and coaxing his voice could be, how near. The very sound of it made Banford's blood boil.

"Come on for a minute," he said, looking down into her uplifted, unsure face. And she rose to her feet as if drawn up by his young, ruddy face that was looking down on her.

"I should think you're never going out at this time of night, Nellie!" cried Banford.

"Yes, just for a minute," said the boy, looking round on her, and speaking with an odd sharp yelp in his voice.

March looked from one to the other, as if confused, vague. Banford rose to her feet for battle.

"Why it's ridiculous. It's bitter cold. You'll catch your death in that thin frock. And in those slippers. You're not going to do any such thing."

There was a moment's pause. Banford turtled up like a little fighting cock, facing March and the boy.

"Oh, I don't think you need worry yourself," he replied. "A moment under the stars won't do anybody any damage. I'll get the rug off the sofa in the dining-room. You're coming, Nellie."

His voice had so much anger, and contempt and fury in it as he spoke to Banford: and so much tenderness and proud authority as he spoke to March, that the latter answered:

"Yes, I'm coming."

And she turned with him to the door.

Banford, standing there in the middle of the room, suddenly burst into a long wail and a spasm of sobs. She covered her face with her poor thin hands, and her thin shoulders shook in an agony of weeping. March looked back from the door.

"Jill!" she cried in a frantic tone, like someone just coming awake. And she seemed to start towards her darling.

But the boy had March's arm in his grip, and she could not move. She did not know why she could not move. It was as in a dream when the heart strains and the body cannot stir.

"Never mind," said the boy softly. "Let her cry. Let her cry. She will have to cry sooner or later. And the tears will relieve her feelings. They will do her good."

So he drew March slowly through the doorway. But her last look was back to the poor little figure which stood in the middle of the room with covered face and thin shoulders shaken with bitter weeping.

In the dining-room he picked up the rug and said:

"Wrap yourself up in this."

She obeyed—and they reached the kitchen door, he holding her soft and firm by the arm, though she did not know it. When she saw the night outside she started back.

"I must go back to Jill," she said. "I *must*! Oh yes, I must!"

Her tone sounded final. The boy let go of her and she turned indoors. But he seized her again and arrested her.

"Wait a minute," he said. "Wait a minute. Even if you go you're not going yet."

"Leave go! Leave go!" she cried. "My place is at Jill's side. Poor little thing, she's sobbing her heart out."

"Yes," said the boy bitterly. "And your heart too, and mine as well."

"Your heart?" said March. He still gripped her and detained her.

"Isn't it as good as her heart?" he said. "Or do you think it's not?"

"Your heart?" she said again, incredulous.

"Yes mine! Mine! Do you think I haven't *got* a heart?"—And with his hot grasp he took her hand and pressed it under his left breast. "There's my heart," he said, "if you don't believe in it."

It was wonder which made her attend. And then she felt the deep, heavy, powerful stroke of his heart, terrible, like something from beyond. It was like something from beyond, something awful from outside, signalling to her. And the signal paralysed her. It beat upon her very soul, and made her helpless. She forgot Jill. She could not think of Jill any more. She could not think of her. That terrible signalling from outside!

The boy put his arm round her waist.

"Come with me," he said gently. "Come and let us say what we've got to say."

And he drew her outside, closed the door. And she went with him darkly down the garden path. That he should have a beating heart! And that he should have his arm round her, outside the blanket! She was too confused to think who he was or what he was.

He took her to a dark corner of the shed, where was a tool-box with a lid, long and low.

"We'll sit here a minute," he said.

And obediently she sat down by his side.

"Give me your hand," he said.

She gave him both her hands, and he held them between his own. He was young, and it made him tremble.

"You'll marry me. You'll marry me before I go back, won't you?" he pleaded.

"Why, aren't we both a pair of fools?" she said.

He had put her in the corner, so that she should not look out and see the lighted window of the house, across the dark yard and garden. He tried to keep her all there inside the shed with him.

"In what way a pair of fools?" he said. "If you go back to Canada with me, I've got a job and a good wage waiting for me, and it's a nice place, near the mountains. Why shouldn't you marry me? Why shouldn't we marry? I should like to have you there with me. I should like to feel I'd got somebody there, at the back of me, all my life."

"You'd easily find somebody else, who'd suit you better," she said.

"Yes, I might easily find another girl. I know I could. But not one I really wanted. I've never met one I really wanted, for good. You see, I'm thinking of all my life. If I marry, I want to feel it's for all my life. Other girls: well, they're just girls, nice enough to go a walk with now and then. Nice enough for a bit of play. But when I think of my life, then I should be very sorry to have to marry one of them, I should indeed."

"You mean they wouldn't make you a good wife."

"Yes, I mean that. But I don't mean they wouldn't do their duty by me. I mean—I don't know what I mean. Only when I think of my life, and of you, then the two things go together."

"And what if they didn't?" she said, with her odd sardonic touch.

"Well I think they would."

They sat for some time silent. He held her hands in his, but he did not make love to her. Since he had realised that she was a woman, and vulnerable, accessible, a certain heaviness had possessed his soul. He did not want to make love to her. He shrank from any such performance, almost with fear. She was a woman, and vulnerable, accessible to him finally, and he held back from that which was ahead, almost with dread. It was a kind of darkness he knew he would enter finally, but of which he did not want as yet even to think. She was the woman, and he was responsible for the strange vulnerability he had suddenly realised in her.

"No," she said at last, "I'm a fool. I know I'm a fool."

"What for?" he asked.

"To go on with this business."

"Do you mean me?" he asked.

"No, I mean myself. I'm making a fool of myself, and a big one."

"Why, because you don't want to marry me, really?"

"Oh, I don't know whether I'm against it, as a matter of fact. That's just it. I don't know."

He looked at her in the darkness, puzzled. He did not in the least know what she meant.

"And don't you know whether you like to sit here with me this minute, or not?" he asked.

"No, I don't, really. I don't know whether I wish I was somewhere else, or whether I like being here. I don't know, really."

"Do you wish you were with Miss Banford? Do you wish you'd gone to bed with her?" he asked, as a challenge.

She waited a long time before she answered.

"No," she said at last. "I don't wish that."

"And do you think you would spend all your life with her—when your hair goes white, and you are old?" he said.

"No," she said, without much hesitation. "I don't see Jill and me two old women together."

"And don't you think, when I'm an old man, and you're an old woman, we might be together still, as we are now?" he said.

"Well, not as we are now," she replied. "But I could imagine—no, I can't. I can't imagine you an old man. Besides, it's dreadful!"

"What, to be an old man?"

"Yes of course."

"Not when the time comes," he said. "But it hasn't come. Only it will. And when it does, I should like to think you'd be there as well."

"Sort of old age pensions," she said drily.

Her kind of witless humour always startled him. He never knew what she meant. Probably she didn't quite know herself.

"No," he said, hurt.

"I don't know why you harp on old age," she said. "I'm not ninety."

"Did anybody ever say you were?" he asked, offended.

They were silent for some time, pulling different ways in the silence.

"I don't want you to make fun of me," he said.

"Don't you?" she replied, enigmatic.

"No, because just this minute I'm serious. And when I'm serious, I believe in not making fun of it."

"You mean nobody else must make fun of you," she replied.

"Yes, I mean that. And I mean I don't believe in making fun of it myself. When it comes over me so that I'm serious, then—there it is, I don't want it to be laughed at."

She was silent for some time. Then she said, in a vague, almost pained voice:

"No, I'm not laughing at you."

A hot wave rose in his heart.

"You believe me, do you?" he asked.

"Yes, I believe you," she replied, with a twang of her old tired nonchalance, as if she gave in because she was tired.—But he didn't care. His heart was hot and clamorous.

"So you agree to marry me before I go?—perhaps at Christmas?"

"Yes, I agree."

"There!" he exclaimed. "That's settled it."

And he sat silent, unconscious, with all the blood burning in all his veins, like fire in all the branches and twigs of him. He only pressed her two hands to his chest, without knowing. When the curious passion began to die down, he seemed to come awake to the world.

"We'll go in, shall we?" he said: as if he realised it was cold.

She rose without answering.

"Kiss me before we go, now you've said it," he said.

And he kissed her gently on the mouth, with a young, frightened kiss. It made her feel so young, too, and frightened, and wondering: and tired, tired, as if she were going to sleep.

They went indoors. And in the sitting-room, there, crouched by the fire like a queer little witch, was Banford. She looked round with reddened eyes as they entered, but did not rise. He thought she looked frightening, unnatural, crouching there and looking round at them. Evil he thought her look was, and he crossed his fingers.

Banford saw the ruddy, elate face of the youth: he seemed strangely tall and bright and looming. And March had a delicate look on her face, she wanted to hide her face, to screen it, to let it not be seen.

"You've come at last," said Banford uglily.

"Yes, we've come," said he.

"You've been long enough for anything," she said.

"Yes, we have. We've settled it. We shall marry as soon as possible," he replied.

"Oh, you've settled it, have you! Well, I hope you won't live to repent it," said Banford.

"I hope so too," he replied.

"Are you going to bed *now*, Nellie?" said Banford.

"Yes, I'm going now."

"Then for goodness sake come along."

March looked at the boy. He was glancing with his very bright eyes at her and at Banford. March looked at him wistfully. She wished she could stay with him. She wished she had married him already, and it was all over. For oh, she felt suddenly so safe with him. She felt so strangely safe and peaceful in his presence. If only she could sleep in his shelter, and not with Jill. She felt afraid of Jill. In her dim, tender state, it was agony to have to go with Jill and sleep with her. She wanted the boy to save her. She looked again at him.

And he, watching with bright eyes, divined something of what she felt. It puzzled and distressed him that she must go with Jill.

"I shan't forget what you've promised," he said, looking clear into her eyes, right into her eyes, so that he seemed to occupy all her self with his queer, bright look.

She smiled to him, faintly, gently. She felt safe again—safe with him.

But in spite of all the boy's precautions, he had a set-back. The morning he was leaving the farm he got March to accompany him to the market-town, about six miles away, where they went to the registrar and had their names stuck up as two people who were going to marry. He was to come at Christmas, and the wedding was to take place then. He hoped in the spring to be able to take March back to Canada with him, now the war was really over. Though he was so young, he had saved some money.

"You never have to be without *some* money at the back of you, if you can help it," he said.

So she saw him off in the train that was going West: his camp was on Salisbury plains. And with big dark eyes she watched him go, and it seemed as if everything real in life was retreating as the train retreated with his queer, chubbed, ruddy face, that seemed so broad across the cheeks, and which never seemed to change its expression, save when a cloud of sulky anger hung on the brows, or the bright eyes fixed themselves in their stare. This was what happened now.

He leaned there out of the carriage window as the train drew off, saying goodbye and staring back at her, but his face quite unchanged. There was no emotion on his face. Only his eyes tightened and became fixed and intent in their watching, as a cat when suddenly she sees something and stares. So the boy's eyes stared fixedly as the train drew away, and she was left feeling intensely forlorn. Failing his physical presence, she seemed to have nothing of him. And she had nothing of anything. Only his face was fixed in her mind: the full, ruddy, unchanging cheeks, and the straight snout of a nose, and the two eyes staring above. All she could remember was how he suddenly wrinkled his nose when he laughed, as a puppy does when he is playfully growling. But him, himself, and what he was—she knew nothing, she had nothing of him when he left her.

On the ninth day after he had left her he received this letter.

"Dear Henry,

I have been over it all again in my mind, this business of me and you, and it seems to me impossible. When you aren't there I see what a fool I am. When you are there you seem to blind me to things as they actually are. You make me see things all unreal and I don't know what. Then when I am alone again with Jill I seem to come to my own senses and realise what a fool I am making of myself and how I am treating you unfairly. Because it must be unfair to you for me to go on with this affair when I can't feel in my heart that I really love you. I know people talk a lot of stuff and nonsense about love, and I don't want to do that. I want to keep to plain facts and act in a sensible way. And that seems to me what I'm not doing. I don't see on what grounds I am going to marry you. I know I am not head over heels in love with you, as I have fancied myself to be with fellows when I was a young fool of a girl. You are an absolute stranger to me, and it seems to me you will always be one. So on what grounds am I going to marry you? When I think of Jill she is ten times more real to me. I know her and I'm awfully fond of her and I hate myself for a beast if I ever hurt her little finger. We have a life together. And even if it can't last for ever, it is a life while it does last. And it might last as long as either of us lives. Who knows how long we've got to live? She is a delicate little thing, perhaps nobody but me knows how delicate. And as for me, I feel I might fall down the well any day. What I don't seem to see at all is you. When I think of what I've been and what I've done with you I'm afraid I am a few screws loose. I should be sorry to think that softening of the brain is setting in so soon, but that is what it seems like. You are such an absolute stranger and so different from what I'm used to and we don't seem to have a thing in common. As for love the very word seems impossible. I know what love means even in Jill's case, and I know that in this affair with you it's an absolute impossibility. And then going to Canada. I'm sure I must have been clean off my chump when I promised such a thing. It makes me feel fairly frightened of myself. I feel I might do something really silly, that I wasn't responsible for. And end my days in a lunatic asylum. You may think that's all I'm fit for after the way I've gone on, but it isn't a very nice thought for me. Thank goodness Jill is here and her being here makes me feel sane again, else I don't know what I might do, I might have an accident with the gun one evening. I love Jill and she makes me feel safe and sane, with her loving anger against me for being such a fool. Well what I want to say is won't you let us cry the whole thing off? I can't marry you, and really, I won't do such a thing if it seems to me wrong. It is all a great mistake. I've made a complete fool of myself, and all I can do is to apologise to you and ask you please to forget it and please to take no further notice of me. Your fox skin is nearly ready and seems all right. I will post it to you if you will just let me know if this address is still right, and if you will accept my apology for the awful and lunatic way I have behaved with you, and then let the matter rest.

Jill sends her kindest regards. Her mother and father are staying with us over Christmas.

Yours very Sincerely
Ellen March."

The boy read this letter in camp as he was cleaning his kit. He set his teeth and for a moment went almost pale, yellow round the eyes with fury. He said nothing and saw nothing and felt nothing but a livid rage that was quite unreasoning. Balked! Balked again! Balked! He wanted the woman, he had fixed like doom upon having her. He felt that was his doom, his destiny, and his reward, to have this woman. She was his heaven and hell on earth, and he would have none elsewhere. Sightless with rage and thwarted madness he got through the morning. Save that in his mind he was lurking and scheming towards an issue, he would have committed some insane act. Deep in himself he felt like roaring and howling and gnashing his teeth and breaking things. But he was too intelligent. He knew society was on top of him, and he must scheme. So with his teeth bitten together and his nose curiously slightly lifted, like some creature that is vicious, and his eyes fixed and staring, he went through the morning's affairs drunk with anger and suppression. In his mind was one thorn—Banford. He took no heed of all March's outpouring: none. One thorn rankled stuck in his mind: Banford. In his mind, in his soul, in his whole being, one thorn rankling to insanity. And he would have to get it out. He would have to get the thorn of Banford out of his life, if he died for it.

With this one fixed idea in his mind, he went to ask for twenty-four hours leave of absence. He knew it was not due to him. His consciousness was supernaturally keen. He knew where he must go—he must go to the Captain. But how could he get at the Captain? In that great camp of wooden huts and tents, he had no idea where his captain was.

But he went to the officers' canteen. There was his captain standing talking with three other officers. Henry stood in the doorway at attention.

"May I speak to Captain Berryman?"—The captain was Cornish like himself.

"What do you want?" called the captain.

"May I speak to you, Captain?"

"What do you want?" replied the captain, not stirring from among his group of fellow-officers.

Henry watched his superior for a minute without speaking.

"You won't refuse me Sir, will you?" he asked gravely.

"It depends what it is."

"Can I have twenty-four hours leave?"

"No, you've no business to ask."

"I know I haven't. But I must ask you."

"You've had your answer."

"Don't send me away, Captain."

There was something strange about the boy as he stood there so everlasting in the doorway. The Cornish Captain felt the strangeness at once, and eyed him shrewdly.

"Why, what's afoot?" he said, curious.

"I'm in trouble about something. I must go to Blewbury," said the boy.

"Blewbury eh? After the girls?"

"Yes, it is a woman, Captain." And the boy, as he stood there with his head reaching forward a little, went suddenly terribly pale, or yellow, and his lips seemed to give off pain. The captain saw and paled a little also. He turned aside.

"Go on then," he said. "But for God's sake don't cause any trouble of any sort."

"I won't, Captain, thank you."

He was gone. The captain, upset, took a gin and bitters. Henry managed to hire a bicycle. It was twelve o'clock when he left the camp. He had sixty miles of wet and muddy cross-roads to ride. But he was in the saddle and down the road without a thought of food.

At the farm, March was busy with a work she had had some time in hand. A bunch of Scotch-fir-trees stood at the end of the open shed, on a little bank where ran the fence between two of the gorse-shaggy meadows. The furthest of these trees was dead—it had died in the summer and stood with all its needles brown and sere in the air. It was not a very big tree. And it was absolutely dead. So March determined to have it, although they were not allowed to cut any of the timber. But it would make such splendid firing, in these days of scarce fuel.

She had been giving a few stealthy chops at the trunk for a week or more, every now and then hacking away for five minutes, low down, near the ground, so no one should notice. She had not tried the saw, it was such hard work, alone. Now the tree stood with a great yawning gap in his base, perched as it were on one sinew, and ready to fall. But he did not fall.

It was late in the damp December afternoon, with cold mists creeping out of the woods and up the hollows, and darkness waiting to sink in from above. There was a bit of a yellowness where the sun was fading away beyond the low woods of the distance. March took her axe and went to the tree. The small thud-thud of her blows resounded rather ineffectual about the wintry homestead. Banford came out wearing her thick coat, but with no hat on her head, so that her thin, bobbed hair blew on the uneasy wind that sounded in the pines and in the wood.

"What I'm afraid of," said Banford, "is that it will fall on the shed and we s'll have another job repairing that."

"Oh, I don't think so," said March straightening herself and wiping her arm over her hot brow. She was flushed red, her eyes were very wide-open and queer, her upper lip lifted away from her two white front teeth with a curious, almost rabbit-look.

A little stout old man in a black overcoat and a bowler hat came pottering across the yard. He had a pink face and a white beard and smallish, pale-blue eyes. He was not very old, but nervy, and he walked with little short steps.

"What do you think, father?" said Banford. "Don't you think it might hit the shed in falling?"

"Shed, no!" said the old man. "Can't hit the shed. Might as well say the fence."

"The fence doesn't matter," said March, in her high voice.

"Wrong as usual, am I!" said Banford, wiping her straying hair from her eyes.

The tree stood as it were on one spelch of itself, leaning, and creaking in the wind. It grew on the bank of a little dry ditch between the two meadows. On the top of the bank straggled one fence, running to the bushes uphill. Several trees clustered there in the corner of the field near the shed and near the gate which led into the yard. Towards this gate, horizontal across the weary meadows came the grassy, rutted approach from the highroad. There trailed another ricketty fence, long split poles joining the short, thick, wide-apart uprights.

The three people stood at the back of the tree, in the corner of the shed meadow, just above the yard gate. The house with its two gables and its porch stood tidy in a little grassed garden across the yard. A little stout rosy-faced woman in a little red woolen shoulder shawl had come and taken her stand in the porch.

"Isn't it down yet?" she cried, in a high little voice.

"Just thinking about it," called her husband. His tone towards the two girls was always rather mocking and satirical. March did not want to go on with her hitting while he was there. As for him, he wouldn't lift a stick from the ground if he could help it, complaining, like his daughter, of rheumatics in his shoulder. So the three stood there a moment silent in the cold afternoon, in the bottom corner near the yard.

They heard the far-off taps of a gate, and craned to look. Away across, on the green horizontal approach, a figure was just swinging on to a bicycle again, and lurching up and down over the grass, approaching.

"Why it's one of our boys—it's Jack," said the old man.

"Can't be," said Banford.

March craned her head to look. She alone recognised the khaki figure. She flushed, but said nothing.

"No, it isn't Jack, I don't think," said the old man, staring with little round blue eyes under his white lashes.

In another moment the bicycle lurched into sight, and the rider dropped off at the gate. It was Henry, his face wet and red and spotted with mud. He was altogether a muddy sight.

"Oh!" cried Banford, as if afraid. "Why it's Henry!"

"What!" muttered the old man. He had a thick, rapid, muttering way of speaking, and was slightly deaf. "What? What? Who is it? Who is it do you say? That young fellow? That young fellow of Nellie's? Oh! Oh!" And the satiric smile came on his pink face and white eyelashes.

Henry, pushing the wet hair off his steaming brow, had caught sight of them and heard what the old man said. His hot young face seemed to flame in the cold light.

"Oh, are you all there!" he said, giving his sudden, puppy's little laugh. He was so hot and dazed with cycling he hardly knew where he was. He leaned the bicycle against the fence and climbed over into the corner on to the bank, without going in to the yard.

"Well, I must say, we weren't expecting *you*," said the Banford laconically.

"No, I suppose not," said he, looking at March.

She stood aside, slack, with one knee drooped and the axe resting its head loosely on the ground. Her eyes were wide and vacant, and her upper lip lifted from her teeth in that helpless, fascinated rabbit-look. The moment she saw his glowing red face it was all over with her. She was as helpless as if she had been bound. The moment she saw the way his head seemed to reach forward.

"Well, who is it? Who is it, anyway?" asked the smiling, satiric old man in his muttering voice.

"Why Mr Grenfel, whom you've heard us tell about, father," said Banford coldly.

"Heard you tell about, I should think so. Heard of nothing else practically," muttered the elderly man with his queer little jeering smile on his face. "How do you do," he added, suddenly reaching out his hand to Henry.

The boy shook hands just as startled. Then the two men fell apart.

"Cycled over from Salisbury Plain have you?" asked the old man.

"Yes."

"Hm! Longish ride. How long d'it take you, eh? Some time, eh? Several hours, I suppose."

"About four."

"Eh? Four! Yes, I should have thought so. When are you going back then?"

"I've got till tomorrow evening."

"Till tomorrow evening, eh? Yes. Hm! Girls weren't expecting you, were they?"

And the old man turned his pale-blue, round little eyes under their white lashes mockingly towards the girls. Henry also looked round. He had become a little awkward. He looked at March, who was still staring away into the distance as if to see where the cattle were. Her hand was on the pommel of the axe, whose head rested loosely on the ground.

"What were you doing then?" he asked in his soft, courteous voice. "Cutting a tree down?"

March seemed not to hear, as if in a trance.

"Yes," said Banford. "We've been at it for over a week."

"Oh! And have you done it all by yourselves then?"

"Nellie's done it all, I've done none," said Banford.

"Really!—You must have worked quite hard," he said, addressing himself in a curious gentle tone direct to March. She did not answer, but remained half averted staring away towards the woods above as if in a trance.

"*Nellie!*" cried Banford sharply. "Can't you answer?"

"What—me?" cried March, starting round, and looking from one to the other. "Did anyone speak to me?"

"Dreaming!" muttered the old man, turning aside to smile. "Must be in love, eh, dreaming in the daytime!"

"Did you say anything to me?" said March, looking at the boy as from a strange distance, her eyes wide and doubtful, her face delicately flushed.

"I said you must have worked hard at the tree," he replied courteously.

"Oh that! Bit by bit. I thought it would have come down by now."

"I'm thankful it hasn't come down in the night, to frighten us to death," said Banford.

"Let me just finish it for you, shall I?" said the boy.

March slanted the axe-shaft in his direction.

"Would you like to," she said.

"Yes, if you wish it," he said.

"Oh, I'm thankful when the thing's down, that's all," she replied, nonchalant.

"Which way is it going to fall?" said Banford. "Will it hit the shed?"

"No, it won't hit the shed," he said. "I should think it will fall *there*—quite clear. Though it might give a twist and catch the fence."

"Catch the fence!" cried the old man. "What, catch the fence! When it's leaning at that angle?—Why it's further off than the shed. It won't catch the fence."

"No," said Henry, "I don't suppose it will. It has plenty of room to fall quite clear, and I suppose it will fall clear."

"Won't tumble backwards on top of *us*, will it?" asked the old man, sarcastic.

"No, it won't do that," said Henry, taking off his short overcoat and his tunic. "Ducks! Ducks! Go back!"

A line of four brown-speckled ducks led by a brown-and-green drake were stemming away downhill from the upper meadow, coming like boats running on a ruffled sea, cockling their way top speed downwards towards the fence and towards the little group of people, and cackling as excitedly as if they brought news of the Spanish Armada.

"Silly things! Silly things!" cried Banford going forward to turn them off. But they came eagerly towards her, opening their yellow-green beaks and quacking as if they were so excited to say something.

"There's no food. There's nothing here. You must wait a bit," said Banford to them. "Go away. Go away. Go round to the yard."

They didn't go, so she climbed the fence to swerve them round under the gate and into the yard. So off they waggled in an excited string once more, wagging their rumps like the sterns of little gondolas ducking under the bar of the gate. Banford stood on the top of the bank, just over the fence, looking down on the other three.

Henry looked up at her, and met her queer, round-pupilled, weak eyes staring behind her spectacles. He was perfectly still. He looked away, up at the weak, leaning tree. And as he looked into the sky, like a huntsman who is watching a flying bird, he thought to himself: "If the tree falls in just such a way, and spins just so much as it falls, then the branch there will strike her exactly as she stands on top of that bank."

He looked at her again. She was wiping the hair from her brow again, with that perpetual gesture. In his heart he had decided her death. A terrible still force seemed in him, and a power that was just his. If he turned even a hair's breadth in the wrong direction, he would lose the power.

"Mind yourself, Miss Banford," he said. And his heart held perfectly still, in the terrible pure will that she should not move.

"Who me, mind myself?" she cried, her father's jeering tone in her voice. "Why, do you think you might hit me with the axe?"

"No, it's just possible the tree might, though," he answered soberly. But the tone of his voice seemed to her to imply that he was only being falsely solicitous and trying to make her move because it was his will to move her.

"Absolutely impossible," she said.

He heard her. But he held himself icy still, lest he should lose his power.

"No, it's just possible. You'd better come down this way."

"Oh all right. Let us see some crack Canadian tree felling," she retorted.

"Ready then," he said, taking the axe, looking round to see he was clear.

There was a moment of pure, motionless suspense, when the world seemed to stand still. Then suddenly his form seemed to flash up enormously tall and fearful, he gave two swift, flashing blows, in immediate succession, the tree was absolutely severed, turning slowly, spinning strangely in the air and coming down like a sudden darkness on the earth. No one saw what was happening except himself. No one heard the strange little cry which the Banford gave as the dark end of the bough swooped down on her. No one saw her crouch a little and receive the blow on the back of the neck. No one saw her flung outwards and laid, a little twitching heap, at the foot of the fence. No one except the boy. And he watched with intense bright eyes, as he would watch a wild goose he had shot. Was it winged, or dead? Dead!

Immediately he gave a loud cry. Immediately March gave a wild shriek that went far, far down the afternoon. And the father started a strange bellowing sound.

The boy leapt the fence and ran to the figure. The back of the neck and head was a mass of blood, of horror. He turned it over. The body was quivering with little convulsions. But she was dead really. He knew it, that it was so. He knew it in his soul and his blood. The inner necessity of his life was fulfilling itself, it was he who was to live. The thorn was drawn out of his bowels. So, he put her down gently, she was dead.

He stood up. March was standing there petrified and absolutely motionless. Her face was dead white, her eyes big black pools. The old man was scrambling horribly over the fence.

"I'm afraid it's killed her," said the boy.

The old man was making curious, blubbering noises as he huddled over the fence.

"What!" cried March, starting electric.

"Yes I'm afraid," repeated the boy.

March was coming forward. The boy was over the fence before she reached it.

"What do you say, killed her?" she asked in a sharp voice.

"I'm afraid so," he answered softly.

She went still whiter, fearful. The two stood facing one another. Her black eyes gazed on him with the last look of resistance. And then in a last agonised failure she began to grizzle, to cry in a shivery little fashion of a child that doesn't want to cry, but which is beaten from within, and gives that little first shudder of sobbing which is not yet weeping, dry and fearful.

He had won. She stood there absolutely helpless, shuddering her dry sobs and her mouth trembling rapidly. And then, as in a child, with a little crash came the tears and the blind agony of sightless weeping. She sank down on the grass and sat there with her hands on her breast and her face lifted in sightless, convulsed weeping. He stood above her, looking down on her, mute, pale, and everlasting seeming. He never moved, but looked down on her. And among all the torture of the scene, the torture of his own heart and bowels, he was glad, he had won.

After a long time he stooped to her and took her hands.

"Don't cry," he said softly. "Don't cry."

She looked up at him with tears running from her eyes, a senseless look of helplessness and submission. So she gazed on him as if sightless, yet looking up to him. She would never leave him again. He had won her. And he knew it and was glad, because he wanted her for his life. His life must have her. And now he had won her. It was what his life must have.

But if he had won her, he had not yet got her. They were married at Christmas as he had planned, and he got again ten days leave. They went to Cornwall, to his own village, on the sea. He realised that it was awful for her to be at the farm any more.

But though she belonged to him, though she lived in his shadow, as if she could not be away from him, she was not happy. She did not want to leave him: and yet she did not feel free with him. Everything around her seemed to watch her, seemed to press on her. He had won her, he had her with him, she was his wife. And she—she belonged to him, she knew it. But she was not glad. And he was still foiled. He realised that though he was married to her and possessed her in every possible way, apparently, and though she *wanted* him to possess her, she wanted it, she wanted nothing else, now, still he did not quite succeed.

Something was missing. Instead of her soul swaying with new life, it seemed to droop, to bleed, as if it were wounded. She would sit for a long time with her hand in his, looking away at the sea. And in her dark, vacant eyes was a sort of wound, and her face looked a little peaked. If he spoke to her, she would turn to him with a faint new smile, the strange, quivering little smile of a woman who has died in the old way of love, and can't quite rise to the new way. She still felt she ought to *do* something, to strain herself in some direction. And there was nothing to do, and no direction in which to strain herself. And she could not quite accept the submergence which his new love put upon her. If she was in love, she ought to *exert* herself, in some way, loving. She felt the weary need of our day to *exert* herself in love. But she knew that in fact she must no more exert herself in love. He would not have the love which exerted itself towards him. It made his brow go black. No, he wouldn't let her exert her love towards him. No, she had to be passive, to acquiesce, and to be submerged under the surface of love. She had to be like the seaweeds she saw as she peered down from the boat, swaying forever delicately under water, with all their delicate fibrils put tenderly out upon the flood, sensitive, utterly sensitive and receptive within the shadowy sea, and never, never rising and looking forth above water while they lived. Never. Never looking forth from the water until they died, only then washing, corpses, upon the surface. But while they lived, always submerged, always beneath the wave. Beneath the wave they might have powerful roots, stronger than iron, they might be tenacious and dangerous in their soft waving within the flood. Beneath the water they might be stronger, more indestructible than resistant oak trees are on land. But it was always under-water, always under-water. And she, being a woman, must be like that.

And she had been so used to the very opposite. She had had to take all the thought for love and for life, and all the responsibility.

Day after day she had been responsible for the coming day, for the coming year: for her dear Jill's health and happiness and well-being. Verily, in her own small way, she had felt herself responsible for the well-being of the world. And this had been her great stimulant, this grand feeling that, in her own small sphere, she was responsible for the well-being of the world.

And she had failed. She knew that, even in her small way, she had failed. She had failed to satisfy her own feeling of responsibility. It was so difficult. It seemed so grand and easy at first. And the more you tried, the more difficult it became. It had seemed so easy to make one beloved creature happy. And the more you tried, the worse the failure. It was terrible. She had been all her life reaching, reaching, and what she reached for seemed so near, until she had stretched to her utmost limit. And then it was always beyond her.

Always beyond her, vaguely, unrealisably beyond her, and she was left with nothingness at last. The life she reached for, the happiness she reached for, the well-being she reached for all slipped back, became unreal, the further she stretched her hand. She wanted some goal, some finality—and there was none. Always this ghastly reaching, reaching, striving for something that might be just beyond. Even to make Jill happy. She was glad Jill was dead. For she had realised that she could never make her happy. Jill would always be fretting herself thinner and thinner, weaker and weaker. Her pains grew worse instead of less. It would be so for ever. She was glad she was dead.

And if she had married a man it would have been just the same. The woman striving, striving to make the man happy, striving within her own limits for the well-being of her world. And always achieving failure. Little, foolish successes in money or in ambition. But at the very point where she most wanted success, in the anguished effort to make some one beloved human being happy and perfect, there the failure was almost catastrophic. You wanted to make your beloved happy, and his happiness seemed always achievable. If only you did just this, that and the other. And you did this, that, and the other, in all good faith, and every time the failure became a little more ghastly. You could love yourself to ribbons, and strive and strain yourself to the bone, and things would go from bad to worse, bad to worse, as far as happiness went. The awful mistake of happiness.

Poor March, in her goodwill and her responsibility, she had strained herself till it seemed to her that the whole of life and everything was only a horrible abyss of nothingness. The more you reach after the fatal flower of happiness, which trembles so blue and lovely in a crevice just beyond your grasp, the more fearfully you become aware of the ghastly and awful gulf of the precipice below you, into which you will inevitably plunge, as into the bottomless pit, if you reach any further. You pluck flower after flower—it is never *the* flower. The flower itself—its calyx is a horrible gulf, it is the bottomless pit.

That is the whole history of the search for happiness, whether it be your own or somebody else's that you want to win. It ends, and it always ends, in the ghastly sense of the bottomless nothingness into which you will inevitably fall if you strain any further.

And women?—what goal can any woman conceive, except happiness? Just happiness, for herself and the whole world. That, and nothing else. And so, she assumes the responsibility, and sets off towards her goal. She can see it there, at the foot of the rainbow. Or she can see it a little way beyond, in the blue distance. Not far, not far.

But the end of the rainbow is a bottomless gulf down which you can fall forever without arriving, and the blue distance is a void pit which can swallow you and all your efforts into its emptiness, and still be no emptier. You and all your efforts. So, the illusion of attainable happiness!

Poor March, she had set off so wonderfully, towards the blue goal. And the further and further she had gone, the more fearful had become the realisation of emptiness. An agony, an insanity at last.

She was glad it was over. She was glad to sit on the shore and look westwards over the sea, and know the great strain had ended. She would never strain for love and happiness any more. And Jill was safely dead. Poor Jill, poor Jill. It must be sweet to be dead.

For her own part, death was not her destiny. She would have to leave her destiny to the boy.—But then, the boy. He wanted more than that. He wanted a new connection. He wanted her to give herself without defences, to sink and become submerged in him. And she—she wanted to sit still, like a woman on the last milestone, and watch. She wanted to see, to know, to understand. She wanted to be alone: with him at her side.

And he? He did not want her to watch any more, to see any more, to understand any more. He wanted to veil her woman's spirit, as Orientals veil the woman's face. He wanted her to commit herself to him, and to put her independent spirit to sleep. He wanted to take away from her all her effort, all that had seemed her very raison d'être. He wanted to make her submit, yield, blindly pass away out of all her strenuous consciousness. He wanted to take away her consciousness, and make her just his woman. Just his woman.

And she was so tired, so tired, like a child that wants to go to sleep, but which fights against sleep as if sleep were death. She seemed to stretch her eyes wider in the obstinate effort and tension of keeping awake. She *would* keep awake. She *would* know. She *would* consider and judge and decide. She *would* have the reins of her own life between her own hands. She *would* be an independent woman to the last.—But she was so tired, so tired of everything. And sleep seemed near. And there was such rest in the boy.

Yet there, sitting in a niche of the high wild cliffs of west Cornwall, looking over the westward sea, she stretched her eyes wider and wider. Away to the West, Canada, America. She *would* know and she *would* see what was ahead. And the boy, sitting beside her staring down at the gulls, had a cloud between his brows and the strain of discontent in his eyes. He wanted her asleep, at peace in him. He wanted her at peace, asleep in him. And there she was, dying with the strain of her own resistant wakefulness. Yet she would not sleep: no, never. Sometimes he thought bitterly that he ought to have left her. He ought never to have killed Banford. He should have left Banford and March to kill one another.

But that was only impatience: and he knew it. He was waiting, waiting to go west. He was aching almost in torment to leave England, to go west, to take March away. To leave this shore! He believed that as they crossed the seas, as they left this England which he so hated, because in some way it seemed to have stung him with poison, she would go to sleep. She would close her eyes at last, and give in to him.

And then he would have her, and he would have his own life at last. He chafed, feeling he hadn't got his own life. He would never have it till she yielded and slept in him. Then he would have all his own life as a young man and a male, and she would have all her own life as a woman and a female. There would be no more of this awful straining. She would not be a man any more, an independent woman with a man's responsibility. Nay, even the responsibility for her own soul she would have to commit to him. He knew it was so, and obstinately held out against her, waiting for the surrender.

"You'll feel better when once we get over the seas, to Canada, over there," he said to her as they sat among the rocks on the cliff.

She looked away to the sea's horizon, as if it were not real. Then she looked round at him, with the strained, strange look of a child that is struggling against sleep.

"Shall I?" she said.

"Yes," he answered quietly.

And her eyelids drooped with the slow motion, sleep weighing them unconscious. But she pulled them open again to say:

"Yes, I may. I can't tell. I can't tell what it will be like over there."

"If only we could go soon!" he said, with pain in his voice.

THE CAPTAIN'S DOLL

The Captain's Doll

"Hannele—!"

"Ja—a."

"Wo bist du?"

"Hier."

"Wo dann?"

Hannele did not lift her head from her work. She sat in a low chair under a reading-lamp, a basket of coloured silk pieces beside her, and in her hands a doll, or mannikin, which she was dressing. She was doing something to the knee of the mannikin, so that the poor little gentleman flourished head downwards with arms wildly tossed out. And it was not at all seemly, because the doll was a Scotch soldier in tight-fitting tartan trews.

There was a tap at the door, and the same voice, a woman's, calling:

"Hannele?"

"Ja—a!"

"Are you here?—Are you alone?" asked the voice, in German.

"Yes—come in."

Hannele did not sound very encouraging. She turned round her doll as the door opened, and straightened his coat. A dark-eyed young woman peeped in through the door, with a roguish coyness. She was dressed fashionably for the street, in a thick cape-wrap, and a little black hat pulled down to her ears.

"Quite, quite alone!" said the new-comer, in a tone of wonder. "Where is he then?"

"That I don't know," said Hannele.

"And you sit here alone, and wait for him? But no! That I call courage! Aren't you afraid?" Mitchka strolled across to her friend.

"Why shall I be afraid?" said Hannele curtly.

"But no—! And what are you doing? Another puppet? He is a good one, though! Ha—ha—ha! *Him*! It is him! No—no—that is too beautiful! No—that is too beautiful, Hannele. It is *him*—exactly him. Only the trousers."

75

"He wears those trousers too," said Hannele, standing her doll on her knee. It was a perfect portrait of an officer of a Scottish regiment, slender, delicately made, with a slight, elegant stoop of the shoulders, and close-fitting tartan trousers. The face was beautifully modelled, and a wonderful portrait, dark-skinned, with a little close-cut dark moustache, and wide-open dark eyes, and that air of aloofness and perfect diffidence which marks an officer and a gentleman.

Mitchka bent forward, studying the doll. She was a handsome woman with a warm, dark-golden skin and clear black eyebrows over her russet-brown eyes.

"No," she whispered to herself, as if awestruck. "That is him. That is him. Only not the trousers. Beautiful, though, the trousers. Has he really such beautiful fine legs?"

Hannele did not answer.

"Exactly him. Just as finished as he is. Just as complete. He is just like that: finished off.—Has he seen it?"

"No," said Hannele.

"What will he say then?"—She started. Her quick ear had caught a sound on the stone stairs. A look of fear came to her face. She flew to the door and out of the room, closing the door to behind her.

"Who is it?" her voice was heard calling anxiously down the stairs.

The answer came in German. Mitchka immediately opened the door again and came back to join Hannele.

"Only Martin," she said.

She stood waiting. A man appeared in the doorway—erect, military.

"Ah!—Countess Hannele," he said in his quick, precise way, as he stood on the threshold in the distance. "May one come in?"

"Yes, come in," said Hannele.

The man entered with a quick, military step, bowed, and kissed the hand of the woman who was sewing the doll. Then, much more intimately he touched Mitchka's hand with his lips.

Mitchka meanwhile was glancing round the room. It was a very large attic, with the ceiling sloping and then bending in two handsome movements towards the walls. The light from the dark-shaded reading-lamp fell softly on the huge whitewashed vaulting of the ceiling, on the various objects round the walls, and made a brilliant pool of colour where Hannele sat in her soft red dress, with her basket of silks.

She was a fair woman with dark-blond hair and a beautiful fine skin. Her face seemed luminous, a certain quick gleam of life about it as she looked up at the man. He was handsome, clean-shaven, with very blue eyes strained a little too wide. One could see the war in his face.

Mitchka was wandering round the room, looking at everything, and saying: "Beautiful! But beautiful! Such good taste! A man, and such good taste! No, they don't need a woman. No, look here, Martin, the Captain Hepburn has arranged all this room himself. Here you have the man. Do you see? So simple, yet so elegant. He needs no woman—"

The room was really beautiful, spacious, pale, softly-lighted. It was heated by a large stove of dark-blue tiles, and had very little furniture save two large peasant cupboards or presses of painted wood, and a huge writing table on which were writing materials and some scientific apparatus and a cactus plant with fine scarlet blossoms. But it was a man's room. Tobacco and pipes were on a little tray, on the pegs in the distance hung military overcoats and belts, and two guns on a bracket. Then there were two telescopes, one mounted on a stand near a window. Various astronomical apparatus lay upon the table.

"And he reads the stars. Only think—he is an astronomer and reads the stars. Queer, queer people, the English!"

"He is Scottish," said Hannele.

"Yes, Scottish," said Mitchka.—"But, you know, I am afraid when I am with him. He is at a closed end. I don't know where I can get to with him. Aren't you afraid of him too, Hannele? Ach, like a closed road!"

"Why should I be?"

"Ah you! Perhaps you don't know when you should be afraid. But if he were to come and find us here?—No, no—let us go. Let us go, Martin. Come, let us go. I don't want the Captain Hepburn to come and find me in his room. Oh no!"—Mitchka was busily pushing Martin to the door, and he was laughing with the queer mad laugh in his strained eyes. "Oh no! I don't like. I don't like it," said Mitchka, trying her English now. She spoke a few sentences prettily. "Oh no, Sir Captain, I don't want that you come. I don't like it, to be here when you come. Oh no. Not at all. I go. I go, Hannele. I go, my Hannele.—And will you really stay here and wait for him?—But when will he come? You don't know?—Oh dear, I don't like it, I don't like it. I do not wait in the man's room. No, no—Never—jamais—jamais, voyez vous.—Ach, you poor Hannele! And he has got wife and children in England?—Nevair! No, nevair shall I wait for him."

She had bustlingly pushed Martin through the door, and settled her wrap and taken a mincing elegant pose, ready for the street, and waved her hand and made wide, scared eyes at Hannele, and was gone. The Countess Hannele picked up the doll again and began to sew its shoe. What living she now had she earned making these puppets.

But she was restless. She pressed her arms into her lap, as if the holding them bent had wearied her. Then she looked at the little clock on his writing table. It was long after dinner-time—why hadn't he come? She sighed rather exasperated. She was tired of her doll.

Putting aside her basket of silks, she went to one of the windows. Outside the stars seemed white, and very near. Below was the dark agglomeration of the roofs of houses, a fume of light came up from beneath the darkness of roofs, and a faint breakage of noise from the town far below. The room seemed high, remote, in the sky.

She went to the table and looked at his letter-clip with letters in it and at his sealing-wax and his stamp-box, touching things and moving them a little, just for the sake of the contact, not really noticing what she touched. Then she took a pencil, and in stiff Gothic characters began to write her name—Johanna zu Rassentlow—time after time her own name—and then once, bitterly, curiously, with a curious sharpening of her nose: Alexander Hepburn.

But she threw the pencil down, having no more interest in her writing. She wandered to where the large telescope stood near a further window, and stood for some minutes with her fingers on the barrel, where it was a little brighter from his touching it. Then she drifted restlessly back to her chair. She had picked up her puppet when she heard him on the stairs. She lifted her face and watched as he entered.

"Hello, you there!" he said quietly, as he closed the door behind him. She glanced at him swiftly, but did not move nor answer.

He took off his overcoat, with quick, quiet movements, and went to hang it up on the pegs. She heard his step, and looked again. He was like the doll, a tall, slender, well-bred man in uniform. When he turned, his dark eyes seemed very wide open. His black hair was going grey at the temples—the first touch.

She was sewing her doll. Without saying anything, he wheeled round the chair from the writing-table, so that he sat with his knees almost touching her. Then he crossed one leg over the other. He wore fine tartan socks. His ankles seemed slender and elegant, his brown shoes fitted as if they were part of him. For some moments he watched her as she sat sewing. The light fell on her soft, delicate hair, that was full of strands of gold and of tarnished gold and shadow. She did not look up.

In silence he held out his small, naked-looking brown hand, for the doll. On his forearm were black hairs.

She glanced up at him. Curious how fresh and luminous her face looked in contrast to his.

"Do you want to see it?" she asked, in natural English.

"Yes," he said.

She broke off her thread of cotton and handed him the puppet. He sat with one leg thrown over the other, holding the doll in one hand, and smiling inscrutably with his dark eyes. His hair, parted perfectly on one side, was jet black and glossy.

"You've got me," he said at last, in his amused, melodious voice.

"What?" she said.

"You've got me," he repeated.

"I don't care," she said.

"What?—You don't care?"—His face broke into a smile. He had an odd way of answering, as if he were only half attending, as if he were thinking of something else.

"You are very late, aren't you?" she ventured.

"Yes. I am rather late."

"Why are you?"

"Well, as a matter of fact, I was talking with the Colonel."

"About me?"

"Yes. It was about you."

She went pale as she sat looking up into his face. But it was impossible to tell whether there was distress on his dark brow, or not.

"Anything nasty?" she said.

"Well yes. It was rather nasty. Not about you, I mean. But rather awkward for me."

She watched him. But still he said no more.

"What was it?" she said.

"Oh well—only what I expected. They seem to know rather too much about you—about you and me, I mean. Not that anybody cares one bit, you know, unofficially. The trouble is, they are apparently going to have to take official notice."

"Why?"

"Oh well—it appears my wife has been writing letters to the Major-General. He is one of her family acquaintances—known her all his life. And I suppose she's been hearing rumours. In fact I know she has. She said so in her letter to me."

"And what do you say to her then?"

"Oh, I tell her I'm all right—not to worry."

"You don't expect *that* to stop her worrying, do you?" she asked.

"Oh I don't know. Why should she worry?" he said.

"I think she might have some reason," said Hannele. "You've not seen her for a year—And if she adores you—"

"Oh, I don't think she adores me. I think she quite likes me."

"Do you think you matter as little as that to her?"

"I don't see why not.—Of course she likes to feel *safe* about me—"

"But now she doesn't feel safe."

"No—exactly. Exactly. That's the point. That's where it is. The Colonel advises me to go home on leave."

He sat gazing with curious bright, dark, unseeing eyes at the doll which he held by one arm. It was an extraordinary likeness of himself, true even to the smooth parting of his hair and his peculiar way of fixing his dark eyes.

"For how long?" she asked.

"I don't know.—For a month," he replied, first vaguely, then definitely.

"For a month!" She watched him, and seemed to see him fade from her eyes.

"And will you go?" she asked.

"I don't know. I don't know." His head remained bent, he seemed to muse rather vaguely. "I don't know," he repeated. "I can't make up my mind what I shall do."

"Would you like to go?" she asked.

He lifted his brows and looked at her. Her heart always melted in her when he looked straight at her with his black eyes, and that curious, bright unseeing look that was more like second sight than direct human vision. She never knew what he saw when he looked at her.

"No," he said simply. "I don't *want* to go. I don't think I've any desire at all to go to England."

"Why not?" she said.

"I can't say."—Then again he looked at her, and a curious white light seemed to shine on his eyes, as he smiled slowly with his mouth, and said: "I suppose you ought to know, if anybody does."

A glad, half-frightened look came on her face.

"You mean you don't want to leave me?" she asked, breathless.

"Yes. I suppose that's what I mean."

"But you aren't sure?"

"Yes I am, I'm quite sure," he said, and the curious smile lingered on his face, and the strange light shone on his eyes.

"That you don't want to leave me?" she stammered, looking aside.

"Yes, I'm quite sure I don't want to leave you," he repeated. He had a curious, very melodious Scottish voice. But it was the incomprehensible smile on his face that convinced and frightened her. It was almost a gargoyle smile, a strange, lurking, changeless-seeming grin.

She was frightened, and turned aside her face. When she looked at him again, his face was like a mask, with strange, deep-graven lines and a glossy dark skin and a fixed look—as if carved half grotesque in some glossy stone. His black hair on his smooth, beautifully-shaped head seemed changeless.

"Are you rather tired?" she asked him.

"Yes, I think I am." He looked at her with black, unseeing eyes, and a mask-like face. Then he glanced aside as if he heard something. Then he rose with his hand on his belt, saying: "I'll take off my belt, and change my coat, if you don't mind."

He walked across the room, unfastening his broad brown belt. He was in well-fitting, well-cut khaki. He hung up his belt and came back to her wearing an old light tunic, which he left unbuttoned. He carried his slippers in one hand. When he sat down to unfasten his shoes, she noticed again how black and hairy his forearm was, how naked his brown hand seemed. His hair was black and smooth and perfect on his head, like some close helmet, as he stooped down.

He put on his slippers, carried his shoes aside, and resumed his chair, stretching luxuriously.

"There," he said. "I feel better now." And he looked at her. "Well," he said, "and how are you?"

"Me?" she said. "Do I matter?" She was rather bitter.

"Do you matter?" he repeated, without noticing her bitterness. "Why, what a question! Of course you are of the very highest importance. What? Aren't you?" And smiling his curious smile—it made her for a moment think of the fixed sadness of monkeys, of those Chinese carved soapstone apes;—he put his hand under her chin, and gently drew his fingers along her cheek. She flushed deeply.

"But I'm not as important as you, am I?" she asked defiantly.

"As important as me! Why bless you, I'm not important a bit. I'm not important a bit!"—The odd, straying sound of his words mystified her. What did he really mean?

"And I'm even less important than that," she said bitterly.

"Oh no you're not. Oh no you're not. You're very important. You're very important indeed, I assure you."

"And your wife?"—the question came rebelliously. "Your wife? Isn't she important?"

"My wife? My wife?" he seemed to let the word stray out of him as if he did not quite know what it meant. "Why yes, I suppose she is important in her own sphere."

"What sphere?" blurted Hannele, with a laugh.

"Why, her own sphere, of course. Her own house, her own home, and her two children: that's her sphere."

"And you?—where do you come in?"

"At present I don't come in," he said.

"But isn't that just the trouble," said Hannele. "If you have a wife and a home, it's your business to belong to it, isn't it?"

"Yes, I suppose it is, if I want to," he replied.

"And you *do* want to?" she challenged.

"No, I don't," he replied.

"Well then—?" she said.

"Yes, quite," he answered. "I admit, it's a dilemma."

"But what will you *do*?" she insisted.

"Why, I don't know. I don't know yet. I haven't made up my mind what I'm going to do."

"Then you'd better begin to make it up," she said.

"Yes I know that. I know that."

He rose, and began to walk uneasily up and down the room. But the same vacant darkness was on his brow. He had his hands in his pockets. Hannele sat feeling helpless. She couldn't help being in love with the man: with his hands, with his strange, fascinating physique, with his incalculable presence. She loved the way he put his feet down, she loved the way he moved his legs as he walked, she loved the mould of his loins, she loved the way he drooped his head a little, and the strange dark vacancy of his brow, his not-thinking. But now his restlessness only made her unhappy. Nothing would come of it. Yet she had driven him to it.

He took his hands out of his pockets and returned to her like a piece of iron returning to a magnet. He sat down again in front of her and put out his hands to her, looking into her face.

"Give me your hands," he said softly, with that strange, mindless soft suggestive tone which left her powerless to disobey. "Give me your hands, and let me feel that we are together. Words mean so little. They mean nothing. And all that one thinks and plans doesn't amount to anything. Let me feel that we are together, and I don't care about all the rest."

He spoke in his slow, melodious way, and closed her hands in his. She struggled still for voice.

"But you'll *have* to care about it. You'll *have* to make up your mind. You'll just *have* to," she insisted.

"Yes, I suppose I shall. I suppose I shall. But now that we are together, I won't bother. Now that we are together, let us forget it."

"But when we *can't* forget it any more?"

"Well—then I don't know. But—tonight—it seems to me—we might just as well forget it."

The soft, melodious, straying sound of his voice made her feel helpless. She felt that he never answered her. Words of reply seemed to stray out of him, in the need to say *something*. But he himself never spoke. There he was, a continual blank silence in front of her.

She had a battle with herself. When he put his hand again on her cheek, softly, with the most extraordinary soft half-touch, as a kitten's paw sometimes touches one, like a fluff of living air, then, if it had not been for the magic of that almost indiscernible caress of his hand, she would have stiffened herself and drawn away and told him she could have nothing to do with him, while he was so half-hearted and unsatisfactory. She wanted to tell him these things. But when she began he answered invariably in the same soft, straying voice, that seemed to spin gossamer threads all over her, so that she could neither think nor act nor even feel distinctly. Her soul groaned rebelliously in her. And yet, when he put his hand softly under her chin, and lifted her face and smiled down on her with that gargoyle smile of his—she let him kiss her.

"What are you thinking about tonight?" he said. "What are you thinking about?"

"What did your colonel say to you, exactly?" she replied, trying to harden her eyes.

"Oh that!" he answered. "Never mind that. That is of no significance whatever."

"But what *is* of any significance?" she insisted. She almost hated him.

"What is of any significance? Well, nothing, to me, outside of this room, at this minute. Nothing in time or space matters to me."

"Yes, *this minute*!" she repeated bitterly. "But then there's the future. *I've* got to live in the future."

"The future! The future! The future is used up every day. The future to me is like a big tangle of black thread. Every morning you begin to untangle one loose end—and that's your day. And every evening you break off and throw away what you've untangled and the heap is so much less: just one thread less, one day less. That's all the future matters to me."

"Then nothing matters to you. And I don't matter to you. As you say, only an end of waste thread," she resisted him.

"No, there you're wrong. You aren't the future to me."

"What am I then?—the past?"

"No, not any of those things. You're nothing. As far as all that goes, you're nothing."

"Thank you," she said sarcastically, "if I'm nothing."

But the very irrelevancy of the man overcame her. He kissed her with half-discernible, dim kisses, and touched her throat. And the meaninglessness of him fascinated her and left her powerless. She could ascribe no meaning to him, none whatever. And yet his mouth, so strange in kissing, and his hairy forearms, and his slender, beautiful breast with black hair—it was all like a mystery to her, as if one of the men from Mars were loving her. And she was heavy and spell-bound, and she loved the spell that bound her. But also she didn't love it.

———

Countess zu Rassentlow had a studio in one of the main streets. She was really a refugee. And nowadays you can be a Grand duke and a pauper, if you are a refugee. But Hannele was not a pauper, because

84

she and her friend Mitchka had the studio where they made these dolls, and beautiful cushions of embroidered coloured wools, and such-like objects of feminine art. The dolls were quite famous, so the two women did not starve.

Hannele did not work much in the studio. She preferred to be alone in her own room, which was another fine attic, not quite so large as the Captain's, under the same roof. But often she went to the studio in the afternoon, and if purchasers came, then they were offered a cup of tea.

The Alexander doll was never intended for sale. What made Hannele take it to the studio one afternoon, we do not know. But she did so, and stood it on a little bureau. It was a wonderful little portrait of an officer and gentleman, the physique modelled so that it made you hold your breath.

"But *that*—that is genius!" cried Mitchka. "That is a *chef d'œuvre*! That is thy masterpiece, Hannele. That is really marvellous. And beautiful! A beautiful man, what! But no, that is *too* real. I don't understand how you *dare*. I always thought you were *good*, Hannele, so much better-natured than I am. But now you frighten me. I am afraid you are wicked, do you know. It frightens me to think that you are wicked. Aber nein!—But you won't leave him there?"

"Why not?" said Hannele, satiric.

Mitchka made big dark eyes of wonder, reproach, and fear.

"But you *must* not," she said.

"Why not?"

"No, that you *may* not do. You love the man."

"What then?"

"You can't leave his puppet standing there."

"Why can't I?"

"But you are really wicked. Du bist *wirklich* bös. Only think!— and he is an English officer."

"He isn't sacrosanct even then."

"They will expel you from the town. They will deport you."

"Let them then."

"But no! What will you do? That would be horrible if we had to go to Berlin or to Munich and begin again. Here everything has happened so well."

"I don't care," said Hannele.

Mitchka looked at her friend, and said no more. But she was angry. After some time she turned and uttered her ultimatum.

"When you are not there," she said, "I shall put the puppet away in a drawer. I shall show it to nobody, nobody. And I must tell you, it makes me afraid to see it there. It makes me afraid. And you have no right to get me into trouble, do you see. It is not I who look at the English officers. I don't like them, they are too cold and finished off for me. I shall never bring trouble on *myself* because of the English officers—"

"Don't be afraid," said Hannele. "They won't trouble *you*. They know everything we do, well enough. They have their spies everywhere. Nothing will happen to you."

"But if they make you go away—and I am planted here with the studio—"

It was no good, however, Hannele was obstinate.

So, one sunny afternoon there was a ring at the door: a little lady in white, with a wrinkled face that still had its prettiness.

"Good-afternoon!"—in rather lardy-dardy middle-class English. "I wonder if I may see your things in your studio."

"Oh yes!" said Mitchka. "Please to come in."

Entered the little lady in her finery and her crumpled prettiness. She would not be very old: perhaps younger than fifty. And it was odd that her face had gone so crumpled, because her figure was very trim, her eyes were bright, and she had pretty teeth when she laughed. She was very fine in her clothes: a dress of thick knitted white silk, a large ermine scarf with the tails only at the ends, and a black hat over which dripped a trail of green feathers of the osprey sort. She wore rather a lot of jewellery, and two bangles tinkled over her white kid gloves as she put up her fingers to touch her hair, whilst she stood complacently and looked round.

"You've got a *charming* studio—*charming*—perfectly delightful. I couldn't imagine anything more delightful."

Mitchka gave a slight ironic bow, and said, in her odd, plangent English:

"Oh yes. We like it very much also."

Hannele, who had dodged behind a screen, now came quietly forth.

"Oh how do you do!" smiled the elderly lady. "I heard there were two of you. Now which is which, if I may be so bold? This—" and she gave a winsome smile and pointed a white kid finger at Mitchka—"is the—?"

"Annamaria von Prielau-Carolath," said Mitchka, slightly bowing.

86

"Oh!—" and the white kid finger jerked away. "Then this—"

"Johanna zu Rassentlow," said Hannele, smiling.

"Ah yes! Countess von Rassentlow! And this is Baroness von—von—but I shall never remember even if you tell me, for I'm awful at names. Anyhow I shall call one *Countess* and the other *Baroness*. That will do, won't it, for poor me!—Now I should like awfully to see your things, if I may. I want to buy a little present to take back to England with me. I suppose I shan't have to pay the world in duty on things like these, shall I?"

"Oh no," said Mitchka. "No duty. Toys, you know, they—there is—" Her English stammered to an end, so she turned to Hannele.

"They don't charge duty on toys, and the embroideries they don't notice," said Hannele.

"Oh well. Then I'm all right," said the visitor. "I hope I can buy something really nice. I see a perfectly lovely jumper over there, perfectly delightful. But a little too gay for me, I'm afraid. I'm not quite so young as I was, alas." She smiled her winsome little smile, showing her pretty teeth, and the old pearls in her ears shook.

"I've heard so much about your dolls. I hear they're perfectly exquisite, quite works of art. May I see some, please."

"Oh yes," came Mitchka's invariable answer, this exclamation being the foundation stone of all her English.

There were never more than three or four dolls in stock. This time there were only two. The famous Captain was hidden in his drawer.

"Perfectly beautiful! Perfectly wonderful!" murmured the little lady, in an artistic murmur. "I think they're perfectly delightful. It's wonderful of you, Countess, to make them. It is you who make them, is it not? Or do you both do them together?"

Hannele explained, and the inspection and the rhapsody went on together. But it was evident that the little lady was a cautious buyer. She went over the things very carefully, and thought more than twice. The dolls attracted her—but she thought them expensive, and hung fire.

"I do wish," she said wistfully, "there had been a larger selection of the dolls. I feel, you know, there might have been one which I *just loved*. Of course these are *darlings*—darlings they are: and worth every *penny*, considering the work there is in them. And the art, of course. But I have a feeling, don't you know how it is, that if there had been just one or two more, I should have found one which I *absolutely* couldn't live without.—Don't you know how it is?—One is

87

so foolish, of course.—What does Goethe say—'Dort wo du nicht bist . . .'?—My German isn't even a beginning, so you must excuse it. But it means you always feel you would be happy somewhere else, and not just where you are. Isn't that it?—Ah well, it's so very often true—so very often. But not always, thank goodness."—She smiled an odd little smile to herself, pursed her lips, and resumed: "Well now, that's how I feel about the dolls. If only there had been one or two more. Isn't there a single one?"

She looked winsomely at Hannele.

"Yes," said Hannele, "there is one. But it is ordered. It isn't for sale."

"Oh, do you think I might see it? I'm sure it's lovely. Oh I'm dying to see it.—You know what woman's curiosity is, don't you?"—she laughed her tinkling little laugh. "Well, I'm afraid I'm all woman, unfortunately. One is so much harder if one has a touch of the man in one, don't you think, and more able to bear things. But I'm afraid I'm all woman." She sighed and became silent.

Hannele went quietly to the drawer and took out the Captain. She handed him to the little woman. The latter looked frightened. Her eyes became round and childish, her face went yellowish. Her jewels tinkled nervously as she stammered:

"Now *that*—isn't that—" and she laughed a little, hysterical laugh. She turned round, as if to escape.

"Do you mind if I sit down," she said. "I think the standing——" and she subsided into a chair. She kept her face averted. But she held the puppet fast, her small white fingers with their heavy jewelled rings clasped round his waist.

"You know," rushed in Mitchka, who was terrified, "you know, that is a life-picture of one of the Englishmen, of a gentleman, you know. A life-picture, you know."

"A portrait," said Hannele brightly.

"Yes," murmured the visitor vaguely. "I'm sure it is. I'm sure it is a very clever portrait indeed."

She fumbled with a chain, and put up a small gold lorgnette before her eyes, as if to screen herself. And from behind the screen of her lorgnette she peered at the image in her hand.

"But," she said, "none of the English officers, or rather Scottish, wear the close-fitting tartan trews any more—except for fancy dress."

Her voice was vague and distant.

"No, they don't now," said Hannele. "But that is the correct dress. I think they are so handsome, don't you?"

"Well—I don't know. It depends—" and the little woman laughed shakily.

"Oh yes," said Hannele. "It needs well-shapen legs."

"Such as the original of your doll must have had—quite," said the lady.

"Oh yes," said Hannele. "I think his legs are very handsome."

"Quite!" said the lady. "Judging from his portrait, as you call it. —May I ask the name of the gentleman—if it is not too indiscreet?"

"Captain Hepburn," said Hannele.

"Yes of course it is. I knew him at once.—I've known him for many years."

"Oh please," broke in Mitchka. "Oh please not to tell him you have seen it! Oh please! Please not to tell anyone!"

The visitor looked up with a grey little smile.

"But why not?" she said. "Anyhow, I can't tell him at once, because I hear he is away at present. You don't happen to know when he will be back?"

"I believe tomorrow," said Hannele.

"Tomorrow!—"

"And please!" pleaded Mitchka, who looked lovely in her pleading distress. "Please not to tell anybody that you have seen it."

"Must I promise?" smiled the little lady wanly. "Very well then, I won't tell him I've seen it.—And now I think I must be going.—Yes, I'll just take the cushion cover, thank you. Tell me again how much it is, please—"

That evening Hannele was restless. He had been away on some duty for three days. He was returning that night—should have been back in time for dinner. But he had not arrived, and his room was locked and dark. Hannele had heard the servant light the stove some hours ago. Now the room was locked and blank as it had been for three days.

Hannele was most uneasy because she seemed to have forgotten him in the three days whilst he had been away. He seemed to have quite disappeared out of her. She could hardly even remember him. He had become so insignificant to her she was dazed.

Now she wanted to see him again, to know if it was really so. She felt that he was coming. She felt that he was already putting out some influence towards her. But what? And was he real? Why had she made his doll? Why had his doll been so important, if he was nothing? Why had she shown it to that funny little woman this afternoon? Why was she herself such a fool, getting herself into tangles in this place where it was so unpleasant to be entangled? Why was she entangled, after all? It was all so unreal. And particularly *he* was unreal: as unreal as a person in a dream, whom one has never heard of in actual life. In actual life, her own German friends were real. Martin was real, German men were real to her. But this other, he was simply not there. He didn't really exist. He was a nullus, in reality. A nullus—and she had somehow got herself complicated with him.

Was it possible? Was it possible she had been so closely entangled with an absolute nothing? Now he was absent she couldn't even *imagine* him. He had gone out of her imagination, and even when she looked at his doll she saw nothing but a barren puppet. And yet for this dead puppet she had been compromising herself, now, when it was so risky for her to be compromised.

Her own German friends—her own German men—they were men, they were real beings. But this English officer he was neither fish, flesh, fowl, nor good red herring, as they say. He was just a hypothetical presence.—She felt that if he never came back, she would be just as if she had read a rather peculiar but false story, a *tour de force* which works up one's imagination all falsely.

Nevertheless she was uneasy. She had a lurking suspicion that there might be something else. So she kept uneasily wandering out on to the landing, and listening, to hear if he might be coming.

Yes—there was a sound. Yes, there was his slow step on the stairs, and the slow, straying purr of his voice. And instantly she heard his voice she was afraid again. She knew there *was* something there. And instantly she felt the reality of his presence, she felt the unreality of her own German men-friends. The moment she heard the peculiar slow melody of his foreign voice everything seemed to go changed in her, and Martin and Otto and Albrecht, her German friends, seemed to go pale and dim as if one could almost see through them, like unsubstantial things.

This was what she had to reckon with, this recoil from one to the other. When he was present, he seemed so terribly real. When he absent he was completely vague, and her own men of her own race seemed so absolutely the only reality.

But he was talking. Who was he talking to?—She heard the steps echo up the hollow of the stone staircase, slowly, as if wearily, and voices slowly, confusedly mingle. The slow, soft trail of his voice—and then the peculiar quick tones—yes, of a woman. And not one of the maids, because they were speaking English. She listened hard. The quick, and yet slightly hushed, slightly sad-sounding voice of a woman who talks a good deal, as if talking to herself. Hannele's quick ears caught the sound of what she was saying: "Yes, I thought the Baroness a perfectly beautiful creature, perfectly lovely. But so extraordinarily like a Spaniard. Do you remember, Alec, at Malaga? I always thought they fascinated you there, with their mantillas. Perfectly lovely she would look in a mantilla. Only perhaps she is too open-hearted, too impulsive, poor thing. She lacks the Spanish reserve. Poor thing, I feel sorry for her. For them both, indeed. It must be very hard to have to do these things for a living, after you've been accustomed to be made much of for your own sake and for your aristocratic title. It's very hard for them, poor things. Baroness, Countess, it sounds just a little ridiculous, when you're buying woolen embroideries from them. But I suppose, poor things, they can't help it. Better drop the titles altogether, I think—"

"Well, they do, if people will let them. Only English and American people find it so much easier to say Baroness or Countess than Fräulein von Prielau-Carolath, or whatever it is."

"They could say simply Fräulein, as we do to our governesses—or as we used to, when we *had* German governesses," came the voice of *her*.

"Yes, we *could*—" said his voice.

"After all, what is the good, what is the good of titles if you have to sell dolls and woolen embroideries—not so *very* beautiful, either—"

"Oh quite! Oh quite! I think titles are perhaps a mistake, anyhow. But they've always had them," came his slow, musical voice, with its singsong note of hopeless indifference. He sounded rather like a man talking out of his sleep.

Hannele caught sight of the tail of blue-green crane feathers, veering round a turn in the stairs away below, and she beat a hasty retreat.

———

There was a little platform out on the roof, where he used sometimes to stand his telescope and observe the stars or the moon: the moon when possible. It was not a very safe platform, just a little ledge of the roof, outside the window at the end of the top corridor: or rather, the top landing, for it was only the space between the attics. Hannele had the one attic-room at the back, he had the room we have seen, and a little bedroom which was really only a lumber room. Before he came, Hannele had been alone under the roof. His rooms were then lumber-room and laundry-room, where the clothes were dried. But he had wanted to be high up, because of his stars, and this was the place that pleased him.

Hannele heard him quite late in the night, wandering about. She heard him also on the ledge outside. She could not sleep. He disturbed her. The moon was risen, large and bright in the sky. She heard the bells from the cathedral slowly strike two: two great drops of sound in the livid night. And again, from outside on the roof, she heard him clear his throat. Then a cat howled.

She rose, wrapped herself in a dark wrap, and went down the landing to the window at the end. The sky outside was full of moonlight. He was squatted like a great cat peering up his telescope, sitting on a stool, his knees wide apart. Quite motionless he sat in that attitude, like some leaden figure on the roof. The moonlight glistened with a gleam of plumbago on the great slope of black tiles. She stood still in the window, watching. And he remained fixed and motionless at the end of the telescope.

She tapped softly on the window-pane. He looked round, like some tom-cat staring round with wide night-eyes. Then he reached down his hand and pulled the window open.

"Hello," he said quietly. "You not asleep?"

"Aren't *you* tired?" she replied, rather resentful.

"No, I was as wide awake as I could be. *Isn't* the moon fine tonight! What? Perfectly amazing. Wouldn't you like to come up and have a look at her?"

"No thank you," she said hastily, terrified at the thought.

He resumed his posture, peering up the telescope.

"Perfectly amazing," he said, murmuring. She waited for some time, bewitched likewise by the great October moon and the sky full of resplendent white-green light. It seemed like another sort of daytime. And there he straddled on the roof like some cat! It was exactly like day in some other planet.

At length he turned round to her. His face glistened faintly, and his eyes were dilated like a cat's at night.

"You knew I had a visitor?" he said.

"Yes."

"My wife."

"Your *wife*—!"—she looked up really astonished. She had thought it might be an acquaintance—perhaps his aunt—or even an elder sister.—"But she's years older than you," she added.

"Eight years," he said. "I'm forty one."

There was a silence.

"Yes," he mused. "She arrived suddenly, by surprise, yesterday, and found me away. She's staying in the hotel—in the Vier Jahreszeiten."

There was a pause.

"Aren't you going to stay with her?" asked Hannele.

"Yes, I shall probably join her tomorrow."

There was a still longer pause.

"Why not tonight?" asked Hannele.

"Oh well—I put it off for tonight.—It meant all the bother of my wife changing her room at the hotel—and it was late—and I was all mucky after travelling—"

"But you'll go tomorrow?"

"Yes I shall go tomorrow. For a week or so.—After that I'm not sure what will happen."

There was quite a long pause. He remained seated on his stool on the roof, looking with dilated, blank black eyes at nothingness. She stood below in the open window-space, pondering.

"Do you want to go to her at the hotel?" asked Hannele.

"Well, I don't, particularly. But I don't mind, really. We're very good friends. Why we've been friends for eighteen years—we've been married seventeen. Oh, she's a nice little woman.—I don't want to hurt her feelings.—I wish her no harm, you know.—On the contrary, I wish her all the good in the world."

He had no idea of the blank amazement in which Hannele listened to these stray remarks.

"But—" she stammered. "But doesn't she expect you to make *love* to her?"

"Oh yes, she expects that. You bet she does: woman-like."

"And you—?"—the question had a dangerous ring.

"Why I don't mind, really, you know, if it's only for a short time. I'm used to her. I've always been fond of her, you know—and so if it gives her any pleasure—why I like her to get what pleasure out of life she can."

"But *you*—you *yourself*!—Don't *you* feel anything?" Hannele's amazement was reaching the point of incredulity. She began to feel that he was making it up. It was all so different from her own point of view.—To sit there so quiet and to make such statements in all good faith: no, it was impossible.

"I don't consider I count," he said, naïvely.

Hannele looked aside. If that wasn't lying, it was imbecility, or worse. She had for the moment nothing to say. She felt he was a sort of psychic phenomenon like a grasshopper or a tadpole or an ammonite. Not to be regarded from a human point of view.—No, he just wasn't normal.—And she had been fascinated by him!—It was only sheer, amazed curiosity that carried her on to her next question.

"But do you *never* count, then?" she asked, and there was a touch of derision, of laughter in her tone. He took no offence.

"Well—very rarely," he said. "I count very rarely. That's how life appears to me. One matters so *very* little."

She felt quite dizzy with astonishment.—And he called himself a man!

"But if you matter so very little, what do you do anything at all for?" she asked.

"Oh, one has to. And then, why not? Why not do things, even if oneself hardly matters.—Look at the moon. It doesn't matter in the least to the moon whether I exist or whether I don't. So why should it matter to me?"

After a blank pause of incredulity she said:

"I could die with laughter. It seems to me all so ridiculous—no, I can't believe it."

"Perhaps it is a point of view," he said.

There was a long and pregnant silence: we should not like to say pregnant with what.

"And so I don't mean anything to you at all?" she said.

"I didn't say that," he replied.

"Nothing means anything to you," she challenged.

"I don't say that."

"Whether it's your wife—or me—or the moon—toute la même chose."

"No—no—that's hardly the way to look at it—"

She gazed at him in such utter amazement that she felt something would really explode in her if she heard another word. Was this a man?—or what was it? It was too much for her, that was all.

"Well goodbye," she said. "I hope you will have a nice time at the Vier Jahreszeiten."

So she left him still sitting on the roof.

"I suppose," she said to herself, "that is love à l'anglaise. But it's more than I can swallow."

———

"Won't you come and have tea with me—do! Come right along now. Don't you find it bitterly cold? Yes—well now—come in with me and we'll have a cup of nice hot tea in our little sitting-room. The weather changes so suddenly, and really, one needs a little reinforcement. But perhaps you don't take tea?"

"Oh yes. I got so used to it in England," said Hannele.

"Did you now! Well now, were you long in England?"

"Oh yes— —"

The two women had met in the Domplatz. Mrs Hepburn was looking extraordinarily like one of Hannele's dolls, in a funny little cape of odd striped skins, and a little dark-green skirt, and a rather fuzzy sort of hat. Hannele looked almost huge beside her.

"But now you will come in and have tea, won't you? Oh please do. Never mind whether it's *de rigueur* or not. I *always* please myself *what* I do. I'm afraid my husband gets some shocks sometimes—but that we can't help. I won't have anybody laying the law down to me." She laughed her winsome little laugh. "So now come along in, and we'll see if there aren't hot scones as well. I love a hot scone for tea in cold weather. And I hope you do.—That is, if there are any. We don't know yet." She tinkled her little laugh. "My husband may or may not be in. But that makes no difference to you and me, does it?—There, it's just striking half-past four. In England we always have tea at half past. My husband *adores* his tea. I don't suppose our man is five minutes off the half-past, ringing the gong for tea, not once in twelve months. My husband doesn't mind at all if dinner is a little late. But he gets—quite—well, quite 'ratty' if tea is late." She tinkled a laugh. "Though I shouldn't say that. He is the soul of kindness and patience. I don't think I've ever known him do an unkind thing—or hardly, say an unkind word.—But I doubt if he will be in today."

He *was* in, however, standing with his feet apart and his hands in his trouser pockets in the little sitting-room upstairs in the hotel. He raised his eyebrows the smallest degree, seeing Hannele enter.

"Ah, Countess Hannele—my wife has brought you along! Very nice, very nice! Let me take your wrap.—Oh yes, certainly . . ."

"Have you rung for tea, dear?" asked Mrs Hepburn.

"Er—yes. I said as soon as you came in they were to bring it."

"Yes—well—Won't you ring again dear, and say for *three*—"

"Yes—certainly. Certainly."

He rang, and stood about with his hands in his pockets waiting for tea.

"Well now," said Mrs Hepburn, as she lifted the teapot, and her bangles tinkled, and her huge rings of brilliants twinkled, and her big ear-rings of clustered seed-pearls bobbed against her rather withered cheek, "isn't it charming of Countess zu—Countess zu—"

"Rassentlow," said he. "I believe most people say Countess Hannele. I know we always do among ourselves. We say Countess Hannele's shop—"

"Countess Hannele's shop! Now isn't that perfectly delightful: such a romance in the very sound of it.—You take cream—?"

"Thank you," said Hannele.

The tea passed in a cloud of chatter, while Mrs Hepburn manipulated the tea-pot, and lit the spirit-flame, and blew it out, and peeped into the steam of the teapot, and couldn't see whether there was any more tea or not—and—"At home I *know*—I was going to say to a teaspoonful—how much tea there is in the pot. But this teapot—I don't know what it's made of—it isn't silver, I know that—it is so heavy in itself, that it's deceived me several times already. And my husband is a greedy man, a greedy man—he likes at least three cups—and four if he can get them—or *five*!—Yes dear, I've plenty of tea today. You shall have even five, if you don't mind the last two weak.—Do let me fill your cup, Countess Hannele.—I think it's a *charming* name—"

"There's a play called *Hannele*, isn't there?" said he.

When he had had his five cups, and his wife had got her cigarette perched in the end of a long, long slim white holder, and was puffing like a little China woman from the distance, there was a little lull.

"Alec dear," said Mrs Hepburn. "You won't forget to leave that message for me at Mrs Rackham's. I'm so afraid it will be forgotten."

"No dear, I won't forget.—Er—would you like me to go round now?"

Hannele noticed how often he said "er", when he was beginning to speak to his wife. But they *were* such good friends, the two of them.

"Why if you *would*, dear, I should feel perfectly comfortable.—But I don't want you to hurry one bit."

"Oh, I may as well go now."

And he went. Mrs Hepburn detained her guest.

"He *is* so charming to me," said the little woman. "He's really wonderful. And he always has been the same—invariably. So that if he *did* make a little slip—well, you know, I don't have to take it too seriously."

"No," said Hannele, feeling as if her ears were stretching with astonishment.

"It's the war. It's just the war. It's had a terribly deteriorating effect on the men."

"In what way?" said Hannele.

"Why, morally. Really, there's hardly one man left the same as he was before the war. Terribly degenerated."

"Is that so?" said Hannele.

"It is indeed. Why, isn't it the same with the German men and officers?"

"Yes, I think so," said Hannele.

"And I'm sure so, from what I hear.—But of course it is the women who are to blame in the first place. We poor women! We are a guilty race, I am afraid. But I never throw stones. I know what it is myself to have temptations. I'm afraid I should never be able to keep *quite* clear of the men. Just my nature. I have to flirt a little—and when I was younger—well, the men didn't escape me, I assure you. And I was *so* often scorched. But never *quite* singed. My husband never minded. He knew I was *really* safe. Oh yes, I have always been faithful to him. But still—I have been *very* near the flame—" And she laughed her winsome little laugh.

Hannele put her fingers to her ears, to make sure they were not falling off.

"Of course during the war it was terrible. I know that in a certain hospital it was quite impossible for a girl to stay on if she kept straight. The matrons and sisters just turned her out. They wouldn't have her unless she was one of themselves. And you know what that means.—Quite like the convent in Balzac's story—you know which I mean, I'm sure—" And the laugh tinkled gaily.

"But then, what can you expect, when there aren't enough men to go round!—Why I had a friend in Ireland. She and her husband had been an ideal couple, an *ideal* couple. Real playmates. And you can't say more than that, can you.—Well then, he became a major during the war. And she was so looking forward, poor thing, to the perfectly lovely times they would have together when he came home. She is like me, and is lucky enough to have a little income of her own—not a great fortune—but—well—Well now, what was I going to say. Oh yes, she was looking forward to the perfectly lovely times they would have when he came home: building on her dreams, poor thing, as we unfortunate women always do. I suppose we shall never be cured of it—" A little tinkling laugh.—"Well now, not a bit of it. Not a bit of it." Mrs Hepburn lifted her heavily-jewelled little hand in a motion of protest. It was curious, her hands were pretty and white, and her neck and breast, now she wore a little tea-gown, were also smooth and white and pretty, under the medley of twinkling little chains and coloured jewels. Why should her face have played her this nasty trick of going all crumpled? However, it was so.—

"Not one bit of it," reiterated the little lady. "He came home quite changed. She said she could hardly recognise him for the same man. Let me tell you one little incident. Just a trifle, but significant.—He was coming home—this was some time after he was free from the army—he was coming home from London, and he told her to meet him at the boat: gave her the time and everything. Well, she went to the boat, poor thing, and he didn't come. She waited, and no word of explanation or anything. So she couldn't make up her mind whether to go next day and meet the boat again.—However, she decided she wouldn't. So of course, on that boat he arrived. When he got home, he said to her 'Why didn't you meet the boat?'—'Well,' she said, 'I went yesterday, and you didn't come—'—'Then why didn't you meet it again today?'—Imagine it, the sauce! And they had been real playmates. Heartbreaking, isn't it!—'Well,' she said in self-defence, 'why didn't you come yesterday?'—'Oh,' he said, 'I met a woman in town whom I liked, and she asked me to spend the night with her, so I did.'—Now what do you think of that?—Can you conceive of such a thing?"

"Oh no," said Hannele. "I call that unnecessary brutality."

"Exactly! So terrible to *say* such a thing to her! The brutality of it!—Well, that's how the world is today.—I'm thankful my husband isn't that sort. I don't say he's perfect. But whatever else he did, he'd never be unkind, and he *couldn't* be brutal. He just couldn't. He'd never tell me a lie—I know *that*. But callous brutality, no, thank goodness, he hasn't a spark of it in him.—I'm the wicked one, if either of us is wicked.—" The little laugh tinkled. "Oh but he's been perfect to me, perfect. Hardly a cross word. Why, on our wedding night, he kneeled down in front of me and promised, with God's help, to make my life happy. And I must say, as far as possible he's kept his word. It has been his one aim in life, to make my life happy."

The little lady looked away with a bright, musing look, towards the window. She was being a heroine in a romance. Hannele could see her being a heroine, playing the chief part in her own life-romance. It is such a feminine occupation, that no woman takes offence when she is made audience.

"I'm afraid I've more of the woman than the mother in my composition," resumed the little heroine. "I adore my two children. The boy is at Winchester, and my little girl is in a convent in Brittany. Oh they are perfect darlings, both of them. But the man is first in my mind, I'm afraid. I fear I'm rather old-fashioned. But never mind. I can see the attractions in other men—can't I indeed! There was a perfectly exquisite creature—he was a very clever engineer—but much, much more than *that*—But never mind." The little heroine sniffed as if there were perfume in the air, folded her jewelled hands, and resumed: "However—I know what it is myself to flutter round the flame. You know I'm Irish myself, and we Irish can't help it. Oh, I wouldn't be English for anything. Just that little touch of imagination, you know . . ." The little laugh tinkled. "And that's what makes me able to sympathise with my husband even when, perhaps, I shouldn't. Why, when he was at home with me, he never gave a thought, not a thought to another woman. I must say, he used to make *me* feel a little guilty sometimes—But there!—I don't think he ever thought of another woman as being flesh and blood, after he knew me. I could tell. Pleasant, courteous, charming—but other women were not flesh and blood to him, they were just people, callers—that kind of thing. It used to amaze me, when some perfectly lovely creature came, whom I should have been head over heels in love with in a minute—and he, he was charming, delightful, he could see her points, but she was no more to him than, let me say, a pot of carnations, or a beautiful old piece of punto di Milano. Not flesh and blood. Well, perhaps one can feel too safe. Perhaps one needs a tiny pinch of the salt of jealousy. I believe one does. And I have not had one jealous moment for seventeen years.—So that, *really*, when I heard a whisper of something going on here, I felt almost pleased. I felt exonerated for my own little peccadilloes, for one thing. And I felt he was perhaps a little more human. Because, after all, it is nothing but human to fall in love, if you are alone for a long time and in the company of a beautiful woman—and if you're an attractive man yourself—"

Hannele sat with her eyes propped open and her ears buttoned back with amazement, expecting the next revelations.

"Why of course," she said, knowing she was expected to say something.

"Yes, of course," said Mrs Hepburn, eyeing her sharply. "So I thought I'd better come and see how far things had gone. I had nothing but a hint to go on. I knew no name—nothing. I had just a hint that she was German, and a refugee aristocrat—and that he used to call at the studio—" The little lady eyed Hannele sharply, and gave a breathless little laugh, clasping her hands nervously. Hannele sat absolutely blank: really dazed.

"Of course," resumed Mrs Hepburn, "that was enough. That was quite a sufficient clue. I'm afraid my intentions when I called at the studio were not as pure as they might have been. I'm afraid I wanted to see something more than the dolls.—But when you showed me *his* doll, then I knew. Of course there wasn't a shadow of doubt after that. And I saw at once that she loved him, poor thing. She was *so* agitated. And no idea who I was. And you were so unkind to show me the doll. Of course you had no idea who you were showing it to.—But for her, poor thing, it was such a trial. I could see how she suffered. And I must say she's very lovely—she's very, very lovely, with her golden skin and her reddish amber eyes and her beautiful, beautiful carriage. And such a naïve impulsive nature. Gives everything away in a minute. And then her deep voice—'*Oh yes—Oh please*!'—such a child. And such an aristocrat, that lovely turn of her head, and her simple, elegant dress. Oh, she's very charming. And she's just the type I always knew would attract him, if he hadn't got me. I've thought about it many a time—many a time. When a woman is older than a man, she does think these things—especially if he has his attractive points too. And when I've dreamed of the woman he would love if he hadn't got me, it has always been a Spanish type. And the Baroness is extraordinarily Spanish in her appearance. She must have had some noble Spanish ancestor. Don't you think so?"

"Oh yes," said Hannele. "There were such a lot of Spaniards in Austria, too, with the various emperors."

"With Charles V, exactly. Exactly. That's how it must have been. And so she has all the Spanish beauty, and all the German feeling. Of course, for myself, I miss the *reserve*, the haughtiness. But she's very, very lovely, and I'm sure I could never *hate* her. I couldn't even if I tried. And I'm not going to try.—But I think she's much too dangerous for my husband to see much of her. Don't you agree, now?"

"Oh, but really," stammered Hannele. "There's nothing in it, really."

"Well," said the little lady, cocking her head shrewdly aside, "I shouldn't like there to be any *more* in it."

And there was a moment's dead pause. Each woman was reflecting. Hannele wondered if the little lady was just fooling her.

"Anyhow," continued Mrs Hepburn, "the spark is there, and I don't intend the fire to spread.—I am going to be very, very careful, myself, not to fan the flames. The last thing I should think of would be to make my husband scenes. I believe it would be fatal."

"Yes," said Hannele, during the pause.

"I am going very carefully.—You think there isn't much in it—between him and the Baroness—?"

"No—no—I'm sure there isn't," cried Hannele, with a full voice of conviction. She was almost indignant at being slighted so completely herself, in the little lady's suspicions.

"Hm!—mmm!" hummed the little woman, sapiently nodding her head slowly up and down. "I'm not so sure! I'm not so sure that it hasn't gone pretty far—"

"Oh no—!" cried Hannele, in real irritation of protest.

"Well," said the other. "—In any case, I don't intend it to go any further."

There was dead silence for some time.

"There's more in it than you say. There's more in it than you say," ruminated the little woman. "I know *him*, for one thing. I know he's got a cloud on his brow. And I know it hasn't left his brow for a single minute.—And when I told him I had been to the studio, and showed him the cushion-cover, I knew he felt guilty. I am not so easily deceived. We Irish all have a touch of second sight, I believe.—Of course I haven't challenged him. I haven't even mentioned the doll—By the way, *who* ordered the doll? *Do* you mind telling me—?"

"No, it wasn't ordered," confessed Hannele.

"Ah—I thought not—I thought not!" said Mrs Hepburn, lifting

her finger. "At least, I knew no outsider had ordered it. Of course I knew."—And she smiled to herself.

"So," she continued, "I had too much sense to say anything about it. I don't believe in stripping wounds bare. I believe in gently covering them and letting them heal.—But I *did* say I thought her a lovely creature—". The little lady looked brightly at Hannele.

"Yes," said Hannele.

"And he was very vague in his answer. 'Yes, not bad,' he said. I thought to myself Aha, my boy, you don't deceive me with your *not bad*. She's very much more than not bad. I said so, too. I wanted, of course, to let him know I had a suspicion."

"And do you think he knew?"

"Of course he did. Of course he did.—'She's much too dangerous,' I said, 'to be in a town where there are so many strange men: married and unmarried.' And then he turned round to me and gave himself away, oh, so plainly. '*Why*?' he said. But such a haughty, distant tone. I said to myself 'It's time, my dear boy, you were removed out of the danger-area.' But I answered him: Surely somebody is bound to fall in love with her.—Not at all,—he said,—she keeps to her own countrymen.—You don't tell *me*,—I answered him,—with her pretty broken English! It is a wonder the two of them are allowed to stay in the town.—And then again he rounded on me. Good gracious! he said. Would you have them turned out just because they're beautiful to look at, when they have nowhere else to go, and they make their bit of a livelihood here?—I assure you, he hasn't rounded on me in that overbearing way, not once before, in all our married life. So I just said quietly: I should like to protect *our own men*.—And he didn't say anything more. But he looked at me under his brows, and went out of the room."

There was a silence. Hannele waited with her hands in her lap, and Mrs Hepburn mused, with her hands in *her* lap. Her face looked yellow, and *very* wrinkled.

"Well now," she said, breaking again suddenly into life. "What are we to do?—I mean what is to be done?—You are the Baroness' nearest friend. And I wish her *no* harm, none whatsoever—"

"What can we do?" said Hannele, in the pause.

"I have been urging my husband for some time to get his discharge from the army," said the little woman. "I know he could have it in three months' time. But like so many more men, he has no income of his own, and he doesn't want to feel dependent. Perfect nonsense!—So he says he wants to stay on in the army.—I have never known him before go against my real wishes—"

"But it *is* better for a man to be independent," said Hannele.

"I know it is. But it is also better for him to be *at home*.—And I could get him a post in one of the observatories. He could do something in meteorological work."

Hannele refused to answer any more.

"Of course," said Mrs Hepburn, "if he *does* stay on here, it would be much better if the Baroness left the town."

"I'm sure she will never leave of her own choice," said Hannele.

"I'm sure she won't either. But she might be made to see that it would be very much *wiser* of her to move of her own free will."

"Why?" said Hannele.

"Why because, she might any time be removed by the British authorities."

"Why should she?" said Hannele.

"I think the women who are a menace to our men should be removed."

"But she is *not* a menace to your men."

"Well, I have my own opinion on that point."

Which was a decided deadlock.

"I'm sure I've kept you an awful long time with my chatter," said Mrs Hepburn. "But I did want to make everything as simple as possible. As I said before, I can't feel any ill-will against her. Yet I can't let things just go on. Heaven alone knows where they may end.—Of course if I can persuade my husband to resign his commission and come back to England—Anyhow, we will see.—I'm sure I am the last person in the world to bear malice."

The tone in which she said it conveyed a dire threat.

Hannele rose from her chair.

"Oh, and one other thing," said her hostess, taking out a tiny lace handkerchief and touching her nose delicately with it. "Do you think—" dab, dab, "that I might have that *doll*—you know—?"

"That—?"

"Yes, of my husband"—the little lady rubbed her nose with her kerchief.

"The price is three guineas—" said Hannele.

"Oh indeed!"—the tone was very cold. "I thought it was not for sale." Hannele put on her wrap.

"You'll send it round—will you?—if you will be so kind."

"I must ask my friend, first."

"Yes of course.—But I'm sure she will be so kind as to send it me. It is a little—er—indelicate, don't you think!"

"No," said Hannele. "No more than a painted portrait."

"Don't you?" said her hostess coldly. "Well even a painted portrait I think I should like in my own possession. This *doll*—"

Hannele waited, but there was no conclusion.

"Anyhow," she said, "the price is three guineas: or the equivalent in Marks."

"Very well," said the little lady, "you shall have your three guineas when I get the doll."

––––––––

Hannele went her way pondering. A man never is quite such an abject specimen as his wife makes him look, talking about "my husband". Therefore, if any woman wishes to rescue her husband from the clutches of another female, let her only invite this female to tea and talk quite sincerely about "my husband, you know." Every man has made a ghastly fool of himself with a woman, at some time or other. No woman ever forgets. And most women will give the show away, with real pathos, to another woman. For instance the picture of Alec at his wife's feet on his wedding night, vowing to devote himself to her lifelong happiness—this picture strayed across Hannele's mind time after time, whenever she thought of her dear captain. With disastrous consequences to the captain.—Of course if he had been at her own feet, then Hannele would have thought it almost natural: almost a necessary part of the show of love. But at the feet of that other little woman!—And what was that other little woman *wearing*?—Her wedding night! Hannele hoped before heaven it wasn't some awful little nighty of frail flowered silk. Imagine it, that little lady! Perhaps in a chic little boudoir cap of "punto di Milano", and this slip of frail flowered silk: and the man, perhaps, in his braces! Oh merciful heaven, save us from other people's indiscretions.—No, let us be sure it was in proper evening dress—twenty years ago—very low cut, with a full skirt gathered behind and trailing a little, and a little feather-erection in her high-dressed hair, and all those jewels: pearls of course: and he in a dinner-jacket and a white waistcoat: probably in an hotel bedroom in Lugano, or Biarritz. And she? Was she standing with one small hand on his shoulder?—or was she seated on the couch in the bedroom?

Oh dreadful thought!—And yet, it was almost inevitable, that scene.—Hannele had never been married, but she had come quite near enough to the realisation of the event, to know that such a scene *was* practically inevitable. An indispensable part of any honeymoon. Him on his knees, with his heels up!

And how black and tidy his hair must have been then!—and no grey at the temples at all. Such a good-looking bridegroom. Perhaps with a white rose in his button-hole still.—And she could see him kneeling there, in his new black trousers, and a wing collar. And she could see his head bowed. And she could hear his plangent, musical voice saying: "With God's help, I will make your life happy. I will live for that and for nothing else." And then the little lady must have had tears in her eyes, and she must have said, rather superbly: "Thank you dear. I'm perfectly sure of it."

Ach! Ach!! Husbands should be left to their own wives: and wives should be left to their own husbands. And *no* stranger should ever be made a party to these terrible bits of connubial staging. Nay, thought Hannele, that scene was really true. It actually took place. And with the man of that scene I have been in love! With the devoted husband of that little lady. Oh God, oh God, how was it possible! Him on his knees, on his knees, with his heels up!

Am I a perfect fool? she thought to herself. Am I really just an idiot, gaping with love for him? How *could* I? How could I? The very way he says "Yes dear!" to her! The way he does what she tells him! The way he fidgets about the room with his hands in his pockets! The way he goes off when she sends him away because she wants to talk to me. And he knows she wants to talk to me. And he knows what she *might* have to say to me. Yet he goes off on her errand without a question, like a servant. "I will do exactly whatever you wish, darling." He must have said those words time after time, to the little lady. And fulfilled them, also. Performed all his pledges and his promises.

Ach! Ach! Hannele wrung her hands to think of *herself* being mixed up with him. And he had seemed to her so manly. He seemed to have so much silent male passion in him. And yet—the little lady! "My husband has *always* been *perfectly sweet* to me." Think of it! On his knees too. And his "Yes dear! Certainly. Certainly." Not that he was afraid of the little lady. He was just committed to her, as he might have been committed to gaol, or committed to paradise.

Had she been dreaming, to be in love with him? Oh, she wished so much she had never been it. She *wished* she had never given herself away. To him!—given herself away to him!—and so abjectly! Hung upon his words and his motions, and looked up to him as if he were Caesar. So he had seemed to her: like a mute Caesar. Like Germanicus. Like—she did not know what—

How had it all happened? What had taken her in? Was it just his good looks?—No, not really. Because they were the kind of staring good looks she didn't really care for.—He must have had charm. He must have charm. Yes, he *had* charm.—When it worked.

His charm had not worked on her now for some time—never since that evening after his wife's arrival. Since then he had seemed to her—rather awful. Rather awful—stupid—an ass—a limited, rather vulgar person. That was what he seemed to her when his charm wouldn't work. A limited, rather inferior person. And in a world of Schiebers and profiteers and vulgar, pretentious persons, this was the worst thing possible. A limited, inferior, slightly pretentious individual! The husband of the little lady!—And oh heaven, she was so deeply implicated with him. He had not, however, spoken with her in private since his wife's arrival. Probably he would never speak with her in private again. She hoped to heaven, never again. The awful thing was the past, that which had been between him and her. She shuddered when she thought of it. The husband of the little lady!

But surely there was something to account for it!—Charm, just charm. He had a charm. And then, oh heaven, when the charm left off working! It had left off so completely at this moment, in Hannele's case, that her very mouth tasted salt. What *did* it all amount to?

What was his charm, after all? How could it have affected her?—She began to think of him again, at his best: his presence, when they were alone high up in that big, lonely attic near the stars. His room!—the big whitewashed walls, the faint scent of tobacco, the silence, the sense of the stars being near, the telescopes, the cactus with fine scarlet flowers: and above all the strange, remote, insidious silence of his presence, that was so congenial to her also. The curious way he had of turning his head to listen—to listen to what?—as if he heard something in the stars. The strange look, like destiny, in his wide-open, almost staring dark eyes. The beautiful line of his brow, that seemed always to have a certain cloud on it. The slow elegance of his straight beautiful legs as he walked, and the exquisiteness of his dark, slender chest! Ah, she could feel the charm mounting over her again. She could feel the snake biting her heart. She could feel the arrows of desire rankling.

But then—and she turned from her thoughts, back to this last little tea-party in the Vier Jahreszeiten. She thought of his voice: "Yes dear. Certainly. Certainly I will."—And she thought of the stupid, inferior look on his face. And the something of a servant-like way in which he went out to do his wife's bidding.

And then the charm was gone again, as the glow of sunset goes off a burning city and leaves it a sordid industrial hole. So much for charm!

So much for charm. She had better have stuck to her own sort of men, Martin, for instance, who was a gentleman and a daring soldier and a queer soul and pleasant to talk to. Only he hadn't any *magic*. Magic? The very word made her writhe. Magic? Swindle. Swindle, that was all it amounted to. Magic!

And yet—let us not be too hasty. If the magic had *really* been there, on those evenings in that great lofty attic—Had it?—Yes. Yes, she was bound to admit it. There had been magic. If there had been magic in his presence and in his contact, the husband of the little lady—But the distaste was in her mouth again.

So she started afresh, trying to keep a tight hold on the tail of that all-too-evanescent magic of his. Dear, it slipped so quickly into disillusion. Nevertheless. If it had existed it did exist. And if it did exist, it was worth having. You could call it an illusion if you liked. But an illusion which is a real experience is worth having. Perhaps this disillusion was a greater illusion than the illusion itself. Perhaps all this disillusion of the little lady and the husband of the little lady was falser than the illusion and magic of those few evenings. Perhaps the long disillusion of life is falser than the brief moments of real illusion. After all—the delicate darkness of his breast, the mystery that seemed to come with him as he trod slowly across the floor of his room, after changing his tunic—Nay, nay, if she could keep the illusion of his charm, she would give all disillusion to the devil. Nay, only let her be under the spell of his charm. Only let the spell be upon her. It was all she yearned for. And the thing she had to fight was the vulgarity of disillusion. The vulgarity of the little lady, the vulgarity of the husband of the little lady, the vulgarity of his insincerity, his "Yes dear. Certainly. Certainly!"—this was what she had to fight. He *was* vulgar and horrible, then.—But also, the queer figure that sat alone on the roof watching the stars! The wonderful red flower of the cactus. The mystery that advanced with him as he came across the room after changing his tunic. The glamour and sadness of him, his silence, as he stooped unfastening his boots. And the strange gargoyle smile, fixed, when he caressed her with his hand under the chin!—Life is all a choice. And if she chose the glamour, the magic, the charm, the illusion, the spell?—Better death than that other, the husband of the little lady. When all was said and done, was he as much the husband of the little lady as he was that other, queer, delicate-breasted Caesar of her own knowledge? Which was he?

No, she was *not* going to send her the doll. The little lady should never have the doll.

What a doll she would make herself! Heavens, what a wizened jewel!

———

Captain Hepburn still called occasionally at the house for his post. The maid always put his letters in a certain place in the hall, so that he should not have to climb the stairs.

Among his letters—that is to say, along with another letter, for his correspondence was very meagre—he one day found an envelope with a crest. Inside this envelope two letters.

"Dear Captain Hepburn,

I had the enclosed letter from Mrs Hepburn. I don't intend her to have the doll which is your portrait, so I shall not answer this note. Also I don't see why she should try to turn us out of the town. She talked to me after tea that day, and it seems she believes that Mitchka is your lover. I didn't say anything at all—except that it wasn't true. But she needn't be afraid of *me*. I don't want you to trouble yourself. But you may as well *know* how things are.

Johanna z. R."

The other letter was on his wife's well-known heavy paper, and in her well-known, large, "aristocratic" hand.

"My dear Countess

I wonder if there has been some mistake, or some misunderstanding. Four days ago you said you would send round that *doll* we spoke of, but I have seen no sign of it yet. I thought of calling at the studio, but did not wish to disturb the Baroness. I should be very much obliged if you could send the doll at once, as I do not feel easy while it is out of my possession. You may rely on having a cheque by return.

108

Our old family friend, Major General Barlow, called on me yesterday, and we had a most interesting conversation on our *Tommies*, and the protection of their morals here. It seems we have full power to send away any person or persons deemed undesirable, with twenty-four hours' notice to leave. But of course all this is done as quietly and with the intention of causing as little scandal as possible.

Please let me have the doll by tomorrow, and perhaps some hint as to your future intentions.

With very best wishes from one who only seeks to be your friend.

Yours very sincerely

Evangeline Hepburn."

And then a dreadful thing happened: really a very dreadful thing. Hannele read of it in the evening newspaper of the town—the *Abendblatt*. Mitchka came rushing up with the paper at ten o'clock at night, just when Hannele was going to bed.

Mrs Hepburn had fallen out of her bedroom window, from the third floor of the hotel, down on to the pavement below, and was killed. She was dressing for dinner. And apparently she had in the morning washed a certain little camisole, and put it on the window-sill to dry. She must have stood on a chair reaching for it, when she fell out of the window. Her husband, who was in the dressing-room, heard a queer little noise, a sort of choking cry, and came into her room to see what it was. And she wasn't there. The window was open and the chair by the window. He looked round, and thought she had left the room for a moment, so returned to his shaving. He was half shaved when one of the maids rushed in.—When he looked out of the window down into the street he fainted, and would have fallen too if the maid had not pulled him in in time.

The very next day the captain came back to his attic. Hannele did not know, until quite late at night when he tapped on her door. She knew his soft tap immediately.

"Won't you come over for a chat?" he said.

She paused for some moments before she answered. And then perhaps surprise made her agree: surprise and curiosity.

"Yes, in a minute," she said, closing her door in his face.

She found him sitting quite still, not even smoking, in his quiet attic. He did not rise, but just glanced round with a faint smile. And she thought his face seemed different, more flexible. But in the half-light she could not tell. She sat at some little distance from him.

"I suppose you've heard," he said.

"Yes."

After a long pause, he resumed:

"Yes. It seems an impossible thing to have happened. Yet it *has* happened."

Hannele's ears were sharp. But strain them as she might she could not catch the meaning of his voice.

"A terrible thing. A *very* terrible thing," she said.

"Yes."

"Do you think she fell quite accidentally?" she said.

"Must have done. The maid was in just a minute before, and she seemed as happy as possible.—I suppose reaching over that broad window-ledge, her brain must suddenly have turned. I can't imagine why she didn't call me. She could never bear even to look out of a high window. Turned her ill instantly if she saw a space below her. She used to say she couldn't really look at the moon, it made her feel as if she would fall down a dreadful height. She never dared do more than glance at it. She always had the feeling, I suppose, of the awful space beneath her, if she were on the moon."

Hannele was not listening to his words, but to his voice. There was something a little automatic in what he said. But then that is always so when people have had a shock.

"It must have been terrible for you too," she said.

"Oh yes. At the time it was awful. Awful. I felt the smash right inside me, you know."

"Awful!" she repeated.

"But now," he said, "I feel very strangely about it. I feel happy about it. I feel happy for her sake, if you can understand that. I feel she has got out of some great tension. I feel she's free now for the first time in her life. She was a gentle soul, and an original soul, but she was like a fairy who is condemned to live in houses and sit on furniture and all that, don't you know. It was never her nature."

"No?" said Hannele, herself sitting in blank amazement.

"I always felt she was born in the wrong period—or on the wrong planet. Like some sort of delicate creature you take out of a tropical forest the moment it is born, and from the first moment teach it to perform tricks. You know what I mean. All her life she performed the tricks of life, clever little monkey she was at it too. Beat me into fits. But her own poor little soul, a sort of fairy soul, those queer Irish creatures, was cooped up inside her all her life, tombed in. There it was, tombed in, while she went through all the tricks of life, that you have to go through if you are born today."

"But—" stammered Hannele—"what would she have done if she *had* been free?"

"Why, don't you see, there *is* nothing for her to do in the world today. Take her language, for instance. She never ought to have been speaking English. I don't know what language she ought to have spoken. Because if you take the Irish language, they only learn it back from English. They think in English, and just put Irish words on top.—But English was never her language. It bubbled off her lips, so to speak. And she had no other language. Like a starling that you've made talk from the very beginning, and so it can only shout these talking noises, don't you know. It can't whistle its own whistling to save its life. Couldn't do it. It's lost it. All its own natural mode of expressing itself has collapsed, and it can only be artificial."

There was a long pause.

"Would she have been wonderful, then, if she had been able to talk in some unknown language?" said Hannele jealously.

"I don't say she would have been wonderful. As a matter of fact we think a talking starling is much more wonderful than an ordinary starling. I don't myself, but most people do. And she would have been a sort of starling. And she would have had her own language and her own ways. As it was, poor thing, she was always arranging herself and fluttering and chattering inside a cage. And she never knew she was in the cage, any more than we know we are inside our own skins."

"But," said Hannele, with a touch of mockery. "How do you know you haven't made it all up—just to console yourself?"

"Oh, I've thought it long ago," he said.

"Still," she blurted, "you may have invented it all—as a sort of consolation for—for—for your life."

"Yes, I may," he said. "But I don't think so. It was her eyes. Did you ever notice her eyes? I often used to catch her eyes. And she'd be talking away, all the language bubbling off her lips. And her eyes were so clear and bright and different. Like a child's, that is listening to something, and is going to be frightened. She was always listening—and waiting—for something else. I tell you what, she was exactly like that fairy in the Scotch song, who is in love with a mortal, and sits by the high road in terror waiting for him to come, and hearing the plovers and the curlews.—Only nowadays motor-lorries go along the moor roads, and the poor thing is struck unconscious, and carried into our world in a state of unconsciousness, and when she comes round, she has to talk our language and behave as we behave and she can't remember anything else, so she goes on and on, till she falls with a crash, back to her own world."

Hannele was silent, and so was he.

"You loved her then?" she said at length.

"Yes. But in this way. When I was a boy I caught a bird, a black-cap, and I put it in a cage. And I loved that bird. I don't know why, but I loved it. I simply loved that bird. All the gorse, and the heather, and the rock, and the hot smell of yellow gorse-blossom, and the sky that seemed to have no end to it, when I was a boy, everything that I almost was *mad* with, as boys are, seemed to me to be in that little, fluttering black-cap. And it would peck its seed as if it didn't quite know what else to do; and look round about, and begin to sing. But in quite a few days it turned its head aside and died. Yes, it died.—I never had the feeling again, that I got from that black-cap when I was a boy—not until I saw her. And then I felt it all again. I felt it all again. And it was the same feeling. I knew, quite soon I knew, that she would die. She would pick her seed and look round in the cage just the same. But she would die in the end.—Only it would last much longer.—But she would die in the cage, like the black-cap."

"But she loved the cage. She loved her clothes and her jewels. She must have loved her house and her furniture and all that with a perfect frenzy."

"She did. She did. But like a child with playthings. Only they were big, marvellous playthings to her. Oh yes, she was never away from them. She never forgot her things—her trinkets and her furs and her furniture. She never got away from them for a minute. And everything in her mind was mixed up with them."

"Dreadful!" said Hannele.

"Yes, it was dreadful," he answered.

"Dreadful," repeated Hannele.

"Yes quite. Quite! And it got worse. And her way of talking got worse. As if it bubbled off her lips.—But her eyes never lost their brightness, they never lost that fairy look. Only I used to see fear in them. Fear of everything—even all the things she surrounded herself with. Just like my black-cap used to look out of his cage—so bright and sharp, and yet as if he didn't know that it was just the cage that was between him and the outside. He thought it was inside himself, the barrier. He thought it was part of his own nature, to be shut in. And she thought it was part of her own nature.—And so they both died."

"What I can't see," said Hannele, "is what she would have done outside her cage. What other life could she have, except her *bibelots* and her furniture and her talk—?"

"Why none. There *is* no life outside, for human beings."

"Then there's nothing," said Hannele.

"That's true. In a great measure, there's nothing."

"Thank you," said Hannele.

There was a long pause.

"And perhaps I was to blame. Perhaps I ought to have made some sort of a move. But I didn't know what to do. For my life, I didn't know what to do, except try to make her happy. She had enough money—and I didn't think it mattered if she shared it with me. I always had a garden—and the astronomy. It's been an immense relief to me, watching the moon. It's been wonderful. Instead of looking inside the cage, as I did at my bird, or at her—I look right out—into freedom—into freedom—"

"The moon, you mean?" said Hannele.

"Yes, the moon."

"And that's your freedom?"

"That's where I've found the greatest sense of freedom," he said.

"Well, I'm not going to be jealous of the moon," said Hannele at length.

"Why should you. It's not a thing to be jealous of."

In a little while, she bade him good-night, and left him.

The chief thing that the captain knew, at this juncture, was that a hatchet had gone through the ligatures and veins that connected him with the people of his affection, and that he was left with the bleeding ends of all his vital human relationships. Why it should be so, he did not know. But then one never can know the whys and the wherefores of one's passional changes.

He only knew that it was so. The emotional flow between him and all the people he knew and cared for was broken, and for the time being he was conscious only of the cleavage. The cleavage that had occurred between him and his fellow men, the cleft that was now between him and them. It was not the fault of anybody or anything. He could neither reproach himself nor them. What had happened had been preparing for a long time. Now suddenly the cleavage. There had been a long slow weaning away: and now this sudden silent rupture.

What it amounted to principally was that he did not want even to see Hannele. He did not want to think of her even. But neither did he want to see anybody else, or to think of anybody else. He shrank with a feeling almost of disgust from his friends and acquaintances, and their expressions of sympathy. It affected him with instantaneous disgust, when anybody wanted to share emotions with him. He did not want to share emotions or feelings of any sort. He wanted to be by himself, essentially, even if he was moving about among other people.

So he went to England, to settle his own affairs, and out of duty to see his children. He wished his children all the well in the world—everything except any emotional connection with himself. He decided to take his girl away from the convent at once, and to put her into a jolly English school. His boy was all right where he was.

The captain had now an income sufficient to give him his independence, but not sufficient to keep up his wife's house. So he prepared to sell the house and most of the things in it. He decided also to leave the army as soon as he could be free. And he thought he would wander about for a time, till he came upon something he wanted.

So the winter passed, without his going back to Germany. He was free of the army. He drifted along, settling his affairs. They were of no very great importance. And all the time he never wrote once to Hannele. He could not get over his disgust that people insisted on his sharing their emotions. He could not bear their emotions, neither their activities. Other people might have all the emotions and feelings and earnestnesses and busy activities they liked. Quite nice even that they had such a multifarious commotion for themselves. But the moment they approached him to spread their feelings over him or to entangle him in their activities a helpless disgust came up in him, and until he could get away, he felt sick, even physically.

This was no state of mind for a lover. He could not even think of

Hannele. Anybody else he felt he need not think about. He was deeply, profoundly thankful that his wife was dead. It was an end of pity now; because, poor thing, she had escaped and gone her own way into the void, like a flown bird.

———

Nevertheless, a man hasn't finished his life at forty. He may, however, have finished one great phase of his life.

And Alexander Hepburn was not the man to live alone. All our troubles, says somebody wise, come upon us because we cannot be alone. And that is all very well. We must all be *able* to be alone, otherwise we are just victims. But when we *are* able to be alone, then we realise that the only thing to do is to start a new relationship with another—or even the same—human being. That people should all be stuck up apart, like so many telegraph poles, is nonsense.

So with our dear Captain. He had his convulsion into a sort of telegraph-pole isolation: which was absolutely necessary for him. But then he began to bud with a new yearning for—for what? For love?

It was a question he kept nicely putting to himself. And really, the nice young girls of eighteen or twenty attracted him very much: so fresh, so impulsive, and looking up to him as if he were something wonderful. If only he could have married two or three of them, instead of just one!

Love!—When a man has no particular ambition, his mind turns back perpetually, as a needle towards the pole. That tiresome word Love. It means so many things. It meant the feeling he had had for his wife. He had loved her. But he shuddered at the thought of having to go through such love again.—It meant also the feeling he had for the awfully nice young things he met here and there: fresh, impulsive girls ready to give all their hearts away. Oh yes, he could fall in love with half a dozen of them. But he knew he'd better not.

At last he wrote to Hannele: and got no answer. So he wrote to Mitchka and still got no answer. So he wrote for information—and there was none forthcoming, except that the two women had gone to Munich.

For the time being, he left it at that. To him, Hannele did not exactly represent rosy love. Rather a hard destiny. He didn't adore her. He did not feel one bit of adoration for her. As a matter of fact, not all the beauties and virtues of woman put together with all the gold in the Indies would have tempted him into the business of adoration any more. He had gone on his knees once, vowing with faltering tones to try and make the adored one happy. And now—never again. Never.

The temptation this time was, to be adored. One of those fresh young things would have adored him as if he were a god. And there was something *very* alluring about the thought. Very. Very alluring. To be god-almighty in your own house, with a lovely young thing adoring you, and you giving off beams of bright effulgence like a Gloria! Who wouldn't be tempted: at the age of forty? And this was why he dallied.

But in the end, he suddenly took the train to Munich. And when he got there he found the town beastly uncomfortable, the Bavarians rude and disagreeable, and no sign of the missing females, not even in the Café Stephanie. He wandered round and round.

And then one day, oh heaven, he saw his doll in a shop window: a little art shop. He stood and stared quite spell-bound.

"Well if that isn't the devil," he said. "Seeing yourself in a shop-window!"

He was so disgusted that he would not even go into the shop.

Then, every day for a week did he walk down that little street and look at himself in the shop window. Yes, there he stood, with one hand in his pocket. And the figure had one hand in its pocket. There he stood, with his cap pulled rather low over his brow. And the figure had its cap pulled low over its brow. But thank goodness his own cap now was a civilian tweed. But there he stood, his head rather forward, gazing with fixed dark eyes. And himself in little, that wretched figure, stood there with its head rather forward, staring with fixed dark eyes. It was such a real little *man*, that it fairly staggered him. The oftener he saw it, the more it staggered him. And the more he hated it. Yet it fascinated him, and he came again to look.

And it was always there. A lonely little individual lounging there with one hand in its pocket, and nothing to do, among the bric-à-brac and the bibelôts. Poor devil, stuck so incongruously in the world. And yet losing none of his masculinity. A male little devil, for all his forlornness. But such an air of isolation, of not-belonging. Yet taut and male, in his tartan trews. And what a situation to be in! —lounging with his back against a little Japanese lacquer cabinet, with a few old pots on his right hand and a tiresome brass ink-tray on his left, while pieces of not-very-nice filet lace hung their length up and down the background. Poor little devil: it was like a deliberate satire.

And then one day it was gone. There was the cabinet and the filet lace and the tiresome ink-stand tray: and the little gentleman wasn't there. The captain at once walked into the shop.

"Have you sold that doll?—that unknown soldier?" he added, without knowing quite what he was saying.

The doll was sold.

"Do you know who bought it?"

The girl looked at him very coldly, and did not know.

"I once knew the lady who made it. In fact the doll was *me*," he said.

The girl now looked at him with sudden interest.

"Don't you think it was like me?" he said.

"Perhaps—" she began to smile.

"It was me. And the lady who made it was a friend of mine. Do you know her name?"

"Yes."

"Gräfin zu Rassentlow," he cried, his eyes shining.

"Oh yes. But her dolls are famous."

"Do you know where she is? Is she in Munich?"

"That I don't know."

"Could you find out?"

"I don't know. I can ask."

"Or the Baroness von Prielau-Carolath."

"The Baroness is dead."

"Dead!"

"She was shot in a riot in Salzburg. They say a lover— —"

"How do you know?"

"From the newspapers."

"Dead! Is it possible. Poor Hannele."

There was a pause.

"Well," he said, "if you would enquire about the address—I'll call again."

Then he turned back from the door.

"By the way, do you mind telling me how much you sold the doll for?"

The girl hesitated. She was by no means anxious to give away any of her trade details. But at length she answered reluctantly:

"Five hundred Marks."

"So cheap," he said. "Good-day. Then I will call again."

———

Then again he got a trace. It was in the Chit-Chat column of the *Muenchener Neue Zeitung*: under Studio-Comments. "Theodor Worpswede's latest picture is a still-life, containing an entertaining group of a doll, two sun-flowers in a glass jar, and a poached egg on toast. The contrast between the three substances is highly diverting and instructive, and this is perhaps one of the most interesting of Worpswede's works. The doll, by the way, is one of the creations of our fertile Countess Hannele. It is the figure of an English, or rather Scottish officer, in the famous tartan trousers which, clinging closely to the legs of the lively Gaul, so shocked the eminent Julius Caesar and his cohorts. We of course are no longer shocked, but full of admiration for the creative genius of our dear Countess. The doll itself is a masterpiece, and has begotten another masterpiece in Theodor Worpswede's Still-life.—We have heard, by the way, a rumour of Countess zu Rassentlow's engagement. Apparently the Herr Regierungsrat von Poldi, of that most beautiful of summer-resorts, Kaprun, in the Tyrol, is the fortunate man—"

———

The captain bought the Still-life. This new version of himself along with the poached egg and the sunflowers was rather frightening. So he packed up for Austria, for Kaprun, with his picture, and had a fight to get the beastly thing out of Germany, and another fight to get it into Austria. Fatigued and furious he arrived in Salzburg, seeing no beauty in anything. Next day he was in Kaprun.

It was an elegant and fashionable watering-place before the war: a lovely little lake in the midst of the Alps, an old Tyrolese town on the water-side, green slopes sheering up opposite, and away beyond, a glacier. It was still crowded and still elegant. But alas, with a broken, bankrupt, desperate elegance and almost empty shops.

The captain felt rather dazed. He found himself in an hotel full of Jews of the wrong rich sort, and wondered what next. The place was beautiful, but the life wasn't.

———

The Herr Regierungsrat was not at first sight prepossessing. He was approaching fifty, and had gone stout and rather loose, as so many men of his class and race do. Then he wore one of those dreadful full-bottom coats, a kind of poor relation to our full-skirted frock coat: it would best be described as a family coat. It flapped about him as he walked, and he looked at first glance lower middle-class.

But he wasn't. Of course, being in office in the collapsed Austria, he was a republican. But by nature he was a monarchist, nay, an imperialist, as every true Austrian is. And he was a true Austrian. And as such, he was much finer and subtler than he looked. As one got used to him, his rather fat face with its fine nose and slightly bitter, pursed mouth came to have a resemblance to the busts of some of the later Roman emperors. And as one was with him, one came gradually to realise that out of all his baggy bourgeois appearance came something of a *grande geste*. He could not help it. There was something sweeping and careless about his soul: big, rather assertive, and ill-bred-seeming; but in fact, not ill-bred at all, only a little bitter and a good deal indifferent to his surroundings. He looked at first sight so common and *parvenu*. And then one had to realise that he was a member of a big old empire, fallen into a sort of epicureanism, and a little bitter.—There was no littleness, no meanness, and no real coarseness. But he was a great talker, and relentless towards his audience.

Hannele was attracted to him by his talk. He began as soon as dinner appeared: and he went on, carrying the decanter and the wine-glass with him out on to the balcony of the villa, over the lake, on and on until midnight. The summer night was still and warm: the lake lay deep and full, and the old town twinkled away across. There was the faintest tang of snow in the air, from the great glacier-peaks that were hidden in the night opposite. Sometimes a boat with a lantern twanged a guitar. The clematis flowers were quite black, like leaves, dangling from the terrace.

It was so beautiful, there in the very heart of the Tyrol. The hotels glittered with lights: electric light was still cheap. There seemed a fulness and a loveliness in the night. And yet for some reason it was all terrible and devastating: the life-spirit seemed to be squirming bleeding all the time.

And on and on talked the Herr Regierungsrat, with all the witty volubility of the more versatile Austrian. He was really very witty, very human, and with a touch of salty cynicism that reminded one of a real old Roman of the Empire. That subtle stoicism, that unsentimental epicureanism, that kind of reckless hopelessness of course fascinated the women. And particularly Hannele. He talked on and on—about his work before the war, when he held an important post and was one of the governing class—then about the war—then about the hopelessness of the present: and in it all there seemed a bigness, a carelessness based on indifference, and a hopelessness that laughed at its very self. The real old Austria had always fascinated Hannele. As represented in the witty, bitter-indifferent Herr Regierungsrat it carried her away.

And he, of course, turned instinctively to her, talking in his rapid, ceaseless fashion, with a laugh and a pause to drink and a new start taken. She liked the sound of his Austrian speech: its racy careless-ness, its salty indifference to standards of correctness. Oh yes, here was the *grande geste* still lingering.

He turned his large breast towards her, and made a quick gesture with his fat, well-shapen hand, blurted out another subtle, rough-seeming romance, pursed his mouth, and emptied his glass once more. Then he looked at his half-forgotten cigar and started again.

There was something almost boyish and impulsive about him: the way he turned to her, and the odd way he seemed to open his big breast to her. And again, he seemed almost eternal, sitting there in his chair with knees planted far apart. It was as if he would never rise again, but would remain sitting for ever, and talking. He seemed as if he had no legs, save to sit with. As if to stand on his feet and walk would not be natural to him.

Yet he rose at last, and kissed her hand with the grand gesture that France or Germany have never acquired: carelessness, profound indifference to other people's standards, and then such a sudden stillness, as he bent and kissed her hand. Of course she felt a queen in exile.

And perhaps it is more dangerous to feel yourself a queen in exile than a queen *in situ*. She fell in love with him, with this large, stout, loose widower of fifty, with two children. He had no money except some Austrian money that was worth nothing outside Austria. He could not even go to Germany. There he was, fixed in this hollow in the middle of the Tyrol.

But he had an ambition still, old Roman of the decadence that he was. He had year by year and without making any fuss collected the material for a very minute and thorough history of his own district: the Chiemgau and the Pinzgau. Hannele found that his fund of information on this subject was inexhaustible, and his intelligence was so delicate, so human, and his scope seemed so wide, that she felt a touch of reverence for him. He wanted to write this history. And she wanted to help him.

For of course, as things were he would never write it. He was Regierungsrat: that is, he was the petty local governor of his town and immediate district. The Amthaus was a great old building, and there young ladies in high heels flirted among masses of papers with bare-kneed young gentlemen in Tyrolese costume, and occasionally they parted, to take a pleasant, interesting attitude and write a word or two, after which they fluttered together for a little more interesting diversion. It was extraordinary how many finely built, handsome young people of an age fitted for nothing but love-affairs, ran the governmental business of this department. And the Herr Regierungsrat sailed in and out of the big old rooms, his wide coat flying like wings and making the papers flutter, his rather wine-reddened, old-Roman face smiling with its bitter look. And of course it was a witticism he uttered first, even if Hungary was invading the frontier, or cholera was in Vienna.

When he was on his legs he walked nimbly, briskly, and his coat-bottoms always flew. So he waved through the town, greeting somebody at every few strides, grinning, and yet with a certain haughty reserve. Oh yes, there was a certain salty *hauteur* about him, which made the people trust him. And he spoke the vernacular so racily.

Hannele felt she would like to marry him. She would like to be near him. She would like him to write his history. She would like him to make her feel a queen in exile. No one had ever *quite* kissed her hand as he kissed it: with that sudden stillness and strange, chivalric abandon of himself. How he would abandon himself to her!— terribly—wonderfully—perhaps a little horribly. His wife, whom he had married late, had died after seven years of marriage. Hannele could understand that too. One or the other must die.

She became engaged. But something made her hesitate before marriage. Being in Austria was like being on a wrecked ship, that *must* sink after a certain short length of time. And marrying the Herr Regierungsrat was like marrying the doomed captain of the doomed ship. The sense of fatality was part of the attraction.

But yet she hesitated. The summer weeks passed. The strangers flooded in and crowded the town, and ate up the food like locusts. People no longer counted the paper money, they weighed it by the kilogram. Peasants stored it in a corner of the meal-bin, and mice came and chewed holes in it. Nobody knew where the next lot of food was going to come from: yet it always came. And the lake teemed with bathers. When the captain arrived he looked with amazement on the crowds of strapping, powerful fellows who bathed all day long, magnificent blond flesh of men and women. No wonder the old Romans stood in astonishment before the huge blond limbs of the savage Germans.

Well, the life was like a madness. The hotels charged fifteen-hundred Kronen a day: the women, old and young, paraded in the peasant-costume, in flowery cotton dresses with gaudy, expensive silk aprons: the men wore the Tyrolese costume, bare knees and little short jackets. And for the men, the correct thing was to have the leathern hose and the blue linen jacket as old as possible. If you had a hole in your leathern seat, so much the better.

Everything so physical. Such magnificent naked limbs and naked bodies, and in the streets, in the hotels, everywhere, bare, white arms of women and bare, brown, powerful knees and thighs of men. The sense of flesh everywhere, and the endless ache of flesh. Even in the peasants who rowed across the lake, standing and rowing with a slow, heavy, gondolier motion at the one curved oar, there was the same endless ache of physical yearning.

———

It was August when Alexander met Hannele. She was walking under a chintz parasol, wearing a dress of blue cotton with little red roses, and a red silk apron. She had no hat, her arms were bare and soft, and she had white stockings under her short dress. The Herr Regierungsrat was at her side, large, nimble, and laughing with a new witticism.

Alexander, in a light summer suit and Panama hat, was just coming out of the bank, shoving twenty thousand Kronen into his pocket. He saw her coming across from the Amtsgericht, with the Herr Regierungsrat at her side, across the space of sunshine. She was laughing, and did not notice him.

She did not notice till he had taken off his hat and was saluting her. Then what she saw was the black, smooth, shining head, and she went pale. His black, smooth, close head—and all the blue Austrian day seemed to shrivel before her eyes.

"How do you do, Countess! I hoped I should meet you."

She heard his slow, sad-clanging, straying voice again, and she pressed her hand with the umbrella stick against her breast. She had forgotten it—forgotten his peculiar slow voice. And now it seemed like a noise that sounds in the silence of night. Ah, how difficult it was, that suddenly the world could split under her eyes and show this darkness inside. She wished he had not come.

She presented him to the Herr Regierungsrat, who was stiff and cold. She asked where the captain was staying. And then, not knowing what else to say, she said:

"Won't you come to tea?"

She was staying in a villa across the lake. Yes, he would come to tea.

He went. He hired a boat and a man to row him across. It was not far. There stood the villa, with its brown balconies one above the other, the bright red geraniums and white geraniums twinkling all round, the tress of purple clematis tumbling at one corner. All the green window-doors were open: but nobody about. In the little garden by the water's edge the rose-trees were tall and lank, drawn up by the dark green trees of the background. A white table with chairs and garden seats stood under the shadow of a big willow tree, and a hammock with cushions swung just behind. But no-one in sight. There was a little landing bridge on to the garden: and a fairly large boat-house at the garden end.

The captain was not sure that the boat-house belonged to the villa. Voices were shouting and laughing from the water's surface, bathers swimming. A tall, naked youth with a little red cap on his head and a tiny red loin-cloth round his slender young hips was standing on the steps of the boat-house calling to the three women who were swimming near. The dark-haired woman with the white cap swam up to the steps and caught the boy by the ankle. He cried and laughed and remonstrated, and poked her in the breast with his foot.

"Nein, nein, Hardu!" she cried as he tickled her with his toe. "Hardu! Hardu! Hör' auf!—Leave off—!"—and she fell with a crash back into the water. The youth laughed a loud, deep laugh of a lad whose voice is newly broken.

"Was macht er dann?" cried a voice from the waters. "What is he doing?" It was a dark-skinned girl swimming swiftly, her big dark eyes watching amused from the water-surface.

"Jetzt Hardu hör' auf. Nein. Jetzt ruhig!—Now leave off! Now be quiet." And the dark-haired woman was climbing out in the sunshine on to the pale, raw-wood steps of the boat-house, the water glistening on her dark-blue, stockinette, soft-moulded back and loins: while the boy, with his foot stretched out, was trying to push her back into the water. She clambered out, however, and sat on the steps in the sun, panting slightly. She was dark and attractive looking, with a mature beautiful figure, and handsome, strong woman's legs.

In the garden appeared a black-and-white maid-servant with a tray.

"Kaffee, gnädige Frau!"

The voice came so distinct over the water.

"Hannele! Hannele! Kaffee!" called the woman on the steps of the bathing house.

"Tante Hannele! Kaffee!" called the dark-eyed girl, turning round in the water, then swimming for home.

"Kaffee! Kaffee!" roared the youth, in anticipation.

"Ja—a! Ich kom—mm," sang Hannele's voice from the water.

The dark-eyed girl, her hair tied up in a silk bandana, had reached the steps and was climbing out, a slim young fish in her close dark suit. The three stood clustered on the steps, the elder woman with one arm over the naked shoulders of the youth, the other arm over the shoulders of the girl. And all in chorus they sang:

"Hannele! Hannele! Hannele!—Wir warten auf dich."

The boat-man had left off rowing, and the boat was drifting slowly in. The family became quiet, because of the intrusion. The attractive-looking woman turned and picked up her blue bath-robe, of a mid-blue colour that became her. She swung it round her as if it were an opera cloak. The youth stared at the boat.

The captain was watching Hannele. With a white kerchief tied round her silky, brownish hair, she was swimming home. He saw her white shoulders, and her white, wavering legs below in the clear water. Round the boat fishes were suddenly jumping.

The three on the steps beyond stood silent, watching the intruding boat with resentment. The boatman twisted his head round and watched them. The captain, who was facing them, watched Hannele. She swam slowly and easily up, caught the rail of the steps, and stooping forward, climbed slowly out of the water. Her legs were large and flashing white and looked rich, the rich white thighs with the blue veins behind, and the full, rich softness of her stooping loins.

"Ach—!—Schön! Schön! 'S war schön! Das Wasser ist gut," her voice was heard, half singing as she took her breath—"It was lovely."

"Heiss," said the woman above. "Zu warm.—Too warm."

The youth made way for Hannele, who drew herself erect at the top of the steps, looking round, panting a little, and putting up her hand to the knot of her kerchief on her head. Her legs were magnificent and white.

"Kuck' die Leut die da bleiben," said the woman in the blue wrap, in a low voice. "Look at the people stopping there."

"Ja!" said Hannele negligently. Then she looked. She started as if in fear, looked round, as if to run away, looked back again, and met the eyes of the captain, who took off his hat.

She cried, in a loud frightened voice:

"Oh but—I thought it was *tomorrow*!"

"No—today," came the quiet voice of the captain over the water.

"*Today*! Are you *sure*—?" she cried, calling to the boat.

"Quite sure. But we'll make it tomorrow if you like," he said.

"Today! Today!" she repeated in bewilderment. "No! Wait a minute." And she ran into the boat-house.

"Was ist es?" asked the dark woman, following her. "What is it?"

"A friend—a visitor—Captain Hepburn," came Hannele's voice.

The boat-man now rowed slowly to the landing stage. The dark woman, huddled in her blue wrap as in an opera-cloak, walked proudly and unconcernedly across the background of the garden, and up the steps to the first balcony. Hannele, her feet slip-slopping in loose slippers, clutching an old yellow wrap round her, came to the landing stage and shook hands.

"I am so sorry. It is so stupid of me. I was sure it was tomorrow," she said.

"No, it was today. But I wish for your sake it had been tomorrow," he replied.

"No. No. It doesn't matter. You won't mind waiting a minute, will you? You mustn't be angry with me for being so stupid."

So she went away, the heel-less slippers flipping up to her naked heels. Then the big-eyed, dusky girl stole into the house: and then the naked youth, who went with sang froid. He would make a fine, handsome man: and he knew it.

————

Hepburn and Hannele were to make a small excursion to the glacier which stood there always in sight, coldly grinning in the sky. The weather had been very hot, but this morning there were loose clouds in the sky. The captain rowed over the lake soon after dawn. Hannele stepped into the little craft, and they pulled back to the town. There was a wind ruffling the water, so that the boat leaped and chuckled. The glacier, in a recess among the folded mountains, looked cold and angry. But morning was very sweet in the sky, and blowing very sweet with a faint scent of the second hay, from the low lands at the head of the lake. Beyond stood naked grey rock like a wall of mountains, pure rock, with faint thin slashes of snow. Yesterday it had rained on the lake. The sun was going to appear from behind the Breitsteinhorn, the sky with its clouds floating in blue light and yellow radiance was lovely and cheering again. But dark clouds seemed to spout up from the Pinzgau valley. And once across the lake, all was shadow, when the water no longer gave back the sky-morning.

The day was a feast day, a holiday. Already so early three young men from the mountains were bathing near the steps of the Badeanstalt. Handsome, physical fellows, with good limbs rolling and swaying in the early morning water. They seemed to enjoy it too. But to Hepburn it was always as if a dark wing were stretched in the sky, over these mountains, like a doom. And these three young, lusty naked men swimming and rolling in the shadow.

Hepburn's was the first boat stirring. He made fast in the hotel boat-house, and he and Hannele went into the little town. It was deep in shadow, though the light of the sky, curdled with cloud, was bright overhead. But dark and chill and heavy lay the shadow in the black-and-white town, like a sediment.

The shops were all shut, but peasants from the hills were already strolling about, in their holiday dress: the men in their short leather trousers, like football drawers, and bare brown knees, and great boots: their little grey jackets faced with green, and their green hats with the proud chamois-brush behind. They seemed to stray about like lost souls, and the proud chamois-brush behind their hats, this proud, cocky, perking-up tail, like a mountain-buck with his tail up, was belied by the lost-soul look of the men, as they loitered about with their hands shoved in the front-pockets of their trousers.— Some women also were creeping about: peasant women, in the funny little black hats that had thick gold under the brim and long black streamers of ribbon, broad, black water-wave ribbon starting from a bow under the brim behind and streaming right to the bottom of the skirt. These women in their thick dark dresses with tight bodices, and massive heavy full skirts, and bright or dark aprons, strode about with the heavy stride of the mountain women, the heavy, quick, forward-leaning motion. They were waiting for the town-day to begin.

Hepburn had a knapsack on his back, with food for the day. But bread was wanting. They found the door of the bakery open, and got a loaf: a long, hot loaf of pure white bread, beautiful sweet bread. It cost seventy Kronen. To Hepburn it was always a mystery where this exquisite bread came from, in a lost land.

In the little square where the clock stood were bunches of people, and a big motor-omnibus, and a motor car that would hold about eight people. Hepburn had paid his seven hundred Kronen for the two tickets. Hannele tied up her head in a thin scarf, and put on her thick coat. She and Hepburn sat in front by the peaked driver. And at seven o'clock away went the car, swooping out of the town, past the handsome old Tyrolese Schloss, or manor, black-and-white, with its little black spires pricking up, past the station, and under the trees by the lake-side. The road was not good, but they ran at a great speed, out past the end of the lake, where the reeds grew, out into the open valley-mouth, where the mountains opened in two clefts. It was cold in the car. Hepburn buttoned himself up to the throat and pulled his hat down on his ears. Hannele's scarf fluttered. She sat without saying anything, erect, her face fine and keen, watching ahead. From the deep Pinzgau valley came the river roaring and raging, a glacier river of pale, seething ice-water. Over went the car, over the log bridge, darting towards the great slopes opposite. And then a sudden immense turn, a swerve under the height of the mountain side, and again a darting lurch forward, under the pear-trees of the highroad, past the big old ruined castle that so magnificently watched the valley mouth and the foaming river, on, rushing under the huge roofs of the balconied peasant houses of a village, then swinging again to take another valley mouth, there where a little village clustered all black and white on a knoll, with a white church that had a black steeple, and a white castle with black spines, and clustering, ample black-and-white houses of the Tyrol. There is a grandeur even in the peasant houses, with their great wide passage halls where the swallows build, and where one could build a whole English cottage.

So the motor-car darted up this new, narrow, wilder, more sinister valley. A herd of almost wild young horses, handsome reddish things, burst around the car, and one great mare with full flanks went crashing up the road ahead, her heels flashing to the car, while her foal whinneyed and screamed from behind. But no, she could not turn from the road. On and on she crashed, forging ahead, the car behind her. And then at last she did swerve aside, among the thin alder trees by the wild river-bed.

"If it isn't a cow, it's a horse," said the driver, who was thin and weaselish and silent, with his ear-flaps over his ears.

But the great mare had shaken herself in a wild swerve, and screaming and whinneying was plunging back to her foal. Hannele had been frightened.

The car rushed on, through water-meadows, along a naked white bit of mountain road. Ahead was a darkness of mountain front and pine trees. To the right was the stony, furious, lion-like river, tawny-coloured here, and the slope up beyond. But the road for the moment was swinging fairly level through the stunned water-meadows of the savage valley. There were gates to open, and Hepburn jumped down to open them, as if he were the foot-boy. The heavy Jews of the wrong sort, seated behind, of course did not stir.

At a house on a knoll the driver sounded his horn, and out rushed children crying Papa! Papa!—then a woman with a basket. A few brief words from the weaselish man, who smiled with warm, manly blue eyes at his children, then the car leaped forward. The whole bearing of the man was so different, when he was looking at his own family. He could not even say thank-you when Hepburn opened the gates. He hated and even despised his human cargo of middle-class people. Deep, deep is class-hatred, and it begins to swallow all human feeling in its abyss. So, stiff, silent, thin, capable, and neuter towards his fares sat the little driver with the flaps over his ears, and his thin nose cold.

The car swept round, suddenly, into the trees: and into the ravine. The river shouted at the bottom of a gulf. Bristling pine-trees stood around. The air was black and cold and forever sunless. The motor-car rushed on, in this blackness, under the rock-walls and the fir-trees.

Then it suddenly stopped. There was a huge motor-omnibus ahead, drab and enormous-looking. Tourists and trippers of last night coming back from the glacier. It stood like a great rock. And the smaller motor-car edged past, tilting into the rock-gutter under the face of stone.

So, after a while of this valley of the shadow of death, lurching in steep loops upwards, the motor-car scrambling wonderfully, struggling past trees and rock upwards, at last they came to the end. It was a huge inn or tourist-hotel of brown wood: and here the road ended in a little wide bay surrounded and overhung by trees. Beyond was a garage and a bridge over a roaring river: and always the overhung darkness of trees and the intolerable steep slopes immediately above.

Hannele left her big coat. The sky looked blue above the gloom. They set out across the hollow-resounding bridge, over the everlasting mad rush of ice-water, to the immediate upslope of the path, under dark trees. But a little old man in a sort of sentry-box wanted fifty or sixty Kronen: apparently for the upkeep of the road, a sort of toll.

The other tourists were coming—some stopping to have a drink first. The second omnibus had not yet arrived. Hannele and Hepburn were the first two, treading slowly up that dark path, under the trees. The grasses hanging on the rock face were still dewy. There were a few wild raspberries, and a tiny tuft of bilberries with black berries here and there, and a few tufts of unripe cranberries. The many hundreds of tourists who passed up and down did not leave much to pick. Some mountain hare-bells, like bells of blue water, hung coldly glistening in their darkness. Sometimes the hairy mountain-bell, pale-blue and bristling, stood alone, curving his head right down, stiff and taut. There was an occasional big, moist, lolling daisy.

So the two climbed slowly up the steep ledge of a road. This valley was just a mountain cleft, cleft sheer in the hard, living rock, with black trees like hair flourishing in this secret, naked place of the earth. At the bottom of the open wedge forever roared the rampant, insatiable water. The sky from above was like a sharp wedge forcing its way into the earth's cleavage, and that eternal ferocious water was like the steel edge of the wedge, the terrible tip biting in into the rocks' intensity. Who would have thought that the soft sky of light, and the soft foam of water could thrust and penetrate into the dark strong earth?—But so it was. Hannele and Hepburn, toiling up the steep little ledge of a road that hung half-way down the gulf, looked back, time after time, back down upon the brown timbers and shingle roofs of the hotel, that now, away below, looked damp and wedged in like boulders. Then back at the next tourists struggling up. Then down at the water, that rushed like a beast of prey. And then, as they rose higher, they looked up also, at the livid great sides of rock, livid bare rock that sloped from the sky-ridge in a hideous sheer swerve downwards.

In his heart of hearts Hepburn hated it. He hated it, he loathed it, it seemed almost obscene, this livid naked slide of rock, unthinkably huge and massive, sliding down to this gulf where bushes grew like hair in the darkness, and water roared. Above, there were thin slashes of snow.

So the two climbed slowly on, up the eternal side of that valley, sweating with the exertion. Sometimes the sun, now risen high, shone full on their side of the gulley. Tourists were trickling down-hill too: two maidens with bare arms and bare heads and huge boots: men tourists with great knapsacks and edelweiss in their hats: giving Bergheil for a greeting. But the captain said Good-day. He refused this Bergheil business. People swarming touristy on these horrible mountains made him feel almost sick.

He and Hannele also were not in good company together. There was a sort of silent hostility between them. She hated the effort of climbing; but the high air, the cold in the air, the savage cat-howling sound of the water, those awful flanks of livid rock, all this thrilled and excited her to another sort of savageness. And he, dark, rather slender and feline, with something of the physical suavity of a delicate-footed race, he hated beating his way up the rock, he hated the sound of the water, it frightened him, and the high air bit him in his chest, like a viper.

"Wonderful! Wonderful!" she cried, taking great breaths in her splendid chest.

"Yes.—And horrible. Detestable," he said, as if lurking among it all and trying to retain a certain invisibility.

She turned with a flash, and the high, strident sound of the mountains in her voice.

"If you don't like it," she said, rather jeering, "why ever did you come?"

"I had to try," he said.

"And if you don't like it," she said, "why should you try to spoil it for me?"

"I hate it," he answered.

They were climbing more into the height, more into the light, into the open, in the full sun. The valley-cleft was sinking below them. Opposite was only the sheer livid slide of the naked rock, tipping from the pure sky. At a certain angle they could see away beyond, the lake lying far off and small, the wall of those other rocks like a curtain of stone, dim and diminished to the horizon. And the sky with curdling clouds and blue sunshine intermittent.

"Wonderful, wonderful, to be high up," she said, breathing great breaths.

"Yes," he said. "It *is* wonderful. But very detestable. I want to live near the sea-level. I am no mountain-topper."

"Evidently not," she said.

"Bergheil!" cried a youth with bare arms and bare chest, bare head, terrific fanged boots, a knapsack and an alpenstock, and all the bronzed wind and sun of the mountain snow in his skin and his faintly-bleached hair. With his great heavy knapsack, his rumpled thick stockings, his ghastly fanged boots, Hepburn found him repulsive.

"Guten Tag," he answered coldly.

"Grüss Gott," said Hannele.

And the young Tannhäuser, the young Siegfried, this young Balder beautiful strode climbing down the rocks, marching and swinging with his alpenstock. And immediately after the youth came a maiden, with hair on the wind and her shirt-breast open, striding in corduroy breeches, rumpled worsted stockings, thick boots, a knapsack and an alpenstock. She passed without greeting. And our pair stopped in angry silence and watched her dropping down the mountain side.

———

Ah well, everything comes to an end, even the longest up-climb. So, after much sweat and effort and crossness, Hepburn and Hannele emerged on to the rounded bluff where the road wound out of that hideous great valley-cleft, into upper regions. So they emerged more on the level, out of the trees as out of something horrible, on to a naked great bank of rock and grass.

"Thank the Lord!" said Hannele.

So they trudged on round the bluff, and then in front of them saw what is always, always wonderful, one of those shallow upper valleys, naked, where the first waters are rocked. A flat, shallow, utterly desolate valley, wide as a wide bowl under the sky, with rock slopes and grey stone slides and precipices all around, and the zig-zag of snow-stripes and ice-roots descending, and then rivers, streams and rivers rushing from many points downwards, down out of the ice roots and the snow-dagger-points, waters rushing in newly-liberated frenzy downwards, down in waterfalls and cascades and threads, down into the wide shallow bed of the valley, strewn with rocks and stones innumerable, and not a tree, not a visible bush.

Only, of course, two hotels or restaurant places. But these no more than low, sprawling, peasant-looking places lost among the stones, with stones on their roofs so that they seemed just a part of the valley bed. There was the valley, dotted with rock and rolled-down stone, and these two house-places, and woven with innumerable new waters, and one hoarse stone-tracked river in the desert, and the thin road-track winding along the desolate flat, past first one house, then the other, over one stream, then another, on to the far rock-face above which the glacier seemed to loll like some awful great tongue put out.

"Ah, it is wonderful!" he said, as if to himself.

And she looked quickly at his face, saw the queer, blank, sphinx-look with which he gazed out beyond himself. His eyes were black and set, and he seemed so motionless, as if he were eternal facing these upper facts.

She thrilled with triumph. She felt he was overcome.

"It *is* wonderful," she said.

"Wonderful. And forever wonderful," he said.

"Ah, in *winter*—" she cried.

His face changed, and he looked at her.

"In winter you couldn't get up here," he said.

They went on. Up the slopes cattle were feeding: came that isolated tong-tong-tong of cowbells, dropping like the slow clink of ice on the arrested air. The sound always woke in him a primeval, almost hopeless melancholy. Always made him feel *navré*. He looked round. There was no tree, no bush, only great grey rocks and pale boulders scattered in place of trees and bushes.—But yes, clinging on one side like a dark close beard were the Alpenrose shrubs.

"In May," he said, "that side there must be all pink with Alpenroses."

"I *must* come. I *must* come!" she cried.

There were tourists dotted along the road: and two tiny low carts drawn by silky, long-eared mules. These carts went right down to meet the motor-cars, and to bring up provisions for the glacier hotel: for there was still another big hotel ahead.

Hepburn was happy in that upper valley, that first rocking cradle of early water. He liked to see the great fangs and slashes of ice and snow thrust down into the rock, as if the ice had bitten into the flesh of the earth. And from the fang-tips the hoarse water crying its birth-cry, rushing down.

By the turfy road and under the rocks were many flowers: wonderful harebells, big and cold and dark, almost black, and seeming like purple-dark ice: then little tufts of tiny pale-blue bells, as if some fairy frog had been blowing spume-bubbles out of the ice: then the bishops-crosier of the stiff, bigger, hairy mountain-bell: then many stars of pale-lavender gentian, touched with earth-colour: and then monkshood, yellow, primrose yellow monkshood and sudden places full of dark monkshood. That dark-blue, black-blue, terrible colour of the strange rich monkshood made Hepburn look and look and look again. How did the ice come by that lustrous blue-purple intense darkness?—and by that royal poison?—that laughing-snake gorgeousness of much monkshood.

By one of the loud streams, under a rock in the sun, with scented minty or thyme flowers near, they sat down to eat some lunch. It was about eleven o'clock. A thin bee went in and out the scented flowers and the eyebright. The water poured with all the lust and speed of unloosed water over the stones. He took a cupful for Hannele, bright and icy, and she mixed it with the red Hungarian wine.

Down the road strayed the tourists like pilgrims, and at the closed end of the valley they could be seen, quite tiny, climbing the cut-out road that went up like a stair-way. Just by their movement you perceived them. But on the valley-bed they went like rolling stones, little as stones. A very elegant mule came stepping by, following a middle aged woman in tweeds and a tall, high-browed man in knickerbockers. The mule was drawing a very amusing little cart, a chair, rather like a round office-chair upholstered in red velvet, and mounted on two wheels. The red velvet had gone gold and orange and like fruit-juice, being old: really a lovely colour. And the muleteer, a little shabby creature, waddled beside excitedly.

"Ach," cried Hannele, "that looks almost like before the war: almost as peaceful."

"Except that the chair is too shabby, and that they all feel exceptional," he remarked.

There in that upper valley, there was no sense of peace. The rush of the waters seemed like weapons, and the tourists all seemed in a sort of frenzy, in a frenzy to be happy, or to be thrilled. It was a feeling that desolated the heart.

The two sat in the changing sunshine under their rock, with the mountain flowers scenting the snow-bitten air, and they ate the eggs and sausage and cheese, and drank the bright-red Hungarian wine. It seemed lovely: almost like before the war. Almost the same feeling of eternal holiday, as if the world was made for man's everlasting holiday. But not quite. Never again quite the same. The world is not made for man's everlasting holiday.

As Alexander was putting the bread back into his shoulder-sack, he exclaimed:

"Oh, look here!"

She looked, and saw him drawing out a flat package wrapped in paper: evidently a picture.

"A picture!" she cried.

He unwrapped the thing, and handed it to her. It was Theodor Worpswede's *Still-leben*: not very large, painted on a board.

Hannele looked at it, and went pale.

"It's *good*," she cried, in an equivocal tone.

"Quite good," he said.

"Especially the poached egg," she said.

"Yes, the poached egg is almost living."

"But where did you find it?"

"Oh, I found it in the artist's studio—" And he told her how he had traced her.

"How extraordinary!" she cried. "But why did you buy it?"

"I don't quite know."

"Did you *like* it?"

"No, not quite that."

"You could *never* hang it up."

"No, never," he said.

"But do you think it is good as a work of art?"

"I think it is quite clever as a painting. I don't like the spirit of it, of course. I'm too Catholic for that."

"No—No—" she faltered. "It's rather horrid really. That's why I wonder why you bought it."

"Perhaps to prevent anyone else's buying it," he said.

"Do you mind very much, then?" she asked.

"No, I don't mind very much.—I didn't quite like it that you sold the doll," he said.

"I needed the money," she said quietly.

"Oh quite."

There was a pause for some moments.

"I felt you'd sold *me*," she said, quiet and savage.

"When?"

"When your wife appeared. And when you *disappeared*."

Again there was a pause: his pause this time.

"I did write to you," he said.

"When?"

"Oh—in March, I believe."

"Oh yes. I had that letter." Her tone was just as quiet, and even savager.

So there was a pause that belonged to both of them. Then she rose.

"I want to be going," she said. "We shall never get to the glacier at this rate."

He packed up the picture, slung on his knapsack, and they set off. She stooped now and then to pick the starry, earth-lavender gentians from the road-side. As they passed the second of the valley hotels, they saw the man and wife sitting at a little table outside eating bread and cheese, while the mule-chair with its red velvet waited aside on the grass. They passed a whole grove of black-purple nightshade— monkshood—on the left, and some long, low cattle-huts which, with the stones on their roofs, looked as if they had grown up as stones grow in such places through the grass. In the wild, desert place some black pigs were snouting.

So they wound into the head of the valley, and saw the steep face ahead, and high up, like vapour or foam dripping from the fangs of a beast, waterfalls vapouring down from the deep fangs of ice. And there was one end of the glacier, like a great bluey-white fur just slipping over the slope of the rock.

As the valley closed in again the flowers were very lovely, especially the big, dark, icy bells, like harebells, that would sway so easily, but which hung dark and with that terrible motionlessness of upper mountain flowers. And the road turned to get on to the long slant in the cliff-face, where it climbed like a stair. Slowly, slowly the two climbed up. Now again they saw the valley below, behind. The mule-chair was coming, hastening, the lady seated tight facing backwards, as the chair faced and wrapped in rugs. The tall, fair, middle-aged husband in knickerbockers strode just behind, bare-headed.

Alexander and Hannele climbed slowly, slowly up the slant, under the dripping rock-face where the white and veined flowers of the Grass of Parnassus still rose straight and chilly in the shadow, like water which had taken on itself white flower-flesh. Above they saw the slipping edge of the glacier, like a terrible great paw, bluey. And from the skyline dark grey clouds were fuming up, fuming up, as if breathed black and icily out from some ice-cauldron.

"It is going to rain," said Alexander.

"Not much," said Hannele shortly.

"I hope not," said he.

And still she would not hurry up that steep slant, but insisted on standing to look. So the dark, ice-black clouds fumed solid, and the rain began to fly on a cold wind. The mule-chair hastened past, the lady sitting comfortably with her back to the mule, a little pheasant-trimming glinting in her tweed hat, while her Tannhäuser husband reached for his dark, cape-frilled mantle.

Alexander had his dust-coat, but Hannele had nothing but a light knitted jersey-coat, such as women wear indoors. Over the hollow crest above came the cold steel rain. They pushed on up the slope. From behind came another mule, and a little old man hurrying, and a little cart like a handbarrow on which were hampers with cabbage and carrots and pears and joints of meat, for the hotel above.

"Wird es viel sein?" asked Alexander of the little gnome. "Will it be much?"

"Was meint der Herr?" replied the other. "What does the gentle-man say?"

"Der Regen, wird er lang dauern?—Will the rain last long?"

"Nein. Nein. Dies ist kein langer Regen."

So, with his mule which had to stand exactly at that spot to make droppings, the little man resumed his way, and Hannele and Alexander were the last on the slope. The air smelt steel-cold of rain, and of hot mule-droppings. Alexander watched the rain beat on the shoulders and on the blue skirt of Hannele.

"It is a pity you left your big coat down below," he said.

"What good is it saying so now!" she replied, pale at the nose with anger.

"Quite," he said, as his eyes glowed and his brow blackened. "What good suggesting anything at any time, apparently!"

She turned round on him in the rain, as they stood perched nearly at the summit of that slanting cliff-climb, with a glacier-paw hung almost invisible above, and waters gloating aloud in the gulf below. She faced him, and he faced her.

"What have you ever suggested to me?" she said, her face naked as the rain itself with an ice-bitter fury. "What have you ever suggested to me?"

"When have you ever been open to suggestion?" he said, his face dark and his eyes curiously glowing.

"I? I? Pah! Haven't I waited for you to suggest something?— And all you can do is to come here with a picture to reproach me for having sold your doll. Ha! I'm glad I sold it. A foolish empty figure it was too, a foolish staring thing. What should I do but sell it? Why should I keep it, do you imagine?"

"Why do you come here with me today, then?"

"Why do I come here with you today?" she replied. "I come to see the mountains, which are wonderful, and give me strength. And I come to see the glacier. Do you think I come here to see *you*? Why should I? You are always in some hotel or other away below."

"You came to see the glacier and the mountains *with* me," he replied.

"Did I? Then I made a mistake. You can do nothing but find fault even with god's mountains."

A dark flame suddenly went over his face.

"Yes," he said, "I hate them, I hate them. I hate their snow and their affectation."

"*Affectation*!" she laughed. "Oh! Even the mountains are affected for you, are they?"

"Yes," he said. "Their loftiness and their uplift. I hate their uplift. I hate people prancing on mountain-tops and feeling exalted. I'd like to make them all stop up there, on their mountain-tops, and chew ice to fill their stomachs. I wouldn't let them down again, I wouldn't. I hate it all, I tell you, I hate it."

She looked in wonder on his dark, glowing, ineffectual face. It seemed to her like a dark flame burning in the daylight and in the ice-rain: very ineffectual and unnecessary.

"You must be a little mad," she said superbly, "to talk like that about the mountains. They are so much bigger than you."

"No," he said. "No! They are not."

"What!" she laughed aloud. "The mountains are not bigger than you? But you are extraordinary."

"They are not bigger than me," he cried. "Any more than you are bigger than me if you stand on a ladder. They are not bigger than me. They are less than me."

"Oh! Oh!" she cried in wonder and ridicule. "The mountains are *less* than you!"

"Yes," he cried, "they are less."

He seemed suddenly to go silent and remote as she watched him. The speech had gone out of his face again, he seemed to be standing a long way off from her, beyond some border-line. And in the midst of her indignant amazement she watched him with wonder and a touch of fascination. To what country did he belong then?—to what dark, different atmosphere.

"You must suffer from megalomania," she said. And she said what she felt.

But he only looked at her out of dark, dangerous, haughty eyes.

They went on their way in the rain in silence. He was filled with a passionate silence and imperiousness, a curious dark, masterful force that supplanted thought in him. And she, who always pondered, went pondering: "Is he mad? What does he mean? Is he a madman?—He wants to bully me. He wants to bully me into something. What does he want to bully me into? Does he want me to love him?"

At this final question she rested. She decided that what he wanted was that she should love him. And this thought flattered her vanity and her pride, and appeased her wrath against him. She felt quite mollified towards him.

But what a way he went about it! He wanted her to love him. Of this she was sure. He had always wanted her to love him, even from the first. Only he had not made up his *mind* about it. He had not made up his mind. After his wife had died he had gone away to make up his mind. Now he had made it up. He wanted her to love him. And he was offended, mortally offended because she had sold his doll.

So, this was the conclusion to which Hannele came. And it pleased her, and it flattered her. And it made her feel quite warm towards him, as they walked in the rain. The rain, by the way, was abating. The spume over the hollow crest to which they were approaching was thinning considerably. They could again see the glacier paw hanging out, a little beyond. The rain was going to pass. And they were not far now from the hotel, and the third level of the Lammerboden.

He wanted her to love him. She felt again quite glowing and triumphant inside herself, and did not care a bit about the rain on her shoulders. He wanted her to love him. Yes, that was how she had to put it. He didn't want to *love* her. No. He wanted *her* to love *him*.

But then, of course, woman-like, she took his love for granted. So many men had been so very ready to love her. And this one—to her amazement, to her indignation, and rather to her secret satisfaction—just blackly insisted that *she* must love *him*. Very well—she would give him a run for his money. That was it: he blackly insisted that *she* must love *him*. What he felt was not to be considered. *She* must love *him*. And be bullied into it. That was what it amounted to. In his silent, black, overbearing soul, he wanted to compel her, he wanted to have power over her. He wanted to make her love him so that he had power over her. He wanted to bully her, physically, sexually, and from the inside.

And she! Well, she was just as confident that she was not going to be bullied. She would love him: probably she would: most probably she did already. But she was not going to be bullied by him in any way whatsoever. No, he must go down on his knees to her if he wanted her love. And then she would love him. Because she *did* love him. But a dark-eyed little master and bully she would never have.

And this was her triumphant conclusion. Meanwhile the rain had almost ceased, they had almost reached the rim of the upper level, towards which they were climbing, and he was walking in that silent diffidence which made her watch him because she was not sure what he was feeling, what he was thinking, or even what he was. He was a puzzle to her: eternally incomprehensible in his feelings and even his sayings. There seemed to her no logic and no reason in what he felt and said. She could never tell what his next mood would come out of. And this made her uneasy, made her watch him. And at the same time it piqued her attention. He had some of the fascination of the incomprehensible. And his curious inscrutable face—it wasn't really only a meaningless mask, because she had seen it half an hour ago melt with a quite incomprehensible and rather, to her mind, foolish passion. Strange, black, inconsequential passion. Asserting with that curious dark ferocity that he was bigger than the mountains. Madness! Madness! Megalomania.

But because he gave himself away, she forgave him and even liked him. And the strange passion of his, that gave out incomprehensible flashes, *was* rather fascinating to her. She felt just a tiny bit sorry for him. But she wasn't going to be bullied by him. She wasn't going to give in to him and his black passion. No, never. It must be love on equal terms, or nothing. For love on equal terms she was quite ready. She only waited for him to offer it.

In the hotel was a buzz of tourists. Alexander and Hannele sat in the restaurant drinking hot coffee and milk, and watching the maidens in cotton frocks and aprons and bare arms, and the fair youths with maidenly necks and huge voracious boots, and the many Jews of the wrong sort and the wrong shape. These Jews were all being very Austrian, in Tyrol costume that didn't sit on them, assuming the whole gesture and intonation of aristocratic Austria, so that you might think they *were* Austrian aristocrats, if you weren't properly listening, or if you didn't look twice. Certainly they were lords of the Alps, or at least lords of the Alpine hotels this summer, let prejudice be what it might. Jews of the wrong sort. And yet even they imparted a wholesome breath of sanity, disillusion, unsentimentality to the excited "Bergheil" atmosphere. Their dark-eyed, sardonic presence seemed to say to the maidenly-necked mountain youths: "Don't sprout wings of the spirit too much, my dears."

The rain had ceased. There was a wisp of sunshine from a grey sky. Alexander left the knapsack, and the two went out into the air. Before them lay the last level of the upclimb, the Lammerboden. It was a rather gruesome hollow between the peaks, a last shallow valley about a mile long. At the end the enormous static stream of the glacier poured in from the blunt mountain-top of ice. The ice was dull, sullen-coloured, melted on the surface by the very hot summer: and so it seemed a huge, arrested, sodden flood, ending in a wave-wall of stone-speckled ice upon the valley bed of rocky débris. A gruesome desert of stone and blocks of rock, the little valley bed, with a river raving through. On the left rose the grey rock, but the glacier was there too, sending down great paws of ice. It was like some great, deep-furred ice-bear lying spread upon the top heights, and reaching down terrible paws of ice into the valley; like some immense sky-bear fishing in the earth's solid hollows, from above. Hepburn it just filled with terror. Hannele too it scared, but it gave her a sense of ecstasy. Some of the immense, furrowed paws of ice held down between the rock were vivid blue in colour, but of a frightening, poisonous blue, like crystal copper-sulphate. Most of the ice was a sullen, semi-translucent greeny grey.

The two set off to walk through the mussy desolate stone-bed, under rocks and over waters, to the main glacier. The flowers were even more beautiful on this last reach. Particularly the dark harebells were large and almost black and ice-metallic, one could imagine they gave a dull ice-chink. And the Grass of Parnassus stood erect, white-veined big cups held terribly naked and open to this ice-air.

From behind the great blunt summit of ice that blocked the distance at the end of the valley a pale-grey, woolly mist or cloud was fusing up, exhaling huge like some grey-dead aura into the sky, and covering the top of the glacier. All the way along the valley people were threading, strangely insignificant, among the grey dishevel of stone and rock, like insects. Hannele and Alexander went ahead quickly, along the tiring track.

"Are you glad now that you came?" she said, looking at him triumphant.

"Very glad I came," he said. His eyes were dilated with excitement that was ordeal or mystic battle rather than the Bergheil ecstasy. The curious vibration of his excitement made the scene strange, rather horrible to her. She too shuddered. But it still seemed to her to hold the key to all glamour and ecstasy, the great silent, living glacier. It seemed to her like a grand beast.

As they came near they saw the wall of ice: the glacier end, thick crusted and speckled with stone and dirt-débris. From underneath, secret in stones, water rushed out. When they came quite near, they saw the great monster was sweating all over, trickles and rivulets of sweat running down his sides of pure, slush-translucent ice. There it was, the glacier, ending abruptly in the wall of ice under which they stood. Near to, the ice was pure, but water-logged, all the surface rather rotten from the hot summer. It was sullenly translucent, and of a watery, darkish bluey-green colour. But near the earth it became again bright coloured, gleams of green like jade, gleams of blue like thin, pale sapphire, in little caverns above the wet stones where the water trickled forever.

Alexander wanted to climb on to the glacier. It was his one desire: to stand upon it. So under the pellucid wet wall they toiled among rocks upwards, to where the guide-track mounted the ice. Several other people were before them—mere day-tourists—and all uncertain about venturing any further. For the ice-slope rose steep and slithery, pure, sun-pocked, sweating ice. Still, it was like a curved back. One could scramble on to it, on and on up to the first level, like the flat on top of some huge paw.

There stood the little cluster of people, facing the uphill of sullen, pure, sodden-looking ice. They were all afraid: naturally. But being human, they all wanted to go beyond their fear. It was strange that the ice looked so pure, like flesh. Not bright, because the surface was soft like a soft, deep epidermis. But pure ice away down to immense depths.

Alexander, after some hesitation, began gingerly to try the ice. He was frightened of it. And he had no stick, and only smooth-soled boots. But he had a great desire to stand on the glacier. So, gingerly and shakily, he began to struggle a few steps up the pure slope. The ice was soft on the surface, he could kick his heel in it and get a little sideways grip. So, staggering and going sideways he got up a few yards, and was on the naked ice-slope.

Immediately the youths and the fat man below began to tackle it too: also two maidens. For some time, however, Alexander gingerly and scramblingly led the way. The slope of ice was steeper, and rounded, so that it was difficult to stand up in any way. Sometimes he slipped, and was clinging with burnt finger-ends to the soft ice-mass. Then he tried throwing his coat down, and getting a foot-hold on that. Then he went quite quickly by bending down and getting a little grip with his fingers, and going ridiculously as on four legs.

Hannele watched from below, and saw the ridiculous exhibition, and was frightened, and amused, but more frightened. And she kept calling, to the great joy of the Austrians down below:

"Come back. Do come back."

But when he got on to his feet again he only waved his hand at her, half crossly, as she stood away down there in her blue frock.—The other fellows with sticks and nail boots had now taken heart and were scrambling like crabs past our hero, doing better than he.

He had come to a rift in the ice. He sat near the edge and looked down. Clear, pure ice, fused with pale colour, and fused into intense copper-sulphate blue away down in the crack. It was not like crystal, but fused as one fuses a borax bead under a blow-flame. And keenly, wickedly blue in the depths of the crack.

He looked upwards. He had not half mounted the slope. So on he went, upon the huge body of the soft-fleshed ice, slanting his way sometimes on all fours, sometimes using his coat, usually hitting-in with the side of his heel. Hannele down below was crying him to come back. But two other youths were now almost level with him.

So he struggled on till he was more or less over the brim. There he stood and looked at the ice. It came down from above in a great hollow world of ice. A world: a terrible place of hills and valleys and slopes, all motionless, all of ice. Away above the grey mist-cloud was looming bigger. And near at hand were long huge cracks, side by side, like gills in the ice. It would seem as if the ice breathed through these great ridged gills. One could look down into the series of gulfs, fearful depths, and the colour burning that acid, intense blue, intenser as the crack went deeper. And the crests of the open gills ridged and grouped pale blue above the crevices. It seemed as if the ice breathed there.

The wonder, the terror, and the bitterness of it. Never a warm leaf to unfold, never a gesture of life to give off. A world sufficient unto itself in lifelessness, all this ice.

He turned to go down, though the youths were passing beyond him. And seeing the naked translucent ice heaving downwards in a vicious curve, always the same dark translucency underfoot, he was afraid. If he slipped, he would certainly slither the whole way down, and break some of his bones. Even when he sat down, he had to cling with his fingernails in the ice, because if he had started to slide he would have slid the whole way down on his trouser-seat, precipitously, and have landed heaven knows how.

Hannele was watching from below. And he was frightened, perched seated on the shoulder of ice and not knowing how to get off. Above he saw the great blue gills of ice ridging the air. Down below were two blue cracks—then the last wet level claws of ice upon the stones. And there stood Hannele and the three or four people who had got so far.

However, he found that by striking in his heels sideways with sufficient sharpness he could keep his footing no matter how steep the slope. So he started to jerk his way zig-zag downwards.

As he descended, arrived a guide with a black beard and all the paraphernalia of ropes and pole and bristling boots. He and his gentleman began to strike their way up the ice. With those bristling nails like teeth in one's boots, it was quite easy: and a pole to press on to.

Hannele, who had got sick of waiting, and who was also

frightened, had gone scuttling on the return journey. He hurried after her, thankful to be off the ice, but excited and gratified. Looking round, he saw the guide and the man on the ice watching the ice-world and the weather. Then they too turned to come down. The day wasn't safe.

———

Pondering, rather thrilled, they threaded their way through the desert of rock and rushing water back to the hotel. The sun was shining warmly for a moment, and he felt happy, though his finger-ends were bleeding a little from the ice.

"But one day," said Hannele, "I should love to go with a guide right up, high, right into the glacier."

"No," said he. "I've been far enough. I prefer the world where cabbages will grow on the soil. Nothing grows on glaciers."

"They say there are glacier-fleas, which only live on glaciers," she said.

"Well, to me the ice didn't look good to eat, even for a flea."

"You never know," she laughed.—"But you're glad you've been, aren't you?"

"Very glad. Now I need never go again."

"But you *did* think it wonderful?"

"Marvellous. And awful, to my mind."

———

They ate venison and spinach in the hotel, then set off down again. Both felt happier. She gathered some flowers, and put them in her handkerchief so they should not die. And again they sat by the stream, to drink a little wine.

But the fume of cloud was blowing up again thick from behind the glacier. Hannele was uneasy. She wanted to get down. So they went fairly quickly. Many other tourists were hurrying downwards also. The rain began—a sharp handful of drops flung from beyond the glacier. So Hannele and he did not stay to rest, but dropped easily down the steep dark valley towards the motor-car terminus.

There they had tea—rather tired but comfortably so. The big hotel-restaurant was hideous, and seemed sordid. So in the gloom of a grey, early twilight they went out again and sat on a seat, watching the tourists and the trippers and the motor-car men. There were three Jews from Vienna: and the girl had a huge white woolly dog, as big as a calf, and white and woolly and silly and amiable as a toy. The men of course came patting it and admiring it, just as men always do, in life and in novels. And the girl, holding the leash, posed and leaned backwards in the attitudes of heroines on novel-covers. She said the white wool monster was a Siberian steppe-dog. Alexander wondered what the steppes made of such a wuffer. And the three Jews pretended they were elegant Austrians out of popular romances.

"Do you think," said Alexander, "you will marry the Herr Regierungsrat?"

She looked round, making wide eyes.

"It looks like it, doesn't it!" she said.

"Quite," said he.

Hannele watched the woolly white dog. So of course it came wagging its ever-amiable hindquarters towards her. She looked at it still, but did not touch it.

"What makes you ask such a question?" she said.

"I can't say. But even so, you haven't really answered. Do you really fully intend to marry the Herr Regierungsrat? Is that your final intention at this moment?"

She looked at him again.

"But before I answer," she said, "oughtn't I to know why you ask?"

"Probably you know already," he said.

"I assure you I don't."

He was silent for some moments. The huge woolly dog stood in front of him and breathed enticingly, with its tongue out. He only looked at it blankly.

"Well," he said, "if you were not going to marry the Herr Regierungsrat, I should suggest that you should marry me."

She stared away at the auto-garage, a very faint look of amusement, or pleasure, or ridicule on her face: or all three. And a certain shyness.

"But why?" she said.

"Why what?" he returned.

"Why should you suggest that I should marry you?"

"*Why?*" he replied, in his lingering tones. "*Why?*—Well, for what purpose does a man usually ask a woman to marry him?"

"For what *purpose!*" she repeated, rather haughtily.

"For what reason, then?" he corrected.

She was silent for some moments. Her face was closed and a little numb-looking, her hands lay very still in her lap. She looked away from him, across the road.

"There is usually only one reason," she replied, in a rather small voice.

"Yes?" he replied curiously. "What would you say that was?"

She hesitated. Then she said, rather stiffly:

"Because he really loved her, I suppose. That seems to me the only excuse for a man asking a woman to marry him."

Followed a dead silence, which she did not intend to break. He knew he would have to answer, and for some reason he didn't want to say what was obviously the thing to say.

"Leaving aside the question of whether you love me or I love you—" he began.

"I certainly *won't* leave it aside," she cried.

"And I certainly won't consider it," he said, just as obstinately.

She turned now and looked full at him, with amazement, ridicule, and anger in her face.

"I really think you must be mad," she said.

"I doubt if you do think that," he replied. "It is only a method of retaliation, that is. I think you understand my point very clearly."

"Your point!" she cried. "Your point! Oh, so you have a point in all this palavering?"

"Quite!" said he.

She was silent with indignation for some time. Then she said angrily:

"I assure you I do *not* see your point. I don't see any point at all. I see only impertinence."

"Very good," he replied. "The point is whether we marry on a basis of love."

"Indeed! Marry! We, marry! I don't think that is by any means the point."

He took his knapsack from under the seat, between his feet. And from the knapsack he took the famous picture.

"When," he said, "we were supposed to be in love with one another, you made that doll of me, didn't you?" And he sat looking at the odious picture.

"I never for one moment deluded myself that you *really* loved me," she said bitterly.

"Take the other point, whether *you* loved *me* or not," said he.

"How could I love you, when I couldn't believe in your love for me?" she cried.

He put the picture down between his knees again.

"All this about love," he said, "is very confusing, and very complicated."

"Very! In *your* case. Love to me is simple enough," she said.

"Is it? Is it? And was it simple love which made you make that doll of me?"

"Why shouldn't I make a doll of you? Does it do you any harm? And *weren't* you a doll, good heavens! You *were* nothing but a doll. So what hurt does it do you?"

"Yes, it does. It does me the greatest possible damage," he replied.

She turned on him with wide-open eyes of amazement and rage.

"Why? Pray why? Can you tell me why?"

"Not quite, I can't," he replied, taking up the picture and holding it in front of him. She turned her face from it as a cat turns its nose away from a lighted cigarette. "But when I look at it—when I look at this—then I *know* that there's no love between you and me."

"Then why are you talking at me in this shameful way," she flashed at him, tears of anger and mortification rising to her eyes. "You want your little revenge on me, I suppose, because I made that doll of you."

"That may be so, in a small measure," he said.

"That is *all*. That is all and everything," she cried. "And that is all you came back to me for—for this petty revenge.—Well, you've had it now.—But please don't speak to me any more.—I shall see if I can go home in the big omnibus."

She rose and walked away. He saw her hunting for the motor-bus conductor. He saw her penetrate into the yard of the garage. And he saw her emerge again, after a time, and take the path to the river. He sat on in front of the hotel. There was nothing else to do.

The tourists who had arrived in the big bus now began to collect. And soon the huge drab vehicle itself rolled up, and stood big as a house before the hotel door. The passengers began to scramble in to their seats. The two men of the white dog were going: but the woman of the white dog, and the dog, were staying behind. Hepburn wondered if Hannele had managed to get herself transferred. He doubted it, because he knew the omnibus was crowded.

Moreover, he had her ticket.

The passengers were packed in. The conductor was collecting the tickets. And at last the great bus rolled away. The bay of the road-end seemed very empty. Even the woman with the white dog had gone. Soon the other car, the Luxus, so-called, must appear. Hepburn sat and waited. The evening was falling chilly, the trees looked gruesome.

At last Hannele sauntered up again, unwillingly.

"I think," she said, "you have my ticket."

"Yes, I have," he replied.

"Will you give it me, please."

He gave it to her. She lingered a moment. Then she walked away.

There was the sound of a motor-car. With a triumphant purr the Luxus came steering out of the garage yard, and drew up at the hotel door. Hannele came hastening also. She went straight to one of the hinder doors—she and Hepburn had their seats in front, beside the driver. She had her foot on the step of the back seat. And then she was afraid. The little sharp faced driver—there was no conductor— came round looking at the car. He looked at her with his sharp, metallic eye of a mechanic.

"Are all the people going back, who came?" she asked, shrinking.

"Jawohl."

"It is full?—this car?"

"Jawohl."

"There's no other place?"

"Nein."

Hannele shrank away. The driver was absolutely laconic.

Six of the passengers were here: four were already seated. Hepburn sat still by the hotel door, Hannele lingered in the road by the car, and the little driver, with a huge woolen muffler round his throat, was running round and in and out looking for the two missing passengers. Of course there were two missing passengers. No, he could not find them.—And off he trotted again, silently, like a weasel after two rabbits. And at last, when everybody was getting cross, he unearthed them and brought them scuttling to the car.

Now Hannele took her seat, and Hepburn beside her. The driver snapped up the tickets and climbed in past them. With a vindictive screech the car slid away down the ravine. Another beastly trip was over, another infernal joyful holiday done with.

"I think," said Hepburn, "I may as well finish what I had to say?"

"What?" cried Hannele, fluttering in the wind of the rushing car.

"I may as well finish what I had to say," shouted he, his breath blown away.

"Finish then," she screamed, the ends of her scarf flickering behind her.

"When my wife died," he said loudly, "I knew I couldn't love any more."

"Oh—h!" she screamed ironically.

"In fact," he shouted, "I realised that, as far as I was concerned, love was a mistake."

"*What* was a mistake?" she screamed.

"Love," he bawled.

"Love!" she screamed. "A mistake?" Her tone was derisive.

"For me personally," he said, shouting.

"Oh, only for you personally," she cried, with a pouf of laughter.

The car gave a great swerve, and she fell on the driver. Then she righted herself. It gave another swerve, and she fell on Alexander. She righted herself angrily. And now they ran straight on: and it seemed a little quieter.

"I realised," he said, "that I had always made a mistake, undertaking to love."

"It must have been an undertaking, for *you*," she cried.

"Yes, I'm afraid it was. I never really wanted it. But I thought I did. And that's where I made my mistake."

"Whom have you ever loved?—even as an undertaking?" she asked.

"To begin with, my mother: and that was a mistake. Then my sister: and that was a mistake. Then a girl I had known all my life: and that was a mistake. Then my wife: and that was my most terrible mistake. And then I began the mistake of loving you."

"Undertaking to love me, you mean," she said. "But then you never did properly undertake it. You never really *undertook* to love *me*."

"Not quite, did I?" said he.

And she sat feeling angry that he had never made the undertaking.

"No," he continued. "Not quite. That is why I came back to you. I don't want to love you. I don't want marriage on a basis of love."

"On a basis of what, then?"

"I think you know without my putting it into words," he said.

"Indeed I assure you I don't. You are much too mysterious," she replied.

Talking in a swiftly-running motor-car is a nerve-wracking business. They both had a pause, to rest, and to wait for a quieter stretch of road.

"It isn't very easy to put it into words," he said.—"But I tried marriage once on a basis of love: and I must say, it was a ghastly affair in the long run. And I believe it would be so, for me, *whatever* woman I had."

"There must be something wrong with you, then," said she.

"As far as love goes, yes.—And yet I want marriage. I want marriage. I want a woman to honour and obey me—"

"If you are quite reasonable and *very* sparing with your commands," said Hannele. "And very careful how you give your orders."

"In fact, I want a sort of patient Griseldis. I want to be honoured and obeyed. I don't want love."

"How Griseldis managed to honour that fool of a husband of hers, even if she obeyed him, is more than I can say," said Hannele. "I'd like to know what she *really* thought of him.—Just what any woman thinks of a bullying fool of a husband."

"Well," said he, "that's no good to me."

They were silent now until the car stopped at the station. There they descended and walked on under the trees by the lake.

"Sit on a seat," he said, "and let us finish."

Hannele, who was really curious to hear what he would say, and who, woman-like, was fascinated by a man when he began to give away his own inmost thoughts—no matter how much she might jeer afterwards—sat down by his side. It was a grey evening, just falling dark. Lights twinkled across the lake, the hotel over there threaded its strings of light. Some little boats came rowing quietly to shore. It was a grey, heavy evening, with that special sense of dreariness with which a public holiday usually winds up.

"Honour, and obedience: and the proper physical feelings," he said. "To me that is marriage. Nothing else."

"But what are the proper physical feelings, but love?" asked Hannele.

"No," he said. "A woman wants you to adore her, and be in love with her—and I shan't. I will not do it again, if I live a monk for the rest of my days. I will neither adore you nor be in love with you—"

"You won't get a chance, thank you.—And what do you call the proper physical feelings, if you are not in love? I think you want something vile."

"If a woman honours me—absolutely from the bottom of her nature honours me—and obeys me because of that, then, I take it, my desire for her goes very much deeper than if I was in love with her, or if I adored her."

"It's the same thing. If you love, then everything is there—all the lot: your honour and obedience and everything. And if love isn't there, nothing is there," she said.

"That isn't true," he replied. "A woman may love you, she may adore you, but she'll neither honour you nor obey you. The most loving and adoring woman today could any minute start and make a doll of her husband—as you made of me."

"Oh that eternal doll! What makes it stick so in your mind?"

"I don't know. But there it is. It wasn't malicious. It was flattering, if you like. But it just sticks in me like a thorn: like a thorn.—And there it is, in the world, in Germany somewhere—And you can say what you like, but *any* woman, any woman today, no matter *how* much she loves her man—she could start any minute and make a doll of him. And the doll would be her hero: and her hero would be no more than her doll.—My wife might have done it. She did do it, in her mind. She had her doll of me right enough. Why, I've heard her talk about me to other women. And her doll was a great deal sillier than the one you made.—But it's all the same—if a woman loves you, she'll make a doll out of you. She'll never be satisfied till she's made your doll. And when she's got your doll, that's all she wants.—And that's what love means.—And so, I won't be loved. And I won't love. I won't have anybody loving me. It is an insult. I feel I've been insulted for forty years: by love, and the women who've loved me. I won't be loved. And I won't love.—I'll be honoured and I'll be obeyed: or nothing."

"Then it'll most probably be nothing," said Hannele sarcastically. "For I assure you, I've nothing but love to offer."

"Then keep your love," said he.

She laughed shortly.

"And you?" she cried. "You! Even suppose you *were* honoured and obeyed. I suppose all you've got to do is to sit there like a Sultan and sup it up."

"Oh no, I have many things to do. And woman or no woman, I'm going to start to do them."

The Captain's Doll

"What pray?"

"Why nothing very exciting. I'm going out to East Africa to join a man who's breaking his neck to get his three thousand acres of land under control. And when I've done a few more experiments and observations, and got all the necessary facts, I'm going to do a book on the moon. Woman or no woman, I'm going to do that."

"And the woman?—supposing you got the poor thing."

"Why, she'll come along with me, and we'll set ourselves up out there."

"And she'll do all the honouring and obeying and house-keeping incidentally, while you ride about in the day and stare at the moon in the night."

He did not answer. He was staring away across the lake.

"What will you do for the woman, poor thing, while she's racking herself to pieces honouring you and obeying you and doing frightful housekeeping in Africa: because I know it can be *awful*: awful."

"Well—" he said slowly—"she'll be my wife, and I shall treat her as such. If the marriage service says love and cherish—well, in that sense I shall do so—"

"Oh!" cried Hannele. "What, *love* her? Actually love the poor thing?"

"Not in that sense of the word, no. I shan't adore her or be in love with her. But she'll be my wife, and I shall love and cherish her as such."

"Just because she's your wife. Not because she's herself. Ghastly fate for any miserable woman," said Hannele.

"I don't think so. I think it's her highest fate."

"To be your wife?"

"To be a wife—and to be loved and cherished as a wife—not as a flirting woman."

"To be loved and cherished just because you're his wife! No thank you. All I can admire is the conceit and impudence of it."

"Very well then—there it is," he said, rising.

She rose too, and they went on towards where the boat was tied. As they were rowing in silence over the lake, he said:

"I shall leave tomorrow."

She made no answer. She sat and watched the lights of the villa draw near. And then she said:

"I'll come to Africa with you. But I won't promise to honour and obey you."

152

"I don't want you otherwise," he said, very quietly.

The boat was drifting to the little landing stage. Hannele's friends were hallooing to her from the balcony.

"Hallo!" she cried. "Ja! Da bin ich. Ja—'s war wunderschön."

Then to him she said:

"You'll come in?"

"No," he said, "I'll row straight back."

From the villa they were running down the steps to meet Hannele.

"But won't you have me even if I love you?" she asked him.

"You must promise the other," he said. "It comes in the marriage service."

"Hat's geregnet? Wie war das Wetter? Warst du auf dem Gletscher?" cried the voices from the garden.

"Nein—kein Regen. Wunderschön! Ja, er war ganz auf dem Gletscher," cried Hannele in reply. And to him, *sotto voce*:

"Don't be a solemn ass. Do come in."

"No," he said, "I don't want to come in."

"Do you want to go away tomorrow? Go if you *do*. But anyway I won't say it *before* the marriage service. I needn't, need I?"

She stepped from the boat on to the plank.

"Oh," she said, turning round. "Give me that picture, please, will you? I want to burn it."

He handed it to her.

"And come tomorrow, will you?" she said.

"Yes, in the morning."

He pulled back quickly into the darkness.

THE LADYBIRD

The Ladybird

How many swords had Lady Beveridge in her pierced heart! Yet there always seemed room for another. Since she had determined that her heart of pity and kindness should never die. If it had not been for this determination she herself might have died of sheer agony, in the years 1916 and 1917, when her boys were killed, and her brother, and death seemed to be mowing with wide swaths through her family. But let us forget.

Lady Beveridge loved humanity, and come what might, she would continue to love it. Nay, in the human sense, she would love her enemies. Not the criminals among the enemy, the men who committed atrocities. But the men who were enemies through no choice of their own. She would be swept into no general hate.

Somebody had called her the soul of England. It was not ill said: though she was half Irish. But of an old, aristocratic, loyal family famous for its brilliant men. And she, Lady Beveridge, had for years as much influence on the tone of English politics as any individual alive. The close friend of the real leaders in the House of Lords and in the Cabinet, she was content that the men should act, so long as they breathed from her as from the rose of life the pure fragrance of truth and genuine love. She had no misgivings regarding her own spirit.

She, she would never lower her delicate silken flag. For instance, throughout all the agony of the war she never forgot the enemy prisoners, she was determined to do her best for them. During the first years she still had influence. But during the last years of the war power slipped out of the hands of her and her sort, and she found she could do nothing any more: almost nothing. Then it seemed as if the many swords had gone home into the heart of this little, unyielding Mater Dolorosa. The new generation jeered at her. She was no longer a fashionable little aristocrat. Since the war her drawing-room was out of date.

But we anticipate. The years 1916 and 1917 were the years when the old spirit died for ever in England. But Lady Beveridge struggled on. She was being beaten.

It was in the winter of 1917—or in the late autumn. She had been for a fortnight sick, stricken, paralysed by the fearful death of her youngest boy. She felt she *must* give in, and just die. And then she remembered how many others were lying in agony.

So she rose, trembling, frail, to pay a visit to the hospital where lay the enemy sick and wounded, near London. Countess Beveridge was still a privileged woman. Society was beginning to jeer at this little, worn bird of an out-of-date righteousness and aesthetic. But they dared not think ill of her.

She ordered the car and went alone. The Earl, her husband, had taken his gloom to Scotland. So, on a sunny, wan November morning Lady Beveridge descended at the hospital, Hurst Place. The guard knew her, and saluted as she passed. Ah, she was used to such deep respect! It was strange that she felt it so bitterly, when the respect became shallower. But she did. It was like the beginning of the end to her.

The matron went with her into the ward. Alas, the beds were all full, and men were even lying on pallets on the floor. There was a desperate, crowded dreariness and hopelessness in the place: as if nobody wanted to make a sound or utter a word. Many of the men were haggard and unshaven, one was delirious, and talking fitfully in the Saxon dialect. It went to Lady Beveridge's heart. She had been educated in Dresden, and had had many dear friendships in the city. Her children also had been educated there. She heard the Saxon dialect with pain.

She was a little, frail, bird-like woman, elegant, but with that touch of the blue-stocking of the nineties which was unmistakeable. She fluttered delicately from bed to bed, speaking in perfect German, but with a thin, English intonation: and always asking if there was anything she could do. The men were mostly officers and gentlemen. They made little requests which she wrote down in a book. Her long, pale, rather worn face and her nervous little gestures somehow inspired confidence.

One man lay quite still, with his eyes shut. He had a black beard. His face was rather small and sallow. He might be dead. Lady Beveridge looked at him earnestly, and fear came into her face.

"Why, Count Dionys!" she said, fluttered. "Are you asleep?"

It was Count Johann Dionys Psanek, a Bohemian. She had

known him when he was a boy, and only in the spring of 1914 he and his wife had stayed with Lady Beveridge in her country house in Leicestershire.

The black eyes opened: large, black, unseeing eyes, with curved black lashes. He was a small man, small as a boy, and his face too was rather small. But all the lines were fine, as if they had been fired with a keen male energy. Now the yellowish swarthy paste of his flesh seemed dead, and the fine black brows seemed drawn on the face of one dead. The eyes however were alive: but only just alive, unseeing and unknowing.

"You know me, Count Dionys? You know me, don't you?" said Lady Beveridge, bending forward over the bed.

There was no reply for some time. Then the black eyes gathered a look of recognition, and there came the ghost of a polite smile.

"Lady Beveridge."—The lips formed the words. There was practically no sound.

"I am so glad you can recognise me.—And I am so sorry you are hurt. I am so sorry."

The black eyes watched her from that terrible remoteness of death, without changing.

"There is nothing I can do for you? Nothing at all?" she said, always speaking German.

And after a time, as from a distance, came the answer from his eyes, a look of weariness, of refusal, and a wish to be left alone; he was unable to strain himself into consciousness. His eyelids dropped.

"I am so sorry," she said. "If ever there is anything I can do—"

The eyes opened again, looking at her. He seemed at last to hear, and it was as if his eyes made the last weary gesture of a polite bow. Then slowly his eyelids closed again.

Poor Lady Beveridge felt another sword-thrust of sorrow in her heart, as she stood looking down at the motionless face, and at the black fine beard. The black hairs came out of his skin thin and fine, not very close together. A queer, dark, aboriginal little face he had, with a fine little nose: not an Aryan, surely. And he was going to die.

He had a bullet through the upper part of his chest, and another bullet had broken one of his ribs. He had been in the hospital five days.

Lady Beveridge asked the matron to ring her up if anything happened. Then she drove away, saddened. Instead of going to

Beveridge House, she went to her daughter's flat near the park—near Hyde Park. Lady Daphne was poor. She had married a commoner, son of one of the most famous politicians in England, but a man with no money. And Earl Beveridge had wasted most of the large fortune that had come to him, so that the daughter had very little, comparatively.

Lady Beveridge suffered, going in the narrow doorway into the rather ugly flat. Lady Daphne was sitting by the electric fire in the small yellow drawing-room, talking with a visitor. She rose at once, seeing her little mother.

"Why, mother, ought you to be out? I'm sure not."

"Yes, Daphne darling. Of course I ought to be out."

"How are you?" The daughter's voice was slow and sonorous, protective, sad. Lady Daphne was tall, only twenty-five years old. She had been one of the beauties, when the war broke out, and her father had hoped she would make a splendid match. Truly, she had married fame: but without money. Now, sorrow, pain, thwarted passion had done her great damage. Her husband was missing in the East. Her baby had been born dead. Her two darling brothers were dead. And she was ill, always ill.

A tall beautifully-built girl, she had the fine stature of her father. Her shoulders were still straight. But how thin her white throat! She wore a simple black frock stitched with coloured wool round the top, and held in a loose coloured girdle: otherwise no ornaments. And her face was lovely, fair, with a soft exotic white complexion and delicate pink cheeks. Her hair was soft and heavy, of a pallid gold quality, ash-blond. Her hair, her complexion were so perfectly cared for as to be almost artificial, like a hot-house flower.

But alas, her beauty was a failure. She was threatened with phthisis, and was far too thin. Her eyes were the saddest part of her. They had slightly reddened rims, nerve-worn, with heavy, veined lids that seemed as if they did not want to keep up. The eyes themselves were large and of a beautiful green-blue colour. But they were dull, languid, almost glaucous.

Standing as she was, a tall, finely built girl, looking down with affectionate care on her mother, she filled the heart with ashes. The little pathetic mother, so wonderful in her way, was not really to be pitied for all her sorrow. Her life was in her sorrows and her efforts on behalf of the sorrows of others. But Daphne was not born for grief and philanthropy. With her splendid frame, and her lovely, long, strong legs she was Artemis or Atalanta rather than Daphne. There was a certain width of brow and even of chin that told a strong, reckless nature, and the curious, distraught slant of her eyes told of a wild energy dammed up inside her.

That was what ailed her: her own wild energy. She had it from her father, and from her father's desperate race. The earldom had begun with a riotous, daredevil border soldier, and this was the blood that flowed on: And alas, what was to be done with it?

Daphne had married an adorable husband: truly an adorable husband. Whereas she needed a daredevil. But in her *mind* she hated all daredevils, she had been brought up by her mother to admire only the good.

So, her reckless, anti-philanthropic passion could find no outlet— and *should* find no outlet, she thought. So her own blood turned against her, beat on her own nerves, and destroyed her. It was nothing but frustration and anger which made her ill, and made the doctors fear consumption. There it was, drawn on her rather wide mouth: frustration, anger, bitterness. There it was the same in the roll of her green-blue eyes, a slanting, averted look: the same anger furtively turning back on itself. This anger reddened her eyes and shattered her nerves. And yet, her whole will was fixed in her adoption of her mother's creed, and in condemnation of her handsome, proud, brutal father who had made so much misery in the family. Yes, her will was fixed in the determination that life should be gentle and good and benevolent. Whereas her blood was reckless, the blood of daredevils. Her will was the stronger of the two. But her blood had its revenge on her. So it is with strong natures today: shattered from the inside.

"You have no news, darling?" asked the mother.

"No. My father-in-law had information that British prisoners had been brought into Hasrun, and that details would be forwarded by the Turks. And there was a rumour from some Arab prisoners that Basil was one of the British brought in wounded."

"When did you hear this?"

"Primrose came in this morning."

"Then we can hope, dear."

"Yes."

Never was anything more dull and bitter than Daphne's affirmative of hope. Hope had become almost a curse to her. She wished there need be no such thing. Ha, the torment of hoping, and the *insult* to one's soul. Like the importunate widow dunning for her deserts. Why could it not all be just clean disaster, and have done with it? This dilly-dallying with despair was worse than despair. She had hoped so much: ah, for her darling brothers she had hoped with such anguish. And the two she loved best were dead. So were most others she had hoped for, dead. Only this uncertainty about her husband still rankling.

"You feel better, dear?" said the little, unquenched mother.

"Rather better," came the resentful answer.

"And your night?"

"No better."

There was a pause.

"You are coming to lunch with me, Daphne darling?"

"No, mother dear. I promised to lunch at the Howards with Primrose. But I needn't go for a quarter of an hour. Do sit down.—"

Both women seated themselves near the electric fire. There was that bitter pause, neither knowing what to say. Then Daphne roused herself to look at her mother.

"Are you sure you were fit to go out?" she said. "What took you out so suddenly?"

"I went to Hurst Place, dear. I had the men on my mind, after the way the newspapers have been talking."

"Why ever do you read the newspapers!" blurted Daphne, with a certain burning, acid anger.—"Well," she said, more composed. "And do you feel better now you've been?"

"So many people suffer besides ourselves, darling."

"I know they do. Makes it all the worse. It wouldn't matter if it were only just us.—At least, it would matter, but one could bear it more easily.—To be just one of a crowd all in the same state—"

"And some even worse, dear—"

"Oh quite!—And the worse it is for all, the worse it is for one."

"Is that so, darling? Try not to see too darkly. I feel if I can give just a little bit of myself to help the others—you know—it alleviates me. I feel that what I can give to the men lying there, Daphne, I give to my own boys. I can only help them now through helping others. But I can still do that, Daphne, my girl."

And the mother put her little white hand into the long, white, cold hand of her daughter. Tears came to Daphne's eyes, and a fearful stony grimace to her mouth.

"It's so wonderful of you that you can feel like that," she said.

"But you feel the same, my love. I know you do."

"No I don't. Every one I see suffering these same awful things, it makes me wish more for the end of the world. And I quite see that the world won't end—"

"But it will get better, dear. This time is like a great sickness—like a terrible pneumonia tearing the breast of the world."

"Do you believe it will get better? I don't."

"It will get better. Of course it will get better. It is perverse to think otherwise, Daphne. Remember what *has* been before, even in Europe. Ah Daphne, we must take a bigger view."

"Yes, I suppose we must."

The daughter spoke rapidly, from the lips, in a resonant, monotonous tone. The mother spoke from the heart.

"And Daphne, I found an old friend among the men at Hurst Place."

"Who?"

"Little Count Dionys Psanek. You remember him?"

"Quite. What's wrong?"

"Wounded rather badly—through the chest. So ill."

"Did you speak to him?"

"Yes. I recognised him in spite of his beard."

"Beard!"

"Yes—a black beard. I suppose he could not be shaven. It seems strange that he is still alive, poor man."

"Why strange? He isn't old. How old is he?"

"Between thirty and forty. But so ill, so wounded, Daphne. And so small. So small, so sallow—*smorto*, you know the Italian word. The way dark people look. There is something so distressing in it."

"Does he look *very* small now—uncanny?" asked the daughter.

"No, not uncanny. Something of the terrible far-awayness of a child that is very ill and can't tell you what hurts it. Poor Count Dionys, Daphne. I didn't know, dear, that his eyes were so black, and his lashes so curved and long. I had never thought of him as beautiful."

"Nor I. Only a little comical. Such a dapper little man."

"Yes. And yet now, Daphne, there is something remote and in a sad way heroic in his dark face. Something primitive."

"What did he say to you?"

"He couldn't speak to me. Only with his lips, just my name."

"So bad as that?"

163

"Oh yes. They are afraid he will die."

"Poor Count Dionys. I liked him. He was a bit like a monkey, but he had his points. He gave me a thimble on my seventeenth birthday. Such an amusing thimble."

"I remember, dear."

"Unpleasant wife, though.—Wonder if he minds dying far away from her. Wonder if she knows."

"I think not. They didn't even know his name properly. Only that he was a colonel of such and such a regiment—"

"Fourth cavalry," said Daphne.—"Poor Count Dionys. Such a lovely name, I always thought: Count Johann Dionys Psanek. Extraordinary dandy he was. And an amazingly good dancer, small, yet electric. Wonder if he minds dying."

"He was so full of life, in his own little animal way. They say small people are always conceited. But he doesn't look conceited now, dear. Something ages old in his face—and, yes, a certain beauty, Daphne."

"You mean long lashes—"

"No. So still, so solitary—and ages old, in his race. I suppose he must belong to one of those curious little aboriginal races of Central Europe. I felt quite new beside him."

"How nice of you," said Daphne.

Nevertheless, next day Daphne telephoned to Hurst Place to ask for news of him. He was about the same. She telephoned every day. Then she was told he was a little stronger. The day she received the message that her husband was wounded and a prisoner in Turkey, and that his wounds were healing, she forgot to telephone for news of the little enemy Count. And the following day she telephoned that she was coming to the hospital to see him.

He was awake, more restless, more in physical excitement. They could see the tension of pain between his brows, and a curious peaked look of the nausea of pain round his nose. His face seemed to Daphne curiously hidden behind the black beard, which nevertheless was thin, each hair coming thin and fine, singly, from the sallow, slightly translucent skin. In the same way his moustache made a thin black line round his mouth. His eyes were wide open, very black, and of no legible expression. He watched the two women coming down the crowded, dreary room, as if he did not see them. His eyes seemed too wide.

It was a cold day, and Daphne was huddled in a black sealskin coat with a skunk collar pulled up to her ears, and a dull gold cap with wings pulled down on her brow. Lady Beveridge wore her sable coat, and had that odd, untidy elegance which was natural to her, rather like a ruffled chicken.

Daphne was upset by the hospital. She looked from right to left in spite of herself, and everything gave her a dull feeling of horror: the terror of these sick, wounded enemy men. She loomed tall and obtrusive in her furs by the bed, her little mother at her side.

"I hope you don't mind my coming!" she said in German to the sick man. Her tongue felt rusty, speaking the language.

"Who is it then?" he asked.

"It is my daughter, Lady Daphne. You remember *me*, Lady Beveridge! This is my daughter, whom you knew in Saxony. She was so sorry to hear you were wounded."

The black eyes rested on the little lady. Then they returned to the looming figure of Daphne. And a certain fear grew on the sick brow. It was evident the presences loomed and frightened him. He turned his face aside. Daphne noticed how his fine black hair grew uncut over his small, animal ears.

"You don't remember me, Count Dionys?" she said dully.

"Yes," he said. But he kept his face averted.

She stood there feeling confused and miserable, as if she had made a *faux pas* in coming.

"Would you rather be left alone?" she said. "I'm sorry."

Her voice was monotonous. She felt suddenly stifled in her closed furs, and threw her coat open, showing her thin white throat and plain black slip dress on her flat breast. He turned again unwillingly to look at her. He looked at her as if she were some strange creature standing near him.

"Goodbye," she said. "Do get better."

She was looking at him with a queer, slanting, downward look of her heavy eyes, as she turned away. She was still a little red round the eyes, with her nervous exhaustion.

"You are so tall," he said, still frightened.

"I was always tall," she replied, turning half to him again.

"And I small," he said.

"I am so glad you are getting better," she said.

"I am not glad," he said.

"Why? I'm sure you are. Just as we are glad because we want you to get better."

"Thank you," he said. "I have wished to die."

"Don't do that, Count Dionys. Do get better," she said, in the rather deep, laconic manner of her girlhood. He looked at her with a farther look of recognition. But his short, rather pointed nose was lifted with the disgust and weariness of pain, his brows were tense. He watched her with that curious flame of suffering which is forced to give a little outside attention, but which speaks only to itself.

"Why did they not let me die?" he said. "I wanted death now."

"No," she said. "You mustn't. You must live. If we *can* live we must."

"I wanted death," he said.

"Ah well," she said. "Even death we can't have when we want it: or when we think we want it."

"That is true," he said, watching her with the same wide black eyes. "Please to sit down. You are so tall as you stand."—It was evident he was a little frightened still by her looming, overhanging figure.

"I'm sorry I am too tall," she said, smiling, taking a chair which a man-nurse had brought her. Lady Beveridge had gone away to speak with the men. Daphne sat down, not knowing what to say further. The pitch-black look in the Count's wide eyes puzzled her.

"Why do you come here? Why does your lady mother come?" he said.

"To see if we can do anything," she answered.

"When I am well, I will thank your ladyships."

"All right," she replied. "When you are well I will let my lord the Count thank me. Please do get well."

"We are enemies," he said.

"Who? You and I and my mother?"

"Are we not? The most difficult thing is to be sure of anything.—If they had let me die!"

"That is at least ungrateful, Count Dionys."

"*Lady Daphne*! Yes!—*Lady Daphne*! Beautiful, the name is. You are always called Lady Daphne? I remember you were so bright a maiden."

"More or less," she said, answering his question.

"Ach! We should all have new names now. I thought of a name for myself, but I have forgotten it. No longer Johann Dionys. That is shot away. I am Karl or Wilhelm or Ernst or Georg. Those are names I hate. Do you hate them?"

"I don't like them—but I don't hate them. And you mustn't leave off being Count Johann Dionys. If you do I shall have to leave off being Daphne. I like your name so much."

"Lady Daphne! Lady Daphne!" he repeated. "Yes, it rings well, it sounds beautiful to me.—I think I talk foolishly. I hear myself talking foolishly to you."—He looked at her anxiously.

"Not at all," she said.

"Ach! I have a head on my shoulders that is like a child's windmill, and I can't prevent its making foolish words. Please to go away, not to hear me. I can hear myself."

"Can't I do anything for you?" she asked.

"No no! No no! If I could be buried deep, very deep down, where everything is forgotten! But they draw me up, back to the surface. I would not mind if they buried me alive, if it were very deep, and dark, and the earth heavy above."

"Don't say that," she replied, rising.

"No, I am saying it when I don't wish to say it. Why am I here? Why am I here? Why have I survived into this? Why can I not stop talking?"

He turned his face aside. The black, fine, elvish hair was so long, and pushed up in tufts from the smooth brown nape of his neck. Daphne looked at him in sorrow. He could not turn his body. He could only move his head. And he lay with his face hard averted, the fine hair of his beard coming up strange from under his chin and from his throat, up to the socket of his ear. He lay quite still, in this posture. And she turned away, looking for her mother. She had suddenly realised that the bonds, the connections between him and his life in the world had broken, and he lay there a bit of loose, palpitating humanity, shot away from the body of humanity.

It was ten days before she went to the hospital again. She had wanted never to go again, to forget him, as one tries to forget incurable things. But she could not forget him. He came again and again into her mind. She had to go back. She had heard that he was recovering very slowly.

He looked really better. His eyes were not so wide open, they had lost that black, inky exposure which had given him such an unnatural look, unpleasant. He watched her guardedly. She had taken off her furs, and wore only her dress and a dark, soft feather cap.

"How are you?" she said, keeping her face averted, unwilling to meet his eyes.

"Thank you, I am better. The nights are not so long."

She shuddered, knowing what long nights meant. He saw the worn look in her face too, the reddened rims of her eyes.

"Are you not well? Have you some trouble?" he asked her.

"No no," she answered.

She had brought a handful of pinky, daisy-shaped flowers.

"Do you care for flowers?" she asked.

He looked at them. Then he slowly shook his head.

"No," he said. "If I am on horseback, riding through the marshes or through the hills, I like to see them below me. But not here. Not now. Please do not bring flowers into this grave. Even in gardens, I do not like them. When they are upholstery to human life!"

"I will take them away again," she said.

"Please do. Please give them to the nurse."

Daphne paused.

"Perhaps," she said, "you wish I would not come to disturb you."

He looked into her face.

"No," he said. "You are like a flower behind a rock, near an icy water. No, you do not live too much.—I am afraid I cannot talk sensibly. I wish to hold my mouth shut. If I open it, I talk this absurdity. It escapes from my mouth."

"It is not so very absurd," she said.

But he was silent—looking away from her.

"I want you to tell me if there is really nothing I can do for you," she said.

"Nothing," he answered.

"If I can write any letter for you."

"None," he answered.

"But your wife—and your two children—Do they know where you are?"

"I should think not."

"And where are they?"

"I do not know. Probably they are in Hungary."

"Not at your home?"

"My castle was burnt down in a riot. My wife went to Hungary with the children. She has her relatives there. She went away from me. I wished it too. Also for her, I wished to be dead. Pardon me the personal tone—"

Daphne looked down at him—the queer, obstinate little fellow.

"But you have somebody you wish to tell—somebody you want to hear from?"

"Nobody. Nobody. I wish the bullet had gone through my heart. I wish to be dead. It is only I have a devil in my body, that will not die."

She looked at him as he lay with closed, averted face.

"Surely it is not a devil which keeps you alive," she said. "It is something good."

"No, a devil," he said.

She sat looking at him with long, slow, wondering look.

"Must one hate a devil that makes one live?" she asked.

He turned his eyes to her with a touch of a satiric smile.

"If one lives, no—" he said.

She looked away from him the moment he looked at her. For her life she would not have met his dark eyes direct.

She left him, and he lay still. He neither read nor talked, throughout the long winter nights and the short winter days. He only lay for hours with black, open eyes, seeing everything around with a touch of disgust, and heeding nothing.

Daphne went to see him now and then. She never forgot him for long. He seemed to come into her mind suddenly, as if by sorcery.

One day he said to her:

"I see you are married. May I ask you who is your husband?"

She told him. She had had a letter also from Basil. The Count smiled slowly.

"You can look forward," he said, "to a happy reunion, and new, lovely children, Lady Daphne. Is it not so?"

"Yes, of course," she said.

"But you are ill," he said to her.

"Yes—rather ill."

"Of what—?"

"Oh—?" she answered fretfully, turning her face aside. "They talk about lungs." She hated speaking of it. "Why, how do you know I am ill?" she added quickly.

Again he smiled slowly.

"I see it in your face, and hear it in your voice. One would say the Evil Eye had cast a spell on you."

"Oh no," she said hastily. "But do I look ill?"

"Yes. You look as if something had struck you across the face, and you could not forget it."

"Nothing has," she said. "Unless it's the war."

"The war!" he repeated.

"Oh well, don't let us talk of it," she said.

Another time he said to her:

"The year has turned. The sun must shine at last, even in England. I am afraid of getting well too soon. I am a prisoner, am I not? But I wish the sun would shine. I wish the sun would shine on my face."

"You won't always be a prisoner. The war will end. And the sun *does* shine, even in the winter in England," she said.

"I wish it would shine on my face," he said.

So that when in February there came a blue, bright morning, the morning that suggests yellow crocuses and the scent of a mezereon tree and the smell of damp, warm earth, Daphne hastily got a taxi and drove out to the hospital.

"You have come to put me in the sun," he said the moment he saw her.

"Yes, that's what I came for," she said.

She spoke to the matron, and had his bed carried out where there was a big window that came low. There he was put full in the sun. Turning, he could see the blue sky, and the twinkling tops of purplish, bare trees.

"The world! The world!" he murmured.

He lay with his eyes shut, and the sun on his swarthy, transparent, immobile face. The breath came and went through his nostrils invisibly. Daphne wondered how he could lie so still, how he could look so immobile. It was true as her mother had said: he looked as if he had been cast in the mould when the metal was white hot, all his lines were so clean. So small, he was, and in his way perfect.

Suddenly his dark eyes opened and caught her looking.

"The sun makes even anger open like a flower," he said.

"Whose anger?" she said.

"I don't know. But I can make flowers, looking through my eyelashes. Do you know how?"

"You mean rainbows?"

"Yes, flowers."

And she saw him, with a curious smile on his lips, looking through his almost closed eyelids at the sun.

"The sun is neither English nor German nor Bohemian," he said. "I am a subject of the sun. I belong to the fire-worshippers."

"Do you?" she replied.

"Yes truly, by tradition." He looked at her smiling. "You stand there like a flower that will melt," he added.

She smiled slowly at him, with a slow, cautious look of her eyes, as if she feared something.

"I am much more solid than you imagine," she said.

Still he watched her.

"One day," he said, "before I go, let me wrap your hair round my hands, will you?" He lifted his thin, short dark hands. "Let me wrap your hair round my hands, like a bandage. They hurt me. I don't know what it is. I think it is all the gun explosions. But if you let me wrap your hair round my hands. You know, it is the hermetic gold—but so much of water in it, of the moon. That will soothe my hands.—One day, will you—?"

"Let us wait till the day comes," she said.

"Yes," he answered, and was still again.

"It troubles me," he said after a while, "that I complain like a child, and ask for things. I feel I have lost my manhood for the time being. The continual explosion of guns and shells! It seems to have driven my soul out of me like a bird frightened away at last.—But it will come back, you know. And I am so grateful to you, you are good to me when I am soulless, and you don't take advantage of me. Your soul is quiet and heroic."

"Don't," she said. "Don't talk!"

The expression of shame and anguish and disgust crossed his face.

"It is because I can't help it," he said. "I have lost my soul, and I can't stop talking to you. I can't stop. But I don't talk to anyone else. I try not to talk, but I can't prevent it. Do you draw the words out of me?"

Her wide, green-blue eyes seemed like the heart of some curious, full-open flower, some Christmas rose with its petals of snow and flush. Her hair glinted heavy, like water-gold. She stood there passive and indomitable, with the wide-eyed persistence of her wintry, blond nature.

Another day when she came to see him, he watched her for a time, then he said:

"Do they all tell you you are lovely, you are beautiful?"

"Not quite all," she replied.

"But your husband?"

"He has said so."

"Is he gentle? Is he tender? Is he a dear lover?"

She turned her face aside, displeased.

"Yes," she replied curtly.

He did not answer. And when she looked again he was lying with his eyes shut, a faint smile seeming to curl round his short, transparent nose. She could faintly see the flesh through his beard, as water through reeds. His black hair was brushed smooth as glass, his black eyebrows glinted like a curve of black glass on the swarthy opalescence of his brow.

Suddenly he spoke, without opening his eyes.

"You have been very kind to me," he said.

"Have I? Nothing to speak of."

He opened his eyes and looked at her.

"Everything finds its mate," he said. "The ermine and the pole-cat and the buzzard. One thinks so often that only the dove and the nightingale and the stag with his antlers have gentle mates. But the pole-cat and the ice-bears of the north have their mates. And a white she-bear lies with her cubs under a rock as a snake lies hidden, and the male-bear slowly swims back from the sea, like a clot of snow or a shadow of white cloud passing on the speckled sea. I have seen her too, and I did not shoot her. Nor him when he landed with fish in his mouth, wading wet and slow and yellow-white over the black stones."

"You have been in the north seas?"

"Yes. And with the eskimo in Siberia, and across the Tundras. And a white sea-hawk makes a nest on a high stone, and sometimes looks out with her white head, over the edge of the rock. It is not only a world of men, Lady Daphne."

"Not by any means," said she.

"Else it were a sorry place."

"It is bad enough," said she.

"Foxes have their holes. They have even their mates, Lady Daphne, that they bark to and are answered. And an adder finds his female. Psanek means an outlaw, did you know?"

"I did not."

"Outlaws, and brigands, have often the finest woman-mates."

"They do," she said.

"I will be Psanek, Lady Daphne. I will not be Johann Dionys any more. I will be Psanek. The law has shot me through."

"You might be Psanek and Johann and Dionys as well," she said.

"With the sun on my face?—Maybe—" he said; looking to the sun.

There were some lovely days in the spring of 1918. In March the Count was able to get up. They dressed him in a simple, dark-blue uniform. He was not very thin, only swarthy-transparent, now his beard was shaven and his hair was cut. His smallness made him noticeable, but he was masculine, perfect in his small stature. All the smiling dapperness that had made him seem like a monkey to Daphne when she was a girl had gone now. His eyes were dark and haughty, he seemed to keep inside his own reserves, speaking to nobody if he could help it, neither to the nurses nor the visitors nor to his fellow-prisoners, fellow-officers. He seemed to put a shadow between himself and them, and from across this shadow he looked with his dark, beautifully-fringed eyes, as a proud little beast from the shadow of its lair. Only to Daphne he laughed and chatted.

She sat with him one day in March on the terrace of the hospital, on a morning when white clouds went endlessly and magnificently about a blue sky, and the sunshine fell warm after the blots of shadow.

"When you had a birthday, and you were seventeen, didn't I give you a thimble?" he asked her.

"Yes. I have it still."

"With a gold snake at the bottom, and a Mary-beetle of green stone at the top, to push the needle with."

"Yes."

"Do you ever use it?"

"No. I sew so rarely."

"Would it displease you to sew something for me?"

"You won't admire my stitches.—What would you wish me to sew?"

"Sew me a shirt that I can wear. I have never before worn shirts from a shop, with a maker's name inside. It is very distasteful to me."

She looked at him—his haughty little brows.

"Shall I ask my maid to do it?" she said.

"Oh please no! Oh please no, do not trouble. No, please, I would not want it unless you sewed it yourself, with the Psanek thimble."

She paused before she answered. Then came her slow:

"Why?"

He turned and looked at her with dark, searching eyes.

"I have no reason," he said, rather haughtily.

She left the matter there. For two weeks she did not go to see him. Then suddenly one day she took the bus down Oxford Street and bought some fine white flannel. She decided he must wear flannel.

That afternoon she drove out to Hurst Place. She found him sitting on the terrace, looking across the garden at the red suburb of London smoking fumily in the near distance, interrupted by patches of uncovered ground and a flat, tin-roofed laundry.

"Will you give me measurements for your shirt?" she said.

"The number of the neck-band of this English shirt is fifteen. If you ask the matron she will give you the measurement.—It is a little too large, too long in the sleeves, you see—" and he shook his shirt cuff over his wrist. "Also too long altogether."

"Mine will probably be unwearable when I've made them," said she.

"Oh no. Let your maid direct you. But please do not let her sew them."

"Will you tell me why you want me to do it?"

"Because I am a prisoner, in other people's clothes, and I have nothing of my own. All the things I touch are distasteful to me. If your maid sews for me, it will still be the same. Only you might give me what I want, something that buttons round my throat and on my wrists."

"And in Germany—or in Austria—?"

"My mother sewed for me. And after her, my mother's sister who was the head of my house."

"Not your wife?"

"Naturally not. She would have been insulted. She was never more than a guest in my house. In my family there are old traditions—but with me they have come to an end.—I had best try to revive them."

"Beginning with traditions of shirts?"

"Yes. In our family the shirt should be made and washed by a woman of our own blood: but when we marry, by the wife. So when I married I had sixty shirts, and many other things—sewn by my mother and my aunt, all with my initial, and the ladybird, which is our crest."

"And where did they put the initial?"

"Here—!" He put his finger on the back of his neck, on the swarthy, transparent skin. "I fancy I can feel the embroidered ladybird still. On our linen we had no crown: only the ladybird."

She was silent, thinking.

"You will forgive what I ask you?" he said. "Since I am a prisoner and can do no other, and since fate has made you so that you understand the world as I understand it. It is not really indelicate, what I ask you. There will be a ladybird on your finger when you sew, and those who wear the ladybird understand."

"I suppose," she mused, "it is as bad to have your bee in your shirt as in your bonnet."

He looked at her with round eyes.

"Don't you know what it is to have a bee in your bonnet?" she said.

"No."

"To have a bee buzzing among your hair! To be out of your wits," she smiled at him.

"So!" he said. "Ah, the Psaneks have had a ladybird in their bonnets for many hundred years."

"Quite, quite mad," she said.

"It may be," he answered. "But with my wife I was quite quite sane for ten years. Now give me the madness of my ladybird. The world I was sane about has gone raving. The ladybird I was mad about is wise still."

"At least, when I sew the shirts, if I sew them," she said, "I shall have the ladybird at my finger's end."

"You want to laugh at me."

"But surely you know you are funny, with your family insect."

"My family insect? Now you want to be rude to me."

"How many spots must it have?"

"Seven."

"Three on each wing. And what do I do with the odd one?"

"You put that one between its teeth, like the cake for Cerberus."

"I'll remember that."

When she brought the first shirt, she gave it to the matron. Then she found Count Dionys sitting on the terrace. It was a beautiful spring day. Near at hand were tall elm trees, and some rooks cawing.

"What a lovely day!" she said. "Are you liking the world any better?"

"The world?" he said, looking up at her with the same old discontent and disgust on his fine, transparent nose.

"Yes," she replied, a shadow coming over her face.

"Is this the world—all those little red-brick boxes in rows, where couples of little people live, who decree my destiny—?"

"You don't like England?"

"Ah England! Little houses like little boxes, each with its domestic Englishman and his domestic wife, each ruling the world because all are alike, so alike—"

"But England isn't all houses."

"Fields then! Little fields with innumerable hedges. Like a net with an irregular mesh, pinned down over this island, and everything under the net.—Ah Lady Daphne, forgive me. I am ungrateful. I am so full of bile, of spleen, you say. My only wisdom is to keep my mouth shut."

"Why do you hate everything?" she said, her own face going bitter.

"Not everything. If I were free! If I were outside the law. Ah, Lady Daphne, how does one get outside the law?"

"By going inside oneself," she said. "Not outside."

His face took on a greater expression of disgust.

"No no. I am a man, I am a man, even if I am little. I am not a spirit, that coils itself inside a shell. In my soul is anger, anger, anger. Give me room for my anger. Give me room for that." His black eyes looked keenly into her. She rolled her eyes as if in a half-trance. And in a monotonous, tranced voice she said:

"Much better get over your anger.—And *why* are you angry?"

"There is no why. If it were love, you would not ask me, *why do you love*? But it is anger, anger, anger. What else can I call it? And there is no why."

Again he looked at her with his dark, sharp, questioning, tormented eyes.

"Can't you get rid of it?" she said, looking aside.

"If a shell exploded and blew me into a thousand fragments," he said, "it would not destroy the anger that is in me. I know that. No, it will never dissipate. And to die is no release. The anger goes on gnashing and whimpering in death. Lady Daphne, Lady Daphne, we have used up all the love, and this is what is left."

"Perhaps *you* have used up all your love," she replied. "You are not everybody."

"I know it. I speak for me and you."

"Not for me," she said rapidly.

He did not answer, and they remained silent.

At length she turned her eyes slowly to him.

"Why do you say you speak for me?" she said, in an accusing tone.

"Pardon me. I was hasty."

But a faint touch of superciliousness in his tone showed he meant what he had said. She mused, her brow cold and stony.

"And why do you tell *me* about your anger?" she said. "Will that make it better?"

"Even the adder finds his mate. And she has as much poison in her mouth as he."

She gave a little sudden squirt of laughter.

"Awfully poetic thing to say about one," she said.

He smiled, but with the same corrosive quality.

"Ah," he said, "you are not a dove. You are a wild-cat with open eyes, half dreaming on a bough, in a lonely place, as I have seen her. And I ask myself—What are her memories, then?"

"I wish I were a wild-cat," she said suddenly.

He eyed her shrewdly, and did not answer.

"You want more war?" she said to him bitterly.

"More trenches? More Long Berthas, more shells and poison-gas, more machine-drilled science-manœuvred so-called armies? Never. Never. I would rather work in a factory that makes boots and shoes. And I would rather deliberately starve to death than work in a factory that makes boots and shoes."

"Then what do you want?"

"I want my anger to have room to grow."

"How?"

"I do not know. That is why I sit still here, day after day. I wait."

"For your anger to have room to grow?"

"For that."

"Goodbye, Count Dionys."

"Goodbye, Lady Daphne."

She had determined never to go and see him again. She had no sign from him. Since she had begun the second shirt, she went on with it. And then she hurried to finish it, because she was starting a round of visits that would end in the summer sojourn in Scotland. She intended to post the shirt. But after all she took it herself.

She found that Count Dionys had been removed from Hurst Place to Voynich Hall, where other enemy officers were interned. The being thwarted made her more determined. She took the train next day to go to Voynich Hall.

When he came into the ante-room where he was to receive her, she felt at once the old influence of his silence and his subtle power.

His face had still that swarthy-transparent look of one who is unhappy, but his bearing was proud and reserved. He kissed her hand politely, leaving her to speak.

"How are you?" she said. "I didn't know you were here. I am going away for the summer."

"I wish you a pleasant time," he said. They were speaking English.

"I brought the other shirt," she said. "It is finished at last."

"That is a greater honour than I dared expect," he said.

"I'm afraid it may be more honorable than useful. The other didn't fit, did it?"

"Almost," he said. "It fitted the spirit, if not the flesh," he smiled.

"I'd rather it had been the reverse, for once," she said. "Sorry."

"I would not have it one stitch different."

"Can we sit in the garden?"

"I think we may."

They sat on a bench. Other prisoners were playing croquet not far off. But these two were left comparatively alone.

"Do you like it better here?" she said.

"I have nothing to complain of," he said.

"And the anger?"

"It is doing well, I thank you," he smiled.

"You mean getting better?"

"Making strong roots," he said, laughing.

"Ah, so long as it only makes roots—!" she said.

"And your ladyship, how is she?"

"My ladyship is rather better," she replied.

"Much better, indeed," he said, looking into her face.

"Do you mean I *look* much better?" she asked quickly.

"Very much.—It is your beauty you think of. Well, your beauty is almost itself again."

"Thanks."

"You brood on your beauty as I on my anger. Ah, your ladyship, be wise, and make friends with your anger. That is the way to let your beauty blossom."

"I was not unfriends with you, was I?" she said.

"With me?" His face flickered with a laugh. "Am I your anger? Your wrath incarnate? So then, be friends with the angry me, your ladyship. I ask nothing better."

"What is the use," she said, "being friends with the *angry* you? I would much rather be friends with the happy you."

178

"That little animal is extinct," he laughed. "And I am glad of it."

"But what remains? Only the angry you? Then it is no use my trying to be friends."

"You remember, dear Lady Daphne, that the adder does not suck his poison all alone, and the pole-cat knows where to find his she-polecat. You remember that each one has his own dear mate," he laughed. "Dear, deadly mate."

"And what if I do remember those bits of natural history, Count Dionys?"

"The she-adder is dainty, delicate, and carries her poison lightly. The wild-cat has wonderful green eyes that she closes with memory like a screen. The ice-bear hides like a snake with her cubs, and her snarl is the strangest thing in the world."

"Have you ever heard me snarl?" she asked suddenly.

He only laughed, and looked away.

They were silent. And immediately the strange thrill of secrecy was between them. Something that had gone beyond sadness into another, secret, thrilling communion which she would never admit.

"What do you do all day here?" she asked.

"Play chess—play this foolish croquet—play billiards—and read—and wait—and remember."

"What do you wait for?"

"I don't know."

"And what do you remember?"

"Ah, that.—Shall I tell you what amuses me? Shall I tell you a secret?"

"Please don't, if it's anything that matters."

"It matters to nobody but me. Will you hear it?"

"If it does not implicate me in any way."

"It does not.—Well, I am a member of a certain old secret society—no, don't look at me, nothing frightening—only a society like the free-masons."

"And—?"

"And—well, as you know, one is initiated into certain so-called secrets and rites. My family has always been initiated. So I am an initiate too. Does it interest you?"

"Why, of course."

"Well—. I was always rather thrilled by these secrets. Or some of them. Some seemed to me farfetched. The ones that thrilled me even never had any relation to actual life. When you knew me in

Dresden and Prague, you would not have thought me a man invested with awful secret knowledge, now would you?"

"Never."

"No. It was just a little exciting side-show. And I was a grimacing little society man. But now they become true. It becomes true."

"The secret knowledge?"

"Yes."

"What, for instance?"

"Take actual fire.—It will bore you. Do you want to hear?"

"Go on."

"This is what I was taught. The true fire is invisible. Flame, and the red fire we see burning, has its back to us. It is running away from us.—Does that mean anything to you?"

"Yes."

"Well then, the yellowness of sunshine—light itself—that is only the glancing aside of the real original fire. You know that is true. There would be no light if there were no refraction, no bits of dust and stuff to turn the dark fire into visibility.—You know that's a fact.—And that being so, even the sun is dark. It is only his jacket of dust that makes him visible.—You know that too.—And the true sunbeams coming towards us flow darkly, a moving darkness of the genuine fire. The sun is dark, the sunshine flowing to us is dark. And light is only the inside-out of it all, the lining, and the yellow beams are only the turning away of the sun's directness that was coming to us.—Does that interest you at all?"

"Yes," she said dubiously.

"Well, we've got the world inside out. The true living world of fire is dark, throbbing, darker than blood. Our luminous world that we go by is only the white lining of this."

"Yes, I like that," she said.

"Well! Now listen. The same with love. This white love that we have is the same. It is only the reverse, the whited sepulchre of the true love. True love is dark, a throbbing together in darkness, like the wild-cat in the night, when the green screen opens and her eyes are on the darkness."

"No, I don't see that," she said, in a slow, clanging voice.

"You, and your beauty—that is only the inside-out of you. The real you is the wild-cat invisible in the night, with red fire perhaps coming out of its wide, dark eyes. Your beauty is your whited sepulchre."

"You mean cosmetics," she said. "I've used none at all today—not even powder."

He laughed.

"Very good," he said. "Consider me. I used to think myself small but handsome, and the ladies used to admire me moderately, never very much. A smart little fellow, you know. Well, that was just the inside-out of me. I am a black tom-cat howling in the night, and it is then that fire comes out of me. This me you look at is my whited sepulchre.—What do you say—?"

She was looking into his eyes. She could see the darkness swaying in the depths. She perceived the invisible, cat-like fire stirring deep inside them, felt it coming towards her. She turned her face aside. Then he laughed, showing his strong white teeth, that seemed a little too large, rather dreadful.

She rose to go.

"Well," she said. "I shall have the summer in which to think about the world inside out.—Do write if there is anything to say. Write to Thoresway.—Goodbye!"

"Ah your eyes!" he said. "They are like jewels of stone."

Being away from the Count, she put him out of her mind. Only she was sorry for him a prisoner in that sickening Voynich Hall. But she did not write. Nor did he.

As a matter of fact her mind was now much more occupied with her husband. All arrangements were being made to effect his exchange. From month to month she looked for his return. And so she thought of him.

Whatever happened to her, she thought about it, thought and thought a great deal. The consciousness of her mind was like tablets of stone weighing her down. And whoever would make a new entry into her must break these tablets of stone piece by piece. So it was that in her own way she thought often enough of the Count's world inside-out. A curious latency stirred in her consciousness, that was not yet an idea.

He said her eyes were like jewels of stone. What a horrid thing to say! What did he want her eyes to be like?—He wanted them to dilate and become all black pupil, like a cat's at night. She shrank convulsively from the thought, and tightened her breast.

He said her beauty was her whited sepulchre. Even that, she knew what he meant. The fluid invisibility of her, he wanted to love. But ah, her pearl-like beauty was so dear to her, and it was so famous in the world.

He said her white love was like moonshine, harmful, the reverse of love. He meant Basil, of course. Basil always said she was the moon. But then Basil loved her for that. The ecstasy of it! She shivered, thinking of her husband. But it had also made her nerve-worn, her husband's love. Ah, nerve-worn.

What then would the Count's love be like? Something so secret and different. She would not be lovely and a queen to him. He hated her loveliness. The wild cat has its mate. The little wildcat that he was. Ah—!

She caught her breath, determined not to think. When she thought of Count Dionys she felt the world slipping away from her. She would sit in front of a mirror, looking at her wonderfully cared-for face, that had appeared in so many society magazines. She loved it so, it made her feel so vain. And she looked at her blue-green eyes—the eyes of the wildcat on a bough. Yes, the lovely bluegreen iris drawn tight like a screen. Supposing it should relax. Supposing it should unfold, and open out the dark depths, the dark, dilated pupil! Supposing it should?

Never! She always caught herself back. She felt she might be killed, before she could give way to that relaxation that the Count wanted of her. She could not. She just could not. At the very thought of it some hypersensitive nerve started with a great twinge in her breast, she drew back, forced to keep her guard. Ah no, Monsieur le Comte, you shall never take her ladyship off her guard.

She disliked the thought of the Count. An impudent little fellow. An impertinent little fellow! A little madman, really. A little outsider.—No, no. She would think of her husband: an adorable, tall, well-bred Englishman, so easy and simple, and with the amused look in his blue eyes. She thought of the cultured, casual trail of his voice. It set her nerves on fire. She thought of his strong, easy body—beautiful, white-fleshed, with the fine sprinkling of warm-brown hair like tiny flames. *He* was the Dionysos, full of sap, milk and honey and northern golden wine: he, her husband. Not that little unreal Count.—Ah, she dreamed of her husband, of the love-days, and the honey-moon, the lovely, simple intimacy. Ah the marvellous revelation of that intimacy, when he left himself to her so generously. Ah, she was his wife for this reason, that he had given himself to her so greatly, so generously. Like an ear of corn he was there for her gathering—her husband, her own lovely English husband. Ah, when would he come again, when would he come again!

She had letters from him—and how he loved her. Far away, his life was all hers. All hers, flowing to her as the beam flows from a white star right down to us, to our heart. Her lover, her husband.

He was now expecting to come home soon. It had all been arranged. "I hope you won't be disappointed in me when I do get back," he wrote. "I am afraid I am no longer the plump and well-liking young man I was. I've got a big scar at the side of my mouth, and I'm as thin as a starved rabbit, and my hair's going grey. Doesn't sound attractive, does it? And it isn't attractive. But once I can get out of this infernal place, and once I can be with you again, I shall come in for my second blooming. The very thought of being quietly in the same house with you, quiet and in peace, makes me realise that if I've been through hell, I have known heaven on earth and can hope to know it again. I am a miserable brute to look at now. But I have faith in you. You will forgive me my appearance, and that alone will make me feel handsome—"

She read this letter many times. She was not afraid of his scar or his looks. She would love him all the more.

Since she had started making shirts—those two for the Count had been an enormous labour, even though her maid had come to her assistance forty times: but since she had started making shirts, she thought she might continue. She had some good suitable silk: her husband liked silk underwear.

But still she used the Count's thimble. It was gold outside and silver inside, and was too heavy. A snake was coiled round the base, and at the top, for pressing the needle, was inlet a semi-translucent apple-green stone, perhaps jade, carved like a scarab, with little dots. It was too heavy. But then she sewed so slowly. And she liked to feel her hand heavy, weighted. And as she sewed she thought about her husband, and she felt herself in love with him. She thought of him, how beautiful he was, and how she would love him now he was thin, she would love him all the more. She would love to trace his bones, as if to trace his living skeleton. The thought made her rest her hands in her lap, and drift into a muse. Then she felt the weight of the thimble on her finger, and took it off, and sat looking at the green stone. The ladybird. The ladybird. And if only her husband would come soon, soon. It was wanting him that had made her so ill. Nothing but that. She had wanted him so badly. She wanted him now. Ah, if she could go to him now, and find him, wherever he was, and see him and touch him and take all his love.

As she mused, she put the thimble down in front of her, took up a little silver pencil from her workbasket, and on a bit of blue paper that had been the band of a small skein of silk she wrote the lines of the silly little song:

> "Wenn ich ein Vöglein wär'
> Und auch zwei Flüglein hätt',
> Flög' ich zu dir—"

That was all she could get on her bit of paleblue paper.

> "If I were a little bird
> And had two little wings
> I'd fly to thee—"

Silly enough, in all conscience. But she did not translate it, so it did not seem quite so silly.

At that moment her maid announced Lady Bingham—her husband's sister. Daphne crumpled up the bit of paper in a flurry, and in another minute Primrose, his sister, came in. The newcomer was not a bit like a primrose, being long-faced and clever, smart, but not a bit elegant, in her new clothes.

"Daphne dear, what a domestic scene! I suppose it's rehearsal. Well, you may as well rehearse, he's with Admiral Burns on the Ariadne. Father just heard from the Admiralty: quite fit. He'll be here in a day or two.—Splendid, isn't it!—And the war is going to end. At least it seems like it. You'll be safe of your man now, dear. Thank heaven when it's all over. What are you sewing?"

"A shirt," said Daphne.

"A shirt! Why how clever of you. I should never know which end to begin. Who showed you?"

"Millicent."

"And how did *she* know? She's no business to know how to sew shirts: nor cushions nor sheets either. Do let me look.—Why how perfectly marvellous you are!—every bit by hand too. Bassie isn't worth it, dear, really he isn't. Let him order his shirts in Oxford Street. Your business is to be beautiful, not to sew shirts. What a dear little pin-poppet, or rather needle-woman! I say, a satire on us, that is. But what a darling, with mother of pearl wings to her skirts! And darling little gold-eyed needles inside her. You screw her head off, and you find she's full of pins and needles. Woman for you!—Mother says won't you come to lunch tomorrow. And won't you come to Brassey's to tea with me at this minute. Do, there's a dear—I've got a taxi—"

Daphne bundled her sewing loosely together.

When she tried to do a bit more, two days later, she could not find her thimble. She asked her maid, whom she could absolutely trust. The girl had not seen it. She searched everywhere. She asked her nurse—who was now her housekeeper and footman. No, nobody had seen it. Daphne even asked her sister-in-law.

"Thimble, darling? No, I don't remember a thimble. I remember a dear little needle lady, whom I thought such a precious satire on us women. I didn't notice a thimble."

Poor Daphne wandered about in a muse. She did not want to believe it lost. It had been like a talisman to her. She tried to forget it. Her husband was coming, quite soon, quite soon. But she could not raise herself to joy. She had lost her thimble. It was as if Count Dionys accused her in her sleep, of something, she did not quite know what.

And though she did not really want to go to Voynich Hall, yet like a fatality she went, like one doomed. It was already late autumn, and some lovely days. This was the last of the lovely days. She was told that Count Dionys was in the small park, finding chestnuts. She went to look for him. Yes there he was in his blue uniform stooping over the brilliant yellow leaves of the sweet chestnut tree, that lay around him like a fallen nimbus of glowing yellow, under his feet, as he kicked and rustled, looking for the chestnut burrs. And with his short brown hands he was pulling out the small chestnuts and putting them in his pockets. But as she approached he peeled a nut to eat it. His teeth were white and powerful.

"You remind me of a squirrel laying in a winter store," said she.

"Ah, Lady Daphne—I was thinking, and did not hear you."

"I thought you were gathering chestnuts—even eating them."

"Also!" he laughed. He had a dark, sudden charm when he laughed, showing his rather large white teeth. She was not quite sure whether she found him a little repulsive.

"Were you *really* thinking?" she said, in her slow, resonant way.

"Very truly."

"And weren't you enjoying the chestnut a bit?"

"Very much. Like sweet milk. Excellent, excellent—" he had the fragments of the nut between his teeth, and bit them freely. "Will you take one too—" He held out the little, pointed brown nuts on the palm of his hand.

She looked at them doubtfully.

"Are they as tough as they always were?" she said.

"No, they are fresh and good. Wait, I will peel one for you."

They strayed about through the thin clump of trees.

"You have had a pleasant summer?—you are strong?"

"Almost *quite* strong," said she. "Lovely summer, thanks. I suppose it's no good asking you if you have been happy?"

"Happy?—" He looked at her direct.—His eyes were black, and seemed to examine her. She always felt he had a little contempt of her. "Oh yes," he said, smiling. "I have been very happy."

"So glad."

They drifted a little further, and he picked up an apple-green chestnut burr out of the yellow-brown leaves, handling it with sensitive fingers that still suggested paws to her.

"How did you succeed in being happy?" she said.

"How shall I tell you? I felt that the same power which put up the mountains could pull them down again—no matter how long it took."

"And was that all?"

"Was it not enough?"

"I should say decidedly too little."

He laughed broadly, showing the strong, negroid teeth.

"You do not know all it means," he said.

"The thought that the mountains were going to be pulled down?" she said. "It will be so long after my day—"

"Ah, you are bored," he said. "But I—I found the God who pulls things down: especially the things that men have put up. Do they not say that life is a search after God, Lady Daphne? I have found my God."

"The God of destruction," she said, blanching.

"Yes—not the devil of destruction, but the god of destruction. The blessed God of destruction. It is strange—" he stood before her, looking up at her—"but I have found my God. The God of anger, who throws down the steeples and the factory chimneys. Ah Lady Daphne, he is a man's God, he is a man's God. I have found my God, Lady Daphne."

"Apparently. And how are you going to serve him?"

A naïve glow transfigured his face.

"Oh, I will help. With my heart I will help while I can do nothing with my hands. I say to my heart: Beat, hammer, beat with little strokes. Beat, hammer of God, beat them down. Beat it all down."

Her brows knitted, her face took on a look of discontent.

"Beat what down?" she asked harshly.

"The world, the world of man. Not the trees—these chestnuts for example—" he looked up at them, at the tufts and loose pinions of yellow—"not these—nor the chattering sorcerers, the squirrels— nor the hawk that comes. Not those."

"You mean beat England—?" she said.

"Ah no! Ah no! Not England any more than Germany—perhaps not as much. Not Europe any more than Asia."

"Just the end of the world?"

"No no. No no. What grudge have I against a world where little chestnuts are as sweet as these! Do you like yours? Will you take another?"

"No thanks."

"What grudge have I against a world where even the hedges are full of berries, bunches of black berries that hang down, and red berries that thrust up. Never would I hate the world. But the world of man. Lady Daphne—" his voice sank to a whisper. "*I hate it. Zzz!*" he hissed. "*Strike, little heart! Strike, strike, hit, smite!* Oh Lady Daphne!"—his eyes dilated with a ring of fire.

"What?" she said, scared.

"I believe in the power of my red, dark heart. God has put the hammer in my breast—the little eternal hammer. Hit—hit—hit! It hits on the world of man. It hits, it hits! And it hears the thin sound of cracking. The thin sound of cracking. Hark!"

He stood still and made her listen. It was late afternoon. The strange laugh of his face made the air seem dark to her. And she could easily have believed that she heard a faint fine shivering, cracking, through the air, a delicate crackling noise.

"You hear it? Yes?—Oh, may I live long! May I live long, so that my hammer may strike and strike, and the cracks go deeper, deeper! Ah, the world of man! Ah the joy, the passion in every heart-beat! Strike home, strike true, strike sure. Strike to destroy it. Strike! Strike! To destroy the world of man. Ah God."

He stood before her with his teeth set together, and his black eyes leaping thin flames upon her, like a little demon.

"Don't you think it is rather silly," she said, "to set your heart on destruction? There's been destruction enough, surely."

"Indiscriminate, ridiculous cannon. But the acute destruction hasn't begun yet. Wait, wait, till the steeples and tall chimneys all rock on the air like trees in a wind! Ah, *crash*! That is what my soul longs for. And God is with me. God is with me."

He seemed almost to dance on the grass beside her.

"I don't think so at all," she said. "I think you have just become perverse, nothing more."

"Wait," he said, "wait! Only wait. God is with me."

"They say the war is going to end. Do you think it is true?"

"Oh yes. Quite sure. This war is enough—it is finished."

"I wish I were as sure," she said, sighing.

"Be sure," he said.

"'We are not sure of sorrow, And joy was never sure'," she quoted. "Do you know Swinburne?—My husband is coming home. I expect him every day—any day—"

"Ah! That is very joyful for you."

"Yes, indeed," she said, in that tone of conviction which had so much sullenness underneath.

"Ah now," he said, "you can brush your hair, that is like underwater gold, and perfume the slack lily of your long white body, and rest your green eyes like green lotus flowers on water. Now you can sway before the mirrors, sick, sick with love of love, and longing to be loved. Ah now—"

"Why not—" she said, looking at him.

He looked back at her with dark, fiery contempt.

"Beat, beat on her, little heart, my heart," he said. "Beat on her and destroy her, then. It is time she fell to dust."

"But why?" she laughed.

"Ah well, you plucked lily! Ah well, loll in your fine jar of crystal. You plucked lily! You plucked lily. Already the scent of you is a half-dead lily."

"Why plucked?" she said, a little bitterly.

"Plucked lily! Plucked lily!" he repeated.

"Isn't that better than a silly hammer?" she said.

"But I, even I, I know you have a root. You, and your leaning white body, you are dying like a lily in a drawing-room, in a crystal jar. But shall I tell you of your root, away below and invisible? My hammer strikes fire, and your root opens its lily-scales and cries for the sparks of my fire, for my fire, for my fire, for your aching lily-root—Ah *you*, don't I know you? And am I not a prisoner. Prisoner of war. Ah God, prisoner of peace. Do I not know you, Lady Daphne? Do I not? Do I not?"

She was silent for some moments, looking away at the twinkling lights of a station beyond.

"Not the white plucked lily of your body. I have gathered no flower for my ostentatious life.—But in the colddark, your lily root, Lady Daphne. Ah yes, you will know it all your life, that I know where your root lies buried, with its sad, sad quick of life.—What does it matter!"

They had walked slowly towards the house. She was silent. Then at last she said, in a peculiar voice:

"And you would never want to kiss me?"

"Ah no!" he answered sharply.

She held out her hand.

"Good—bye, Count Dionys," she drawled, fashionably.

He bowed over her hand, but did not kiss it.

"Goodbye, Lady Daphne."

She went away, with her brow set hard. And henceforth she thought only of her husband, of Basil. She made the Count die out of her.—Basil was coming, he was near. He was coming back from the east, from war and death. Ah, he had been through awful fire of experience. He would be something new, something she did not know. He was something new, a stranger lover who had been through terrible fire, and had come out strange and new, like a god. Ah, new and terrible his love would be, pure and intensified by the awful fire of suffering. A new lover—a new bridegroom—a new, superhuman, wedding-night. She shivered in anticipation, waiting for her husband. She hardly noticed the wild excitement of the Armistice. She was waiting for something more wonderful to her.

And yet the moment she heard his voice on the telephone, her heart contracted with fear. It was his well-known voice, deliberate, diffident, almost drawling, with the same subtle suggestion of deference, and the rather exaggerated Cambridge intonation, up and down. But there was a difference: a new icy note that went through her veins like death.

"Is that you, Daphne? I shall be with you in half an hour. Is that all right for you? Yes, I've just landed, and shall come straight to you. Yes, a taxi. Shall I be too sudden for you, darling? No? Good, oh good! Half an hour, then!—I say Daphne?—There won't be anyone else there, will there? Quite alone! Good! I can ring up Dad afterwards.—Yes splendid, splendid. Sure you're all right, my darling? I'm at death's door till I see you.—Yes. Goodbye—half-an-hour. Goodbye."

When Daphne had hung up the receiver she sat down almost in a faint. What was it that so frightened her? His terrible, terrible cultured voice, like cold blue steel. She had no time to think. She rang for her maid.

"Oh, my lady, it isn't bad news?" cried Millicent when she caught sight of her mistress white as death.

"No, good news. Major Apsley will be here in half an hour. Help me to dress. Ring to Murry's first to send in some roses, red ones, and some lilac-coloured iris—two dozen of each, at once."

Daphne went to her room. She didn't know what to wear, she didn't know how she wanted her hair dressed. She spoke hastily to her maid. She chose a violet coloured dress. She did not know what she was doing. In the middle of dressing the flowers came, and she left off to put them in the bowls. So that when she heard his voice in the hall, she was still standing in front of the mirror reddening her lips and wiping it away again.

"Major Apsley, my lady!" murmured the maid, in excitement.

"Yes, I can hear. Go and tell him I shall be *one* minute."

Daphne's voice had become slow and sonorous, like bronze, as it always did when she was upset. Her face looked almost haggard, and in vain she dabbed with the rouge.

"How does he look?" she asked curtly when her maid came back.

"A long scar here—" said the maid, and she drew her finger from the left-hand corner of her mouth into her cheek, slanting downwards.

"Make him look very different?" asked Daphne.

"Not so *very* different, my lady," said Millicent, gently. "His eyes are the same, I think." The girl also was distressed.

"All right," said Daphne. She looked at herself a long last look as she turned away from the mirror. The sight of her own face made her feel almost sick. She had seen so much of herself. And yet even now she was fascinated by the heavy droop of her lilac-veined lids over her slow, strange, large, green-blue eyes. They *were* mysterious-looking. And she gave herself a long, sideways glance, curious and Chinese. How was it possible there was a touch of the Chinese in her face?—she so purely an English blonde, an Aphrodite of the foam, as Basil had called her in poetry. Ah well!—She left off her thoughts and went through the hall to the drawing room.

He was standing nervously in the middle of the room, in his uniform. She hardly glanced at his face—and saw only the scar.

"Hullo Daphne—" he said, in a voice full of the expected emotion. He stepped forward and took her in his arms, and kissed her forehead.

"So glad! So glad it's happened at last," she said, hiding her tears.

"So glad what has happened, darling?" he asked, in his deliberate manner.

"That you're back." Her voice had the bronze resonance, she spoke rather fast.

"Yes, I'm back, Daphne darling—as much of me as there is to bring back."

"Why?" she said. "You've come back whole, surely?" She was frightened.

"Yes, apparently I have. Apparently. But don't let's talk of that. Let's talk of you, darling. How are you? Let me look at you. You are thinner, you are older—But you are more wonderful than ever. Far more wonderful."

"How?" said she.

"I can't exactly say how. You were only a girl. Now you are a woman. I suppose it's all that's happened. But you are wonderful as a woman, Daphne darling—more wonderful than all that's happened. I couldn't have believed you'd be so wonderful. I'd forgotten—or else I'd never known. I say, I'm a lucky chap really. Here I am, alive and well, and I've got you for a wife.—It's brought you out like a flower.—I say, darling, there is more now than Venus of the foam—grander. How beautiful you are! But you look like the beauty of all life—as if you were moon-mother of the world—Aphrodite.— God is good to me after all, darling. I ought never to utter a single complaint.—How lovely you are—how lovely you are, my darling! I'd forgotten you—and I thought I knew you so well—Is it true, that you belong to me? Are you really mine?"

They were seated on the yellow sofa. He was holding her hand, and his eyes were going up and down, from her face to her throat and her breast. The sound of his words, and the strong, cold desire in his voice excited her, pleased her, and made her heart freeze. She turned and looked into his lightblue eyes. They had no longer the amused light, nor the young look. They burned with a hard, focussed light, whitish.

"It's all right. You *are* mine, aren't you, Daphne darling?" came his cultured, musical voice, that had always the well-bred twang of diffidence.

She looked back into his eyes.

"Yes, I am yours," she said, from the lips.

"Darling! Darling!" he murmured, kissing her hand.

Her heart beat suddenly so terribly, as if her breast would be ruptured, and she rose in one movement and went across the room. She leaned her hand on the mantel-piece and looked down at the electric fire. She could hear the faint, faint noise of it. There was silence for a few moments.

Then she turned and looked at him. He was watching her intently. His face was gaunt, and there was a curious deathly sub-pallor, though his cheeks were not white. The scar ran livid from the side of his mouth. It was not so very big. But it seemed like a scar in him himself, in his brain as it were. In his eyes was that hard, white, focussed light that fascinated her and was terrible to her. He *was* different. He was like death: like risen death. She felt she dared not touch him. White death was still upon him. She could tell that he shrank with a kind of agony from contact. "Touch me not, I am not yet ascended unto the Father."—Yet for contact he had come. Something, someone seemed to be looking over his shoulder. His own young ghost looking over his shoulder. Oh god! She closed her eyes, seeming to swoon. He remained leaning forward on the sofa, watching her.

"Aren't you well, darling?" he asked. There was a strange, incomprehensible coldness in his very fire. He did not move to come near her.

"Yes, I'm well. It is only that after all it is so sudden. Let me get used to—you," she said, turning aside her face from him. She felt utterly like a victim of his white, awful face.

"I suppose I must be a bit of a shock to you," he said. "I hope you won't leave off loving me. It won't be that, will it?"

The strange coldness in his voice! And yet the white, uncanny fire.

"No, I shan't leave off loving you," she admitted, in a low tone, as if almost ashamed. She *dared* not have said otherwise. And the saying it made it true.

"Ah, if you're sure of that—," he said. "I'm a rather unlovely sight to behold, I know, with this wound-scar. But if you can forgive it me, darling—. Do you think you can?" There was something like compulsion in his tone.

She looked at him, and shivered slightly.

"I love you—more than before," she said hurriedly.

"Even the scar?"—came his terrible voice, inquiring.

She glanced again, with that slow, Chinese side-look, and felt she would die.

"Yes," she said, looking away at nothingness. It was an awful moment to her. A little, slightly imbecile smile widened on her face.

He suddenly knelt at her feet, and kissed the toe of her slipper, and kissed the instep, and kissed the ankle in the thin black stocking.

"I knew," he said in a muffled voice. "I knew you would make good. I knew if I had to kneel, it was before you. I knew you were divine, you were the one—Cybele—Isis. I knew I was your slave. I knew. It has all been just a long initiation. I had to learn how to worship you."

He kissed her feet again and again, without the slightest self-consciousness, or the slightest misgiving. Then he went back to the sofa, and sat there looking at her, saying:

"It isn't love, it is worship. Love between me and you will be a sacrament, Daphne. *That's* what I had to learn. You are beyond me. A mystery to me. My God, how great it all is. How marvellous!"

She stood with her hand on the mantel-piece, looking down and not answering. She was frightened—almost horrified:—but she was thrilled deep down to her soul. She really felt she could glow white and fill the universe like the moon, like Astarte, like Isis, like Venus. The grandeur of her own pale power. The man religiously worshipped her, not merely amorously. She was ready for him—for the sacrament of his supreme worship.

He sat on the sofa with his hands spread on the yellow brocade and pushing downwards behind him, down between the deep upholstery of the back and the seat. He had long, white hands with pale freckles. And his fingers touched something. With his long white fingers he groped and brought it out. It was the lost thimble. And inside it was the bit of screwed-up blue paper.

"I say, is that *your* thimble?" he asked, delighted.

She started, and went hurriedly forward for it.

"Where was it?" she said, agitated.

But he did not give it to her. He turned it round and pulled out the bit of blue paper. He saw the faint pencil marks on the screwed-up ball, and unrolled the band of paper, and slowly deciphered the verse.

> "Wenn ich ein Vöglein wär'
> Und auch zwei Flüglein hätt',
> Flög' ich zu dir—"

"How awfully touching that is," he said. "A Vöglein with two little Flüglein! But what a precious darling child you are!—Whom did you want to fly to, if you were a Vöglein?" He looked up at her with a curious smile.

"I can't remember," she said, turning aside her head.

"I hope it was to me," he said. "Anyhow I shall consider it was, and shall love you all the more for it. What a darling child!—a Vöglein if you please, with two little wings! Why how beautifully absurd of you, darling!"

He folded the scrap of paper carefully, and put it in his pocket-book, keeping the thimble all the time between his knees.

"Tell me when you lost it, Daphne," he said, examining the bauble.

"About a month ago—or two months."

"About a month ago—or two months—And what were you sewing?—Do you mind if I ask? I like to think of you then. I was still in that beastly El Hasrun. What were you sewing, darling, two months ago, when you lost your thimble?"

"A shirt."

"I say, a shirt! Whose shirt?"

"Yours."

"There. Now we've run it to earth. Were you really sewing a shirt for me! Is it finished? Can I put it on at this minute?"

"That one isn't finished, but the first one is."

"I say, darling—let me go and put it on. To think I should have it next my skin! I shall feel you all round me, all over me. I say how marvellous that will be! Won't you come?"

"Won't you give me the thimble?" she said.

"Yes, of course. What a noble thimble it is, too! Who gave it you?"

"Count Dionys Psanek."

"Who was he?"

"A Bohemian Count, in Dresden. He once stayed with us in Thoresway—with a tall wife. Didn't you meet them?"

"I don't think I did. I think I did. I don't remember. What was he like?"

"A little man with black hair and a rather low dark forehead—rather dressy."

"No, I don't remember him at all.—So he gave it you.—Well, I wonder where he is now?—Probably rotted, poor devil."

"No, he's interned in Voynich Hall. Mother and I have been to see him several times. He was awfully badly wounded."

"Poor little beggar! In Voynich Hall! I'll look at him before he goes. Odd thing, to give you a thimble. Odd gift! You were a girl then, though. Do you think he had it made, or do you think he found it in a shop?"

"I think it belonged to the family. The ladybird at the top is part of their crest—and the snake as well, I think."

"A ladybird! Funny thing for a crest. The Americans would call it a bug. I must look at him before he goes.—And you were sewing a shirt for me! And then you posted me this little letter into the sofa. Well, I'm jolly glad I received it, and that it didn't go astray in the post, like so many things. 'Wenn ich ein Vöglein wär''—you perfect child! But that is the beauty of a woman like you: you are so superb and beyond worship, and then such an exquisite naïve child. Who could help worshipping you and loving you: immortal and mortal together.—What, you want the thimble? Here!—Wonderful, wonderful white fingers. Ah darling, you are more goddess than child, you long, limber Isis with sacred hands. White, white, and immortal! Don't tell me your hands could die, darling: your wonderful Proserpine fingers. They are immortal as February and snowdrops. If you lift your hand the spring comes.—I *can't* help kneeling before you, darling. I am no more than a sacrifice to you, an offering. I *wish* I could die in giving myself to you, give you all my blood on your altar, for ever."

She looked at him with a long slow look, as he turned his face up to her. His face was white with ecstasy. And she was not afraid. Somewhere, saturnine, she knew it was absurd. But she chose not to know. A certain swoon-sleep was on her. With her slow, green-blue eyes she looked down on his ecstasised face, almost benign. But in her right hand unconsciously she held the thimble fast, she only gave him her left hand. He took her hand and rose to his feet in that curious priestly ecstasy which made him more than a man or a soldier, far, far more than a lover to her.

Nevertheless his homecoming made her begin to be ill again. Afterwards, after his love, she had to bear herself in torment. To her shame and her heaviness, she knew she was not strong enough, or pure enough, to bear this awful outpouring adoration-lust. It was not her fault she felt weak and fretful afterwards, as if she wanted to cry and be fretful and petulant, wanted someone to save her. She could not turn to Basil, her husband. After his ecstasy of adoration-lust for her, she recoiled from him. Alas, she was not the goddess, the superb person he named her. She was flawed with the fatal humility of her age. She could not harden her heart and burn her soul pure of this humility, this misgiving. She could not *finally* believe in her own woman-godhead—only in her own female mortality.

That fierce power of continuing alone, even with your lover, the fierce power of the woman in excelsis—alas, she could not keep it. She could rise to the height for the time, the incandescent, transcendent, moon-fierce womanhood. But alas, she could not stay intensified and resplendent in her white, womanly powers, her female mystery. She relaxed, she lost her glory, and became fretful. Fretful and ill and never to be soothed. And then naturally her man became ashy and somewhat acrid, while she ached with nerves, and could not eat.

Of course she began to dream about Count Dionys: to yearn wistfully for him. And it was absolutely a fatal thought to her, that he was going away. When she thought that, that he was leaving England soon—going away into the dark for ever—then the last spark seemed to die in her. She felt her soul perish, whilst she herself was worn and soulless like a prostitute. A prostitute goddess. And her husband, the gaunt, white, intensified priest of her, who never ceased from being before her, like a lust.

"Tomorrow," she said to him, gathering her last courage and looking at him with a side look, "I want to go to Voynich Hall."

"What, to see Count Psanek? Oh good! Yes, very good! I'll come along as well. I should like very much to see him. I suppose he'll be getting sent off back before long."

It was a fortnight before Christmas, very dark weather. Her husband was in khaki. She wore black furs, and a black lace veil over her face, so that she seemed mysterious. But she lifted the veil and looped it behind, so that it made a frame for her face. She looked very lovely like that—her face pure like the most white hellebore flower, touched with winter pink, amid the blackness of her drapery and furs. Only she was rather too much like the picture of a modern beauty: too much the actual thing. She had half an idea that Dionys would hate her for her effective loveliness. He would see it and hate it. The thought was like a bitter balm to her. For herself, she loved her loveliness almost with obsession.

The Count came cautiously forward, glancing from the lovely

figure of Lady Daphne to the gaunt, well-bred Major at her side. Daphne was so beautiful in her dark furs, the black lace of her veil thrown back over her close-fitting, dull-gold-threaded hat, and her face fair like a winter flower in a cranny of darkness. But on her face, that was smiling with a slow self-satisfaction of beauty and of knowledge that she was dangling the two men, and setting all the imprisoned officers wildly on the alert, the Count could read that acrid dissatisfaction and insufficiency. And he looked away to the livid scar on the Major's face.

"Count Dionys, I wanted to bring my husband to see you. May I introduce him to you. Major Apsley—Count Dionys Psanek."

The two men shook hands, rather stiffly.

"I can sympathise with you being fastened up in this place," said Basil in his slow, easy fashion. "I hated it, I assure you, out there in the east."

"But your conditions were much worse than mine," smiled the Count.

"Well perhaps they were. But prison is prison, even if it were heaven itself."

"Lady Apsley has been the one angel of my heaven," smiled the Count.

"I'm afraid I was as inefficient as most angels," said she.

The small smile never left the Count's dark face. It was true as she said, he was low-browed, the black hair growing low on his brow, and his eyebrows making a thick bow above his dark eyes, which had again long black lashes. So that the upper part of his face seemed very dusky-black. His nose was small and somewhat translucent. There was a touch of mockery about him, which was intensified even by his small, energetic stature. He was still carefully dressed in the dark-blue uniform, whose shabbiness could not hinder the dark flame of life which seemed to glow through the cloth from his body. He was not thin—but still had a curious swarthy translucency of skin in his low-browed face.

"What would you have been more?" he laughed, making equivocal dark eyes at her.

"Oh, of course, a delivering angel—a cinema heroine," she replied, closing her eyes and turning her face aside.

All the while the whitefaced, tall Major watched the little man with a fixed, half-smiling scrutiny. The foreigner seemed not to notice. He turned to the Englishman.

"I am glad that I can congratulate you, Major Apsley, on your safe and happy return to your home."

"Thanks. I hope I may be able to congratulate you in the same way before long."

"Oh yes," said the Count. "Before long I shall be shipped back."

"Have you any news of your family?" interrupted Daphne.

"No news," he replied briefly, with sudden gravity.

"It seems you'll find a fairish mess out in Austria," said Basil.

"Yes probably. It is what we had to expect," replied the Count.

"Well, I don't know. Sometimes things do turn out for the best.—I feel that's as good as true in my case," said the Major.

"Things have turned out for the best?" said the Count, with an intonation of polite enquiry.

"Yes. Just for me personally, I mean—to put it quite selfishly. After all, what we've learned is that a man can only speak for himself. And I feel it's been dreadful, but it's not been lost. It was an ordeal one had to go through," said Basil.

"You mean the war?"

"The war and everything that went with it."

"And when you've been through the ordeal?" politely inquired the Count.

"Why, you arrive at a higher state of consciousness, and therefore of life. And so, of course, at a higher plane of love. A surprisingly higher plane of love, that you had never suspected the existence of, before."

The Count looked from Basil to Daphne—who was posing her head a little self-consciously.

"Then indeed the war has been a valuable thing," he said.

"Exactly!" cried Basil. "I am another man."

"And Lady Apsley?" queried the Count.

"Oh—" her husband faced round to her—"she is *absolutely* another woman—and *much* more wonderful, more marvellous."

The Count smiled and bowed slightly.

"When we knew her ten years ago, we should have said then that it was impossible," said he, "for her to be more wonderful."

"Oh quite!" returned the husband. "It always seems impossible. And the impossible is always happening.—As a matter of fact, I think the war has opened another cycle of life to us—a wider ring."

"It may be so," said the Count.

"You don't feel it so yourself?" The major looked with his keen, white attention into the dark, low-browed face of the other man. The Count looked smiling at Daphne.

"I am only a prisoner still, Major, therefore I feel my ring quite small."

"Yes of course you do. Of course.—Well, I do hope you won't be a prisoner much longer. You must be dying to get back into your own country."

"I shall be glad to be free. Also," he smiled, "I shall miss my prison and my visits from the angels."

Even Daphne could not be sure whether he was mocking her. It was evident the visit was unpleasant to him. She could see he did not like Basil. Nay more, she could feel that the presence of her tall, gaunt, idealistic husband was hateful to the little swarthy man. But he passed it all off in smiles and polite speeches.

On the other hand, Basil was as if fascinated by the Count. He watched him absorbedly all the time, quite forgetting Daphne. She knew this. She knew that she was quite gone out of her husband's consciousness, like a lamp that has been carried away into another room. There he stood completely in the dark, as far as she was concerned, and all his attention focussed on the other man. On his pale, gaunt face was a fixed smile of amused attention.

"But don't you get awfully bored?" he said—"between the visits?"

The Count looked up with an affectation of frankness.

"No, I do not," he said. "I can brood, you see, on the things that come to pass."

"I think that's where the harm comes in," replied the Major. "One sits and broods, and is cut off from everything, and one loses one's contact with reality. That's the effect it had on me, being a prisoner."

"Contact with reality—what is that?"

"Well—contact with anybody, really—or anything—"

"Why must one have contact?"

"Well, because one must," said Basil.

The Count smiled slowly.

"But I can sit and watch fate flowing, like black water, deep down in my own soul," he said. "I feel that there, in the dark of my own soul, things are happening."

"That may be. But whatever happens, it is only one thing, really. It is a contact between your own soul and the soul of one other being, or of many other beings. Nothing else can happen to man.—That's how I figured it out for myself. I may be wrong. But that's how I figured it out, when I was wounded and a prisoner."

The Count's face had gone dark and serious.

"But is this contact an aim in itself?" he asked.

"Well," said the Major—he had taken his degree in philosophy—"it seems to me it is. It results inevitably in some form of activity. But the cause and the origin and the life-impetus of all action, activity, whether constructive or destructive, seems to me to lie in the dynamic contact between human beings. You bring to pass a certain dynamic contact between men, and you get war. Another sort of dynamic contact, and you get them all building a cathedral, as they did in the Middle Ages—"

"But was not the war, or the cathedral, the real aim, and the emotional contact just the means?" said the Count.

"I don't think so," said the Major, his curious white passion beginning to glow through his face. The three were seated in a little card-room, left alone by courtesy of the other men. Daphne was still draped in her dark, too-becoming drapery. But alas, she sat now ignored by both men. She might just as well have been an ugly little nobody, for all the notice that was taken of her. She sat in the window-seat of the dreary small room with a look of discontent on her exotic, rare face, that was like a delicate white and pink hot-house flower. From time to time she glanced with long, slow looks from man to man: from her husband, whose pallid, intense, white glowing face was pressed forward across the table; to the Count, who sat back in his chair, as if in opposition, and whose dark face seemed clubbed together in a dark, unwilling stare. Her husband was *quite* unaware of anything but his own white intensity. But the Count still had a grain of secondary consciousness which hovered round and remained aware of the woman in the window-seat. The whole of his face, and his forward-looking attention was concentrated on Basil. But somewhere at the back of him he kept track of Daphne. She sat uneasy, in discontent, as women always do sit when men are consumed together in a combustion of words. At the same time, she followed the argument. It was curious that, while her sympathy at this moment was with the Count, it was her husband whose words she believed to be true. The contact, the emotional contact was the real thing, the so-called "aim" was only a by-product. Even wars and cathedrals, in her mind, were only by-products. The real thing was what the warriors and cathedral-builders had had in common, as a great uniting feeling: the thing they felt for one another: and for their women in particular, of course.

"There are a great many kinds of contact, nevertheless," said Dionys.

"Well, do you know," said the Major, "it seems to me there is really only one supreme contact, the contact of love. Mind you, the love may take on an infinite variety of forms. And in my opinion, no form of love is wrong, so long as it is love, and you yourself *honour* what you are doing. Love has an extraordinary variety of forms! And that is all that there is in life, it seems to me.—But I grant you, if you deny the *variety* of love you deny love altogether. If you try to specialise love into one set of accepted feelings, you wound the very soul of love. Love *must* be multiform, else it is just tyranny, just death."

"But why call it all *love?*" said the Count.

"Because it seems to me it *is* love: the great power that draws human beings together, no matter what the result of the contact may be.—Of course there is hate, but hate is only the recoil of love."

"Do you think the old Egypt was established on love?" asked Dionys.

"Why of course! And perhaps the most multiform, the most comprehensive love that the world has seen. All that we suffer from now is that our way of love is narrow, exclusive, and therefore not love at all; more like death and tyranny."

The Count slowly shook his head, smiling slowly and as if sadly.

"No," he said. "No. It is no good. You must use another word than love."

"I don't agree at all," said Basil.

"What word then?" blurted Daphne.

The Count looked at her.

"How shall I say? I know no word. But to a man something is absolute. His will, his good-will is absolute to him. Beyond the interference of any other creature." He looked with his obstinate dark eyes into her eyes. It was curious, she disliked his words intensely, but she liked him. On the other hand, she believed absolutely what her husband said, yet her physical sympathy was against him.

"Do you agree, Daphne?" asked Basil.

"Not a bit," she replied, with a heavy look at her husband.

"Nor I," said Basil. "It seems to me, if you love, you abandon your will, give it up to the soul of love. If you mean your will is the will to love, I quite agree. But if you mean that your will, your god-will, is purely autocratic—I don't agree, and never shall. It seems to me just there where we have gone wrong. Kaiser Wilhelm II wanted power—"

"No no," said the Count. "He was a mountebank. He had no conception of the sacredness of power."

"He proved himself very dangerous."

"Oh yes. But peace can be even more dangerous still."

"Tell me, then. Do you believe that you, as an aristocrat, should have feudal power over a few hundreds of other men, who happen to be born serfs, or not aristocrats?"

"Not as a hereditary aristocrat, but as a *man* who is by nature an aristocrat," said the Count, "it is my sacred duty to hold the destiny of other men in my hands, and to shape the issue.—But I can never fulfil that duty till men willingly put their lives in my hands."

"You don't expect them to, do you?" smiled Basil.

"At this moment, no."

"Or at any moment!" The Major was sarcastic.

"At a certain moment the men who are really living will come beseeching to put their lives into the hands of the greater men among them, beseeching the greater men to take the sacred responsibility of power."

"Do you think so?—Perhaps you mean men will at last begin to choose leaders whom they still *love*," said Basil. "I wish they would."

"No, I mean that they will at last yield themselves before men who are greater than they: become vassals, by choice."

"Vassals!" exclaimed Basil, smiling. "You are still in the feudal ages, Count."

"Vassals. Not to any hereditary aristocrat—Hohenzollern or Hapsburg or Psanek," smiled the Count. "But to the man whose soul is born able, able to be alone, to choose and to command. At last the masses will come to such men and say 'You are greater than we. Be our lords. Take our life and our death in your hands, and dispose of us according to your will. Because we see a light in your face, and a burning on your mouth.'"

The Major smiled for many moments, really piqued and amused, watching the Count, who did not turn a hair.

"I say, you must be awfully naïve, Count, if you believe the modern masses are ever going to behave like that.—I assure you, they never will."

"If they did," said the Count, "would you call it a new reign of love, or something else?"

"Well of course, it would contain an element of love. There would have to be an element of love in their feeling for their leaders."

"Do you think so? I thought that love assumed an equality in difference. I thought that love gave to every man the right to judge the acts of other men—'*This was not an act of love, therefore it was wrong.*' Does not democracy, and love, give to every man that right?"

"Certainly," said Basil.

"Ah, but my chosen aristocrat would say to those who choose him: 'If you choose me, you give up forever your right to judge me. If you have truly chosen to follow me, you have thereby rejected all your right to criticise me. You can no longer either approve or disapprove of me. You have performed the sacred act of choice. Henceforth you can only obey.'"

"They wouldn't be able to help criticising, for all that," said Daphne, blurting in her say.

He looked at her slowly, and for the first time in her life she was doubtful of what she was saying.

"The day of Judas," he said, "ends with the day of love."

Basil woke up from a sort of trance.

"I think of course, Count," he said, "that it's an awfully amusing idea. A retrogression slap back to the dark ages."

"Not so," said the Count. "Men—the mass of men—were never before free to perform the sacred act of choice. Today—soon—they may be free—"

"Oh I don't know. Many tribes chose their kings and chiefs."

"Men have never before been quite free to choose: and to know what they are doing—"

"You mean they've only made themselves free in order voluntarily to saddle themselves with new lords and masters?"

"I do mean that."

"In short, life is just a vicious circle—"

"Not at all. An ever-widening circle, as you say. Always more wonderful."

"Well, it's all frightfully interesting and amusing—don't you think so Daphne?—By the way, Count, where would women be? Would they be allowed to criticise their husbands?"

"Only before marriage," smiled the Count. "Not after."

"Splendid!" said Basil. "I'm all for that bit of your scheme, Count. I hope you're listening, Daphne."

"Oh yes. But then I've only married *you*. I've got my right to criticise all the other men," she said, in a dull, angry voice.

"Exactly. Clever of you! So the Count won't get off!—Well now, what do you think of the Count's aristocratic scheme for the future, Daphne? Do you approve?"

"Not at all. But then little men have always wanted power," she said, cruelly.

"Oh, big men as well, for that matter," said Basil, conciliatory.

"I have been told before," smiled the Count; "little men are always bossy.—I am afraid I have offended Lady Daphne?"

"No," she said. "Not really. I'm amused, really. But I always dislike any suggestion of bullying."

"Indeed, so do I," said he.

"The Count didn't mean bullying, Daphne," said Basil. "Come, there is really an allowable distinction between responsible power and bullying."

"When men put their heads together about it," said she.

She was haughty and angry, as if she were afraid of losing something. The Count smiled mischievously at her.

"You are offended, Lady Daphne! But why? You are safe from any spark of my dangerous and extensive authority."

Basil burst into a roar of laughter.

"It *is* rather funny, you to be talking of power and of not being criticised," he said. "But I would like to hear more: I would like to hear more."

As they drove home, he said to his wife:

"You know I like that little man. He's a quaint little bantam. And he sets one thinking."

Lady Daphne froze to four degrees below zero, under the north-wind of this statement, and not another word was to be thawed out of her.

Curiously enough, it was now Basil who was attracted by the Count, and Daphne who was repelled. Not that she was so bound up in her husband. Not at all. She was feeling rather sore against men altogether. But as so often happens, in this life based on the wicked triangle, Basil could not follow his enthusiasm for the Count save in his wife's presence. When the two men were alone together, they were awkward, resistant, they could hardly get out a dozen words to one another. When Daphne was there, however, to complete the circuit of the opposing current, things went like a house on fire.

This, however, was not much consolation to Lady Daphne. Merely to sit as a passive medium between two men who are squibbing philosophical nonsense to one another: no, it was not good enough! She almost hated the Count: low-browed little man, belonging to the race of prehistoric slaves. But her grudge against her white-faced, spiritually intense husband was sharp as vinegar. Let down: she was let down between the pair of them.

What next? Well, what followed was entirely Basil's fault. The winter was passing: it was obvious the war was really over, that Germany was finished. The Hohenzollern had fizzled out like a very poor squib, the Hapsburg was popping feebly in obscurity, the Romanov was smudged out without a sputter. So much for imperial royalty. Henceforth democratic peace.

The Count, of course, would be shipped back now like returned goods that had no market any more. There was a world peace ahead. A week or two, and Voynich Hall would be empty.

Basil, however, could not let matters follow their simple course. He was intrigued by the Count. He wanted to entertain him as a guest before he went. And Major Apsley could get anything in reason, at this moment. So he obtained permission for the poor little Count to stay a fortnight at Thoresway, before being shipped back to Austria. Earl Beveridge, whose soul was black as ink since the war, would never have allowed the little alien enemy to enter his house, had it not been for the hatred which had been roused in him, during the last two years, by the degrading spectacle of the so-called patriots who had been howling their mongrel indecency in the public face. These mongrels had held the press and the British public in abeyance for almost two years. Their one aim was to degrade and humiliate anything that was proud or dignified remaining in England. It was almost the worst nightmare of all, this coming to the top of a lot of public filth which was determined to suffocate the souls of all dignified men.

Hence, the Earl, who never intended to be swamped by unclean scum, whatever else happened to him, stamped his heels in the ground and stood on his own feet. When Basil said to him, would he allow the Count to have a fortnight's decent peace in Thoresway before all was finished, Lord Beveridge gave a slow consent, scandal or no scandal. Indeed, it was really to defy scandal that he took such a step. For the thought of his dead boys was bitter to him: and the thought of England fallen under the paws of smelly mongrels was bitterer still.

Lord Beveridge was at Thoresway to receive the Count, who arrived escorted by Basil. The English Earl was a big, handsome man, rather heavy, with a dark, sombre face that would have been haughty if haughtiness had not been made so ridiculous. He was a passionate man, with a passionate man's sensitiveness, generosity, and instinctive overbearing. But *his* dark passionate nature, and his violent sensitiveness had been subjected now to fifty-five years subtle repression, condemnation, repudiation, till he had almost come to believe in his own wrongness. His little, frail wife, all love for humanity, she was the genuine article. Himself, he was labelled selfish, sensual, cruel—etc. etc. So by now he always seemed to be standing aside, in the shadow, letting himself be obliterated by the pallid rabble of the democratic hurry. That was the impression he gave, of a man standing back, half ashamed, half haughty, semi-hidden in the dark background.

He was a little on the defensive as Basil came in with the Count.

"Ah—how do you do, Count Psanek!" he said, striding largely forward and holding out his hand. Because he was the father of Daphne, the Count felt a certain tenderness for the taciturn Englishman.

"You do me too much honour, my lord, receiving me in your house," said the small Count proudly.

The Earl looked at him slowly, without speaking: seemed to look down on him, in every sense of the word.

"We are still men, Count. We are not beasts altogether."

"You wish to say that my countrymen are so very nearly beasts, Lord Beveridge?" smiled the Count, curling his fine nose.

Again the Earl was slow in replying.

"You have a low opinion of my manners, Count Psanek."

"But perhaps a just appreciation of your meaning, Lord Beveridge," smiled the Count, with the reckless little look of contempt on his nose.

Lord Beveridge flushed dark, with all his native anger offended.

"I am glad Count Psanek makes my own meaning clear to me," he said.

"I beg your pardon a thousand times, Sir, if I give offense in doing so," replied the Count.

The Earl went black, and felt a fool. He turned his back on the Count. And then he turned round again, offering his cigar-case:

"Will you smoke?" he said. There was kindness in his tone.

"Thank you," said the Count, taking a cigar.

"I dare say," said Lord Beveridge, "that all men are beasts in some way. I am afraid I have fallen into the common habit of speaking by rote, and not what I really mean. Won't you take a seat?"

"It is only as a prisoner that I have learned that I am *not* truly a beast. No, I am myself. I am not a beast," said the Count, seating himself.

The Earl eyed him curiously.

"Well," he said, smiling, "I suppose it is best to come to a decision about it."

"It is necessary, if one is to be safe from vulgarity."

The Earl felt a twinge of accusation. With his agate-brown, hard looking eyes he watched the black-browed little Count.

"You are probably right," he said.

But he turned his face aside.

They were five people at dinner—Lady Beveridge was there as hostess.

"Ah Count Dionys," she said with a sigh, "do you really feel that the war is over?"

"Oh yes," he replied quickly. "*This* war is over. The armies will go home. *Their* cannon will not sound any more. Never again like this."

"Ah, I hope so," she sighed.

"I am sure," he said.

"You think there'll be no more war?" said Daphne.

For some reason she had made herself very fine, in her newest dress of silver and black and pink-chenille, with bare shoulders and her hair fashionably done. The Count in his shabby uniform turned to her. She was nervous, hurried. Her slim white arm was near him, with the bit of silver at the shoulder. Her skin was white like a hothouse flower. Her lips moved hurriedly.

"Such a war as this there will never be again," he said.

"What makes you so sure?" she replied, glancing into his eyes.

"The machine of war has got out of our control. We shall never start it again, till it has fallen to pieces. We shall be afraid."

"Will everybody be afraid?" said she, looking down and pressing back her chin.

"I think so."

"We will hope so," said Lady Beveridge.

"Do you mind if I ask you, Count," said Basil, "what you feel about the way the war has ended? The way it has ended for *you*, I mean."

"You mean that Germany and Austria have lost the war? It was bound to be. We have all lost the war. All Europe."

"I agree there," said Lord Beveridge.

"We've all lost the war—?" said Daphne, turning to look at him. There was pain on his dark, low-browed face. He suffered having the sensitive woman beside him. Her skin had a hot-house delicacy that made his head go round. Her shoulders were broad, rather thin, but the skin was white and so sensitive, so hot-house delicate. It affected him like the perfume of some white, exotic flower. And she seemed to be sending her heart towards him. It was as if she wanted to press her breast to his. From the breast she loved him, and sent out love to him. And it made him unhappy, he wanted to be quiet, and to keep his honour before these hosts.

He looked into her eyes, his own eyes dark with knowledge and pain. She, in her silence and her brief words seemed to be holding them all under her spell. She seemed to have cast a certain muteness on the table, in the midst of which she remained silently master, leaning forward to her plate, and silently mastering them all.

"Don't I think we've all lost the war?" he replied, in answer to her question. "It was a war of suicide. Nobody could win it. It was suicide for all of us."

"Oh I don't know," she replied. "What about America and Japan?"

"They don't count. They only helped *us* to commit suicide. They did not enter, vitally."

There was such a look of pain on his face, and such a sound of pain in his voice, that the other three closed their ears, shut off from attending. Only Daphne was making him speak. It was she who was drawing the soul out of him, trying to read the future in him as the augurs read the future in the quivering entrails of the sacrificed beast.

She looked direct into his face, searching his soul.

"You think Europe has committed suicide?" she said.

"Morally."

"Only morally?" came her slow, bronze-like words, so fatal.

"That is enough," he smiled.

"Quite," she said, with a slow droop of her eyelids. Then she turned away her face. But he felt the heart strangling inside his breast. What was she doing now? What was she thinking? She filled him with uncertainty and with uncanny fear.

"At least," said Basil, "those infernal guns are quiet."

"For ever," said Dionys.

"I wish I could believe you, Count," said the Major.

The talk became more general—or more personal. Lady Beveridge asked Dionys about his wife and family. He knew nothing save that they had gone to Hungary in 1916, when his own house was burnt down. His wife might even have gone to Bulgaria with Prince Bogorik. He did not know.

"But your children, Count!" cried Lady Beveridge.

"I do not know. Probably in Hungary, with their grandmother. I will go when I get back."

"But have you never *written?*—never enquired?"

"I could not write. I shall know soon enough—everything."

"You have no son?"

"No. Two girls."

"Poor things!"

"Yes."

"I say, isn't it an odd thing to have a ladybird on your crest?" asked Basil, to cheer up the conversation.

"Why queer? Charlemagne had bees. And it is a Marienkäfer—a Mary-beetle. The beetle of Our Lady. I think it is quite a heraldic insect, Major," smiled the Count.

"You're proud of it?" said Daphne, suddenly turning to look at him again, with her slow, pregnant look.

"I am, you know. It has such a long genealogy—our spotted beetle. Much longer than the Psaneks. I think, you know, it is a descendant of the Egyptian scarabeus, which is a very mysterious emblem. So I connect myself with the Pharaohs: just through my ladybird."

"You feel your ladybird has crept through so many ages," she said.

"Imagine it!" he laughed.

"The scarab *is* a piquant insect," said Basil.

"Do you know Fabre?" put in Lord Beveridge. "He suggests that the beetle rolling a little ball of dung before him, in a dry old field, must have suggested to the Egyptians the First Principle that set the globe rolling. And so the scarab became the symbol of the creative principle—or something like that."

"That the earth is a tiny ball of dry dung is good," said Basil.

"Between the claws of a ladybird," added Daphne.

"That is what it is, to go back to one's origins," said Lady Beveridge.

"Perhaps they meant that it was the principle of decomposition which first set the ball rolling," said the Count.

"The ball would have to be *there* first," said Basil.

"Certainly. But it hadn't started to roll. Then the principle of decomposition started it." The Count smiled as if it were a joke.

"I am no Egyptologist," said Lady Beveridge, "so I can't judge."

The Earl and Countess Beveridge left next day. Count Dionys was left with the two young people in the house. It was a beautiful Elizabethan mansion, not very large, but with those magical rooms that are all a twinkle of small-paned windows, looking out from the dark panelled interior. The interior was cosy, panelled to the ceiling, and the ceiling moulded and touched with gold. And then the great square bow of the window with its little panes intervening like magic between oneself and the world outside, the crest in stained glass crowing its colour, the broad window-seat cushioned in faded green. Dionys wandered round the house like a little ghost, through the succession of small and large, twinkling sitting-rooms and lounge rooms in front, down the long wide corridor with the wide stair-head at each end, and up the narrow stairs to the bedrooms above, and on to the roof.

It was early spring, and he loved to sit on the leaded, pale-grey roof that had its queer seats and slopes, a little pale world in itself. Then to look down over the garden and the sloping lawn to the ponds massed round with trees, and away to the elms and furrows and hedges of the shires. On the left of the house was the farm-stead, with ricks and great-roofed barns and dark-red cattle. Away to the right, beyond the park, was a village among trees, and the spark of a grey church-spire.

He liked to be alone, feeling his soul heavy with its own fate. He would sit for hours watching the elm-trees standing in rows like giants, like warriors across the country. The Earl had told him that the Romans brought these elms to Britain. And he seemed to see the spirit of the Romans in them still. Sitting there alone in the spring sunshine, in the solitude of the roof, he saw the glamour of this England of hedgerows and elm-trees, and the laborers with slow horses slowly drilling the seed, crossing the brown furrow: and the roofs of the village, with the church-steeple rising beside a big black yew-tree: and the chequer of fields away to the distance.

And the charm of the old manor around him, the garden with its grey stone walls and yew hedges—broad, broad yew hedges—and a peacock pausing to glitter and scream in the busy silence of an English spring, when celandines open their yellow under the hedges, and violets are in the secret, and by the broad paths of the garden polyanthus and crocuses vary the velvet and flame, and bits of yellow wall-flower shake raggedly, with a wonderful triumphance, out of the cracks of the wall. There was a fold somewhere near, and he could hear the treble bleat of the growing lambs, and the deeper, contented baa-ing of the ewes.

This was Daphne's home, where she had been born. She loved it with an ache of affection. But now it was hard to forget her dead brothers. She wandered about in the sun, with two old dogs paddling after her. She talked with everybody, gardener, groom, stableman, with the farm-hands. That filled a large part of her life—straying round talking with the work-people. They were of course respectful to her—but not at all afraid of her. They knew she was poor, that she could not afford a car or anything. So they talked to her very freely: perhaps a little too freely. Yet she let it be. It was her one passion at Thoresway, to hear the dependants talk and talk—about everything. The curious feeling of intimacy across a breach fascinated her. Their lives fascinated her: what they thought, what they *felt*.—There, what they felt. That fascinated her. There was a gamekeeper she could have loved—an impudent, ruddy-faced, laughing, ingratiating fellow; she could have loved him, if she had not been isolated beyond the breach of her birth, her culture, her consciousness. Her *consciousness* seemed to make a great gulf between her and the lower classes, the unconscious classes. She accepted it as her doom. She could never meet in real contact anyone but a super-conscious, finished being like herself: or like her husband: or her brothers. Her father had some of the unconscious dark blood-warmth of primitive people. But he was like a man who is damned. And the Count, of course. The Count had something that was hot and invisible, a dark flame of life that might warm the cold white fire of her own blood. But—.

They avoided each other. All three, they avoided one another. Basil too went off alone. Or he immersed himself in poetry. Sometimes he and the Count played billiards. Sometimes all three walked in the park. Often Basil and Daphne walked to the village, to post. But truly, they avoided one another, all three. The days slipped by.

At evening they sat together in the small west-room, that had books and a piano and comfortable shabby furniture of faded rose-coloured tapestry: a shabby room. Sometimes Basil read aloud. Sometimes the Count played the piano. And they talked. And Daphne stitch by stitch went on with a big embroidered bed-spread, which she might finish if she lived long enough. But they always went to bed early. They were really always avoiding one another.

Dionys had a bedroom in the east bay—a long way from the rooms of the others. He had a habit, when he was quite alone, of singing, or rather crooning to himself the old songs of his childhood. It was only when he felt he was quite alone: when other people seemed to fade out of him, and all the world seemed to dissolve into darkness, and there was nothing but himself, his own soul, alive in the middle of his own small night, isolate for ever. Then, half unconscious, he would croon in a small, high-pitched, squeezed voice, a sort of high dream-voice, the songs of his childhood dialect. It was a curious noise: the sound of a man who is alone in his own blood: almost the sound of a man who is going to be executed.

Daphne heard the sound one night when she was going down-stairs again with the corridor lantern, to find a book. She was a bad sleeper, and her nights were a torture to her. She too, like a neurotic, was nailed inside her own fretful self-consciousness. But she had a very keen ear. So she started as she heard the small, bat-like sound of the Count's singing to himself. She stood in the midst of the wide corridor, that was wide as a room, carpeted with a faded lavender coloured carpet, with a piece of massive dark furniture at intervals by the wall, and an oak arm-chair, and sometimes a faded, reddish oriental rug. The big horn lantern which stood at nights at the end of the corridor she held in her hand. The intense "peeping" sound of the Count, like a witchcraft, made her forget everything. She could not understand a word, of course. She could not understand the noise even. After listening for a long time, she went on downstairs. When she came back again he was still, and the light was gone from under his door.

After this, it became almost an obsession to her, to listen for him. She waited with fretful impatience for ten o'clock, when she could retire. She waited more fretfully still, for her maid to leave her, and for her husband to come and say goodnight. Basil had the room across the corridor. And then in resentful impatience she waited for the sounds of the house to become still. Then she opened her door to listen.

And far away, as if from far, far away in the unseen, like a ventriloquist sound or a bat's uncanny peeping, came the frail, almost inaudible sound of the Count's singing to himself before he went to bed. It *was* inaudible to anyone but herself. But she, by concentration, seemed to hear supernaturally. She had a low arm-chair by the door, and there, wrapped in a huge old black silk shawl, she sat and listened. At first she could not hear. That is, she could hear the sound. But it was only a sound. And then, gradually, gradually she began to follow the thread of it. It was like a thread which she followed out of the world: out of the world. And as she went, slowly, by degrees, far, far away, down the thin thread of his singing, she knew peace—she knew forgetfulness. She could pass beyond the world, away beyond where her soul balanced like a bird on wings, and was perfected.

So it was, in her upper spirit. But underneath was a wild, wild yearning, actually to go, actually to be given. Actually to go, actually to die the death, actually to cross the border and be gone, to be gone. To be gone from this her self, from this Daphne, to be gone from father and mother, brothers and husband and home and land and world: to be gone. To be gone to the call from the beyond: the call. It was the Count calling. He was calling her. She was sure he was calling her. Out of herself, out of her world, he was calling her.

Two nights she sat just inside her room, by the open door, and listened. Then when he finished she went to sleep, a queer, light, bewitched sleep. In the day she was bewitched. She felt strange and light, as if pressure had been removed from around her. Some pressure had been clamped round her all her life. She had never realised it till now, now it was removed, and her feet felt so light, and her breathing delicate and exquisite. There had always been a pressure against her breathing. Now she breathed delicate and exquisite, so that it was a delight to breathe. Life came in exquisite breaths, quickly, as if it delighted to come to her.

The third night he was silent—though she waited and waited till the small hours of the morning. He was silent, he did not sing. And then she knew the terror and blackness of the feeling that he might never sing any more. She waited like one doomed, throughout the day. And when the night came she trembled. It was her greatest nervous terror, lest the spell should be broken, and she should be thrown back to what she was before.

Night came, and the kind of swoon upon her. Yes, and the call from the night. The call! She rose helplessly and hurried down the corridor. The light was under his door. She sat down in the big oak armchair that stood near his door, and huddled herself tight in her black shawl. The corridor was dim with the big, star-studded, yellow lantern-light. Away down she could see the lamp light in her doorway; she had left her door ajar.

But she saw nothing. Only she wrapped herself close in the black shawl, and listened to the sound from the room. It called. Oh it called her! Why could she not go? Why could she not cross through the closed door?

Then the noise ceased. And then the light went out, under the door of his room. Must she go back? Must she go back? Oh impossible. As impossible as that the moon should go back on her tracks, once she has risen. Daphne sat on, wrapped in her black shawl. If it must be so, she would sit on through eternity. Return she never would.

And then began the most terrible song of all. It began with a rather dreary, slow, horrible sound, like death. And then suddenly came a real call—fluty, and a kind of whistling and a strange whirr at the changes, most imperative, and utterly inhuman. Daphne rose to her feet. And at the same moment up rose the whistling throb of a summons out of the death moan.

Daphne tapped low and rapidly at the door. "Count! Count!" she whispered. The sound inside ceased. The door suddenly opened. The pale, obscure figure of Dionys.

"Lady Daphne!" he said in astonishment, automatically standing aside.

"You called," she murmured rapidly, and she passed intent into his room.

"No, I did not call," he said gently, his hand on the door still.

"Shut the door," she said abruptly.

He did as he was bid. The room was in complete darkness. There was no moon outside. She could not see him.

"Where can I sit down?" she said abruptly.

"I will take you to the couch," he said, putting out his hand and touching her in the dark. She shuddered.

She found the couch and sat down. It was quite dark.

"What were you singing?" she said rapidly.

"I am so sorry. I did not think anyone could hear."

"What was it you were singing?"

"A song of my country."

"Had it any words?"

"Yes, it is a woman who was a swan, and who loved a hunter by the marsh. So she became a woman and married him and had three children. Then in the night one night the king of the swans called to her to come back, or else he would die. So slowly she turned into a swan again, and slowly she opened her wide, wide wings, and left her husband and her children."

There was silence in the dark room. The Count had been really startled, startled out of his mood of the song into the day-mood of human convention. He was distressed and embarrassed by Daphne's presence in his dark room. She, however, sat on and did not make a sound. He too sat down in a chair by the window. It was everywhere dark. A wind was blowing in gusts outside. He could see nothing inside his room: only the faint, faint strip of light under the door. But he could feel her presence in the darkness. It was uncanny, to feel her near in the dark, and not to see any sign of her, nor to hear any sound.

She had been wounded in her bewitched state, by the contact with the everyday human being in him. But now she began to relapse into her spell, as she sat there in the dark. And he too, in the silence, felt the world sinking away from him once more, leaving him once more alone on a darkened earth, with nothing between him and the infinite dark space. Except now her presence. Darkness answering to darkness, and deep answering to deep. An answer, near to him, and invisible.

But he did not know what to do. He sat still and silent as she was still and silent. The darkness inside the room seemed alive like blood. He had no power to move. The distance between them seemed absolute.

Then suddenly, without knowing, he went across in the dark, feeling for the end of the couch. And he sat beside her on the couch. But he did not touch her. Neither did she move. The darkness flowed about them thick like blood, and time seemed dissolved in it. They sat with the small, invisible distance between them, motionless, speechless, thoughtless.

Then suddenly he felt her fingertips touch his arm, and a flame
went over him that left him no more a man. He was something seated
in flame, in flame unconscious, seated erect, like an Egyptian
king-god in the statues. Her finger-tips slid down him, and she
herself slid down in a strange silent rush, and he felt her face against
his closed feet and ankles, her hands pressing his ankles. He felt her
brow and hair against his ankles, her face against his feet, and there
she clung in the dark, as if in space below him. He still sat erect and
motionless. Then he bent forward and put his hand on her hair.

"Do you come to me?" he murmured. "Do you come to me?"

The flame that enveloped him seemed to sway him silently.

"Do you really come to me?" he repeated. "But we have nowhere
to go."

He felt his bare feet wet with her tears. Two things were
struggling in him, the sense of eternal solitude, like space, and the
rush of dark flame that would throw him out of his solitude, towards
her.

He was thinking too. He was thinking of the future. He had no
future in the world: of that he was conscious. He had no future in
this life. Even if he lived on, it would only be a kind of enduring.—
But he felt that in the afterlife the inheritance was his. He felt the
afterlife belonged to him.

Future in the world he could not give her. Life in the world he had
not to offer her. Better go on alone. Surely better go on alone.

But then the tears on his feet: and her face that would watch him
as he left her! No no.—The next life was his. He was master of the
afterlife. Why fear for this life? Why not take the soul she offered
him? Now and forever, for the life that would come when they both
were dead. Take her into the underworld. Take her in to the dark
Hades with him, like Francesca and Paolo. And in hell hold her
fast, queen of the underworld, himself master of the underworld.
Master of the life to come. Father of the soul that would come after.

"Listen," he said to her softly. "Now you are mine. In the dark
you are mine. And when you die you are mine. But in the day you are
not mine, because I have no power in the day. In the night, in the
dark, and in death, you are mine. And that is forever. No matter if I
must leave you. I shall come again from time to time. In the dark you
are mine. But in the day I cannot claim you. I have no power in the
day, and no place. So remember. When the darkness comes, I shall
always be in the darkness of you. And as long as I live, from time to

time I shall come to find you, when I am able to, when I am not a prisoner. But I shall have to go away soon. So don't forget—you are the night-wife of the ladybird, while you live and even when you die."

Later, when he took her back to her room, he saw her door still ajar.

"You shouldn't leave a light in your room," he murmured.

In the morning there was a curious remote look about him. He was quieter than ever, and seemed very far away. Daphne slept late. She had a strange feeling as if she had slipped off all her cares. She did not care, she did not grieve, she did not fret any more. All that had left her. She felt she could sleep, sleep, sleep—for ever. Her face too was very still, with a delicate look of virginity that she had never had before. She had always been Aphrodite, the self-conscious one. And her eyes, the green-blue, had been like slow, living jewels, resistant. Now they had unfolded from the hard flower-bud, and had the wonder, and the stillness of a quiet night.

Basil noticed it at once.

"You're different, Daphne," he said. "What are you thinking about?"

"I wasn't thinking," she said, looking at him with candour.

"What were you doing then?"

"What does one do when one doesn't think? Don't make me puzzle it out, Basil."

"Not a bit of it, if you don't want to."

But he was puzzled by her. The sting of his ecstatic love for her seemed to have left him. Yet he did not know what else to do but to make love to her. She went very pale. She submitted to him, bowing her head because she was his wife. But she looked at him with fear, with sorrow, with real suffering. He could feel the heaving of her breast, and knew she was weeping. But there were no tears on her face, she was only death-pale. Her eyes were shut.

"Are you in pain?" he asked her.

"No. No!" She opened her eyes, afraid lest she had disturbed him. She did not want to disturb him.

He was puzzled. His own ecstatic, deadly love for her had received a check. He was out of the reckoning.

He watched her when she was with the Count. Then she seemed so meek—so maidenly—so different from what he had known of her. She was so still, like a virgin girl. And it was this quiet, intact quality of virginity in her which puzzled him most, puzzled his emotions and his ideas. He became suddenly ashamed to make love to her. And because he was ashamed, he said to her as he stood in her room that night:

"Daphne, are you in love with the Count?"

He was standing by the dressing-table, uneasy. She was seated in a low chair by the tiny dying wood fire. She looked up at him with wide, slow eyes. Without a word, with wide, soft, dilated eyes she watched him. What was it that made him feel all confused? He turned his face aside, away from her wide, soft eyes.

"Pardon me dear. I didn't intend to ask such a question. Don't take any notice of it," he said. And he strode away and picked up a book. She lowered her head and gazed abstractedly into the fire, without a sound. Then he looked at her again, at her bright hair that the maid had plaited for the night. Her plait hung down over her soft pinkish wrap. His heart softened to her as he saw her sitting thus. She seemed like his sister. The excitement of desire had left him, and now he seemed to see clear and feel true for the first time in his life. She was like a dear, dear sister to him. He felt that she was his blood-sister, nearer to him than he had imagined any woman could be. So near—so dear—and all the sex and the desire gone. He didn't want it—he hadn't wanted it. This new pure feeling was so much more wonderful.

He went to her side.

"Forgive me, darling," he said, "for having questioned you."

She looked up at him with the wide eyes, without a word. His face was good and beautiful. Tears came to her eyes.

"You have the right to question me," she said sadly.

"No," he said. "No darling. I have no right to question you.— Daphne! Daphne darling! It shall be as *you* wish, between us. Shall it? Shall it be as you wish?"

"You are the husband, Basil," she said sadly.

"Yes darling. But—" he went on his knees beside her—"perhaps darling—something has changed in us. I feel as if I ought never to touch you again—as if I never *wanted* to touch you—in that way—I feel it was wrong, darling. Tell me what you think."

"Basil—don't be angry with me."

"It isn't anger—it's pure love, darling—it is."

"Let us not come any nearer to one another than this, Basil— physically—shall we?" she said. "And don't be angry with me, will you?"

"Why," he said. "I think myself the sexual part has been a mistake. I had rather love you—as I love you now. I *know* that this is true love. The other was always a bit whipped up. I *know* I love you now, darling: now I'm free from that other.—But what if it comes upon me, that other, Daphne?"

"I am always your wife," she said quietly. "I am always your wife. I want always to obey you, Basil: what you wish."

"Give me your hand, dear."

She gave him her hand. But the look in her eyes at the same time warned him and frightened him. He kissed her hand and left her.

It was to the Count she belonged. This had decided itself in her down to the depths of her soul. If she could not marry him and be his wife in the world, it had nevertheless happened to her for ever. She could no more question it. Question had gone out of her.

Strange how different she had become—a strange new quiescence. The last days were slipping past. He would be going away—Dionys: he with the still, remote face, the man she belonged to in the dark and in the light, for ever. He would be going away. He said it must be so. And she acquiesced. The grief was deep, deep inside her. He must go away. Their lives could not be one life, in this world's day. Even in her anguish she knew it was so. She knew he was right. He was for her infallible. He spoke the deepest soul in her.

She never *saw* him, as a lover. When she saw him, he was the little officer, a prisoner, quiet, claiming nothing in all the world. And when she went to him as his lover, his wife, it was always dark. She only knew his voice and his contact in darkness. "My wife in darkness," he said to her. And in this too she believed him. She would not have contradicted him, no, not for anything on earth: lest, contradicting him she should lose the dark treasure of stillness and bliss which she kept in her breast even when her heart was wrung with the agony of knowing he must go.

No, she had found this wonderful thing after she had heard him singing: she had suddenly collapsed away from her old self, into this darkness, this peace, this quiescence that was like a full dark river flowing eternally in her soul. She had gone to sleep from the *nuit blanche* of her days. And Basil, wonderful, had changed almost at once. She feared him, lest he might change back again. She would always have him to fear. But deep inside her she only feared for this love of hers for the Count: this dark, everlasting love that was like a full river flowing forever inside her. Ah, let that not be broken.

219

She was so still inside her. She could sit so still, and feel the day slowly, richly changing to night. And she wanted nothing, she was short of nothing. If only Dionys need not go away! If only he need not go away!

But he said to her, the last morning:

"Don't forget me. Always remember me. I leave my soul in your hands and your womb. Nothing can ever separate us, unless we betray one another. If you have to give yourself to your husband, do so, and obey him. If you are true to me, innerly, innerly true, he will not hurt us. He is generous, be generous to him. And never fail to believe in me. Because even on the other side of death I shall be watching for you. I shall be king in Hades when I am dead. And you will be at my side. You will never leave me any more, in the afterdeath. So don't be afraid in life. Don't be afraid. If you have to cry tears, cry them. But in your heart of hearts know that I shall come again, and that I have taken you for ever. And so, in your heart of hearts be still, be still, since you are the wife of the ladybird." He laughed as he left her, with his own beautiful, fearless laugh. But they were strange eyes that looked after him.

He went in the car with Basil back to Voynich Hall.

"I believe Daphne will miss you," said Basil.

The Count did not reply for some moments.

"Well, if she does," he said, "there will be no bitterness in it."

"Are you sure?" smiled Basil.

"Why—if we are sure of anything," smiled the Count.

"She's changed, isn't she?"

"Is she?"

"Yes, she's quite changed since you came, Count."

"She does not seem to me so very different from the girl of seventeen, whom I knew."

"No—perhaps not. I didn't know her then. But she's very different from the wife I have known."

"A regrettable difference—?"

"Well—no, not as far as she goes. She is much quieter inside herself. You know, Count, something of me died in the war. I feel it will take me an eternity to sit and think about it all."

"I hope you may think it out to your satisfaction, Major."

"Yes—I hope so too. But that is how it has left me—feeling as if I needed eternity now to brood about it all, you know. Without the need to act—or even to love, really. I suppose love is action."

"Intense action," said the Count.

"Quite so. I know really how I feel. I only ask of life to spare me from further effort of action of any sort—even love. And then to fulfil myself, brooding through eternity. Of course I don't mind *work*, mechanical action. That in itself is a form of inaction."

"A man can only be happy following his own inmost need," said the Count.

"Exactly!" said Basil. "I will lay down the law for nobody, not even for myself. And live my day—"

"Then you will be happy in your own way. I find it so difficult to keep from laying the law down for myself," said the Count. "Only the thought of death and the after life saves me from doing it any more."

"As the thought of eternity helps me," said Basil. "I suppose it amounts to the same thing."

Appendix

THE ENDING OF THE FIRST VERSION OF 'THE FOX'

In the morning, however, she only remembered it as a distant memory. She arose and was busy preparing the house and attending to the fowls. Their guest came downstairs in his shirt-sleeves. He was young and fresh, but he walked with his head thrust forward, so that his shoulders seemed raised and rounded, as if he had a slight curvature of the spine. It must have been only a manner of bearing himself, for he was young and vigorous. He washed himself and went outside, whilst the women were preparing breakfast.

He saw everything, and examined everything. His curiosity was quick and insatiable. He compared the state of things with that which he remembered before, and cast over in his mind the effect of the changes. He watched the fowls and the ducks, to see their condition, he noticed the flight of wood-pigeons overhead: they were very numerous; he saw the few apples high up, which March had not been able to reach; he remarked that they had borrowed a draw-pump, presumably to empty the big soft-water cistern which was on the north side of the house.

"It's a funny, dilapidated little place," he said to the girls, as he sat at breakfast.

His eyes were wide and childish, with thinking about things. He did not say much, but ate largely. March kept her face averted. She, too, in the early morning, could not be aware of him, though something about the glint of his khaki reminded her of the brilliance of her dream-fox.

During the day the girls went about their business. In the morning, he attended to the guns, shot a rabbit and a wild duck that was flying high, towards the woods. In the afternoon, he went to the village. He came back at tea-time. He had the same alert, forward-reaching look on his roundish face. He hung his hat on a peg with a little swinging gesture. He was thinking about something.

"Well," he said to the girls, as he sat at table. "What am I going to do?"

"What do you mean, what are you going to do?" said Banford.

"Where am I going to stay?" he said.

"I don't know," said Banford. "Where do you think of staying?"

"Well—" he hesitated—"I should like to stay here, if you could do .with me, and if you'd charge me the same as they would at the Swan.—That's what I should *like*—"

He put the matter to them. He was rather confused. March sat, with her elbows on the table, her two hands supporting her chin, looking at him unconsciously. Suddenly he lifted his clouded blue eyes, and instantaneously looked straight into March's eyes. He was startled as well as she. He too recoiled a little. March felt the same knowing, domineering spark leap out of his eyes and take possession of her psyche. She shut her eyes.

"Well, I don't know—" Banford was saying. She seemed reluctant, as if she were afraid of being imposed upon. She looked at March. But, with her weak, troubled sight, she only saw the usual semi-abstraction on her friend's face. "Why don't you speak, Nellie?" she said.

But March was wide-eyed and silent, and the youth, as if fascinated, was watching her without moving his eyes.

"Go on—answer something," said Banford. And March turned her head slightly aside, as if coming to consciousness, or trying to come to consciousness.

"What do you expect me to say?" she asked automatically.

"Say what you think," said Banford.

"It's all the same to me," said March.

And again there was silence. A pointed light seemed to be on the boy's eyes, penetrating like a needle.

"So it is to me," said Banford.

But he had dropped his head, and was oblivious of what she was saying.

"Well, I suppose you can please yourself, Henry," Banford concluded.

Still he did not reply, but lifting his head, with a strange, cunning look, watched March, only watched her. She sat with face slightly averted, and mouth suffering, quite dim in her consciousness. Banford became a little puzzled. Even she perceived the steady concentration of the youth's eyes, their fixed, knowing, unabashed attention, as he looked at March, whose mouth quivered a little, not with tears—indescribably.

"Cut a bit more bread, Nellie," said Banford uneasily.

And March automatically reached for the knife. The boy dropped his head again, so that they only saw its shapely round dome.

One or two days went by, and the boy stayed on. Banford was quite charmed by him. He was so soft and courteous in speech, not wanting to say much himself, preferring to hear what she had to say, and to laugh in his quick, half mocking way. He helped a little with the work—but not too much. He loved to be out alone with the gun in his hands, to watch, to see. For his sharp-eyed, impersonal curiosity was insatiable, and he was most free when he was quite alone, half-hidden, watching.

Particularly he watched March. She was a strange character to him. Her figure, like a graceful young man's, piqued him. Her dark eyes made something rise in his soul, with a curious elate triumph, when he looked into them, a triumph he was afraid to let be seen, it was so keen and secret. And then her odd, shrewd speech made him laugh outright. He felt he must go further, he was inevitably impelled.—But he put away the thought of her, and went off towards the wood's edge with the gun.

The dusk was falling as he came home, and with the dusk, a fine, late-November rain. He saw the fire-light leaping in the window of the sitting-room, a leaping light in the little cluster of dark buildings. And suddenly, he wanted to stay here permanently, to have this place for his own. And then the thought entered him like a bullet: why not marry March? He stood still in the middle of the field for some moments, the dead rabbit hanging still in his hand, arrested by this thought. His mind opened in amazement—then his soul gave an odd little laugh, and something in him began to burn. He wanted to marry her. Even a sense of ridicule hardly affected him. Secretly, he was keen, subtly and secretly keen, to have her.

He scarcely thought of his intention openly to himself. Yet in his mind he began to scheme, to scheme endlessly: what it would be like; what she would probably say to him: could he stay on the farm when he had got his ticket. He would like to be on a little place of his own, to do as he liked. For all things, he hated most a master. The quick scheming of his mind soon resolved itself. The sense of ridicule was the strongest deterrent: there was something ridiculous in the idea, to him. And he was very much afraid that she might reject him. But when he thought of the actual proposal something beat up with keen and secret desire in him. He knew he could *make* her obey his will. And again he burned.

He went about just the same for two more days. Only it was evident he had something on his mind. But his nature was secretive, it would be impossible to speak to him, or even to surmise about him. He seemed to draw a cloak of invisibleness about him.—At the end of the second day however he determined to speak. The great nerves in his thighs and at the base of his spine seemed to burn like live wire.

He had been sawing logs for the fire, in the afternoon. Darkness came very early: it was still a cold, raw mist. It was getting almost too dark to see. A pile of short sawed logs lay beside the trestle. March came to carry them indoors, or into the shed, as he was busy sawing the last log. He was working in his shirt sleeves, and did not notice her approach. She came unwilling, as if shy. He saw her stooping to the bright-ended logs, and he stopped sawing. A fire like lightning flew down his legs, in the nerves.

"March?" he said, in his quiet young voice.

She looked up from the logs she was piling.

"Yes?" she said.

He looked down on her in the dusk. He could see her not too distinctly.

"I wanted to ask you something," he said.

"Did you? What was it?" she said.

"Why—" his voice seemed to draw out soft and subtle, it penetrated her nerves—"why, what do you think it is?"

She stood up, placed her hands on her hips, and stood looking at him transfixed, without answering. Again he burned with a sudden power.

"Well," he said, and his voice was so soft it seemed rather like a subtle touch, like the merest touch of a cat's paw, a feeling rather than a sound. "Well—I wanted to ask you to marry me."

March felt him rather than heard him. She was trying in vain to turn aside her face. A great relaxation seemed to have come over her. She stood silent, her head slightly on on side. He seemed to be bending towards her, invisibly smiling. It seemed to her fine sparks came out of him.

Then very suddenly, she said:

"What do you mean? I'm old enough to be your mother."

"I know how old you are," came his soft voice, as it were imperceptibly stroking her. "You're thirty-three—and I'm nearly twenty-one. That's not old enough to be my mother.—I knew you'd say that.—What difference does it make?"

She could hardly attend to the words, the sound of his voice had such effect on her, taking away all her power, loosing her into a strange relaxation. She struggled somewhere for her own power. But she knew she was lost—lost—lost. The word seemed to rock in her as if in a narcotic dream. Suddenly again she spoke.

"You don't know what you're talking about," she said, in a brief and transient stroke of scorn.

"Ha!—don't I? Don't I though! Yes I do. Yes I do," he said softly, as if he produced his voice in her blood. "Yes I do know what I'm talking about. I ask you to marry me, because—I want you—you see—"

The swoon passed over her as he slowly concluded. She felt she had been born too late, and must give up. She could not help herself—she gave up in a deathly darkness, through which his voice came, resonant in her as if she were its medium:

"I want you—you see—that's why—" he proceeded, soft and slow. He had achieved his work. Her eyelids were dropped, her face half-averted and unconscious. She was in his power. He stepped forward and put his arm around her.

"Say then," he said. "Say then you'll marry me. Say—say?"

He was softly insistent.

"What?" she asked, faint, from a distance, like one in pain.

His voice was now unthinkably near and soft.

"Say yes."

"Yes—yes," she murmured slowly, half articulate, as if semi-conscious, and as if in pain, like one who dies.

He held her, and he seemed to glisten above her. He was so young—and so old. This also seemed to occupy her consciousness: he was so young—and so old—so old. She was in his power.

He did not kiss or caress her. Suddenly he pressed her hard, and brought her to herself.

"We'll carry in these logs," he said. "We'd better tell Banford."

Without knowing, she obeyed him.

It was he who told Banford.

"Well," he said. "What do you think?" And his face glistened like a were-wolf at poor Banford. He had that power for strangely smiling without altering a muscle of his face, exultantly, domineeringly smiling.

"What?" said Banford.

"March and I are going to get married."

"Don't be so silly," said Banford.

"No silliness. It's quite right—isn't it March?"

And March, with her wide, dark, lost eyes, and her inscrutable pale face, glanced at him and answered "Yes."

Banford was utterly overcome. Her eyes nearly fell out of her head. She laughed, and she was angry. But the boy sat there in his shirt-sleeves, like a man, and both women were at his mercy. All the time there was this indescribable shining on his face, a sort of whitish gleam, which Banford could have vouched for, and which repelled her. But he made her discuss all arrangements with him. They decided the marriage should take place by special licence, in a few days time.

Somewhere, Banford now disliked him intensely, almost mystically. But she did what he wanted. She was quite helpless. And the sight of the wide-eyed, lost March angered her and almost broke her heart. But she was powerless as if enmeshed in fine electric cobwebs.

He was very jaunty in his silence as he took all the necessary measures, very jaunty and self-satisfied, very cocky in his quiet way. The women were at his mercy. He did not make love to March. He did not even want to be with her very much. He almost kept her at a distance. But he held her completely, none the less.

One day she said to him, as they happened to be busy together.

"You remind me so much of the fox." She put aside her strands of hair mistily. His face turned suddenly on her, with its gleam.

"Which fox?" he said, laughing.

"The one that fetched the fowls."

"Do I remind you of *that?*" he said, laughing strangely, and putting his hand on her arm. She almost winced. But she watched him fixedly. "Do you think I've come for your fowls?" he continued, still laughing invisibly. He put his hand behind her neck and drew her head towards him. He kissed her for the first time, on the mouth. Then he laughed aloud. "Well," he said, "tomorrow we shall be married."

And on the morrow they were married, although to Banford it seemed utterly impossible. Yet it was so. And he seemed so cocky, in his quiet, secret way. And Banford was so curiously powerless against him, and March was so curiously happy. This also angered Banford. She could not bear to see the secret, half-dreamy, half knowing look of happiness on March's face. It seemed wicked.

March seemed to her to have a secret wickedness, gentle, receptive wickedness, like a dream.

In March the dream-consciousness now predominated. She lived in another world, the world of the fox. When she dreamed, the fox and the boy were somehow indistinguishable. And all through the day, she lived in his world, the world of the fox and the boy, or the fox and the old man, she never knew which. Her ready superficial consciousness carried her through the world's business all right. But people said she was odd. And she talked so little to her husband.

He had to go away in ten days time after the marriage. She suffered when he was gone, and he suffered in going. But he went in the inevitable decision to come back, and his decisions fulfilled themselves almost like fate, unnoticeably. He would come home by instinct.

Explanatory Notes

7:5 **beast** Not a misprint but a regional plural.

8:7 **puttees** These thin strips of coarse cloth, wound upwards in a spiral from ankle to knee, replaced stockings for many soldiers during the First World War.

8:33 **Daylight Saving Bill** In May 1916 all clocks in Britain were put forward by one hour in order to secure more light in the evenings and maximize efficiency. The practice has continued to this day. In 1916 a common complaint was that the longer, lighter evenings made it more difficult to get the children to bed. March and Banford seem to have the same trouble with their hens.

9:14 **shoot foxes** Before the war shooting foxes would have incurred the displeasure of the local Hunt.

9:32 **the White Horse** DHL's description of Bailey Farm is based on his knowledge of a farm near the village of Hermitage in Berkshire which was run by two women friends of his, Cecily Lambert and Violet Monk. Between December 1917 and November 1919 (when he left England for Italy), DHL was often in Hermitage and occasionally stayed at the farm itself. The White Horse referred to here is cut into the chalk of Uffington Hill, near Wantage, about twelve miles away.

15:2 **Salonika** The British and French landed troops at this port in October 1915, even though Greece was neutral. The aim was to support the Serbs and attack German forces from behind. In the event the Bulgarian army prevented the Allies from making any progress and by the end of the war almost half a million Allied troops were cooped up in Salonika.

15:28 **primmed up** To prim up is to 'set the face or mouth firmly, as if to repel familiarities'. See the *Oxford English Dictionary*, 2nd edn, prepared by J. A. Simpson and E. S. C. Weiner, 10 volumes (Oxford: Clarendon Press, 1989) – hereafter *OED2*.

19:2 **this influenza** The world-wide influenza epidemic arrived in England in the late spring of 1918 with fresh outbreaks in Autumn 1918 and February 1919. There were 150,000 deaths (out of a total of 15 million in the world as a whole).

20:5 **dreamed vividly** Although DHL was often troubled by dreams, and in chapter 14 of *Fantasia of the Unconscious* strenuously debated

Freudian interpretations of them, this and the later dream of March on pp. 40–41 seem to owe less to his own experience, or to psychoanalysis, than to a long tradition of dream narrative in Romantic literature (as exemplified in Coleridge's *Ancient Mariner* or *The Eve of St Agnes* by Keats).

20:17 **In the morning** Up to this point DHL's revisions to his first draft of the story (1919) had been minor: Henry originally said that he had previously lived at Bailey Farm with his father (not grandfather), for example, and in Banford's first conversation with her companion she addresses her as 'March', although thereafter she is 'Nellie'. But from now on DHL began to revise more heavily as he prepared to add his long 'tail'. For the ending of the original story, see the Appendix, where the manuscript of DHL's first version is reprinted from this point on.

28:24 **Captain Mayne Reid** Thomas Mayne Reid (1818–83) was the Irish-born author of numerous adventure novels with titles such as *The Scalp Hunters* (1851), *The White Gauntlet* (1863) and *The Castaways* (1870).

34:16 **bobbed** Hair cut evenly all round to about the length of the chin, very popular during the war and in the 1920s.

45:10 **tam-o'-shanter hat** A beret, with a crown about twice the circumference of the head, supposedly derived from the headgear of Scottish ploughmen and named after the hero of a famous poem by Robert Burns.

45:25 **Bottomless Pit** The phrase comes from the King James Bible: 'And I saw an angel come down from heaven, having the key of the bottomless pit and a great chain in his hand' (Revelation xx.1).

45:32 **the Banford** DHL must have picked up from German or Italian this distinctly un-English habit of using the definite article in front of proper names.

48:27 **land-girl's uniform** The Cambridge edition usefully quotes Cecily Lambert's description of her cousin Violet Monk:

> On the farm she dressed in Land Girl uniform of that date – jodhpurs cadged from a friend, shirt (a man's preferably) and tie, a small felt hat, high brown calf laced boots bought from a West End firm of high class footwear more suitable for the films than the farmyard. Occasionally she wore puttees.

48:39 **piggled** To piggle is 'to trifle or toy with' (*OED2*).

49:12–13 **patent shoes** Made of patent leather, i.e. with a bright glossy surface.

50:32 **chubbed** A variation of 'chubby'. See also 56:37.

53:30 **make love to** In the nineteenth century this phrase almost always meant 'to pay court to'. In DHL's time it was beginning to change its meaning and here suggests something like 'make amorous advances to-wards', 'kiss and fondle', but certainly not 'have sexual intercourse with'. The second use of the phrase at 53:32 is by no means so clear.

54:30 **old-age pensions** In 1908 the Liberal Government passed the Old Age Pensions Act 'which introduced non-contributory pensions "as of right", though on a test of means, and ... laid down the important principle that the strictly limited sections of the aged population who were entitled to pensions were not to be treated as paupers or deprived of any franchise, right or privilege.' See Simon Nowell-Smith (ed.), *Edwardian England: 1901–1914* (Oxford University Press, 1964), p. 87.

56:30 **now the war was really over** The Armistice was signed on 11 November 1918, though it was not until June 1919 that the defeated Germans signed the Peace Treaty of Versailles and the First World War was formally brought to an end.

56:35 **Salisbury plains** At 60:8 Lawrence explains that Henry's camp on Salisbury plain is sixty miles to the west of Hermitage (although the actual distance would be more like fifty miles).

61:11 **spelch** 'A ... splinter of wood' (*OED2*).

64:18 **cockling** In the dialect use of 'cockle' there is sometimes an associa-tion with 'the unsteady equilibrium of a cockle-shell or of a cockle-shell boat on the water' (*OED2*).

66:17 **grizzle** 'To fret, sulk; to cry in a whining whimpering fashion' (*OED2*).

THE CAPTAIN'S DOLL

75:1–5 **"Hannele! ... Wo dann?"** Hannele is a familiar form for Johanna. The exchange goes, 'Where are you?' 'Here.' 'Where, then?'

75:12 **trews** Close-fitting trousers. The manuscript shows that DHL first thought of having Hannele's doll dressed in a kilt.

75:28 **Mitchka** A familiar form for Maria.

85:30 **"Du bist *wirklich* bös"** The German equivalent of the previous sentence.

87:29 **Hannele explained** It is not clear what Hannele explains but unless Mrs Hepburn assumes that *both* the young women make dolls she could not suggest that Mitchka is her husband's mistress.

88:1–2 **'Dort wo du nicht bist'** This is not from Goethe but from Schubert's song 'Der Wanderer'. The line in question goes: 'Dort, wo du nich bist, dort ist das Glück' ('There, where you are not, there is happiness').

92:20 **plumbago** Black lead (as in a pencil), although also the name for a plant (leadwort) with flowers which are sometimes purplish.

93:9–10 **the Vier Jahreszeiten** 'The Four Seasons'.

93:33 **make** *love* The italics help to make clear that this is the more modern meaning of this phrase; see the note on 53:30.

94:10 **ammonite** 'A fossil ... consisting of whorled chambered shells' (*OED2*). DHL is presumably referring to the organism of which the fossil is a record.

94:35–6 **toute la même chose** It's all the same thing (French).

95:14 **Domplatz** The Cathedral Square.

95:19 *de rigueur* Required by the prevailing social conventions (French).

96:11 **seed-pearls** 'Minute pearls having the appearance of seeds' (*OED2*).

96:31 **a play called** *Hannele* The reference is to Gerhart Hauptmann's *Hanneles Himmelfahrt* ('The Ascension of Hannele'), first performed in 1893 and published as *Hannele* in the following year.

97:36 **Balzac's story** Mrs Hepburn is probably referring to one of the stories in Balzac's *Contes drolatiques* ('Les bons propos des religieuses de Poissy') which describes a convent notorious for its sexual licence.

99:13 **Winchester** Location and therefore name of a famous English public school.

99:35 **punto di Milano** Italian name for a special kind of hand-made lace. See also 104:30.

101:1 **Charles V** Holy Roman Emperor (1519–56) but also King of Spain as Charles I (1516–56); founder of the Hapsburg dynasty (see 202:31).

106:5 **Germanicus** The name given to Gaius Caesar (15 BC–19 AD), whose mother was a niece of Augustus and who was himself the father of Caligula. It celebrated the success of his military campaigns in Germany.

106:15 **Schiebers** Racketeers, people who dabbled in the Black Market.

113:10 *bibelots* Knick-knacks (French).

115:8–9 **cannot be alone** The likely source is the seventeenth-century French writer La Bruyère ('*Tout notre mal vient de ne pouvoir être seuls*'), although many others have had the same thought. DHL quotes a slightly altered form of La Bruyère's phrase in his essay on Herman Melville's travel books in *Studies in Classical American Literature* (see p. 151 of the 1971 Penguin edition).

116:15 **Café Stephanie** A famous rendezvous for artists in Munich.

117:1 **filet lace** Lace with a square mesh.

117:20 **Gräfin** Countess.

118:4 **Muenchener Neue Zeitung** 'Munich New Paper'.

118:12 **so shocked the eminent Julius Caesar** In *Movements in European History*, the history book he wrote for schools, DHL notes that when the leader of the Gauls, Vercingetorix, appeared before Caesar, 'It was seen he was a Gaul, for he wore the close tartan breeches no Roman would put on.' (ed. Philip Crompton, Cambridge University Press, 1989, 80:15–16).

118:18 **Herr Regierungsrat** In Austria people are often addressed by their official title. Herr von Poldi's means 'government councillor' (i.e. senior administrative officer).

118:32 **Jews of the wrong rich sort** That this formulation (minus 'rich') is almost ubiquitous in the 1920s; that its use did not prevent DHL from having close friends who were Jewish; or that it could be used by people like Proust, who was half-Jewish himself, is hardly likely to make it seem less offensive now. Compare also 128:18 and especially 140:14–18.

119:6 **a republican** Austria had become a republic in 1918 after the abdication of Charles, the last of the Habsburgs (1887–1922), who in 1916 had proclaimed himself Emperor of Austria as 'Karl I' and King of Hungary as 'Károly IV'.

121:5 **Amthaus** Town Hall.

121:39–40 **by the kilogram** Like Germany, Austria suffered after the war from rampant inflation. In a letter written from Zell am See on 9 August 1921, DHL reported that whereas before the war the Krone had been about 23 to the £1, it was then at 3000 – see *The Letters of D. H. Lawrence*, vol. ii, ed. Warren Roberts, James T. Boulton and Elizabeth Mansfield (Cambridge University Press, 1987), p. 67.

122:13 **leathern hose** Leather shorts or breeches. The unfamiliar English words are a transliteration of the German '*Lederhosen*'. See also 126:28.

122:24 **chintz** Cotton cloth brightly printed with floral patterns in a number of different colours, and usually glazed.

122:31 **Amtsgericht** Court House.

123:10 **a villa across the lake** Between 20 July and 25 August 1921, DHL and Frieda stayed with Frieda's sister and her family in a villa which was across the lake from Zell am See.

124:9 **gnädige Frau** Gracious Lady – still a characteristically Austrian version of formal address.

124:22 **"Wir warten auf dich"** 'We are waiting for you.'

124:41 **"Schön! . . . gut"** 'Beautiful! beautiful! It was beautiful! The water is good.' The 'woman above' then complains that it is 'hot' ("Heiss") – 125:1.

126:16 **Badeanstalt** Open air swimming baths.

130:14 **Bergheil** '*Berg*' means a mountain and '*heil*' safe (amongst other things). Thus: 'safe climbing!', but really, 'Greetings, fellow climber!'

131:16–17 **"Guten Tag," . . . "Grüss Gott"** Hepburn's greeting means 'Good Day' and Hannele's 'May God greet you' (or 'go with you', as English speakers might once have said).

131:18–19 **Tannhäuser . . . Siegfried . . . Balder** The first was a German poet and minstrel of the thirteenth century; the last two are heroic figures from German mythology. DHL would have been familiar with Tannhäuser and Siegfried because he knew the operas by Wagner which bear their names.

132:30 *navré*   Deeply distressed (French).

133:10 **bishops-crosier**   The staff bishops carry with a hook like a question mark at the end.

133:17 **royal poison ... monkshood**   Although monkshood (*aconite*) is an attractive flower, it is also very poisonous.

134:19 **Still-leben**   Still life (German).

134:36 **Catholic**   The capital 'C' suggests that Hepburn must be referring to his religious affiliation or upbringing, which has not previously been mentioned (and will not be mentioned again).

136:6 **Grass of Parnassus**   Another indication of the skilled amateur botanist in DHL. Nearly all his friends would comment on how familiar he was with the different kinds of flowers. This one (*parnassia palustris*) has saucer-shaped white flowers with dark green or purplish-green veins.

136:31 **"Nein. Nein. Dies ist kein langer Regen"**   'No. No. It won't keep on raining long.'

136:37 **left your big coat down below**   See 129:8.

138:41 **Lammerboden**   '*Boden*' usually means 'ground' in German. The valley bottom leading to the foot of the Karlinger Glacier, which DHL and Frieda visited on 20 August 1921, was called the Mooserboden. DHL calls it the Lammerboden because it was the Lammer travel agency which organized trips there. See also 140:23.

141:1 **mussy**   Slippery or messy (in Midlands dialect).

142:35 **a borax bead under a blow-flame**   DHL is remembering a chemistry experiment he would have performed in school or college. In its most usual form, borax powder is taken up on a small loop of wire. When this powder is heated, it fuses within the loop into a glassy bead which is then dipped into a solution or compound. The colour this bead turns when heated again will indicate which metal the solution or compound contains.

150:14 **patient Griseldis**   In the last story in *The Decameron*, Boccaccio describes how the Marquis de Saluzzo chose a wife of humble origins and subjected her to remarkable cruelties which she bore without complaint. The tale was retold on many subsequent occasions so that Griseldis, or Griselda in Boccaccio's Italian, became a byword for saintly endurance in a woman.

153:4 **"'s war wunderschön"**   'It was wonderful.'

153:12–14 **"Hat's geregnet? ... Gletscher?"**   'Did it rain? How was the weather? Did you go on the glacier?' 'No, there was no rain. Wonderful! Yes, he went right on to the glacier.'

THE LADYBIRD

157:1 **pierced heart**   The Virgin Mary is often depicted in medieval or Renaissance painting with her heart pierced through with swords.

157:30 **Mater Dolorosa** 'Sorrowing Mother'. The Latin phrase was tradi-
tionally used for the figure of the Virgin grieving over the dead body of
Jesus.

158:40 **a Bohemian** Bohemia, a kingdom of Central Europe which included Prague, was once part of the Austrian Empire but became a
province of Czechoslovakia when that country was founded in 1918.

159:35 **Aryan** Before acquiring its sinister overtones of racial discrimina-
tion from the Nazis, this word was used to describe the so-called Indo-
European languages (a group broad enough to include Sanskrit as well as
Greek, Persian as well as Latin), or anyone descended from the people
with whom this group originated. For DHL, of course, it is to Count
Dionys's advantage that he is not 'Aryan'.

160:9 **a visitor** DHL seems to forget about this visitor in the scene which
follows.

160:30 **phthisis** Any wasting disease but, most commonly in this period,
pulmonary tuberculosis.

161:1 **Artemis ... Atlanta ... Daphne** Artemis (better known perhaps
by her Roman name of Diana) was a famous huntress in Greek mythology,
as was Atlanta. Daphne, on the other hand, was a river nymph who, to
avoid being hunted down by the amorous Apollo, begged to be transformed into a laurel tree and had her wish granted.

162:1 **dunning** To dun someone is to press them repeatedly for something
(especially money).

163:27 *smorto* Pale as death, ashen (Italian).

165:2 **wings** Ear flaps to a hat which, in the manner of the time, fitted
very tightly. It could only do that, of course, once a woman had decided
to cut her hair short. See also 184:35 for 'wings' in the sense of side-
pieces to a dress.

170:12–13 **mezereon tree** Small shrub with red berries and purple or
pink flowers.

171:11–12 **hermetic gold** The gold is 'hermetic' because it is being
associated with Hermes Trismegistus (the name given by the Neo-
Platonists to the Egyptian God Thoth). He was assumed to have founded
alchemy. The superstitious belief in gold's healing power has been partly
justified in certain modern treatments (gold injections for arthritis, for
example).

173:23 **Mary-beetle** An English version of the German word for a ladybird ('*Marienkäfer*'). See 209:23.

175:29 **the cake for Cerberus** Cerberus was the three-headed dog who in
Greek mythology guarded the entrance to Hades. It became customary to
bury the dead with a piece of honeycake which could be used to conciliate
him. Compare, in DHL's poem 'The Ship of Death', 'Oh build your ship
of death, your little ark/and furnish it with food, with little cakes ...'

(*The Complete Poems of D. H. Lawrence*, ed. V. de Sola Pinto and W. Roberts (Heinemann, 1967), p. 718.

177:17 **Long Berthas** Long-range guns used during the First World War by the Germans (and named after Bertha Krupp, the owner of the firm which manufactured them). More commonly, 'Big Berthas'.

180:18–19 **that's a fact** If light entered a vacuum in which we were living, we would not see it unless it happened to be directed into our eyes. We see the light which we do not look at directly because it is diffused or scattered by 'bits of dust and stuff' in our atmosphere (including molecules of air). The Count is thus partly right; but not sufficiently so to support his contention that sunlight is 'dark'.

181:28–9 **tablets of stone** The ten commandments Moses brought down from Mount Sinai were written on tablets of stone (see Exodus xxxiv.28).

182:32 **the Dionysos** (Dionysus) Greek god of wine and fruitfulness, often opposed in DHL's mind, as he had previously been in Nietzsche's (see especially *The Birth of Tragedy*), with Apollo. Apollo – in spite of his amorous pursuit of Daphne (see note on 161:1) – stood for light and reason; Dionysus for darkness, self-forgetfulness, rapture.

183:7 **well-liking** 'In good condition . . . thriving, healthy, plump' (arch.) (*OED2*)

184:11 **fly to thee** DHL has conveniently translated the words of the German folk song quoted just above. They were included in the *Oxford Book of German Verse* which he reviewed in 1912.

184:31 **Bassie** A strange diminutive for Basil.

184:34 **pin-poppet, or rather needle-woman** A pin-poppet was a cylindrical case for pins and needles. This one is clearly in the form of a woman.

188:13 **Swinburne** The quotation is from Swinburne's 'The Garden of Proserpine' in *Poems and Ballads* (1866).

190:36 **Aphrodite of the foam** In Greek mythology, Aphrodite is the Goddess of Love (her Roman equivalent is Venus). She is supposed to have been born from the sea. (DHL had a particular interest in the famous painting by Botticelli which celebrates this event.)

192:17–18 **"Touch me not . . . Father"** Christ's words to Mary Magdalene after he had risen from the dead (John xx.17).

193:10 **Cybele – Isis** Cybele was an earth-goddess from Phrygia (in what is now Turkey), and Isis a fertility goddess from the Egyptian pantheon. Both were associated with the moon, as was the Syrian earth-goddess Astarte referred to below (193:22).

195:21 **Proserpine** Roman name for the Greek goddess Persephone, daughter of Zeus, who was abducted by the king of the Underworld and thus became his queen. Allowed to return to this world for a few months every year, her annual arrival was synonymous with spring.

196:8 **in excelsis** Lifted up on high (Latin).

200:27 **clubbed together** The verb seems to be used here in the sense of 'combined in a mass' (*OED2*).

202:4 **Kaiser Wilhelm II** Wilhelm II (1859–1941) become King of Prussia and German Emperor in 1888. He fled to Holland in November 1918, after having been forced to abdicate. Hohenzollern was the family name; see 202:31.

202:36–7 **a light in your face, and a burning on your mouth** After Moses came down from Mount Sinai with the ten commandments he had to veil his face because it gave off so much light. See Exodus xxxiv.29–35.

203:22 **day of Judas** In DHL's view, Judas was an inevitable product of Jesus's loving trust.

207:29 **pink-chenille** Chenille (the French word for caterpillar) is 'a kind of velvety cord, having short threads or fibres of silk and wool standing out at right angles from a core of thread or wire, like the hairs of a caterpillar; used in trimming or bordering dresses . . .' (*OED2*).

209:10–11 **Prince Bogorik** Not identified.

209:30 **Egyptian scarabeus** '*Scarabaeus*' is the Latin word for beetle. The Egyptian scarab (also see 183:27) was a sacred symbol often reproduced in the form of carved gemstones.

209:36 **Fabre** Jean Henri Fabre (1823–1915), famous French naturalist who wrote ten volumes of entomological memoirs (*Souvenirs entomologiques*).

211:9 **triumphance** *OED2* gives 'triumphancy' – 'the state or quality of being triumphant' – but not this word (which must, however, mean the same thing).

215:7 **who was a swan** Although there are many similar tales, this precise story (and song) has not been identified and is probably invented.

216:4 **an Egyptian king-god** In 1914, DHL had been very impressed by Egyptian sculptures in the British Museum. See *The Letters of D. H. Lawrence*, vol. ii, ed. George J. Zytaruk and James T. Boulton (Cambridge University Press, 1981), p. 218.

216:30 **Francesca and Paolo** Famous lovers, put to death for adultery in 1289, and movingly depicted in Dante's *Inferno*.

219:36 *nuit blanche* Sleepness night (French).

THE STORY OF PENGUIN CLASSICS

Before 1946 ...'Classics' are mainly the domain of academics and students, without readable editions for everyone else. This all changes when a little-known classicist, E. V. Rieu, presents Penguin founder Allen Lane with the translation of Homer's *Odyssey* that he has been working on and reading to his wife Nelly in his spare time.

1946 *The Odyssey* becomes the first Penguin Classic published, and promptly sells three million copies. Suddenly, classic books are no longer for the privileged few.

1950s Rieu, now series editor, turns to professional writers for the best modern, readable translations, including Dorothy L. Sayers's *Inferno* and Robert Graves's *The Twelve Caesars*, which revives the salacious original.

1960s The Classics are given the distinctive black jackets that have remained a constant throughout the series's various looks. Rieu retires in 1964, hailing the Penguin Classics list as 'the greatest educative force of the 20th century'.

1970s A new generation of translators arrives to swell the Penguin Classics ranks, and the list grows to encompass more philosophy, religion, science, history and politics.

1980s The Penguin American Library joins the Classics stable, with titles such as *The Last of the Mohicans* safeguarded. Penguin Classics now offers the most comprehensive library of world literature available.

1990s The launch of Penguin Audiobooks brings the classics to a listening audience for the first time, and in 1999 the launch of the Penguin Classics website takes them online to a larger global readership than ever before.

The 21st Century Penguin Classics are rejacketed for the first time in nearly twenty years. This world famous series now consists of more than 1300 titles, making the widest range of the best books ever written available to millions – and constantly redefining the meaning of what makes a 'classic'.

The Odyssey continues ...

The best books ever written

PENGUIN ⟨🐧⟩ CLASSICS

SINCE 1946

Find out more at www.penguinclassics.com

PENGUIN CLASSICS

SONS AND LOVERS D. H. LAWRENCE

The marriage of Gertrude and Walter Morel has become a battleground. Repelled by her uneducated and sometimes violent husband, fastidious Gertrude devotes her life to her children, especially to her sons, William and Paul – determined they will not follow their father into working down the coal mines. But conflict is inevitable when Paul seeks to escape his mother's suffocating grasp by entering into relationships with other women. Set in Lawrence's native Nottinghamshire, *Sons and Lovers* (1913) is a highly autobiographical and compelling portrayal of childhood, adolescence and the clash of generations.

In his introduction, Blake Morrison discusses the novel's place in Lawrence's life and his depiction of the mother-son relationship, sex and politics. Using the complete and restored text of the Cambridge edition, this volume includes a new chronology and further reading by Paul Poplawski.

'Lawrence's masterpiece … a revelation' Anthony Burgess

'Momentous – a great book' Blake Morrison

Edited by Helen Baron and Carl Baron
With an introduction by Blake Morrison

PENGUIN CLASSICS

LADY CHATTERLEY'S LOVER D. H. LAWRENCE

Constance Chatterley feels trapped in her sexless marriage to the invalid Sir Clifford. Unable to fulfil his wife emotionally or physically, Clifford encourages her to have a liaison with a man of their own class. But Connie is attracted instead to Mellors, her husband's gamekeeper, with whom she embarks on a passionate affair that brings new life to her stifled existence. Can she find true equality with Mellors, despite the vast gulf between their positions in society? One of the most controversial novels in English literature, *Lady Chatterley's Lover* is an erotically charged and psychologically powerful depiction of adult relationships.

In her introduction, Doris Lessing discusses the influence of Lawrence's sexual politics, his relationship with his wife Frieda and his attitude towards the First World War. Using the complete and restored text of the Cambridge edition, this volume includes a new chronology and further reading by Paul Poplawski.

'No one ever wrote better about the power struggles of sex and love' Doris Lessing

'A masterpiece' *Guardian*

Edited by Michael Squires
With an introduction by Doris Lessing

PENGUIN CLASSICS

THE WOMAN WHO RODE AWAY/ST. MAWR/THE PRINCESS
D. H. LAWRENCE

These three works, all written in 1924, explore the profound effects on protagonists who embark on psychological voyages of liberation. In *St. Mawr*, Lou Witt buys a beautiful, untamable bay stallion and discovers an intense emotional affinity with the horse that she cannot feel with her husband. This superb novella displays Lawrence's mastery of satirical comedy in a scathing depiction of London's fashionable high society. In 'The Woman Who Rode Away' a woman's religious quest in Mexico brings great danger – and astonishing self-discovery, while 'The Princess' portrays the intimacy between an aloof woman and her male guide as she ventures into the wilderness of New Mexico in search of new experiences.

In his introduction, James Lasdun discusses the theme of liberation and the ways in which it is conveyed in these works. Using the restored texts of the Cambridge edition, this volume includes a new chronology by Paul Poplawski.

'Lawrence urged men and women to live ... to glory in the exhilarating terror of this brief life' Frederic Raphael, *Sunday Times*

Edited by Brian Finney, Christa Jansohn and Dieter Mehl
with notes by Paul Poplawski and an introduction by James Lasdun

THE STORY OF PENGUIN CLASSICS

Before 1946 ...'Classics' are mainly the domain of academics and students, without readable editions for everyone else. This all changes when a little-known classicist, E. V. Rieu, presents Penguin founder Allen Lane with the translation of Homer's *Odyssey* that he has been working on and reading to his wife Nelly in his spare time.

1946 *The Odyssey* becomes the first Penguin Classic published, and promptly sells three million copies. Suddenly, classic books are no longer for the privileged few.

1950s Rieu, now series editor, turns to professional writers for the best modern, readable translations, including Dorothy L. Sayers's *Inferno* and Robert Graves's *The Twelve Caesars*, which revives the salacious original.

1960s The Classics are given the distinctive black jackets that have remained a constant throughout the series's various looks. Rieu retires in 1964, hailing the Penguin Classics list as 'the greatest educative force of the 20th century'.

1970s A new generation of translators arrives to swell the Penguin Classics ranks, and the list grows to encompass more philosophy, religion, science, history and politics.

1980s The Penguin American Library joins the Classics stable, with titles such as *The Last of the Mohicans* safeguarded. Penguin Classics now offers the most comprehensive library of world literature available.

1990s The launch of Penguin Audiobooks brings the classics to a listening audience for the first time, and in 1999 the launch of the Penguin Classics website takes them online to a larger global readership than ever before.

The 21st Century Penguin Classics are rejacketed for the first time in nearly twenty years. This world famous series now consists of more than 1300 titles, making the widest range of the best books ever written available to millions – and constantly redefining the meaning of what makes a 'classic'.

The Odyssey continues ...

The best books ever written

PENGUIN (P) CLASSICS

SINCE 1946

Find out more at www.penguinclassics.com